Prey in the Outerlands

Steve Simandle

Acknowledgements

I would like to thank those that have helped to bring this work to its current form. My editors: Stanna Reinke and Tom Byland. Their work was invaluable to me and I thank them for the comments and commas. Everything that's right is because of them but I retain the rights to all the errors. Thanks to my early readers: George Trivette, Jr., Johnny Easter, Bryan Hubbard, Justin White, Jessica Chilton, Deanna Henderson, Nancy Pugh, and Gideon Deschain. Thank you all for your encouragement, comments, patience, and insights.

Most of all, I need to acknowledge the efforts of my faithful wife and loving children – who gave me the space and time to complete this work. I know it has been hard to have mc at home physically but in the Outerlands mentally – thank you for your sacrifices.

Contents

Prologue

Lloyd was a good man, and Specter forced himself to admit that, lately, most of them were.

"Thank you, Lloyd," Specter said as he accepted the food Florentina had packed for him. Specter made himself look the man in the eye. "Thank you for all you do. You're a good man."

"Thank you. I hope you find what you're looking for," Lloyd replied.

As he turned, Specter threw up his hand knowing that Florentina would be watching from the house – along with their children, L.J. and little Fontana.

Cute kids. Totally unaware of the world that was. Lloyd was a good man and that was getting harder and harder to find. He walked down the gravel road back towards the town that was.

After the Breaking – as most people called it now – there were a lot of men like Lloyd. Smart. Charismatic. The type of natural leader who wanted results rather than glory. There were a lot fewer now.

He walked past the rows of what used to be houses, away from the cabin where Lloyd had set up his operations center. Specter stayed one street over from Main Street and nothing much was left. What had been usable had been taken, and that which was not worth it the first time was now prime trade goods. He didn't break stride and yet didn't let his footsteps linger. He had miles to go today, and getting past the town proper was the first part of that. The scenery outside of town was not too dramatic. Had he been driving, this was the part that he would look at but not remember: too similar to the next to be remarkable; too much like the last to stand out.

Once fully outside the town and the surrounding areas the terrain did start to vary. Keeping his same steady pace he went up long, steady slopes and down the other sides. He paused at the top of one especially long rise. He found a nice spot and sat down by a large tree.

He had to go back.

The man Lloyd's group had sent to make sure he got out of town had turned back a while ago. Not a chance that group would let him just walk out of there without making sure he was on his way. Now he looked to see if his follower would double back – no sign yet. He took out the food Florentina had made. A cucumber, a carrot, some leafy greens, even a slice of jerky – he really had made an impression. He ate and watched the trail he'd just walked. His follower was not doubling back. The sun moved closer to bed, beckoning Specter to join him. He got up, ready to be done with this business.

He circled back toward the southeast, knowing he had to move quickly. The homestead wasn't easily accessible this way. The village to the west was just too dicey. He picked up his pace and made twice the time he had coming out. It was rougher terrain, but he had scouted it before and become, if not comfortable with it, at least familiar with it. He measured his breathing and pace and kept at it. He caught sight of smoke from the chimney and used that to hone in on the farmstead. Taking his time now, he got to his perch. He had picked this spot earlier – ranged it. He had a clear view of the house from here, just shy of eight hundred yards from the cabin.

He crouched down with a tree at his back and thought of how it used to be. He thought back to the time when he'd be sitting up in his tree stand waiting for a big buck to cross. Or when the fire at the house would signal a big get-together with friends and family.

He unearthed and unpacked what equipment he needed, noting the wind.

He remembered when he was young. He and his family and friends would go up in the woods – usually to someone's cabin – and they would hunt, cook, eat, and tell lies. Those were different times; times before the Breaking.

He assembled everything he needed, again noting the wind and tracing the smoke from the chimney.

It had been a while since a feeling as strong as this had passed over him. He felt helpless to fight the tide of emotion sweeping him along. Memories of hunting at the cabin, memories of partying at the cabin. Thoughts of those left behind in the past through neglect, desire or – almost worst – just the passing of time.

He shook his head once, violently, to clear his mind.

He looked intently at the cabin, focused in on Lloyd getting some wood inside for the night.

He thought of how the passage of time had changed so much. Honestly, that wasn't true. Time hadn't changed all that. It just stretched over the chasm cut in the wake of the Breaking – the chasm that separated men like him and Lloyd now. Before, they might be hunting together. Now, well, that was broken.

He watched Lloyd stop before picking up one more piece of firewood.

There were some good men like Lloyd left. Some who could gather people, some who could lead. There were some who could inspire loyalty and sacrifice in others. Some who could foment rebellion – those who could stir up trouble for the corporations.

He squeezed the trigger and felt the familiar recoil in his shoulder, like the hand of a friend, comforting in a time of loss.

Those like Lloyd.

He watched as Florentina ran out of the cabin and cradled her husband's now lifeless body, vainly trying to hold his head together.

Those whom it was his job to kill.

Chapter 1.

Specter woke to the sounds of a rainstorm. It was what he had programmed into his alarm clock. When he had gotten back after Lloyd – check that – Number 20, he had gotten the usual two weeks' respite, and now it would be time for him to get his next packet. It was so easy to lose yourself in drink or some other kind of self-medication during the break. That was why it was more important for him to maintain discipline. To drink discipline in the morning, train with it during the day, shower and lather in it, sleep with it at night. Getting lazy meant getting careless, and careless people got dead.

He walked over to the window and looked out at the wide expanse. His apartment here in the Enclave overlooked the outside of the city itself. His view was of fields and orchards stretching right to left and almost to the horizon. You could just make out the trees that marked the end of the Enclave proper and the start of the Outerlands. He always thought it was a bad tactical decision to ring a city with the crop fields and orchards the city needed to survive. *Too hard to protect*, he thought.

But they didn't pay him to be a city planner. They paid him to kill.

He had been trained from an early age how to kill, and he had demonstrated a natural talent for it. But he had forced himself to learn. He had soaked in nearly everything he could that would make him better. He worked hard to become as good as he was. But this might be it.

Early on, when he was approached about being a Hunter, he had been a believer. Then, the Prey were clearly a threat and clearly evil people. No questions – black and white. Looking back, he figured they did that specifically to hook you in. Get you used to it so certain targets just fall in with the rest, and you just decide to get your Thirty in. Maybe.

Lately, though, the targets had been more questionable. The rationale more flimsy, less solid. The moral nature of the person more in question. Lately....

Most of them had been good men.

Well, he had seen the writing on the wall after Number 14. Number 14 was really the first of his ambiguous targets, the first one whose only offense was labeled 'sedition.' How arcane that word was nowadays. Number 14 it turned out had just made a speech at a town meeting speaking about trade with the Enclaves. That was too powerful for the Corps, and he was put on the kill list for it.

After he got back from Number 14, he started making plans and preparations for leaving – forever. He had never known anyone who got to Thirty and enjoyed the promised retirement. He had spent some time looking into it – quietly, of course – and hadn't even heard of anyone making it. Well, pretty soon for him, too, he thought.

He picked up the packet for his next Prey. He read the codename: Maker. Wow. This was the one that could make you famous. Here his next mission was to track down and kill the longest Runner to date. Maybe that was everybody's Number 21 and that's why no one made it to Thirty. He read the byline for the overview: inventor of webarmor. So – the inventor of the body armor that changed warfare more than the machine gun.

Specter looked through his packet. They had the details, the biometrics, and, of course the multiple offenses and justifications. Importantly, the packet contained the Lasts: the last known and independently confirmed contact, the last places he'd stayed, the last people he was known to be in contact with and – like a gift! – the last known recording of the man. He checked the date and – like snow on Christmas! – it was only two years old. Interestingly, it was taken by another Hunter in the process of verifying his identity.

Specter got up, put it in the player and watched the grainy image as it spoke. At least the sound was clear. The image showed a man standing in front of a classroom of older students. This Maker appeared to be very animated. He was either very expressive, very excitable, or very passionate about what he was talking about. Specter turned up the sound.

"The way I see it, it started back before that. There was a trend in politics way before that which catered to business. Once corporations were allowed free speech with their wallets, the money just flowed in. It took a few election cycles to get it down, but money talked. And with the political action committees, it basically made it legal to be on the take. But Corps don't hate each other that much. They hate being told what they can't do or what they have to do. And rich people don't shell out millions unless they can get something. No one hates the other side <u>that</u> much."

"First it was unions, then the retirement age, then social security went bankrupt – sorry – was allowed to go private and tanked while the traders and bankers made millions. Then, to the hue and cry of national debt and austerity measures, most of the social programs got cut to the bone."

He was really into it now. Hands waving, talking quickly, Specter took it for passion.

"There were some groups that spoke out, but big business made sure the airwaves were plastered with their own message. Well, when Yellowstone blew, that was it. The Corps decided it wasn't in their best interest, which meant their bottom line, to send aid. They told their representatives, and it didn't come. When the aftershocks triggered California's earthquake, that cemented it. The continuity plans they had to come up with for terror attacks worked pretty well for the disasters; they still made money while most of the west and Midwest burned."

There was a pause and some muffled sound. *A question maybe*? Specter thought.

"What? Yes, after 9/11 the government mandated every municipality to have a disaster plan, and all companies were 'encouraged' to develop a continuity of operations plan. So, the word from a CEO goes down the chain and some two or three people spend hundreds of man-hours working out a plan. Well, when against their predictions, they needed that disaster plan – turned out they didn't miss much more than a day."

"There were so many disaffected. The country was rife for revolution – the masses were ready to redistribute the wealth at the end of a gun. So many places were left to themselves. Power grids down, bridges out..."

He trailed off here as if remembering something he felt he must. As if in the telling and thereby reliving a painful memory, there's healing. He was far from that, though.

"But the last election cycle – the last one that mattered, anyway – that was when the corporations got what they really wanted. The Corps manipulated the law so that they could offer folks a place to stay while they worked, and the workers agreed to forgo certain rights – like that golden eight-hour workday. And as things go, more and more got taken away. Kids worked at age twelve, healthcare was shouldered by the worker so that it became like indentured servitude. The company would pay, but you'd have to work it off. And that meant, maybe, your grandkids would be free from it. It was like the coal mine's company store in the early 1900's, just the updated version."

"And the kicker – the ultimate – was that if you didn't like it, you didn't have to work there. You could leave."

There was good audio, but the student's comment was unintelligible.

"You'll get to the coal mines later if you haven't already. But, no workers' rights – you had to sign those away before they let you start work. And leave? Oh, no, nothing's wrong with that. But leave and go where? No house to live in, no power, no hospitals, and worst of all, no law. The places not designated as 'Corporate Enclaves' were left to themselves in every way."

Another unintelligible remark. This Hunter needed to work on his surveillance skills.

"No, you're right, it didn't happen overnight. But it was quick – an annexation of a city's power plant and water treatment center by a Corporation. The Corporation would raise rates and force people out of their homes – out into other lands. The 'Outerlands' as everybody started calling them. Pretty soon only the Corporation and their corporate dormitories received the power and water. And that's just one example of how the Corporations pushed people out and established their Enclaves."

Specter thought immediately of Number 14. That was what happened to Number 14. It was easy to find his house because it was sandwiched in between two high rise dormitories and in behind as well. After the threats and the noise and the disregard for his property, Number 14 decided to take it to the town council. In that speech he brought up trade with the Corps and how he should be allowed to trade with them for land and property. The Corp thugs had beaten him to a pulp that night. But Number 14, it turned out, did have some pull, not much, but some. Number 14 reached out to his friends and ... *and then he met me*, Specter thought.

"The whole country – indeed most of the world – was brought back to the 1800's. In the Outerlands it was a twenty-first century world with 1800's technology, all right beside some of the most lavish Enclaves ever known to man. After a while, an uneasy peace developed. People banded together as best they could, defended against the outlaws who also banded together and ransacked and pillaged. In time, life simplified. In the Enclaves you did what you were told; in the Outerlands, you survived. Both simple; both hard."

"Most of the corporate Enclaves had their own protection, but some would utilize criminal gangs to make sure production got met. That was the literal bottom line – that was the driving force – the only thing the boards and the CEOs cared about."

Yet another muffled remark.

"You'd think so, wouldn't you? A large part of that disaster plan involved various memorandums of agreement between companies. Just one example would be fuel. One company agrees that, in an emergency, it will deliver fuel preferentially to a certain power company so they can run their vehicles to repair downed power lines, run generators, et cetera. Those agreements stood when the Breaking happened and evolved into a larger, broader cooperative. Corporations within a certain supply chain saw the benefits of working together exclusively and would form larger *de facto* coalitions. The Corporations maintained a loose affiliation and cut back on competing with each other and started to specialize. In those early years there were some large corporate casualties, but, for the most part, the companies realized that specialization was more profitable. No government run by the Corporations was going to prevent monopolies, so the Corporations struggled to monopolize different areas of the supply chain. Interestingly, this led to a dependence upon other Corporations. For example, if one Corporation focused on making vehicles, they would, by definition, not focus on making clothes. They became dependent on getting clothes from another Corporation. Demand came from within each Corporation to provide the necessary goods for their workforce. Naturally, prominent executives soon saw the profitability in an over-arching affiliation that involved every Corporation – a SuperCorp, if you will."

Specter was surprised at how much of this had been echoed by Lloyd – by Number 20. It was almost exactly the same view of how events had transpired. Certainly the same sentiments. He just hadn't realized it was being taught, but that's what it looked like.

"With fewer people around – I think the eruption, the earthquake, and subsequent tsunami took about one billion people? So with fewer people around, the corporate think tanks decided to invent different ways to make money. When everyone who matters is rich, what do you offer? Experience seemed to be the best answer. That's when the pleasure domes started popping up. Anything you wanted was available in those domes – and the more outrageous, the more people were willing to pay."

"A new type of status developed. When everybody's rich it was – and is – the amount of time you spent at such places that mattered. And the freedom of the Corps made it easy to get rid of protestors/detractors. If you didn't like it and spoke up, you were turned and burned: fired and sent out of the Dome or Enclave, whichever. All enforced by the Corporations' private security/defense contractors, the pri-cons, the single entity with access to webarmor. The culture was such that corporate management structures were designed to select for ruthless pragmatists.

Specter could barely make out the student comment, "What does this have to do with science, again?" Specter chuckled.

"The pragmatism of the Enclave hierarchy demands a different focus on science…"

The recording abruptly cut off. Before Specter could react, though, the picture flashed to life again. The scene showed the Maker seated with other tables behind him, probably a restaurant or an inn. The way the man kept looking directly at the camera made Specter think this footage was from a female Hunter showing some cleavage with a nice necklace (holding the camera) nestled low between her breasts. His suspicion was confirmed when a hand appeared from the right and brought a drink up above the camera. *So, a female Hunter*, Specter thought. The drinks on the table – the tops of multiple glasses were obvious – spoke to his also being inebriated, or working hard at it if not there yet.

"What I was saying to the students was that the pragmatism of the corporations selected for ruthless people to be put in supervisory positions. Assholes who could push their workers harder and harder. The same type of asshole who would think he or she was being highly rewarded with a two-day pleasure dome pass."

"And what recourse for the masses? Come on, you know they used psychology to full effect to keep most mollified. I was surprised how much people preferred electricity and running water to a free existence. To those indoctrinated minds, loyalty to the Corps is the only type of happiness. All the 'work your way up the ladder' and 'pull yourself up by your bootstraps' bullshit they used – heck, still use, for all I know. 'Free' to those brainwashed minds is bad, and failing to comply means certain condemnation."

Then, he took a drink, set his glass down, and you could see his countenance change.

"I don't know why I get so worked up. I can see it, but it's the way the system is. I can't change it; it's a systemic problem. There's no way to fight it without a full-scale revolution, and the pri-cons will put a bloody stop to that and quickly."

The recording abruptly stopped.

There was no more to the tape. Specter turned off the player and checked the overview. Inventor of webarmor, lightweight and strong body armor made from synthetic spider web fibers that would stop even a .50 caliber round. Specter chuckled to himself; he had seen the footage. The armor would stop the bullet but you still had to deal with the momentum of the bullet and all the force of impact.

He read on: mysteriously disappeared one year after California earthquake and resultant tsunami. Specter thought, *got a little upset about not sending aid maybe?* He spent time on the dossier; he had to know his Prey. After laboriously going through all of it, including the background material, he went back to the last contact. He read it again:

Last contact: Hunter [redacted]; deceased.

So he's a killer, Specter thought. *Well, with luck I'll have him dead in two months.*

Chapter 2.

It was a beautiful morning for a hunt. The first rays of sunshine had not seen the lower areas yet and there was just a faint breeze. The woods seemed alive as usual, but there was no sound of big game. From his tree stand, Randal looked out and caught sight of his distance markers. He had been here long enough to gauge his shots and knew he could be deadly from up here. There had been no game, and Randal knew now why.

Someone was approaching.

Randal watched him walk up from way back. He would lose sight of him every now and again, but his approach was steady. Now that the interloper was closer, Randal studied him. His walk was not natural – his gait misleading. He moved differently than most men – there was something predatory in the way he moved. That something was out of place here in the woods, better suited to a battlefield. A hunter of men. That's when he had it!

A Hunter.

He had seen that type of walk before, that type of predatory amble that belied speed and agility. The swagger of one who knows how to kill, and knows he's good at it. He had seen that walk before in the testers of the webarmor, those elite soldiers and killers they sent in for the second wave of testing. More recently, he'd seen the same walk in the Hunter who called herself Katerina.

He pulled his arrow back and felt the tautness of the bowstring. He had no illusions why this guy was here. He let the Hunter walk in closer. Randal gauged his shot and then called out, "Do we have time for breakfast before you kill me?"

The man's question surprised Specter. He'd made no special attempt to keep quiet, but he still thought he should have gotten closer. Taken aback by the question, Specter debated on playing innocent but realized he'd only be playing dumb. His quarry would expect nothing less.

Randal could see him weighing his options. Was he actually thinking about killing him right now? Was he that quick to think he could do it? Was he that quick that he could still be thinking he was on the offensive? At this range, he might have just enough time to dodge the arrow, but....

"Yes, come on down and we'll eat first," Specter said.

Randal released the tension in his bow reluctantly but decidedly. It was on. The game was afoot.

Randal shouldered his bow and quiver and proceeded down the tree. Once on the ground he turned to face his killer. It was a tense moment, but Randal's hand moved by rote habit. "I'm Maker," escaped his lips reflexively, as he offered to shake hands. "Or Randal," he added.

Specter shook his hand. "I'm Specter," was his surprised reply. None of his previous Prey had known their kill order codename.

Randal broke the grip and made for the old house. It was odd enough to shake the hand of the man who was sent to kill you but odder still to have him walking behind you, following in silence. "How did you find me?" Randal asked to stop the silence and his frantic mind.

"You are somewhat of the holy grail of Runners. You've been on the run for longer than any other. What is it now? Five years?" Specter asked.

"Something like that – it doesn't pay to keep track of it. But, really, how _did_ you find me?" Randal asked again.

He asked the question with an intensity that surprised Specter – he was intent on an answer. He obliged, "Vanilla. I tracked the vanilla."

That was it? Randal actually laughed out loud. "Really? Not too many people make vanilla?" asked Randal.

"Interestingly enough, no." was Specter's reply.

"Ha!" Randal said. "I knew it would be rare since you can't grow it around here without the bean and a greenhouse. And I knew that whatever got smuggled out of the Enclaves, if any, would be pricey. But I never expected the demand to be so high. Who knew a few years without vanilla would make it so valuable? I guess you..."

Randal stopped himself. He thought, *this Hunter wants my head, not vanilla. Vanilla was just his ticket to me*, Randal thought. "I guess you never know," he said aloud.

They walked the rest of the way in silence. It wasn't far and when they reached the old house, Randal walked right in, holding the door for Specter. Randal set his bow and quiver along the wall in the hallway knowing he wouldn't pick them up again. He walked straight to the kitchen and then turned. Specter was right behind him. "I've got some ham and biscuits – sound good?" he asked.

"Fine," Specter said.

Randal waved Specter to a seat at the table. Then, he got the ham out, put some water from the pitcher in a pan, and kindled a fire up in the woodstove. "It might take a while to get really hot," he told Specter.

Specter just nodded back at him.

The fire did heat up, though, and the ham cooked well. Randal got some plates from the cupboard and set them out. He walked back over to the bread box and got out four biscuits. Randal grabbed the pan, forked out the ham onto the plates, and put the pan back on the stove. Placing the biscuits in the pan, he took the plates over to the table and set them down. He retrieved another fork, which he gave to Specter. Randal turned the biscuits over with his hand and smelled the aroma of a great breakfast. *This is going to be good*, he thought. He took the pan from the stove and placed it on the table. Then he just sat there with his head bowed.

Was he praying? Specter thought. Specter felt odd, so he spoke first. "So you're the inventor of webarmor?" Specter knew he was loud enough, but Randal didn't move.

Then, suddenly, Randal's head rose up. *Religious man, then*, thought Specter.

Randal looked Specter in the eye. "Not inventor, no, just Maker. It's actually a pretty apt title. You could say all I did was to facilitate and standardize the technology."

"So why'd you run?" Specter asked.

"That's kind of an odd question, don't you think? The simple answer is so they wouldn't kill me," Randal answered. "The more accurate answer would involve Daedalus. Do you know the story of Daedalus and Icarus?"

"They made the Labyrinth," Specter supplied. In having breakfast, Randal didn't seem like most men condemned to die. For one, he was carrying on a conversation – he didn't have that far-off facing death stare. *Something's amiss here*, Specter thought.

"Right, and the king imprisoned them for it so no one would find out how to get out. So, I saw that I was getting the boot, and I had to get out. Kind of like you, right?" Randal asked pointedly.

Specter was surprised. It wasn't something he advertised – Randal must be searching for something. "How so?" Specter replied.

"Well, you have to get your Thirty, right?" Randal began.

Few men could even be aware of that program – how could he know? Specter nodded.

"You must know they won't let you get to thirty. It's just something they can't have happen."

"I know."

"So you've prepared? Set aside a place for yourself? Family? You've got to prepare for them, too – or you have to prepare them, right?"

"I have. I'll get by."

"That's what I thought, too," Randal said.

Specter was surprised how calm Randal was. Randal was...agitated was probably the right word. He had cooked and, unlike most condemned men, he ate his food. He seemed too fidgety for his smooth, measured tone. It was a manner that suggested a plan. Specter asked him a question he hoped would distract him, "Why did you decide to stay here?"

"It was time," Randal replied.

"Time to settle down?" Specter probed.

"Time to stop running," Randal replied.

The resignation was plain on his face. But Specter couldn't place it. It wasn't the resignation of one who has decided to die. God knows he had seen that look before – all too often of late. This was more…then he had it.

It was kill Number 12.

Chapter 3

He had been up close to Number 12. Number 12 had been a gambler. That gambling nature had led to his following, and he <u>had</u> been lucky. But Number 12 had tried to gamble for his life. Specter had made a deal with him – so far as Number 12 knew – that Specter wouldn't kill him. It was a classic role of the dice. Too cliché and could have been sad – but it was too pathetic. Specter let Number 12 believe that if he rolled two sixes he could live. Of course, it wasn't so – but Specter could afford to put his Prey at ease. Number 12 had been excited when Specter agreed, but deflated when Specter laid his revolver on the table. Specter had caught sight of the way Number 12's pants caught on his ankle and knew he had a weapon there. Based on Number 12's gambling nature, he felt it was probably a gun. As the dice were rolling, Number 12 had the same look that Randal now had. That look said: I think I can't win, but I've got to try. As Number 12 went for the gun in his ankle holster, Specter's knife had already gone through his throat. The dice finished rolling and came up twelve.

Now Randal had that same type of look. Specter told him pointedly, "You know how your running is going to end."

Randal surprised him again with his reply.

"You know I can't just accept that without a fight. I've planned, too. I can't go quietly, not today."

And with that simple statement, Specter found himself in yet another fight.

Things happened quickly, but Specter tracked it all. Randal, Specter quickly realized, had indeed been planning for this day. Planning for a while to go up against an opponent like him. When Randal had finished speaking, he shoved the table towards Specter. A simple enough gesture and not wholly unexpected, but what did throw Specter off balance – literally – was the fact that as the table moved, the floor did, too. Not much, but just enough to start his chair tipping backwards. Specter's gun was in his hand when he realized he wouldn't have a shot because the table was going over, too. Randal had planned.

It turned out that Randal's' plan to keep himself alive gave Specter a chance, too. As Specter hit the floor on his back, he caught sight of Randal on the left side of the table but the image was wrong. Randal was too low – if he had ducked down, his head would be lower and tilted. But his head was wrong; he was too low. Specter looked to the window and saw, in the reflection, Randal going through a trap door. Specter spun on his back and got ready to jump over the table and shoot Randal. He looked to the window again and it exploded.

The window, the wall, everything seemed to be going up at once! Specter, having been on the other side of one of those guns before, knew immediately that at least seven private defense contractors were on the ground and another team was still in the air. Pri-cons.

"Didn't think you could handle me on your own?" Randal yelled above the gunfire.

"This ain't me, buddy!" was Specter's reply.

Randal's quick and ludicrous quip back made Specter actually laugh. "Can you tell them they've got the wrong house?"

Specter thought they had about a minute before the house was surrounded when the first explosion sounded outside. Randal had booby-trapped the old house!

"I think you just did," Specter shouted back, just as two more explosions rocked the house.

Specter quickly weighed his options. First, the other team was probably listening in. Second, why would the Corps send in a team just for Randal? Did they want him alive? Still, wouldn't it be easier to...then it hit him right in the gut.

This team was there for him!

He turned his face toward the door and raised his voice, "Hold your fire!"

Specter rolled closer to Randal's side of the table – careful to be as quiet as possible. The floor erupted where he had just been. Specter moved to where Randal was – or, more accurately, where he should have been. Randal was gone!

The kitchen table thumped against his back as bullets tore at it. The drumming of the bullets against the table let Specter know it was about to give way. To his astonishment, the trap door cracked opened and Randal asked a simple question, "I get you out, you let me go?"

"Deal," Specter replied.

The door popped open, and with a quick spin Specter was up, around, and down through the trap door. It didn't turn out to be much – just a lid covering a four foot drop from the bottom of the floor to the ground. Specter let the door flap shut above him as he went to his knees.

Specter looked up and straight into the barrel of Randal's gun. Specter didn't bother to raise his sidearm – Randal had him dead to rights. His mind began searching for his options when Randal repeated his question.

"I get you out, you let me go, right?"

Specter repeated his response, "Yes."

When Randal didn't seem to understand, Specter said, "I can sign something to that effect if you'd like – but we've only got about two minutes before this house is a hole."

That drove Randal to action. He put his gun in a canvas bag and shoved the bag in Specter's chest.

"We go out behind you but we've got to wait a bit more," Randal said.

"Wait for what?" Specter said in exasperation. "We have to get out of here!" Specter moved to where Randal had pointed and saw a rough path leading out from the crawlspace. This would take them out behind the house where, according to his reconnaissance, they would be going into a thicket.

As Specter looked around, Randal started fidgeting with something on the ground. Specter noticed large jars of – of something – on one side of the crawlspace and bags of tomato dust and fertilizer on the other. It was then that Specter realized the sub-flooring was all covered in a black – sticky, as he touched it – covering. Randal started putting everything right under the trapdoor.

A piece of metal caught Specter's eye. It was pressed into the floor covering and was about three inches square. It was crudely stamped:

Good luck finding any trace of me

I'll be haunting you for eternity

Realization struck Specter, and he knew the plan of escape; Randal was going to get it so hot in here that any bodies inside would be cremated. That's why they had to wait as long as they could. His mission had now shifted 180 degrees.

Now he had to make sure that Randal lived – the survival of both of them depended on it.

"Will we be visible from the air?" Specter asked.

"I've got some smoke that should cover us," Randal replied.

Randal's tone worried Specter – amidst everything and Randal's disposition – there was something else that was worrying Randal. Like the lynch pin wasn't going to pull when he needed it to.

"What's the problem, Randal? What's not right?" asked Specter.

Randal's response was quick and trusting – as if he, too, could sense that their shared survival was paramount. At least for now.

"I had some dynamite ready to blow upstairs, but I don't know if it's too shot up to work," Randal said.

"However you set this stuff off will be sure to make that go, too. We just need to be sure they're inside before it goes," Specter said.

The heavy tromp of boots above them was clear indication that the time was now. They both scurried to the back of the house. Randal had two detonators with him, and just before they reached the back wall he stopped, dropped one, and pushed the plunger on the other.

Nothing happened.

Thinking quickly, Specter knocked on the sub-floor with one hand and whispered, "Do it again."

Randal was already resetting the plunger. The sound of boots moved closer. Randal slammed the plunger down and Randal and Specter were thrown to the ground by the concussion.

Specter knew by the very fact he was alive that the explosion had been rigged to eliminate anyone – and anything – above. He saw Randal hit the other plunger, and fire erupted under the trapdoor. Randal turned toward him and shooed him out of the way of the hole in the crawlspace. He started to protest but figured it was Randal's show, and Randal should be the director.

Randal stopped at the wall and pointed with two fingers to his eyes then to the ground. He stepped over about a foot long section of the wall and Specter did the same. Specter's respect for Randal was increasing. Randal had done his homework and wasn't saying anything knowing that the other team would have listening devices trained on the house. Not talking increased their chances, but crashing through the woods was another matter.

Randal grabbed the bag from Specter and started off through the thicket behind the house. As Randal led the way through the thicket, Specter was impressed by how he had carved a way through the dense briars and vegetation. They had gone maybe one hundred feet – hard to tell in that mess – when Specter's ears picked up the sound of a helicopter. *We must be pretty important for them to send a helicopter instead of a platform,* he thought. He grabbed Randal's shoulder and pulled him down. Specter put his finger to his lips and pointed up. Randal caught on quickly and stayed still. Any movement would be caught, but if they stayed still they just might make it.

Specter re-evaluated Randal. Here was a guy who had invented webarmor and then vanished. Only one Hunter had ever found him before now – and Specter was beginning to think that was because Randal wanted to be found. Not much consolation if they got caught out here in the woods. If only there were something back at the house that would distract the pri-cons. So much for wishes.

As the sound of the helicopter faded, Specter tapped Randal on the knee, signaling him to move on. Randal stayed put. Specter tapped him again and motioned for him to move. Randal – still quiet – made a 'no' motion and then pointed at his wrist – like at a watch.

Before Specter could decide to wait or go on with a knocked-out Randal on his back, there was another explosion from the house – more accurately, a chain of explosions. Specter would do well to re-evaluate Randal. Randal grabbed Specter by his shirt, dragged him up, and they took off.

Specter was hard pressed to keep up, even with Randal carrying the bag of whatever he had brought with him. It was clear that Randal knew this path intimately. Like he knew it would save his life one day. Today.

Chapter 4

Randal pushed on and on. The path opened up maybe three hundred feet from the house. It was one of the reasons he had picked the old house. There was the sharp drop off right behind the house, a long gentle downhill slide for about a half mile, and then another steep drop off of about fifty feet to a creek. He stopped there for a quick word with Specter. They looked back and saw smoke from the house. Randal hoped his plan was working. Specter looked flushed but fine. Importantly, Specter looked like he understood that their shared survival was the most important thing right now. Randal made his words quick.

"We've got about five miles of mostly uphill..."

Specter interrupted him, "That'll put us out of their net if we can get there – let's move."

And so they did. Randal had been over this area before. He knew when he'd be challenged, when he could let loose – he knew the trail. Specter, on the other hand, did not. Specter was in fine condition, though, and tried to mimic Randal as best he could. He would speed up when Randal did and found out Randal would hold back before a particularly steep part. They left the old house far behind, but still they would steal glances back at the smoke rising from what used to be. The path Randal was leading them on provided many chances to look back – indicative of good planning on his part. Specter never caught sight of more than that one helicopter, so hopefully they could get far enough out of the Corp's net. Heck, hopefully the Corps thought both of them were already dead.

Specter continued to trace their progress in his mind. The orthographic maps he had studied popped up in his mind. This was one of the ways he would've chosen as an escape route. He had learned to have an idea of where your Prey is going to run.

In Specter's mind, this was a route reserved for smart people. It was uphill, but not exclusively. It was difficult, but that made it harder for pursuit. Most importantly, it put you further from any established towns or places, which made it harder to maintain pursuit over time. This would be the route a smart man would take – if he had the provisions and the constitution to handle the trek. It seemed apparent to Specter that Randal had just that.

And so they went. Up and away. The few downhill portions made their legs feel the full extent of their ascent. They did settle into a steady pace, though, fueled by the need to make sure their escape.

After about a half hour, Randal pulled up, set his bag down, and started walking around. Specter slowed as well. They both looked back to where the old house was. Randal was relieved to see the smoke still rising. In between breaths, Randal explained.

"The longer that fire burns, the better off I am. We are."

"Make them think you're cremated?" Specter asked. "That's what the tomato dust and stuff was for?"

"Yeah," Randal replied, a bit surprised. "Yeah, the sulfur, the jars were pig fat, and the pitch I'd painted on the underside of the floor."

"The sticky stuff?"

"Yes," was Randal's only reply.

"How long does it have to burn?"

Randal's answer was quick. "If it's still burning now – that'll be enough. I hope the explosions made them wait until they could scan for other explosives. That'd be about fifteen to twenty minutes. If the fire had fifteen minutes to burn, it'd be hot enough to cremate bones – hot enough for them not to be sure we got out. Hot enough for them to say I died in that fire.

Specter thought for a moment. "That's why you stayed put this time wasn't it? You had this plan and had no intention of running."

Randal smiled a weary smile. "People don't keep looking for you if they think you're dead." He went back to his bag and started going through it.

Specter started circling around, his hand moving towards his sidearm. If he could at least get behind him, Randal would have to turn around to shoot him.

Randal's right hand felt the grips of his revolver, and he let it rest there. He felt for the canteen with his left, found it, and quickly pulled it out. He could see Specter just imperceptibly shift. Randal tossed the canteen to him as he asked, "Water?"

Specter easily picked the canteen out of the air with his left hand while keeping his right hand directly above his gun. It was clear that Randal still had his right hand in the bag – but he'd still have to turn to get the gun around to shoot him. Specter thought he could still draw and shoot before Randal could do that.

They locked eyes.

Randal broke the silence. "You made me a deal – I got you out and you were to let me go. I've spent a lot of time running and a long time planning so I don't have to run anymore."

Specter knew that. This guy would've killed him without a second thought back there, but this guy's word meant something to him. He had seen it to a degree in his travels but never had had to live by it. He knew he owed Randal – not just for getting him out of the house – but for giving him a plausible explanation of his death; now he was free, too. He had to give Randal his word in a way Randal could trust.

"You probably can't get that gun up before I can pull mine and shoot you." He watched Randal's pupils dilate. "But," he crouched down, "but you did get me out of there and the sound of a gunshot would put us both on the run again." Randal's eyes jerked just a whit to the right and he knew Randal hadn't thought about the sound of a gunshot alerting those searching the old house.

"I've done a lot of traveling myself," continued Specter, "and I would prefer not to die out here before I get rested up." With that, he crouched down and took his right hand – slowly – from his back, opened the canteen, and took a drink. Randal's eyes never left his, neither did his hand leave the bag. Specter held out the canteen to Randal with his left hand. Randal didn't move and didn't break eye contact. Specter withdrew the canteen, took another drink, and capped it.

Specter looked Randal in the eye and said, "We've been thrown in this together. They've wanted you for years – you know that. That team back there was for me – sooner than I thought – but they were after me. Are after me." He let those words hang in the open, twisting in the wind like his past life. "I can't go back home; if they think I'm alive, they will hunt me. You've given me a chance at freedom, freedom from not being hunted."

Specter continued, "Maybe we can help each other out here. At least for a while, my not being hunted means you not being seen or recognized. My safety is tied to us being thought of as dead and ashes."

Randal didn't seem to be moved by any of it.

"We need to keep moving so you need to decide whether we can survive better together or whether you'll go on alone."

He started to wonder if Randal was epileptic and if he was actively seizing.

"This is your one chance because I'm not going to wonder if you're looking for the best time to kill me." He held the canteen out to Randal.

Randal's hand felt so at home and comfortable on the gun hilt. He didn't want to have to trust this – this killer – but his words did make sense. He had never heard of kill teams going after one person unless that person was one of their own – or abnormally dangerous. He had to admit he could benefit from traveling with Specter, even if only for a while. Especially if Specter thought their survival was tied together, he could at least get clear of the search team.

With that decision made, he let the revolver fall out of his hand. He took his hand out of the bag and reached for the canteen. It was awful for Randal to watch Specter visibly relax. He figured if he had tried to pull the gun, Specter would've killed him without even pulling his own gun. One thing Randal had learned in his wanderings was when to trust. He fancied himself a pretty good judge of character, and once he had made the decision to trust he jumped in feet first.

"I've got a cap and ball 1851 Colt Navy revolver in .36 caliber loaded, three extra cylinders all loaded, a flask of powder, a pound of jerky, four biscuits, dried jalapeños, some dried vanilla beans, and a jar of pickles. Also in the bag is a blanket, a tarp, and a change of clothes. My plan was to continue on this way. There's a small town about two days away and I planned on re-supplying there.

"With what?" was all Specter asked.

Randal's frown asked his question.

"With what will you re-supply? You don't have much worth trading – save for the vanilla, maybe," Specter responded.

"Knowledge. I thought that's how you would've tracked me. There's always been something I know for which people are willing to trade," Randal answered.

Specter kept re-evaluating this scientist turned Runner. It was the route that Specter would've taken – complete up to the going to that town to get supplies. He could probably learn something from this guy. He could probably start by trusting him – trusting him full out like Randal trusted him. Granted it had taken some time for Randal to get there, but now he was an open book: trusting. Specter would do well to remember that his own time in the Outerlands was limited – even if considered extensive back in the Enclaves – compared to Randal's. But trust didn't come easily to Specter. One more test and then he'd be all in.

"Too bad about your bow..." he threw out as bait.

"What bow? Oh – wait – no, that had to stay."

Specter asked his next question by raising his eyebrow. Why?

"Well, in order for them to think I burned up in there I had to have most of my stuff in there, believable stuff. I mean, I had to have a means of getting food – that bow – pots, pans, privy. I had no idea how long I'd be under surveillance before someone came, so I had to leave everything there. So I kept the gun hidden in the bag for a long time and picked up the bow so they could find it among the ashes."

"Good thinking. Still a shame about the bow, though. It would've come in handy," Specter replied, still giving him time to pass the test.

"That bow wasn't really much," Randal said. "I've got a better one – the one I call my bow – hidden in a cache about a mile further on. I plan on picking it up along with some other supplies."

Randal passed the test with flying colors. He was trusting Specter with even his hidden cache. It was time for Specter to trust him.

"Well, in for a dime, in for a dollar," Specter began. "I found your cache two days ago and moved it." Randal's surprise was clear – his hand went almost involuntarily back towards his gun. "Don't worry. It's still all there. I just had to have a fallback plan if you slipped away from me. It's a good escape route – the one I would've picked. And since you laid your cards on the table, here's mine."

Specter looked back at the smoke from the old house before he went on. "I knew that was coming sometime – soon – but not this soon. I was sent here to kill you, but my 'job' has obviously been terminated. Keeping you alive is my mission now. We need to get your stuff, but they'll expect you to go to the nearest town if you're alive, so that's out. I brought some extra supplies that I hid near yours so we'll be able to head west, bypass that town, and head for the next town, Renna's Stream. We'll be able to get some horses there and then we can make it out to a place I've got picked out where we can lay low until they call off the search."

Randal took it all in and simply nodded. "We'd better get moving then," he said as he stood up and shouldered his bag. "Your lead, then?"

Specter obliged.

Chapter 5

They reached the cache without incident, the smoke still rising from the old house. Both men felt renewed vigor. They had made it through the immediate danger. They were re-supplied. The smoke marked their "grave," and both felt they could begin again and reclaim their lives.

Specter divided up what was there so each could share the load. He gave Randal his bow and quiver, some provisions, and some blankets. He took the same, buckled on his gun belt, and brought out a wicked-looking crossbow. It was a combination pump shotgun with a crossbow mounted on top. It had an open frame painted in such a way that it reflected no light and just oozed black. Specter held it up proudly for Randal to admire; it was clear that two old friends had been reunited. Randal just smiled and tried to hide his shudder. He reminded himself that even the headsman would take pride in his ax and his ability. He shuddered again in relief that he didn't have Specter as an enemy.

Ready to move out again, Specter donned a flat gray-black duster. Randal recognized the material immediately – webarmor. Specter noticed his glance.

"It'll break up my heat signature. Sorry, I didn't think I'd have company, or I might've packed an extra," Specter said.

"Would you really?" Randal asked. He went on quickly when it sounded less cheerful than he wanted. "Don't worry about it. I've made it this far without having to use it."

Time was short and both men were ready to make the most of the daylight they had left.

They ran on.

The landscape didn't change that much for them. Specter led them along the best path he could find. He consulted his map rarely, stuck to the ridges, and maintained a steady pace. They saw no sign of pursuit and no sign of patrols. They did scare up some small game – squirrels, rabbits, and such – but they didn't see any large animals. At the pace they kept, they were probably loud enough to alert larger game. They did stop twice to eat, but only briefly. And only long enough to get enough down to keep going. Specter did stop at certain points for no other reason Randal could make out but to listen. Apparently, he didn't hear anything he didn't want to because he'd always start out again, Randal following obediently behind.

When the sun set, both men thought they had put enough miles behind them. They both ate a little more as they watched the night set in. Specter directed Randal to sleep first. Randal put out his bedroll confident he wouldn't sleep a wink. He closed his eyes and decided to try some deep breathing. He was jostled awake by Specter.

Specter made him stand up and only whispered "Wake me up at first light." Randal stamped his feet awake and – shocked by the memory of the previous day – found it no trouble to stay awake. Standing helped too, though.

Randal listened to the sounds of the forest. He turned his head to hear those sounds made nearby, craned his neck to hear those sounds that only carried to where they were. He had spent nights in the woods before – even spent nights in the woods when he'd been on the run before. But those times he had been too exhausted to care, so exhausted he had usually slept right through the night, jerking back awake with a shock. Those times he had been alone.

It was different being on the run with someone. It was even more different when it was clear he was the one along for the ride and not making the decisions.

But he had decided to trust Specter. Specter had been the Hunter before – goodness only knew how many times. That meant he would know what to expect and, therefore, would know how to avoid detection. Avoiding detection meant that he might – just might – have a shot at not running anymore. That was worth it. He was content in letting Specter run the show. For now, anyway.

He crouched down against a tree and watched and listened as the day broke across the forest. He got up and nudged Specter's shoulder as the sun peeked over the horizon. Specter jerked and was on his feet almost before Randal could jerk his hand back. Randal was again faced with the fact that Specter could kill him any time he wanted. They ate breakfast, checked the map, and started out as they had ended the day before: Specter leading, Randal following.

The day passed much the same as the day before, but there was no plume of smoke from the old house anymore. The fire was out, and both men knew a search would be imminent. Whether they threw out a large net or kept it confined to the ashes of the house, a search would be done. It was this thought that spurred them on today. The vigor with which they had ended yesterday was replaced by a kind of desperation to be outside the scope of that search.

Stopping only for lunch and dinner – more to catch their breath rather than taste their food – they pushed further. Specter felt confident that if they were spotted and pursued, it would be a large, fully-manned assault. That meant keep going and hope you don't hear gunships. And so they pushed further. The relief at having made it to another sunset was enough to let Randal sleep soundly for the few hours he had. Specter was impressed at how Randal was handling himself. He pushed, and Randal kept up. He didn't talk, and Randal didn't complain. He told him to sleep, and Randal woke him up when he was told. Specter was impressed, but he knew Randal couldn't keep going. Hell, he knew he couldn't keep going much longer. It was a good thing they didn't have much further to go.

That was his same thought as Randal shook him awake. Checking his map as they wolfed down the last of their cold biscuits and jerky, Specter plotted their course and set out. He passed the first stream they came to but stopped at the next one. Too early for lunch, Randal questioned the stop.

"We've been pushing hard for two days," Specter said. "We need to at least change clothes before we go into Renna's Stream." He then directed Randal to go first. Randal did – taking the opportunity to wash up a bit before he put on his next change of clothes. He donned a non-descript brown shirt and some pants. He kept watch while Specter did the same.

Specter came up behind him and tapped his shoulder. "Let's get going," he said. Specter had put on a fresh denim shirt and jeans, and his duster was noticeably absent. Randal asked him about that.

"We're close to the town. They're used to seeing me in denim, and the duster might raise some suspicions," Specter answered. Randal watched as Specter took his gun/crossbow out, broke it down, and rolled the pieces up in the cloak. He did keep his revolvers holstered and buckled on. "The duster would be different enough for some of them to remember it."

"But not another person?" Randal asked.

"Not if you're working for me," replied Specter. "And that's the way we play this – the only thing out of your mouth is 'yes, sir' and 'no, sir' and you don't have to like it. It won't be for long. Clear?"

"Yes, sir," Randal replied.

Chapter 6

Within half an hour they started passing some outlying farms. They slowed to a walk but did not stop. They simply waved and kept moving. The town proper was only a faint light of hope in a bleak sea of memories. Randal could see that this town used to be a quaint, picturesque, quintessential Main Street town before the Breaking. Now, only about four of the twenty or so buildings lining the main street looked occupied. The light persisted, though, like the last embers from a roaring fire that refused to go out long after the warmth and enjoyment from the fire had drained away.

If it was like most other towns after the Breaking, there was a store, a restaurant/bar, an inn of some sort, and a meeting hall used for church, town hall-type gatherings, court proceedings, and the like. Some of the other buildings which looked well-kept might have been used to house workers.

But this was no sight-seeing trip. Specter kept his pace and moved resolutely and directly toward the store. Randal followed him in and didn't speak, just like they had planned.

Randal was actually glad Specter had told him to keep quiet, but he almost said something anyway. Randal observed a transformation in Specter that truly surprised him. As Specter stepped through the doorway of the store he seemed to become another person. The cold eyes and coiled readiness gave way to a friendly, if driven, affability. Specter swept over to the counter, and the change in him was evident even in his gait. He grasped the clerk's hand warmly and appeared genuinely glad to see him again. The mood was infectious.

Randal stood quietly by as the clerk's wife and other workers were called up to receive, in their turn, Specter's warm greetings. The emotions appeared genuine to Randal, and he was forced to re-evaluate his perception of Specter as simply a driven, cold blooded killer. It was logical that Specter might have other facets to his personality which his profession would require him to keep from his Prey. Randal realized there was more to Specter than his personalized weapons and the zeal to use them.

Specter talked further, and Randal was beginning to wonder if they were going to get any supplies or just reminisce. About that time, a stocker went to the back. He appeared a bit later with a well-packed crate. Clearly, Specter had been around often enough to have a usual order. And Randal's presence wasn't enough of a novelty to arouse suspicion. These observations caused Randal to question a few things. Before he could think them through, Specter called him over to pick up the crate. Randal nodded to all in greeting and thanks as he picked up the crate.

His smile for the owner was met with a stern hand. The shop owner put his hand on the crate, and Randal stopped. The owner turned his eyes from Randal to Specter. In those eyes, Randal saw the age the shopkeeper's smile had belied. He saw the concern of one who recognized danger and had borne his share of loss from such danger.

As he spoke, the shopkeeper leveled his gaze on Specter.

"There's something not right on the wind this trip, Mr. Franklin. You and your man here watch out, okay?" With that, he lifted his hand from the crate and gave Randal a nod. Randal picked up the crate as Specter shook hands and embraced the owner. Randal heard Specter mutter "Thank you" as he exited the shop. Specter strode up behind Randal and put his arm around him.

"Known them fifteen years, broke bread with them, and he's one of the few people I trust. He's never said anything like that before. Something's going on," Specter said, back again to the Specter that Randal was familiar with.

He clapped Randal on the back and said "Think alive," as he strode on ahead and led them on their way out of town. Randal had never heard that term, but the sentiment was not lost on him. Whether he would've said 'Look alive,' 'Stay frosty,' or even 'Heads up,' it all meant that this might be the end of the run. And for Specter's demeanor to visibly darken meant that Randal should be just shy of messing his pants.

Chapter 7

Specter veered from Main Street and made for a farmhouse set off the road with a large barn and stables. The mounts! Randal had almost forgotten about needing horses. Specter still appeared affable in talking with the stable owner but also in a rush. A range hand was leaving as Randal walked up. Another hand grabbed the crate from Randal and disappeared further into the barn.

Specter sounded dire as he asked, "Glenn over at the store said he smelled some kind of storm blowing through. Have you felt it?"

The stable owner reminded Randal of those he'd met in his travels. He had the same demeanor of those not shaken by much; like those who had looked death in the eye and still walked away.

"Well, Glenn is known to sense things," he began, "but it's always good advice to be loaded and ready. Don't you think?" he said as he poked his pipe in Specter's direction. "You still have that pig-sticking scatter gun?" he asked Specter. When Specter tapped at his pack the horse dealer was quick to badger him about getting it out. He was good natured through the whole thing, but it was very clear he wanted to see that weapon.

Specter finally obliged and, with the steady hand of one who knew the weapon intimately, he had it together quickly. He showed off the weapon, describing all of its perks: titanium frame, custom pump action, nine shot capacity, et cetera. As he showed off the weapon, the stable hands came back leading two horses, one with the crate secured behind the saddle.

Specter obviously knew his horse because he put his gun in the ranch owner's hands and went up to the horse and started petting its face and neck. The horse responded to seeing his friend, obviously happy. The ranch owner dismissed his hands, and as they gave Randal the reins of the other horse, Specter mounted. The owner clapped Specter on the leg and forced the crossbow into his hands much like an apprehensive squire might have handed his knight a sword.

Specter was a bit taken aback, but Randal, watching him, saw that he understood. This man wanted Specter mounted, armed, and away. Specter's eyes flicked to Randal's. They shared a barely perceptible nod, and Randal then mounted. Randal turned his horse toward the road as Specter bent to shake the rancher's hand and tell him something. Randal couldn't make out what he said, but whatever it was, Specter tore out of there.

Specter led them on out of town and didn't stop until they were quite a way from town. Randal was hard pressed to keep up; he hadn't ridden in a while. Specter pulled up and let Randal come up alongside him. Specter was quick and to the point. "We have to cross over an old highway. Stop where I do. If we're going to have trouble, it'll probably be there."

Specter gigged his horse, and Randal was forced to do the same. They rode on for a little bit, and then Specter slowed to a walk. Rather than come up beside, Randal fell in behind him. They walked the horses for maybe another mile and then Specter abruptly stopped and dismounted. Randal did the same.

Specter checked his guns, put his duster back on, and then put a cowboy hat on that matched his duster in color. He looked to Randal like he was straight out of the late 1800's – well, except for the crossbow. Randal didn't need prompting. He fished the replacement cylinders out of his pack and then grabbed his bow and quiver. They shared another barely perceptible nod and moved out.

They walked only about one hundred feet from where they tethered their horses and found the edge of the tree line. Specter crouched just at the edge and waited for Randal to do the same. Randal crouched down on Specter's right. They were looking at what used to be an interstate highway. The road closest to them sat maybe sixty feet below them down a smooth slope. This was maintained by the Corps; the lack of vegetation on either side of the highway and the median was clear indication that the area had been sprayed. Virtually no plant would grow in that area and no animals had a need to be in there. It was essentially a dead zone.

After a full fifteen minutes of crouching there, Specter spoke in tones barely audible. "There's been some activity here recently and it's set everybody on edge. It's not normal, and that worries people."

Randal only nodded.

After fifteen minutes more, Specter again spoke with his words softer than a whisper. "When we go, we'll ride at a full gallop from here to that opening on the other side." He pointed with his right hand moving ever so slowly.

When Specter did not immediately stand up, Randal resigned himself to wait again. And they did. Randal caught Specter's eye and just raised his eyebrows. He didn't trust himself to be as quiet as Specter. Specter quietly replied, "I know, but something's not right." He waited a moment and then added, "Something's off."

Then they heard the platforms. Specter held his hand flat as if Randal didn't know to stay absolutely still. He was nearly paralyzed!

As the platforms came forward along the old highway, it was easy to see why they elicited such fear. It was a hybrid vehicle with its origin back in World War II. The monofoil platform was designed to afford soldiers a tree top view of the battlefield and a superior vantage point from which to shoot. The big problem, originally, was that, as the platform rose, it also became a great target. Webarmor changed that. You weren't such a target if shooting you only made you mad.

The platforms were powered with four turbine engines and piloted rather like the two-wheeled scooters that people rode at the beach and malls before the Breaking: lean and go forward, stand up and stop, left and right controlled pitch and yaw. The platforms were originally used to oversee outdoor workers – just observation platforms. They evolved into armored and manned platforms used to oversee prisoners and prison work crews. A few more adjustments further modified the platforms for combat. This is what advanced upon them now: two fully armed and manned platforms. Pri-cons.

Chapter 8

Each platform carried eight people: a seven man team plus a pilot. They approached steadily with little more noise than a helicopter. The platform itself was not elaborate. It looked like a flatbed trailer from a semi-truck had been cut in half, a stick placed in the middle, and engines on the corners. The attack team sat with the team leader in front and the pilot in the middle, and three down each side.

The soldiers-for-hire on the platform added to the fear these platforms instilled. These private security contractors, these pri-cons, had replaced the organized military in the years after the Breaking. Each of them were trained to be cold blooded killers. Those who rose in rank were the most skillful and, importantly, most eager to kill. They were all in similar uniform except for the pilot and team leader. The team wore all black webarmor with no insignia. The helmets they wore were a mix between modern military helmets and the German helmets of World War II. The flange on the sides of the helmet came down nearly to the shoulders and the face was covered – except for the mouth – by a large, bullet-proof visor. It was here that information was displayed to the individual including maps, crosshairs, images, whatever they needed. None of that was seen from the outside, though. All that was visible to the outside, however, was a dark visor. The mouth area was left open to accommodate a breathing mask, but those were not needed here. All members of the team were equipped with an evolution of the classic Kalashnikov 7.62mm rifle. The materials used to make the weapon were different, but aside from the polymer stocks, and lighter, stronger metals, it was basically just a souped-up AK-47 rifle. The team leader differed from the team members in wearing a white helmet and carrying both a rifle and a sidearm. The pilot wore a red helmet and carried only a sidearm.

Randal's fear was driven out of him by anger. White-hot, seething anger. These pri-cons didn't even bother to conceal their leaders or to seek cover but stood there arrogantly knowing that they couldn't be stopped. All because they had webarmor and no one else did. They could use basically the same weapons they always had because they were still effective. And their opponents had yet to devise an effective response. Well, he could. As he prepared to rise, he was stopped by Specter's strong right hand on his arm. He kept still. But Specter didn't release his arm.

The first platform seemed to pause directly between where they were and the opening they needed to ride to. The second platform caught up to the first, paused, and then was visibly waved on by the first team leader. The first platform dropped low and the team disembarked in the far highway lane across from Randal and Specter into the median. Randal stole a glance at Specter, but Specter only raised one finger on the hand he was holding Randal with. Wait.

The team on the ground spread out and focused on examining the ground. Randal couldn't make out what they were looking for. *Maybe they lost a hubcap*, he thought. He had been here for at least half an hour before they showed up, and he still hadn't seen anything. Not anything that would summon a platform crew anyway. He tried to focus on the ground in front of the pri-con closest to him – tried to see what he was looking for.

Specter's fingers suddenly locked down on Randal's arm. Randal knew Specter had seen something and wanted him to as well. Randal scanned the scene below him, but didn't pick up anything.

There!

He saw it. It – he – had jumped up on the platform and, using two tomahawks, killed the pilot. He – no, it was a <u>she</u>! – had hit the pilot low, below the webarmor around the Achilles tendon and then jammed the pike of the other tomahawk right up between the pilot's helmet and webarmor. She was off the platform just after the pilot hit the deck. She went off the side opposite of Randal, so he lost sight of her. The platform's engines, still running, must have muffled the pilot's fall because none of the pri-cons facing Randal turned around. Randal scanned for this female killer stupid – or brave – enough to take on a platform team.

He saw her again as a pri-con fell. Apparently the low then high swipes were pretty effective. Randal had never thought that they wouldn't make boots out of webarmor, too. She moved quickly

counter-clockwise to Randal's position and slashed the next pri-con
with both tomahawks to the back of the neck, like a man-made pair
of death scissors. Randal didn't think the hits would penetrate the
webarmor, but the force itself was probably enough to break the pri-
con's neck. Either way, the pri-con dropped like a sack of bricks.

She moved to the next pri-con and almost didn't get there in time.
The pri-con turned towards her, and she cut upward with her right
tomahawk, catching him in the left arm. She followed quickly with
the tomahawk in her left hand, driving the pointed top into the pri-
con's mouth.

Way to keep him quiet, Randal thought.

The woman tilted her left tomahawk up enough so she could
strike his neck with her right. The swift motion cleanly severed that
pri-con's head from his torso. She crouched down and looked to her
right at the remaining pri-cons. She put her tomahawks at her sides –
she must've had some type of belt for them. She took the headless
pri-con's rifle and, shocking Randal, grabbed the decapitated head
and threw it up high into the air towards the front of the platform. In
one fluid motion, she stepped out – towards Randal and Specter –
brought the rifle up and started shooting at the three pri-cons closest
to her. Since they were on the broad side of the platform, she still
had the platform between her and the team leader and the other two
pri-cons on the far side. She must have been aiming for the necks,
because the first just dropped, but the next two fell grasping at their
necks. Everything was happening so quickly it was hard to track. As
she dropped the three soldiers on this side, she crouched and waited
for her thrown head to hit. As the pri-cons on the far side turned to
see the source of the gunfire, the head hit the front end of the
platform. The two pri-cons and the team leader trained their guns on
the head as she popped up and – clack! clack! – got one and – clack!
clack! – got the last.

That was when her luck seemed to run out. She had given the
team leader enough time to sight on her, and she was spun around
and down as he fired. Randal caught sight of blood spray and knew
she had been hit. Randal couldn't make out the words, but he knew
the team leader was talking as he came around to confirm his kill.
Probably calling back the second platform, he thought.

The team leader showed his arrogance. Whether he thought he
had killed her or that his webarmor would protect him, he came
around the front of the platform – on Randal's side – with his rifle

lowered. The woman had just been waiting for him to clear the front. She fired a long burst and seemed to almost take his head off. She'd hit him right in the mouth.

She moved quickly toward the team leader, and Randal could see the blood coming from her left shoulder. Specter finally released his grip from Randal's arm and whispered, "Don't move. Wait."

When she reached the leader, she took off his helmet and started removing his webarmor. Randal thought she was going for the underclothes to make a bandage, but as she worked the webarmor off, she took something from her thigh pocket and put a kind of powder on her shoulder and gave herself a shot of something.

Once she had the webarmor off, she did use the team leader's undershirt. But she used it to wipe out his helmet as she donned the webarmor. She had the webarmor on as the second platform came into Randal's view. She donned the team leader's helmet and turned to meet the second platform. She made some signals with her arms, and Randal saw the other team leader give a thumbs-up. The second platform started to rise above her and cross over her.

As it passed over her, she raised a rifle and started shooting at the underbelly. She must've known where to shoot it because it started smoking, tilted, and just seemed to fall from about thirty feet in the air. The platform exploded just before it hit the ground. The woman rolled out from under the first platform, picked up some more magazines, and retrieved the team leader's side-arm as she walked to where the platform had landed.

Randal watched as the second team recovered from the crash. There was no movement around the platform, but Randal could see that three pri-cons had been thrown from the platform by the explosion. The woman methodically checked every body she came upon, executing any she wasn't sure was dead. The three pri-cons thrown from the blast didn't even come to before she had put a bullet under each one's chin into the helmet.

She looked over the carnage and removed the borrowed helmet and webarmor. She retrieved her tomahawks, tested her shoulder, and set herself like she was off to the woods again.

Randal was about to stand up when he felt Specter's hand on his arm again. Then he noticed two more platforms rushing in on the woman from either side.

Chapter 9

That's not good, Randal thought.

These platforms had no intention of landing. The ground between the woman and the tree line erupted in gunfire. She turned and started to run – towards Randal and Specter – but the platforms tilted, and the median right before the road churned with gunfire in front of her. She stopped just long enough to make it seem like she was giving up, but she took off again. They let her get to the road – just in front of Randal and Specter – when one platform swooped in and physically cut her off. With the other platform hovering above, tilted and giving a clear line of sight to those pri-cons on her side, the woman just stopped. Nothing happened for a while, but as her hands moved toward her tomahawks, all three soldiers on her side of the platform on the ground readied to fire. The team leader must have signaled them to stand down because they eased their weapons, and he jumped down.

The team leader artificially amplified his voice so he could be heard over the platforms. "Shade, lay down your weapons." The woman, Shade, laid down her tomahawks and turned around with her hands up to show she was unarmed. The team leader's voice came through again, "I am going to search you. If you make any move, these men will shoot you. Do you understand?"

She nodded yes. The team leader approached and kicked her tomahawks away with his foot. He then circled around behind her. He began to search her for weapons. Randal's stomach lurched as he thought about what was going to happen. Surprisingly, though, the team leader searched her as he should have and did nothing to molest her. He stepped away and signaled the other platform to land. He then ordered his men to disembark – those on the side closest to Randal first, guns trained on Shade, then those on the side closest to her. The team leader went to speak to the other platform's team leader. They spoke for a while and then separated. The second team leader ordered his men off. Together, the team leaders signaled the pilots to shut down the platforms.

Something was going on. Randal could feel it. Despite the professional manner of the first team leader, Randal knew this had no good end. The pri-cons all gathered in a ring around the woman.

With the platforms off, the first team leader removed his helmet and ordered all to do likewise. Specter and Randal were close enough to hear the team leader's words. "Shade, your position with the Corps has been terminated. Your service to the Corps is appreciated. However, your skill set represents what has been deemed 'operational secrets.' Therefore, you are to be executively removed."

He had the air of one who had given this speech before. In front of a mirror.

"Shade, you will die here today," he said. He then paused to make sure that was a given. "Your skill set is such, though, that I can use it to benefit my team. I have two crews of green recruits, fresh from training, out for their first patrol. What an outstanding training experience for them to find a Hunter on their first patrol!"

Randal couldn't see the man's face, but he could sense the patronizing smile.

"As a training benefit, and a courtesy to you and your service, any man whom you beat in hand-to-hand combat will not be allowed to touch you in any way before your death. Those who do beat you, however, will be allowed their way with you until – umm, say sunset."

Randal felt his stomach turn and his skin crawl. Specter must've felt the same way because he tightened his grip on Randal's arm and gave him the same finger signal. Wait. Randal didn't know if he could wait. But Randal started to think as the men below started removing their equipment and getting ready for the – the further events of the day. Maybe if this guy's word could be trusted, she could beat the crap out of most of those men. That would make it easier to rescue her. Randal had already decided that's what they were going to do.

The pri-cons below formed a circle around the woman, and some of the more eager among them had taken off their webarmor uniforms. In tank tops, boxer shorts, and boots, fully half of the pri-cons stood ready. The team leader called a name, and one of those ready strode forward while his empty space in the ring cinched closed. The pri-con had a swagger, and that might've been the reason the team leader chose him.

The swagger man walked up close to the woman and put his arms on her like a wrestling match. She mirrored him. Locked this way, head to head, she must have said something to him because he jerked his head away from hers and stopped moving. That was the opening she needed. Her right hand shot up and crashed back down into his neck. He crumpled, and she was around and had her foot up and back down into his neck as he hit the ground. The snap was audible even from where Randal was. They all seemed ready to swarm her when the team leader fired his sidearm into the air, then pulled a small rod, and poked the woman with it in her back. She cried out and jerked forward into the arms of those in the ring and was slung backward. She fell to the ground crumpled and twitching.

"Well, that's not fair," whispered Specter. He jerked Randal's arm to get his attention.

"This is risky and she'd be dead if these weren't trainees. If that team leader is stupid enough to keep her alive after she killed one of his men, we can hope that all of them are that dumb. Still, we only have one shot at this or she <u>will</u> be dead. When you see me kill one, you start shooting with your bow. Kill the closest ones first and then pull your revolver and run yelling towards the woman," Specter whispered. Randal understood, slowly nocked an arrow, and turned to look at Specter – but he was gone. The weight of rescuing this woman struck Randal; he would have to kill today.

The team leader pulled the woman up by her hair. He put his face close to hers and simply said, "No killing of my men." He pushed her back and called two names this time. The two pri-cons rushed at her. She caught one in the knee with another audible crack. The next one wrapped her up and tackled her. He hit the ground on top of her and wrestled until he was straddling her. He tried to hold both of her hands in one of his and she took that opening, got one hand free and it shot to his throat like a viper. As he fell backwards she was on her feet ready to finish off both of them when the team leader fired and came in with his cattle prod again. This time the woman just fell and twitched on the ground.

Randal waited as patiently as he could for Specter to start killing these pri-cons. His arrow was ready, but no one was down and he saw no sign of Specter. *He'd better move fast before I lose it,* thought Randal.

Shade regained her feet about the time that Mr. Knee and Mr. Throat were able to hobble off to their place outside of the circle. Mr. Throat kicked at the woman as he left – more like put his foot on her and pushed. It was enough, though; she was off balance and went skidding toward one of the de-uniformed pri-cons. He caught her, but, as she was still off balance, he shifted her around and put her in a head lock. He then swung her out into the circle, spinning her around, and most of those around the ring couldn't hesitate to kick her.

The team leader said nothing, called no more names. He only fired three shots into the air, turned, and walked away. The spinning went over and over – almost interminably long – and it left Randal praying for Specter to make his move.

Two other pri-cons moved in – still with her in a headlock, limp from the hold and the kicks – the pri-con's arm bloody from her scratching. The two picked up her legs and something changed.

Each of these two new ones put one hand on her pants and – knowing what they were about to do – it seemed like every one of them moved closer in as well.

Through it all, it was only then that she called out. It was only once and only brief – as if she knew they would want to hear her cries.

It was then that he noticed the man on the far left – apart from the group, the team leader from the second platform, was wearing some kind of antennae he wasn't before…Specter's crossbow bolt! It was time!

Randal raised up on one knee, took sight of his closest target – Mr. Throat – pulled back and let loose. Randal's arrow took him right between his shoulder blades. Randal re-drew as he fell. His next closest had his webarmor still on, so he aimed for his head. "Think alive" echoed in his mind, and he knew he had to make his shot. He let fly.

It turned out to be low, but sunk into the man's neck – just above his neckline. He dropped like a sack of rocks. Randal was notching another arrow and, as he brought his bow up, he saw a pri-con on the far side of him look up and open his mouth. Before any alert was made, a crossbow bolt appeared in his temple – Specter's kill. Randal looked for his next target when he saw – off to his right – the team leader raising his side arm towards Specter. Randal didn't have time to aim, but he let his arrow go and watched it catch the team leader square in his back. The arrow did not go through the webarmor, but it did knock the team leader off balance and drove the gun from his hand. Randal dropped his bow and pulled his pistol as he started running down the hill, yelling at the top of his lungs.

Chapter 10

Specter's bolt went through the pri-con's temple, thankfully before he could say anything. He was pleasantly surprised at Randal's ability to function and follow orders – especially the orders to kill. He did a quick count as he let his crossbow drop and pulled his knife. He had two, Randal had two, the woman had one. He kept the countdown going in his head when Randal's second mark fell: eleven left. He caught sight of the woman only briefly. She had her clothes on, but she was being pummeled in the face by one of the pri-cons. They didn't have much time before her face was mush – or these new pri-con recruits caught on. Specter pulled one pri-con back from the group by his shoulder – his knife in his neck. He dragged him back to minimize the blood spray. Eleven – ten to go. Specter switched the knife to his left hand and pulled his revolver. He had time to see Randal's arrow hit the team leader, and then he grabbed another contractor, knife to his throat, and raised his gun.

Pow!

He blew the head off of one of the contractors furthest from him. Ten. That stopped everything. And before anyone moved, Randal's yell echoed off the now quiet old highway. Blessedly, Randal's yell came at the perfect time, catching the new recruits off-guard and unsure of where the attack was coming from. *Blessed disarray*, thought Specter. Specter blew two of the stunned pri-cons' heads apart while those further away, distracted, turned to watch Randal running down the hill. Nine, eight. Only two dived for their guns. *The pilots*? he thought . Specter slit the throat of the guard he was holding and let him fall as he pulled his other gun. Seven. Randal was firing his revolver into the crowd, but he'd be lucky to hit anybody.

Specter went methodically through the final six, using their surprise and thankful these weren't battle tested troopers. He started with the two closest to him. He caught the one who tried to charge him with his right. Six. The other tried to run, and he shot him in the back of his head with his left hand. Five. The pri-con who he had seen hitting the woman earlier was still enthralled with his bloodlust and was still hitting her, oblivious of the chaos around him. Specter's bullet entered his head at the man's left temple. There was no longer a right side of his face. Four. With his right hand, Specter tracked one pri-con who had dived for his rifle. As the man raised his weapon towards Randal, Specter's bullet entered his head just behind his right ear. Three. The only two left were the other pri-con who had reacted correctly and gone for his gun and the team leader. The pri-con had gone prone and had a good shot at Randal. Specter didn't have time for a kill shot so he aimed for the rifle and hit it as the pri-con fired. Randal's voice still echoed, so Specter knew it was enough to throw the bullet off. When the pri-con turned to see what had happened, Specter's left hand put a bullet between his eyes. Two. One left.

Specter felt his coat tug at him first on the left but then on the right. He dropped and rolled – the team leader had shot him! As he dropped, he heard Randal's revolver go off.

Hope he went for his head, Specter thought.

Specter rolled with his left gun up (his right was empty). As he looked at the team leader, he saw him clutching his chest. It didn't make sense to Specter – nothing could go through webarmor. As he waited there, ready to end the team leader, Randal fired again, and Specter clearly saw Randal's bullet explode the team leader's chest. The team leader fell with his face towards Specter, the surprise evident on his face.

One and done, thought Specter. *And a heck of a one.*

Specter let the gentle breeze dissipate the black powder smoke. He had no idea what action Randal had seen and didn't want Randal shooting at him. "Pretty nice smoke wagon you've got there," Specter called out of the stillness where he lay.

Randal called back, "Thanks."

Specter got up, looked at Randal, and thought he looked flustered. *Shock?* thought Specter. He had just run down a hill yelling and shooting.

"You okay?" Specter asked him, giving them both time to catch their breath.

"Yeah," Randal replied. "The woman?"

"Probably. I need you to get the horses," Specter said.

"I need his uniform," Randal replied.

"Yeah, we'll get what we can but, right now, I need you to get the horses down here."

"I need to get his uniform," Randal said as he stepped toward the dead team leader.

Specter worried Randal was starting to feel the stress of the combat and he needed Randal to maintain his focus. Specter went full battlefield command on him, "We will get his uniform! Right now you get those horses down here!" The vehemence in his voice stopped Randal. "RIGHT NOW!!" Specter yelled again.

Randal blinked and reason seemed to come back into his gaze. He turned and started to run back up the slope. *Yeah*, Specter thought, *you need that uniform to keep your bullet secret, but I've got to make sure we can get out of here alive.*

Specter started by going back to the woman, Shade. He laid two fingers across her neck and felt a strong pulse. Her clothes were still on, if torn. At least he didn't have to get her pants back on. Her face was swollen badly – maybe even some broken bones. He checked her shoulder. The bullet did go through all the way, but the wound did not appear to be very deep. He recognized the powder she had put on it, and he knew what he had only suspected earlier – she was like him – a Hunter.

Chapter 11

He shook his head, knowing that he was scheduled for termination, too. He had messed with her shoulder enough to know that she was unconscious. That was good because she'd be a handful when she woke up.

Knowing he had to work quickly, he started with face-puncher because he was closest. He picked him up over his shoulder and carried him the twenty feet to the platform. He threw the body on it and went back for another. Randal came bounding back down as he was about halfway through. He seemed clear-eyed and functioning to Specter. "Get all their weapons and loose uniforms," Specter ordered him. He wasn't surprised as Randal went straight for the team leader and got his uniform.

By the time each was through, they had fourteen rifles, four sidearms, and nine webarmor uniforms. Randal had stashed the team leader's uniform in his pack, so Specter took another uniform shirt and started packing the guns in it. They had all the bodies, helmets, and uniforms on the platform. They had their weapons, their retrieved arrows and bolts, her tomahawks, and Randal had stashed the guns and the uniforms in the saddlebags. They had made good time. Each had worked with the fervency of a fugitive. They had left Shade's handiwork alone and untouched. Specter was impressed at how Randal was able to keep himself together after what they'd just been through. *He's seen action*, Specter thought.

Specter went to his pack and pulled out a syringe like the one the woman had injected herself with. Specter went over to her and injected it into her non-injured shoulder. Randal expected her to snap awake, but he knew otherwise when Specter said, "Grab her legs." They carried her over to Specter's horse, and he actually tied her down on his horse – with her feet tied under the horse and her hands tied around its neck. Specter answered Randal's unasked question with, "It'll be easier this way, and it won't hurt her any worse than she is already."

Ready to head out, Specter got an idea.

"Give me that black powder, Randal," Specter asked. Randal obliged and Specter went to the platform. Randal mounted his horse as Specter piddled around. Randal thought they were going to leave all the bodies as they were, but there was Specter, moving them around. Randal brought his mount over. "Posing for a picture?" he asked with no mirth.

"Kind of," Specter replied absently, his mind on something else. Specter handed the gunpowder flask back to Randal. "Get the horses to the other side, will you?" Specter asked. As Randal reached for the reins, Specter's horse whinnied, but he followed right along. They got up to the opening in the woods Specter had pointed out earlier. So long ago it seemed but probably only an hour had passed from when they first dismounted until now.

Randal looked back down over the highway and prayed again that nothing would come by. Specter was on his way up to where they were, but he stopped at one of the first pri-cons Shade had killed. Specter picked up his rifle, sighted and fired at the stacked platform. Nothing happened. Specter looked back, readjusted his aim, and fired again. A spark sprang to life on the platform. Specter dropped the rifle and started running up the hill.

Specter thought of something else as he neared the top. He grabbed one of the woman's tomahawks and ran along the tree line about fifty feet. He came back dragging two saplings in each arm. Specter lashed the saplings to the backs of the saddles. He said, "Let's see if this works – anything might help." When he had secured everything, the fire from below was really going big. "Not much longer, now." Specter said as he mounted. "Let's walk for a bit."

And so they did. They walked the horses and every now and again Randal would check back over their tracks. Specter caught him one time and said, "Tracking's almost a lost art in the Corporations. Something like this might be all we need to make our escape."

They hadn't gone too much further when they heard a large explosion. Specter calmly reached behind him and cut the sapling loose and then he did the same thing for Randal. Putting his knife away, he told Randal, "Now we ride!"

And with that, all thought of being clear was gone. Specter rode hell-bent for leather for most of the next two hours. Randal, usually good with direction, got turned around so many times he would never be able to retrace their path, glad he only had to follow.

As it neared mid-afternoon, they came to a cabin in the woods. Specter dismounted quickly, untied Shade, put her on his back, and went inside with a simple, "Get everything inside, Randal."

Randal did so. It didn't take long. The only stuff they really had was the weapons, the uniforms, the crate of supplies from the store, and their own stuff from the old house. But Randal was a bit upset he had to do it all alone. He just set everything in the front room and, when all was there, went to look for Specter.

Randal found him in a back room that looked like a pantry. He was shocked to see what Specter had been doing to the woman. Specter had her wrapped and secured in some kind of harness that reminded Randal of something used in mountain rescues. He had her rigged to a pulley. Randal flat out could not understand what was going on.

Chapter 12

Specter spoke before a flabbergasted Randal could. "If it were easy, everybody would do it." Checking his ropes again, Specter opened a trap door in the floor and jumped down. Randal stepped over to the edge and saw what looked like a large bored well, about three feet in diameter. Specter lifted the lid aside and, sure enough, Randal could see the water in the bottom of the well, maybe fifty feet down.

Specter got his foot into some kind of rope and started lowering himself into the well! "Don't ask yet," was all he said in explanation. After fifteen to twenty feet, he stopped. Randal looked down the well still wondering what was going on. Specter reached around the piping and was fiddling with something there when Randal saw what he did not believe. A well tile separated behind the pump wiring and the third three foot section of well tile. It just opened up and was lighted behind it. Lighted! Specter got inside the fake section and then stuck his head out.

"Put that hook on the stretcher onto the rope loop right by your head," Specter instructed. His tone indicated he would not accept questions regarding such clear instructions. Randal did what he thought was right and called down, "Okay."

Specter said, "Put her stretcher in the well feet first and send her down."

"Just like that, huh?" Randal asked.

Specter didn't answer.

Randal didn't even know how heavy she'd be. He didn't want to be the rescuer who killed her during his rescue attempt. She was light enough for him to move and, as he rechecked the hook, he found she was light enough to gently ease down the well. He held onto the stretcher and gently made sure the rope would hold her. He was relieved when it did. Specter eased her down until he could grab the foot of the stretcher. Once on his level, he pulled Shade into the alcove behind the well tile and disappeared for a minute.

When he popped back out he sent a basket back up. His only instructions were, "Fill it up." Randal did so with their stuff and soon all of it was down there. Randal wondered how big of a space was down there.

A loop came up instead of the basket, and Specter told Randal, "Put your foot in the loop and come on down."

"Just like that?" Randal asked.

"We've still got to hurry," Specter replied.

Randal did as instructed and started his descent into the well. Specter grabbed his leg when he got near and guided him into the alcove. It was about a ten foot long tunnel about four feet wide. Their stuff was along the side, but Randal saw no sign of the woman.

"Horses?" Specter asked.

"Out front, still tied up, like we got them. But tired and hungry," Randal replied.

Specter was out and up the well without a word. He just climbed the rope up. Once up, he went straight outside and untied the horses. They were good mounts and knew their way home. He slapped their rumps with a hearty "Yah!" And off they went.

Specter then went through the cabin making sure everything was in its place.

They might track them to this cabin but that's where it would end. He stomped around in the other rooms just to stir up the dust and then jumped to the well edge. He closed the trap door after himself and lowered himself a ways down the well. He reached for the large, heavy lid and slid it closed. In the top of the lid – rarely seen – was just enough rot to look reasonable. In truth, it was just enough to slide his rope in the hole around the rebar, secure even though it looked like a child could pull the rebar out. Specter hooked his rope in, held both ends, lowered a bit more, and moved the lid shut. *Almost home*, he thought.

He lowered himself down. Randal guided his feet into the alcove just as he had done for Randal. It was unexpected – he was used to doing this alone – but welcome. Once in, he shoved the well tile shut until it latched. When it did latch, the light went out, and the light in the next room came on. Randal was surprised, Specter had powered lights! Randal hadn't noticed the room before, but there it was, a square room about ten feet on a side and paneled everywhere. It

reminded Randal of a crate box. This was where Shade was lying –
still in her stretcher. He couldn't hold it. *This could work*! Randal
thought. He said, "Thank you, Specter. We can make this work. We
have access to water, we can dig a hole somewhere for a privy, and
we can hide out at least until they give up looking for us. Thanks!"

This took Specter aback. He had seen some folks in tough
situations – many times because he had put them there. But Randal
was smart; Randal hadn't lost touch with the world after the
Breaking. And Randal had fought with him and done well, held up
his end anyway. It was touching to see that genuine emotion. But
Specter didn't handle raw emotion too well. "You think I'd spend
any time in here?" he said – a bit too loud.

"Well," Randal murmured.

"I'll be in a wood box when I'm in a coffin – not until," Specter
said disdainfully.

Randal kept his mouth shut, and Specter was glad he did. Specter
pulled his knife, pried up a board with it, and propped it up with the
knife. He went to the other side of the wall a bit askew from that
board and only said, "Canti-levered." He pushed on the wood plank
and it popped out. He flipped a latch and a section of the wall opened
<u>inward</u> into a large room.

Randal didn't say anything – just looked. His first glance was
wrong. It wasn't a room. It was a full house! This was a great room
with many rooms off of it. This was – he couldn't believe it – a
survival bunker! Randal's feet were moving of their own accord
toward the underground oasis.

Specter's words made him stop. "Help me get her in." They
picked up the stretcher and Specter led the way, walking backwards.
He led them to a room that was outfitted like an actual hospital
room. Randal again re-evaluated. This was a bunker made for a <u>lot</u>
of people. They laid her on the floor, and Specter went to get sheets
and a blanket for the bed. Randal went to work getting her
unfastened from the stretcher. Specter came back in with some
bedding and a large silver bowl. He filled the bowl with hot water
and told Randal to wash her up. Randal was shocked to be in such
opulence. <u>Hot</u> water – from a tap! Randal had almost forgotten what
that was like.

Randal helped Specter get her up on the table. Specter flipped a
switch and a red light started to flash in the ceiling. Randal took a
while to place it. It was a camera. Specter spoke out loud, "We're

recording this for you. I'm Specter. This is Randal. We got to you before they did anything." Specter turned to Randal, "Wash her up. Focus on her shoulder and face and be liberal with the water." And he left the room.

Randal went to work. He removed her torn shirt but left her top on – he didn't know if it was a bra or what. He started in and let the warm water wash away the dried blood and dirt and grime. This was the first chance he had had to be up close to the valiant woman, and he found out she was ugly. Her face was swollen and already starting to bruise and it made her look sickly ugly. Randal cleaned well, though, especially around her shoulder wound. She had a large filigree and ivy tattoo that ran down her right side, from just below her armpit down past her pant line. Randal didn't see any other identifying marks. He was about finished with what he was going to do – her face, shoulder, arms, midriff, and feet – when Specter walked back in with her tomahawks. He held them up to the camera and then placed them on an instrument table, presently empty.

Specter looked at Randal. "Her pants?" he asked. Randal raised his hands as if to say 'not me.' Specter tsked and started undoing her belt. The pri-cons had been kicking her legs repeatedly. He unlaced her pants and gestured for Randal to help. They took her pants off and saw that the tattoo went under her underclothes almost to her mid-thigh. Specter went systematically over both of her legs, ensuring there was no bleeding and no broken bones. Satisfied, he grabbed another washcloth and both he and Randal washed down her legs.

"Did you turn her over?" Specter asked.

"No, I didn't," replied Randal simply.

Specter had Randal help him and they turned her over on her back and continued washing. Specter pulled the hair back from her neck and saw what he expected. The Hunter tattoo.

All Hunters were tattooed with what had come to be known as the Hunter symbol. It was nothing dramatic, simply a crosshair with two lines on the outside. It was done so that the middle horizontal bar of the crosshair formed the middle bar of a capital 'H,' for Hunter. Getting the tattoo was not mandatory, but every Hunter Specter had known had the tattoo. Specter had his tattoo nestled within a tribal design on his right shoulder. Shade, Specter now saw, had incorporated hers by closing the top and bottom of the 'H' and enclosing all within a triangle. Simple and probably only another

Hunter would recognize it, but it would only be visible if she had her hair up.

"Nice Hunter symbol, isn't it?" Randal asked when he saw Specter lingering on the tattoo.

Shocked, Specter only answered, "Yeah."

They dried her off and moved her to a dry bed. Specter placed a blanket over her. He then motioned for Randal to leave the room. Randal walked outside and waited in the hallway.

Randal could hear Specter saying something, but couldn't make out what it was. It reminded Randal of having his sister over and just having to tell her one more thing before bed. Randal thought about that and about Specter's actions towards Shade. He thought about what relationship, what bond, might cause those actions. Was it just mutual respect among fighters? Randal thought about the way Specter moved, how he killed: methodically and efficiently. Then Shade popped into his mind – how methodical and efficient she was at killing.

It was there before him all the time. How could he not have registered that the pri-con's words for Shade were also the words meant for Specter?! These were two killers – two Hunters – in the same place. He stepped farther down the hallway. The stress of combat was affecting him, probably in ways he wasn't even aware of. But one thing was sure: if he was going to die in a crossfire, he was damn well going to have a hot shower first.

Chapter 13

Specter came out of the room and found Randal in the hallway. Specter paused for a minute to consider Randal. How his eyes widened at electric light, his sheer delight over hot water from a tap. Randal had been on the run for longer than any of the other Prey and he was only found this time because he wanted to be. Specter felt like he owed Randal something.

Randal said, "Not every day you find out you're obsolete, is it?"

Specter felt it more than ever. "When's the last time you had a burger and fries?"

"And ketchup?" asked Randal.

"Yeah, ketchup, too."

Randal followed Specter into the kitchen and sat down at the bar. Specter opened an actual operating refrigerator and pulled out two beers and a ketchup bottle. He gave one beer to Randal, said "Cheers," and began telling the story of the bunker while he cooked.

"A man who I was sent to kill actually owned this place. He was a CEO who misappropriated company funds – but in a dramatic, novel way. He fell for the whole 2012 end of the world/ doomsday thing, being prepared, all that – and had started to form what he thought of as a little kingdom."

Specter took out some frozen patties and fries from the freezer and started a pan warming on the stove.

"He was going to rule in a new world – complete with attendants, soldiers, a harem, healers, oracles – and this would be his 'sacred' place. He would, in theory, reach out from here after the cataclysm and build a castle around it for the surrounding subjects."

Specter put the fries in an oven and kept turning the hamburger patties.

"So he had this whole place built, powered, and stocked, but then the apocalypse didn't happen. Not the way he thought it would anyway. Then, after the Breaking, he, being CEO, was fine – he didn't have to care. But he couldn't let it go. His vision of hegemony just had to happen. He set about ways to <u>make</u> some kind of apocalypse happen. He finally settled on a fabricated pandemic. That was enough. That's when I got sent in."

Specter served the food.

"He wanted me to join him, of course."

Randal finally spoke, "And that's when you talked to him. Right?"

Specter just nodded and ate.

After a while Specter said, "We need to talk."

Randal felt a brief chill. He asked, "Not like that talk, I hope."

Specter chuckled. "No, not like that."

He stood up and told Randal, "Come on."

Randal followed him out of the kitchen area and down the hall from the infirmary. They got to a door, and Specter opened it and stood to the side. He motioned Randal down the stairs. As Randal walked down, Specter said from behind him, "We'll talk in the morning. It'll be safer for you to be on another level when she wakes up. In case she's feeling squirrelly." Specter trailed off. "I'm getting tired," he said. "Any room down there is yours and has its own bathroom. Wash up and get some sleep."

Randal looked up from the landing and tiredly said, "Thanks."

Specter added, "You did well today. I know your background from your file but not the things you've been through. I may be off-base, but those pri-cons were going to kill her. We did the right thing."

Randal looked up at Specter and nodded.

Specter felt awkward and didn't like it. "Take it before your god and process it in your mind. We need to be fresh tomorrow."

Randal turned and said 'good night' with his raised hand.

Specter clicked the door handle locked and left Randal on his own. It was a strange lock, locking people from going down rather than from coming up, but it was useful. Randal would come back up and never know the door was locked. But if Shade got up and started Hunting...well, at least she'd have to find a way to get the door open. He walked on down the hall. The floor plan was remarkably like a Catholic finger chaplet. Upon entering, there was a long circular hallway spreading out both right and left with rooms off of the hall. On the opposite side of the entrance, a long hallway ran to the 'king's quarters.' That was the top part of the cross, which was where Specter stayed.

He entered the ante-room, and it looked as he had left it. It actually looked like the bed-chamber, but that was hidden beyond this room. *You have to love paranoid people for layers of protection*, Specter thought. He walked straight to the bed, laid down, rolled around in the covers, and was out the other side. He wondered if he was getting as paranoid. He felt around behind the bed for the release, found it, and activated it. He stepped down into the actual bed-chamber, closing the door behind him. Finally isolated, he almost collapsed. He forced himself to undress and, leaving his guns by the bed, walked into the bathroom and into the walk-in shower. He turned on the water and washed away the blood of the battle, the grime of travel, and the newness of his situation. He forced himself to relive the action of the day, critiquing his actions and non-actions, deliberately tracing the faces of the dead in his mind. He let the water wash away the images of faces once fixed, knowing they'd remain with him from now on. The water did not wash away any tears tonight, though, and he was thankful for that. He dried off, put on some fresh shorts, and then fell into bed. He decided to sleep and dream of bullets that penetrated webarmor.

And so he did.

Chapter 14

Specter woke up feeling rested. He'd just fought off a battalion of that faceless horde of contract soldiers all wearing webarmor with only one of their rifles loaded with those armor piercing bullets. *So much for dreams*, he thought, *but we'll talk about that today.*

He went to his wardrobe and retrieved an outfit. He chose some black cotton pants and a white sleeveless shirt. He would get some training in today. Dressed and barefoot, Specter went forth into the antechamber. Everything as he left it, he continued on into the main hall.

His nose picked up the smell of bacon, and he knew either Randal or Shade was awake. He went opposite of the kitchen to check on Shade first. He found her door closed and, opening it, found her still asleep as they had left her the night before. Specter edged back out of the doorway and closed the door. He went to the entry room to sort through the uniforms from the contractors. After looking through all of them, he remembered that Randal had stashed that uniform in his bag. Specter turned and headed for the kitchen.

Randal was making a really big breakfast. Like a kid in a candy store, Randal had seen many things he wanted and was making some of everything. Randal acknowledged Specter with a nod as he came up and made a plate for him. Specter saw that plenty would be left for Shade when she woke up. He pulled a chair up to the bar and grabbed his fork.

"Wait a second, Specter," Randal said. Then, closing his eyes, he said, "Lord, thank you for this. This food, this place, this time. Amen."

Specter looked at Randal. "You never did that before," he said.

"I did it silently before," Randal replied.

Specter just grunted, and Randal didn't push it. All he needed now was Randal going off all religious on him. He decided to change the subject. "Sleep well?" he asked.

"Once I put the blankets on the floor I got right to sleep. Kept feeling like I was sinking in the bed. Not used to real mattresses anymore." Randal nervously laughed.

Specter had never realized the cost Randal paid for running so long. He asked, "You never had a mattress in all of your travels?"

Randal stopped with a bite of bacon halfway to his mouth, but did not hesitate in his answer. "Not like that one." He thought for a minute as he chewed his bacon. "The last time I had a proper mattress was three years ago." He said wistfully, "Yeah, it was a night I spent in a nice little house. The older lady who was the matriarch of the house was so happy to be able to cook with vanilla again that she actually let me sleep in her bed, and that was a fine rest indeed."

Specter actually laughed out loud. "You actually remember the last time you slept on a mattress?!" He was a bit ashamed as Randal didn't seem to find the humor he did.

Good naturedly, though, Randal said, "I guess it is kind of strange to remember that." He seemed to look deep inside himself. "I seem to remember a lot of 'lasts' in my life." He trailed off and started eating his eggs. These were fresh from the shop keeper. "Your shopkeeper friend, Glenn? He's got some great eggs."

Specter agreed, "He's always had good hens. That's what he did prior to the Breaking – raised chickens."

"Well, they're really good, even if I did cook them," Randal said.

There was a lull in the conversation, during which both men continued to eat. Specter decided his need to know outweighed his need to eat. "So why don't you tell me how it is that your bullets go right through webarmor?"

The voice from the doorway should have startled Specter more than it did.

"Bullets that go through webarmor? That would be a good story to hear," Shade said, leaning in the doorway.

Chapter 15

When Shade woke up, something was different. She remembered getting as many as she could before that one choked her. But – she opened her eyes – she was here, in an infirmary? She shut her eyes again. Judging by the aches she felt, she wasn't dead. She feigned like she needed to change position in her sleep and stretched a bit – added a little moan in there for effect. She wasn't tied down. Well, if they brought her back here to have their way with her, like the team leader had said, they hadn't started yet. She was sore almost everywhere, but not there. Still, she had to make sure she didn't waste a chance. She opened her eyes and closed them quickly three times, each time making sure she could focus on something farther away. Confident in her vision, she took a good long breath and steeled herself.

Up like a flash, she was out of bed and scanning the room. Her tomahawks! *Were they that stupid*?! Ignoring the pain in her legs and shoulder, she retrieved her tomahawks. They provided comfort for her and compensated for her injuries.

She felt their heft and weight and made sure they were intact. Now it was time. If they left her untied with her weapons, they deserved to die. She took another look around to find anything else she could use.

She was rewarded with a note. This didn't appear to be an infirmary in a contractors' headquarters. Did they sell her? No, probably not with her tomahawks. She did as the note said and 'hit play.' She figured she could watch it; she hadn't opened the door, and she did have her tomahawks.

Her button press was rewarded with a lot of humming and whirring. The monitor screen was slashed and wavy. She was just beginning to second guess pushing the button when the screen finally flickered clear. She placed the room in an instant. The audio began, "We're recording this for you..." She did not recognize the men, but she marked their names. She did have to admit that this was a novel way for them to fill in the time when she was unconscious.

She watched as the one, Randal, cleaned her off. She watched as they removed her pants, leaving her underclothes on. She watched as the other one, Specter, checked her legs. She could tell he had knowledge, but not medical training. He was doing what she would do – just verifying what could be treated versus what had to have a doctor's hand. She took note when they looked at the tattoo on the back of her neck and both men knew she was a Hunter.

She listened carefully as Randal was ushered out and Specter addressed the camera.

You need to know your situation. Your shoulder looks the worst. The CoAg powder you put on has stabilized it. Later we can evacuate it and clean it up if you want. That's your call. No indication of a concussion, but we may need to ask you some questions to be sure. Your legs will be sore, but nothing appears to be broken. I don't know how, but it seems they didn't break your nose or any other facial bones. But you're going to look different for a while.

For status, we killed the two platform crews after you were knocked out.

Specter casually, but deliberately, showed his Hunter tattoo to the camera.

We have traveled here, maybe eight miles southwest. We weren't followed, and we're isolated. But the corporations won't be happy about losing four platform

crews and will have close
coverage of this area for a
while. I want you to know that
because you are free to go, but
you're also welcome to stay.

Honestly, I normally
wouldn't do this, but I invoke
the right of Safe House.

Specter stood and bowed before starting:

We have taken you in when
you could not consent.

We have aided you when
you could not refuse.

We ask a two day solace
before a reparation request or
grievance be addressed.

He finished the forms perfectly, as if he had heard them before,
whether spoken to him or by him. He looked down obviously lost in
thought or remembrance.

We can talk more when you wake
up. There are some clothes for you –
coverings anyway. Oh, one last thing:
there're only the three of us here.
Anyone else shouldn't be.

The speech was over and Specter walked toward the door,
pointing to her tomahawks as he walked out. The tape kept running
but she had seen what was important. She walked to the machine and
found the fast forward button. She ran it forward – checking the time
stamp – just to make sure.

So. Two men who, together, killed two platform crews. Two men,
one a Hunter. A Hunter who still felt the need to invoke Safe House.
It appeared straight forward; it was hard to argue with the tape. It all
appeared to be on the level. She tried to think back and remember all
she could, but she still found no memory of them. She went through
the cabinets, found some clothes, strangely all lacy and silky. But
there was a pair of large shorts that looked like men's and a button-
down short-sleeved shirt she could wear as a cover-up. She could
still fight in it if she needed to, but she didn't think she'd have to.

They did give her her tomahawks; that was a nice touch. Funny how having the means to fight actually took the fight out of her.

Well, mostly....

Chapter 16

She opened the door and was immediately hit by the smell of bacon. Her stomach growled loudly enough to give her presence away. *They must not be too close,* she thought. She took in her surroundings, cataloging every possible weapon, every possible piece of cover. It was her nature. She didn't want to just go right up to the kitchen, but skulking around wouldn't exactly hold up her end of Safe House. She strode lightly to the kitchen, trying to make out the words over the low rumble of men's voices. She was rewarded with, "… why don't you tell me how it is that your bullets go right through webarmor?"

That made her forget about the pain and, with her recent interactions with those that wear webarmor, it almost made her forget where she was. With what she was up against, she needed to hear this.

"Bullets that go through webarmor? That would be a good story to hear," she said as she leaned in the doorway. She was surprised to see just a twitch of Specter's hand – she expected more. The reaction Randal gave was almost as surprising in the other direction. He jerked and was up quickly.

"Good morning!" Randal said. "Do you want some breakfast?" His voice was eager but seemed genuine.

"Sure, whatever you've got," she said.

Specter turned towards her and took her all in, measuring her in an instant and then meeting her eye. For her, it was almost like looking into a mirror. She knew from that look that he knew her, and she just met his eye – and, through her training, smiled and winked at him.

He found that wink amusing, but he only let it touch his eyes. He offered her a chair and moved aside to give her room at the bar.

"Coffee or orange juice?" Randal asked.

"Coffee's fine, thank you. What would be better, though, would be your answer to that question about armor-piercing bullets," she prompted.

Randal handed her a plate and sat back down. "So much for the pleasantries, huh? Well, onto the question of the hour." He looked ready to confess to a crime. "Armor piercing is not too accurate, actually. It's more like armor <u>tearing</u>."

Chapter 17

Randal looked at both of them and knew he had their full attention. Specter regarded him with a straight get-on-with-it look while Shade watched him through her bruised face, one eye swollen almost shut, the other bright and alert. To see them side-by-side was rather jarring for Randal so he focused on his toast and began.

"Webarmor was developed before the Breaking. As part of that process, the need arose to bring on partners and investors. The developers were – depending on your point of view – lucky or unlucky enough to have some very wealthy, very paranoid financiers. In fact, two gentlemen decided to support the research in total, not in order to bring the technology to market, but rather to suppress it for their own uses. That is to say, these two gentlemen had mutually agreed upon a certain private contract-based security firm that they wanted to outfit with this new technology."

"Well, the scientists involved didn't want anything to do with that. Not to say they had any illusions that their invention would end wars and conflicts – nothing like that. They just wanted to make sure their side had the webarmor and the other side didn't."

"That was the first problem. The lab was in the United States, so the lead professor laid first claim. The post-doctoral researcher who came up with a lot of it was from China, and the other post-doc who came up with another large part of it was from India. Throw in the German technician who was also deeply involved and you have a real multi-national effort out of that one lab."

"So you're thinking, 'No problem. It was done at a university, so the university owns all of it.'"

"Not so, apparently. In an interesting trade-off, the university did receive a large donation and a recurring deposit in their material science general fund. It wasn't that the school failed to realize the potential of the research. It was afraid of losing the funding. Also, the scientists all received ample funding for whatever they wanted to research plus a healthy bonus payment. In exchange, those two sponsors took legal claim to all intellectual property associated with the webarmor."

"So you're asking, 'why?' Why did these scientists and these college deans, why did they let it go? Was it the obscene amounts of money? No.... They couldn't make it wearable."

"The Chinese post-doc, Hu was his name, found out that the spider web fibers would lay together in certain conditions. Rasdan, the Indian post-doc, found out that with those same conditions, you could layer one whole layer of the fibers over top of another. It'd be like...drink trays! Remember when you could order at a restaurant and you could get drinks in a tray? It'd be like that; those layers would stack together. As serendipity would have it, it was the German tech, Erwin, I think, who inadvertently misaligned those layers one day and had the fiber layers running perpendicular to each other. Well, rather than failing to stack, they actually adhered and 'bonded' together."

"So they found this thin film one morning and then spent the next four months understanding and replicating what they had done. At this point they needed money to continue, and investors were brought in. With both sides eager to proceed, agreements were reached which included additional funding and personal bonuses once they could produce a usable fabric."

"And then they came up with an actual cloth. They had sheets of fabric but they had one huge problem. One insurmountable problem, really. They couldn't <u>cut</u> the cloth. They couldn't <u>sew</u> it. And that, my friends, is a fatal flaw."

"That's not exactly precise. It would be more accurate to say that the metal – whether a cutting machine, sewing needle, scissors, whatever – would cut for a little bit and then would dull and not cut. It was a property of the cloth itself. So it wasn't profitable because it wasn't scalable."

"Well, the two investors, confident that they could throw money at it and make it work, took possession of the entire project. And the university and the researchers let them – in exchange for the money those two wealthy investors dangled in front of them."

"That's where I came in. Those two investors recruited me. They promised me my own lab, untold riches, fame, and all of it. Then, after I agreed, they dropped this in my lap."

"Well, I took as long as I could going through everything, replicating what they did but not getting anywhere. That made them mad – but it really made me madder – because I really thought I could do it. I believed in myself and my ability."

"One day, who knows why – whether by God's hand, serendipity, whatever – I looked at the cloth under a microscope for the thousandth time. It was in a dish under specific conditions. Basically, those conditions were just applying a current, agitating the dish, and having the right chemicals in there. Anyway, I was going to watch how these fibers aligned. So I got a probe, pushed everything around, and watched."

"What caught my eye, though, was the probe. Just basically a needle with a handle, but it turned out to be the key to unlocking the riddle. I had put it in the solution early on and removed it. Well, after a bit, I put it back in the bath and noticed that when I pushed the almost-formed cloth fibers, the probe went right through."

"Magical stuff, right? Yeah, I wasn't so sure either. But I thought it went through because the cloth was not yet fully formed. Because of that, I waited and then did it again. It still went through. I did it a third time and the probe just pushed the cloth down; it didn't go through. I took the probe, wiped it off, and set it aside. For me, it was just the same as always, right? Well, it would have been, but I took some other needles I had and put them in the bath."

"I did ten just to keep it simple and took one out of the bath every minute. I ran all of them through the electron microscope. I saw that the longer the needles were in the bath, the familiar alignment of fibers happened. The pictures were like time-lapse photography. The fibers aligned the way they always did – just this time on the metal. Frustrated and at my wits end, I got mad, shut everything down, and left."

"I went out and had a great pity party for myself. I had such an awesome pity party that the next morning I felt like Death eating a cracker. I managed to make it back into the lab, though. That's when my probe turned into, well, a magic wand. In my frustration and haste to leave the lab the night before, I had thrown everything together, planning on cleaning it in the morning."

"So I had the probe sitting in the dish with just the chemicals, the fully-formed cloth, and some other leftover reaction mixture. The whole lab was a mess, but that was the important part. I took the cloth out of the reaction chamber and just started stabbing that cloth

– my nemesis! But, to my surprise, the probe kept going through the cloth – over and over and over again. So I kept doing it and it kept going through! I started to get really excited, but I needed to be sure I wasn't just still drunk from my pity party."

"It dawned on me as I was poking the cloth that in all the lab notebooks there was never any mention of what had happened before the alignment had been observed. I took the probe right then down to the electron microscope and was rewarded with the picture I needed. The probe was covered in the spider web fibers but the fibers were not aligned. It looked like a club with nails in it, spiky. I thought I had it but – due to my condition – did not print the picture and, in my 'eureka' moment, actually did not save the file. Upset about that, excited about the discovery, and confident I could replicate it all anyway, I went back up to the lab."

"Not having a record of what I'd just done was probably what saved my life."

"By the time I had made it back to the lab, the technicians were there cleaning up my mess. Something was amiss, though. They were used to cleaning up my messes since most of the time the messes were mine, but none were as big as this mess."

"There was a lot of anxiety present in the lab then, mostly related to the lack of progress we were making. When I got back upstairs, one technician was saying we were in trouble, and we might not make it out of this, and I thought he was talking about the work. I let them both have it and demanded that they give me the whole story. That turned them loose, and what they told made me more nervous than a long-tailed cat in a room full of rocking chairs."

"It turns out the professor who had originally put the webarmor together had a recent tragic skiing accident and broke his neck – dead. Hu, the Chinese post-doc, was in Hong Kong for a conference when he was in a hit and run accident and died at the hospital. Rasdan was headed back to India for a family visit and took a little puddle-jumper commuter flight to the airport. There was a problem in flight, the plane crashed and killed all on board. And then the German technician, shot during a convenience store robbery. Interesting that the store was his regular stop – every day – on his way home."

"So everyone with direct knowledge of the webarmor had died mysteriously – within a week – even if they had nothing to do with it anymore or had signed strict non-disclosure agreements. It certainly scared me, so I suggested to my technicians that they both find other, less dangerous employment."

"Knowing the story of Daedalus and in light of what I had just learned, I made my plan. First, I had to verify. That actually turned out to be the easy part. Without those special mixing conditions, the webarmor fibers would not align but would coat a surface and be spiky. That was the key."

Before Randal could continue his story, Specter broke in. "Sounds like bull. It's too simple."

Randal was quick with his reply, "That's the beauty of it! It's such advanced technology that no one had thought to look for the simple answer. In fact, if I hadn't been hung over and my brain working slowly, I might've missed it, just cleaned things up and moved on. But look, look at this."

"The webarmor works because molecularly the fibers of the cloth are aligned one smooth layer over one smooth layer repeatedly. A bullet won't go through that because on a molecular level those smooth layers form a wall."

"Imagine this," he said as he help up a napkin. "This is the webarmor. I hold this on all four corners. Now imagine you throw an orange at me – that's the bullet. I can stop that orange. I can catch that orange. That's the webarmor stopping a bullet. Now, the 'spiky-ness.' Take some nails, large, small, thick, thin and drive those nails into the orange so the pointy ends are sticking out. Now when you throw the orange, the napkin doesn't catch it; the orange tears into and through the napkin."

"First, I verified that I could coat a metal with the spiky stuff. Second, I needed to make a plan so I didn't end up dead. Third, I needed some time to earn enough money for my escape. I knew that, once gone, I would be running for my life."

"I started by telling those two investors – owners, now – that I was close to a breakthrough. They were interested but more concerned about the bottom line. So I examined some of the machinery and found that I could make a liquid coating to cover the cutting edges, the needles, the shears, whatever – all that would be needed to fabricate webarmor."

"The trick for me was to make them think that I had altered the cloth, not the instruments. And it worked. The repeated exposure of the utensils, though, required a re-application about every four months to keep up production. What I thought would be the hardest part, keeping everything in one area, actually turned out to be the easiest. The owners didn't want the technology anywhere but one area."

"I convinced the owners to shut everything down once a quarter, ostensibly to clean and maintain all the machinery. During that time, I would coat all the machines to enable them to cut and sew the webarmor. We made so many uniforms. Going twenty-four–seven with three shifts and making simple small, medium, and large jumpsuits, we were making enough to outfit an army. That first quarter I had to make sure I was still valuable, so I played what politics I could and did all kinds of quality control. It was hard to plan that first quarter due to my having to be at the plant most of the time."

"But I tried to put the time to good use. Good surreptitious use. I put some finished fabric back in the reaction mixture – the soup – without the web fibers, and let it sit and got nothing. But do that and boil the water and – voila! – the fiber layers separate. Then, with some acid and mechanical separation, you can get the constituent parts of a layer to separate. So that all boils down to, no pun intended, the fact that I break the fibers up, get that spiky stuff out and, after I cast my bullets, coat the bullets with it. And, before you ask, I haven't tried to coat other things with it like arrows or knives, but it did work on the machines."

"The reason they want me dead is probably because they can't make any more webarmor."

Chapter 18

Randal had carefully considered this announcement and expected some reaction from his audience. Both Specter and Shade sat still with a look of incredulity on their faces – but for different reasons.

Specter recovered first and asked, "What do you mean, 'no more webarmor'?" while Shade exclaimed, "You are the Maker?!"

Specter may have spoken first, but Shade's incredulity was punctuated with action. She was on her feet as she spoke, her right hand brandishing a tomahawk.

Specter's knife appeared in his hand, and his voice reverberated inside the kitchen, "Stand down!"

Randal flinched but Shade remained standing and poised. Shade's eyes never left Randal's. Specter's words slowed her hand though it still held her tomahawk.

"Do you know how much his bounty is worth?!" she demanded.

To Randal's dismay, Specter sat back down.

This appeared to give Shade the go ahead and simultaneously made her angry.

"Was worth," Specter muttered.

"What?!" Shade shrieked at him, emotions awry. Obviously she was not used to people sitting down when she had bared steel.

Randal looked back at Specter. He saw in Specter's eyes a familiar preoccupation. He had often seen the same expression during his early days of running. Every time he looked in a mirror, really. Specter's countenance revealed the impact of a rejection so severe that they wanted you dead. He was caught in the emotional limbo between realization and reaction. Specter had faced his rejection, maybe he even expected it, but he wasn't sure whether to resist or just accept it.

Randal felt for him. He'd been through it himself. Randal leaned back in his chair and looked at Shade.

She seemed to be more enraged than ever. The sight of her – one eye swollen shut and the other blazing in her black, blue and now red face – was unsettling to Randal.

Specter's calm voice was clear in the room, his tone cutting the tension and requiring them to listen. "Was worth, remember?" Specter began. Echoing the platform leader, he said, "'Shade, your position with the Corps has been terminated. Your service to the Corps is appreciated. However, your skill set represents what has been deemed 'operational secrets.' Therefore, you are to be executively removed.'" Specter paused there. "Remember that before they started trying to beat your face in?" His voice was harsh but effective; Shade was slowly lowering her tomahawk.

"I am the Hunter who found Randal." Shade's head jerked towards Specter when she heard the words. "But you know what? He wanted to be found. Otherwise, he'd still be out there. He plans. There's a reason no one ever caught him before." Specter's words continued to chasten Shade, if not pacify her. "I've seen the degree of his planning. Do you think you could take what he said back to the pri-cons and somehow reinstate yourself with them? Sell that information back to them to buy your freedom?" His tone intensified, "Do you really think this guy just told us everything?"

Specter paused to let his words sink in. Shade visibly caught her breath and then, slowly, sat down. She looked at Randal, realization dawning on her face, and she knew there was no need to ask Randal if he were telling the whole story. It was probably just enough story to get her inside to the pri-cons, maybe deep inside, but with no more information it would be death. She realized that she, like Specter, had underestimated Randal.

Specter filled the gap, "So tell us what you mean about 'they can't make any more webarmor.'"

Randal, calmer now, continued. "Well, it's not like they didn't make enough already. I mean, I kept working there for a while before they tried to, shall we say, terminate my position." Randal was proud of his escape; it was clear in his eyes. "We kept production going for about four years. I'm not sure of the exact number of units because I'm sure they made more after I left. Looking at the platform crews' uniforms, though, those were second year runs." Randal paused in thought.

"Look, they caught on to me. We had year one in which we made straight utility jumpsuits, modified those for the second year, third year we incorporated more general fatigues, cargo-pant type uniforms and that was basically it. We did do some short runs of specialty items like your duster, Specter, even some suit and dress liners and long coats for the paranoid elite and politicians."

"But when they got on to me – when they knew I was altering the machines and not the fabric – I was just ready for the quarterly machine 'cleaning.' Since I ran, that didn't get done, and I guess what I'm saying is that I haven't seen any other type of webarmor around." Randal ran his fingers through his hair showing his consternation. "I don't know if they figured it out or not, but I haven't seen or even heard of anything different."

"Just because you haven't seen it doesn't mean they're not making more," Shade chimed in, obviously more calm now.

Randal was insistent, though, "I'd like to think it shut them down. Remember, I had access to everything – the originals. They had taken care of all the creators, or it was some kind of Pharaoh's curse or something even less believable. They didn't bring anyone else in, and those two technicians I had at the first got out and free of them, I hope. So yeah, I'd like to think that in those three years I was able to doctor, misrepresent, shred, and omit enough material so that no one will create more webarmor." Randal was fervent in his desire to see this technology die.

Specter saw his intensity and asked, "Why, man? Why are you so adamant about it?"

Randal looked relieved to be able to explain. Specter thought about the videotape in which he'd first seen Randal. "Look – Alexander the Great had the phalanx, and he conquered the known world. The Mongols had the stirrup, and they swept over Asia. Advancements in warfare only lead to one side having dominance for a while. The webarmor should be available to all so that full scale slaughter will be harder – so that one side can't go in and just kill everybody they don't like."

"Your dream of peace, Randal?" Shade asked.

"No!" And now it was Randal on his feet.

Specter was again ready to step in if he needed to; he wanted them both alive.

"No," Randal continued, "because that wouldn't happen. If everybody has webarmor, then fewer people die in combat. And maybe there's a chance that so many will get beat up and maimed on both sides that they'll agree to settle and go home. But maybe then a side decides to use chemical or biological warfare. But that takes education and, at least with education, you have a chance that that scientist will second guess her actions before starting a pandemic. At least there's a chance that scientist will tell her leaders that she can't aerosolize anthrax. There's just a chance that those in conflict will find another, non-military, solution."

"But we're not there yet, are we, Randal?" Specter asked, already knowing the answer.

"No," Randal replied and sat back down. "No, now we're at the point where suits of armor rule, and the longbow has not yet been invented."

"Oh, but it has, hasn't it?" Specter said with a forced smile. "You can make those bullets and then we three can go out and rule the world!" he laughed and thumped Randal on the arm to let him know he was joking. Randal only gave a perfunctory smile.

"But you can make more 'spiky' stuff, can't you?" Shade asked, her tone more serious.

Randal twirled his glass in his hands, his mind on that utopia where differences were settled by words and military might was used in disaster relief and rebuilding. "Yes," he finally said, "using those uniforms we got yesterday."

Specter rose and Shade followed. *Or maybe Jesus will come back*, Randal thought as he got up, too. "Lord haste the day," was out of Randal's mouth before he could stop it. He was gathering up dishes, so he didn't see the quick glance Specter and Shade shared.

Chapter 19

As they left the kitchen, Specter took charge. Because it was his place, they let him.

"Okay, then," Specter said, "Randal, grab your gun and an empty cylinder – that's your gun unloaded with an extra cylinder. Don't worry about unloading if you have to. We'll reload later. Meet us back up here."

Randal turned to go, and Specter waited until he was headed downstairs. Specter turned to Shade.

"You and I need to talk," he said simply.

"I overstepped the bounds of Safe House and I apologize. Had you not been there I might be dead now," Shade said.

Specter noticed the way she phrased that. Only a Hunter would say 'might' after being beaten unconscious and surrounded by a bunch of men ordered to kill her. "Accepted," he said. "We need to talk more, though, first about your shoulder, also your face, and then your plans." He paused, she nodded. "We do the first two today, the last before you leave, when you decide."

She nodded in response.

"Good," Specter said as Randal came back up.

"This way," Specter said and led them down the hallway leading toward his quarters. He took the door on the left prior to reaching them and took another immediate left, down a set of stairs, across a short hall, and then right down another set of stairs. He paused before opening the door without turning around and said, "This is the most secure area in this place. Remember that should something happen."

With that, Specter opened the door. They were in a large room and, as deep in the ground as they were, there were still three other doors out of this room. Specter led them to the door opposite the one they came in. This room was white, padded, and about twenty feet square. The walls were interspersed with lines that looked to Randal like they held sensors.

"I know it's padded, but it's like a gym – not like a padded cell. There are sensors throughout the room, including the ceiling, and it's voice activated," Specter explained. He motioned for Randal to give him his revolver. "One handgun," Specter said loudly and held the revolver above his head. "One person. Level one. Target practice. Total three people in room."

The computer answered, and the voice came from everywhere. "Recognized handgun as cap and ball percussion revolver, correct?"

"Yes," Specter answered.

"Method of reload expected to be cylinder replacement, correct?"

"Yes," Specter answered.

"Number of cylinders?"

Specter looked at Randal and put his fingers up asking the question: three? four? Randal held up four fingers.

"Four," Specter said.

"Dry fire on 'one,'" the computer said, and Specter cocked the hammer. "Quiet please," continued the computer, "Three, two, one."

On 'one,' Specter let the hammer fall.

"Level one will commence in ten, nine, eight ..."

The computer counted down, and Shade and Randal stepped back towards the door. Specter hefted the gun in his hand and even twirled it a bit – outlaw gunfighter style. Randal was surprised but figured most Hunters had to be trained in a variety of weapons.

When the computer sounded 'one' an image of a red silhouette target appeared in front of Specter. He cocked the gun, took aim, and let the hammer drop. All ears were assaulted by the sound of a gun firing, and the target showed three concentric black circles dwindling to a dot where the target was hit. For Specter, this was the throat. He cocked the gun again and another target popped up, and he took it down. This went to the sixth target after which flashed a 'reload' sign in white letters. Specter tossed the gun to Randal, who reloaded the cylinder. The computer picked this up and then two targets appeared. Randal, still holding his gun, looked to Specter. Specter gave a 'go ahead' signal and Randal started 'shooting.'

After those targets, Specter said loudly, "Computer, pause." The word 'pause' appeared in large white letters in the middle of the room. Specter clapped Randal on the shoulder. "I know you're a good shot, but practice never hurts. Keep going on this, and I'm going to look at Shade's shoulder. 'Computer, resume,' starts it back up, okay?"

Randal just nodded and then nodded to Shade. They could hear Randal say, "Computer, resume," before Specter was fully out of the door.

"He's going to have fun in there, isn't he?" Shade asked Specter.

"Yeah," Specter said, "I think so."

Chapter 20

On the way back to the infirmary, Specter had Shade follow him to the other bedroom on the main level.

"We need to look at that shoulder, but first, you need a good bath," Specter said as he led her into the bedroom. It was a bedroom painted in a deep, soothing red that spoke of lush relaxation. "It was going to be a harem if you can believe it, but it's the only room with an easy in/easy out bathtub. Plus, it's stocked with clothes. Yes, most of them will be unsuitable for polite company, and all of them will be revealing, but everything is clean. We'll get some laundry going so you won't have to stay in those things," Specter said.

"That might be okay if there are some silky things in there," Shade said with a sly grin. She was glad to see that that threw him off kilter – even if only a little.

"It's your call. Wash up and meet me in the infirmary. Then we'll look at that shoulder," Specter said.

Shade was glad for the time alone. She needed to think. She also needed a bath. She went straight to the closets to find some clothes and found that Specter wasn't joking. Most everything there would barely cover a woman's body and was meant for no other reason than to be taken off. These clothes were great for that, but otherwise useless.

She went to the other side of the room and through the door there. As soon as the door swung open, she knew she would be spending a lot of time in here. It was a gym. The 'sultan' here must've wanted his women to stay fit and supple. Whatever the motivation in building this room, she would put it to good use. She did work hard to stay fit, keep her figure, and remain limber. That reminded her of her shoulder.

She was about to leave and shower up and just put on whatever when, on a whim, she went over to one of the benches along the wall. Pulling on the outside edge yielded nothing, but pushing on the solid piece under the seat pad did. *Pay dirt*! she thought. Under the bench were all the workout clothes that women would need. Real women – not those women who 'worked out' just to turn on their sultan. She took some workout pants, a sports bra, and a tank top. She resigned herself to having to wear a pair of thong underwear from the other room. She smiled. Considering the situation, she could be lying in a shallow grave after being gang-raped. She figured she could put up with the thong after all.

In the shower she let the water wash away her indecision. As she washed and relished the warm bath, she considered her position and plan of action. Specter seemed distantly upset about being fired. She acknowledged that she might go through some emotional issues herself, but, really? Didn't he see it coming just as she did? She thought so because here they were in a bunker he had known about and maintained.

The water running over her shoulder made her wince. It was sore and would have to be opened up. Specter could probably do that, but she could talk him through it if she had to. She thought more about Specter himself. He hadn't been very talkative so far, but he had helped her. It would have been easy to let her go. Maybe he had some plan for retirement? Hole up here and never leave? She spat. Not for her. Maybe she could learn some things from him, though. He did seem at home with that revolver – something she had found troublesome.

That made her think about Randal. She needed to apologize to him for baring steel. What an interesting guy he was – scientist, planner, Runner. Among all the Runners, he was the biggest prize. So how did he get that way? And, for that matter, how did Specter get his card? And armor-piercing bullets. She would not have believed that if Specter hadn't confirmed it. That alone could mean lots of money. It could probably lead to notoriety, too. She had had enough of being chased for a while.

She scrubbed herself clean and started to wash her face, but she again winced in pain having forgotten that her face was black and blue. She was gentle, and it hurt, but she managed to clean her face. She turned off the water and stepped out of the shower.

She dried off, looking at the bruises on her legs. She looked around at the mirror to see her backside. Bruises back there, too, but only bruises. She was proud of her butt; she had worked hard to keep that supple shape. As she turned back, she dried herself on up, spending time on her breasts. *Yes*, she thought, *I look good.*

She turned back towards the mirror for a close-up look at her face – and jumped back. Oh! She <u>had</u> been hit with the ugly stick! She wouldn't be seducing anyone anytime soon. She thought back to Specter. Maybe that was the effect she'd had on him, making him cringe just to look at her! *Oh, well*, she thought as she smiled, *I could've been gang-raped and shot.*

With the pri-cons no doubt circling above, she would have to stay here awhile if she could. She would need her shoulder healed. She would need her strength up. And, importantly, she would need her bruises gone. A pretty woman with a tight body would make a man lust, and as his blood flowed away from his brain, so would discipline and reason. And that was a weapon she needed.

She dressed, secured her tomahawks, and ventured back to the infirmary. Specter was there waiting for her. "Have you been sitting on your hands?" she asked.

Specter smiled and said, "I've been looking forward to seeing you in a flimsy see-through something, but here you've found something else."

Shade smiled through her bruises, "Maybe after this swelling goes down and I can see how to put on some of those things," she said.

"We'll see," he said dismissively. "Right now, though, what do you want to do with that shoulder?"

"It needs to be cleaned out," she said.

So they began. Specter obviously had some experience treating wounds, and he shared it with Shade. She returned the favor, and both learned something.

Specter started by numbing her shoulder with a hypodermic and began to remove the sealant she had put on. "That powder forms a good paste if you can get it just a bit wet or if you're bleeding heavily. Okay, big pinch." And he pulled it out whole. "See?" he said, "You were bleeding enough."

"Aren't you going to wait for it to numb?" she asked.

"No," he said smiling. "It'll be numb when you need it."

Specter started cleaning the wound. Once clean, he manipulated the joint to make sure there were no broken bones or tendon/ligament damage. In actuality, it was just a flesh wound. "It's deep, but it shouldn't hold you back."

"How're you going to run the stitches?" she asked.

"Just loop and go..." he said as he took a towel and ran the suture.

"Run it this way..." she demonstrated. "It cuts down on the scarring."

"Okay," he said and started sewing. When she didn't move at all, he said, "I told you it would be numb when you needed it." He finished by putting some ointment on it and then bandaging and wrapping it well. Specter excused himself and returned with a cold pack. "For your face," he said.

"Thanks a lot!" she joked.

"Some walking or running will help the bruises on your legs," Specter said.

"I found an exercise room off the bedroom. I'll use that," she replied.

"Why don't you use the cold pack now? I'll get Randal from the range, and we'll get lunch going," Specter said. "We need to talk at lunch, okay?"

"Sure. Just give me a call when lunch is ready," she answered.

Specter left the infirmary and started for the range. This talk at lunch would need to be exhaustive and enlightening. Maybe between the three of them they could come up with a plan. Anything would be better than just staying here. They couldn't do that indefinitely either. At least long enough for Shade to fully heal, though.

Chapter 21

Specter reached the range door and listened before opening it. He could hear the manufactured gun shots and was glad the owner had foreseen the need for keeping his protectors sharp. He waited for a 'Reload' moment and knocked on the door. Stepping back he heard Randal's voice, "Pause."

Randal stepped out, flushed and sweaty. Breathing hard and wiping his forehead on his sleeve, Randal said simply, "What?"

Specter looked at him, grinned, and asked "What level?"

Randal looked back and said "Seventeen, but I can't get past it."

Specter was impressed but only said, "Go get washed up. We'll all have lunch and hash some things out, okay?"

"Sure," Randal said. "Do I need to...."

"Nah, I'll get it," said Specter. And he watched as Randal left. *This may actually be beneficial to him,* he thought. He opened the door and said only, "Quit. Shut down." and then closed the door. He would have to get some lunch going. That thought preoccupied him until he got to the kitchen.

His friend at the store had packed some greens and potatoes in with his supplies. Specter started the greens boiling and put quartered potatoes in with them. Also among the supplies was some canned beef and some rice. Specter started the rice and put the meat on to heat. At least they'd eat pretty well. As things were cooking, Specter took the time to reflect.

Three days ago he was about to make his twenty-first kill – this Maker, Randal – the most elusive of all the Runners. Now, he had helped another Hunter to actually kill those with whom he used to serve. They had given no quarter nor chance to reconcile, made no effort to transfer him (or her) to a desk job, or even a personal protection consultant (bodyguard).

Here he was, thrown into a mix with Randal, who he had been fully willing to kill. And vice-versa. But the scientist had been running almost as long as Specter had been Hunting. Now it would be Randal who had more real life experience – Randal who would have good, usable ideas. He would do well to remember that.

Next, they had picked up Shade. But why did they? Had he been angry at the contractors and wanting revenge? Had it been his decision, anyway? Randal wanted to save her because of what would happen to her. He had wanted to help because he saw her situation as unfair – if the pri-cons had given her a fair chance, he might've just passed by.

Perhaps he felt that way about himself; maybe he saw his situation as unfair. How could they just take away all that he had worked for: the reward of not having to kill anymore, his retirement? And now, nothing. And so quickly.

But what would they do now? What could they do? Revenge was out of the question. That was the short path to the grave. Would they still think he and Randal were dead? Hard to know. He felt like he was standing at the center of a spinning wheel where centrifugal force was reversed. Instead of things flying out from the center, they were spinning inward to collect, encroach, press, and suffocate.

He gave his head a violent shake. You took care of the closest threat first, gave yourself some room, and then varied the attack until all threats were eliminated. For him, that was simple. Don't sit in this limbo, but make a plan. He took the greens off the boil, fluffed the rice to make a bed for the meat and went to gather Shade and Randal. They would have a plan before dinner.

Chapter 22

While they were finishing up, Specter collected the plates, put them in the sink, and refilled everyone's water. Shade glanced first at Randal and then Specter. She sensed the mood getting serious and spoke up first.

"I haven't said this specifically, but I thank you both for saving my life. I know what would have happened if not for your help, so I thank you." She tapped her shoulder and waved her hand over the table and said, "And thank you for your hospitality," completing her part of Safe House.

Both men nodded but only Randal said, "You're welcome." Specter could have felt slighted because this was, after all, his bunker. Studying Randal, however, he saw a deeper motive. Randal wanted to make Shade feel welcome, secure, and safe – not to make himself seem like it was all his idea, his doing.

Specter did have questions, though. He asked, "Shade, you had been hiding for a while before that platform team found you, and you had probably been running for a while before we saw you. So. What's your story?"

Shade clearly expected such a question. She cleared her throat and began.

"I have always been a traveler. In this day and age that's not too easy. Growing up my mother would travel all around and take me with her. All I knew about the Contractors was that they traveled. After my mother's death, none of us traveled anymore, and I felt I needed to be a more effective protector. So, when I was old enough, I went to the nearest Enclave and signed up with the pri-cons. It turned out that I have a natural proclivity for fighting and killing. I served my unit with distinction."

"One day, an old instructor found me and told me that he had recommended me for the Hunter program. I had a year to train before the selection began, and he helped me. I worked with him in various arts, forms, literature, training my body and mind. When I got in, he was at the top of my list of people to thank. It turned out that the Corps had an interest in him as well. He was accused of corporate espionage and, due to our close relationship, and" – she flushed a bit – "due to my physical assets, he was my fifth Prey. I was to turn the relationship physical and learn what he knew. Why I did it is another story and my business. But I did, and he opened up. There was no corporate espionage, but he did warn me to get free. The Hunters were running out of Prey, and it was no longer a 'commercially viable' program. It wasn't paying off anymore. He knew why I was there and why he was getting my attentions, so after he told me that, he got up and jumped out of the window - a ninth story window."

Here she paused – but only briefly – she was a Hunter after all.

"I started preparing that day. I watched as my Prey changed from evil and malevolent to less obviously so. I set my plans in place and prepared myself for the day I knew was coming. When it happened, I was on a mission when the platform crews came in lighting it up." Randal and Specter shared a knowing look.

"I had been running for twelve days before I hit the road you found me on."

Specter probed further, "Where were you running to?"

Shade looked slyly at him. "I could ask you the same," she said.

Specter remained stolid.

Shade answered, "I was headed for my hideout, nothing this luxurious, but I did make plans." She took a drink.

"What were you planning on doing once there?" Specter asked.

Shade put down her drink, "Hmm?"

Specter sat back, knowing she had heard him. So Specter asked the same question using different words. "What are you going to do next?" This time he spoke with a bemused tone.

Shade looked surprised and at a loss to answer. "Well, live," she stammered.

Randal joined in at this point. "That is a very salient question, Specter. What is your plan for the future?"

Specter looked at both of them and took a drink before answering. Setting down his glass, he said, "I guess..." he stopped. "I guess that's what I'm trying to figure out."

Before anyone could fill that empty space, Specter went on, "Shade, did you have any contact while you were running?"

"No," she said. "I killed a few of those on that first platform in order to get away – but no other contact. I knew their protocols and methods, so I just tried to stay a step ahead."

"What are you getting at?" asked Randal.

"Just thinking how it could be that two separate operations lose men and then, later, four platforms are taken out, along with their crews. Someone mapping that out is going to back-plan and see how much ground was covered in what amount of time and figure out we made it out alive." His words hung in the room and seemed to penetrate everywhere like fumes from spilled gasoline. "They may even think we're out for revenge."

No one spoke for a while. Each was left alone with their thoughts. No one wanted to speak for fear of touching something off. Despite its relative safety, the bunker seemed to be turning into a coffin.

The thought of never surfacing without being hunted seemed a distinct possibility. Randal, having been Hunted for a while, had already dealt with that emotional reality. Randal's thoughts had turned in another direction.

"Unless they thought it was someone else..." he said.

"Go on," Shade said.

"Well, if they think we're out killing they'll think we want revenge, and we'll be pursued and executed. But if they think some group is doing it, that's a different story. If we could make them think that the last attack was...," he was reaching, "for trade, say, then they'd be forced to take another approach." Randal looked at their faces and knew they didn't think much of the idea, but he knew it would work. It was the same type of certainty that had kept him moving – had kept him alive.

"What and who was on the kill list? I don't need particulars, just how many and/or what crimes?" asked Randal.

Shade answered first, "I started out getting some really evil people – like people who had little fiefdoms and a following. It ended up, I think, just anyone who happened to make the Corps mad."

Specter chimed in, "It seemed to me that I was sent for those who could lead – those who could lead any sort of revolt or uprising." Specter delved further, "Why?"

Randal was thoughtful as he answered, "Well, if you were sent to kill people who could organize a resistance of some kind, wouldn't it stand to reason that one such person would rise up and pose a real threat? Actually organize something like that?"

Shade and Specter sat silently. Randal could see that his words were making an impact.

Randal continued, more animated now, "What did the people on that kill list most want to do? What would be their 'ransom' demand?"

"Contact," Specter and Shade said at the same time. They looked at each other and, again asked together, "Really?" As both smiled, Specter lifted his hand indicating for Shade to go ahead.

She did. "My experience and what I've learned from my Prey is that contact is lost with those in the Outerlands, and most want it back. It's not like you can be granted a work permit in an Enclave and still come home on weekends."

"And I've seen it on the trade side. Things like Outerland art, innovation, and food that many would trade for electricity, clothes, light bulbs, toilet paper. Some kind of interaction," Specter added.

Randal didn't need to think any longer. "So what we do is ambush some more platforms and start leaving notes like 'more will die unless the Enclaves' doors open for trade' and 'working shouldn't mean leaving home.'"

Specter chimed in, "Closed Enclave equals Death."

"Something to that effect, anyway," Randal said. He got a quizzical look on his face. "Why were you terminated?"

"Our skill set represents 'operational secrets,' and we have to be 'executively removed,'" Shade recited.

Randal pressed on, "That's why you have to be killed – not why you were fired." They thought about that. "Maybe it has to do with the level of Prey out there. Haven't you both said that the kill list got more and more sketchy, like you were close to working yourself out of a job?"

Specter and Shade nodded in agreement.

"So maybe the Corps didn't think your targets posed a risk anymore." Randal said, thinking aloud.

"Or that those threats were minor enough to be handled by regular platform crews," Specter added.

"Right," Randal said, "So either way, they would have to expect something to come up and probably they'd have to handle it with platform crews. If we attack those platform crews – here and there – and leave the right kind of signs and misinformation...," Randal trailed off, motioning with his hands for them to finish the thought.

"The Corps will think it's a new threat and not us," Shade finished for him.

"Hopefully not us," Specter amended.

There it was, all out on the table. It seemed like a clear plan that might divert attention from them, but it did involve more killing. Selective killing maybe, but always with the chance of backup arriving before they could get away. It would mean leaving the relative safety and definite luxury of the bunker. So there it was, and each of them didn't like it for his or her own reasons. Randal didn't care for the killing. Shade was worried about combat with her shoulder and the possible repercussions for nearby townsfolk. Specter knew all too well the risks of being identified during a raid, plus the inherent difficulty in killing an entire platform crew.

A light dawned in Specter's mind, but his mouth had raced ahead. "Hey Randal – you can make that goop, right? You can make the coating for bullets that we can use, right?" In his excitement he was up on his feet.

"Yes," Randal said. "I can use the uniforms from before, but I'll need some other stuff as well."

"What stuff, exactly?" Specter asked.

"Well, I'll need power...."

"Check," Specter said.

"...a large vat – maybe twenty gallons at least."

"Old bathtub, check," Specter said.

"No – I have to boil it,"

"With circulator pump, check," Specter answered.

"...a liter of sulfuric acid, ten pounds borax, and a gallon of vinegar."

"Check on the borax and the vinegar. Any way to make the acid?" Specter asked.

"Old car batteries?" asked Randal.

"Check."

"I need that for every two to three uniforms and another mix and dye if you want to create your own webarmor clothes."

Shade got excited, too, "We can do that?"

"Just a sewing machine, the dye, and a steady supply of uniforms," Randal said.

There it was again – right before all of them. A large task and a worrisome future.

But now they would have new tools. *And while it's a poor carpenter who blames his tools,* Specter thought, *it's a poor Hunter who tries to kill too many.* With coated bullets, two Hunters, maybe....

Specter allowed himself to hope.

Chapter 23

The next few days were very hectic around the bunker. Randal spent most of his time down in the shop/repair area of the bunker, opposite the range. He was working on the webarmor uniforms – or rather destroying them. It didn't take long for him to set everything up, but it did take some time to optimize his concentrations. He was careful to keep everything written down. Once done, though, the work progressed smoothly.

The process was monotonous, however, and required dedicated attention. Randal had to stir his mixture every five minutes as the acid dissolved the bonds in the webarmor fibers. After about two hours, he had to filter the fibers, adding the borax and vinegar to the filtrate to keep the fibers buffered and just acidic enough not to re-congeal. This four-hour phase required stirring only every ten minutes. Randal would catch glimpses of Specter and Shade during quick trips back and forth from either the kitchen or the bathroom during these times.

The last step – coating the bullets and blades – was faster but required close attention. Care had to be taken to make sure exactly what needed coating got it and everything else stayed clean. Randal did find some rough approximations of what coatings would work and also what temperatures the metal needed to be before 'quenching' in the webarmor spiky soup. The lead shot he was used to using was simple to coat in comparison.

Randal took advantage in the few minutes he had between stirs to go through Specter's electronic library. After years on the run, Randal had not expected to see anything electronic again, much less an electronic reader. The 'sultan' who had built this place had filled even the expanded memory with every kind of book he hoped he'd never need. There were books and compilations about survival, gardening, navigation, power generation, chemistry, where to find or generate pure chemicals. Randal took extensive notes. He took one of the leather-bound thick blank journals there and appropriated it for himself. After years on the run, Randal knew that a gravy train always ended; he knew to get what he needed before it was gone.

Careful not to neglect his physical needs, Randal worked out twice a day. He still did his usual routine – body weight exercises – but the gym equipment there was also put to good use. He shared these workouts with Randal and Shade. It was Specter's idea, supposed to boost morale and camaraderie, and it was working as far as Randal could tell. It was making Randal more and more aware of being in close proximity to a very fit and very well-proportioned female, too. He was also aware of the interaction Specter had with Shade. Also in the forefront of his mind was the way Specter could deal out death like a card dealer could deal cards. He'd better wait and see how territorial Specter was.

Specter kept the two workout sessions as a mainstay. He never liked to fight beside someone without seeing how they responded to pressure. Working out was a perfect place to test that. Specter also added another session in with just him and Shade. They were special fighting and weapons sessions in which Specter tested Shade's shoulder, showed her knife fighting techniques, and she shared tomahawk training.

Naturally, most of the sessions were form and practice. They did mix it up sometimes, and Specter was relieved to see Shade respond as she should. It was a rare chance for both of them, sparring with an equal in most respects. These were two well-trained killers focused on learning new techniques while keeping their edges sharp and ready for combat, knowing they'd need each other.

Specter did notice an interaction forming between Randal and Shade. She and Specter had to be close, had to be tight, in order to fully rely on each other in a fight, but Specter knew that was the extent of their relationship. They trained to the point that they could intuit each other's moves and, with that closeness and dependence, both knew that sleeping together would ruin that.

Either from experience or fear, both Specter and Shade knew that sex would be a heated and passionate romp that would bind them in animalistic ecstasy. And it would forever alter their combat effectiveness; they would each extend themselves beyond their limits for the other's protection, and that would be fatal for both. So they maintained their distance and fed on their sexual tension, using it to nourish their friendship and maintain their edge.

Randal probably didn't see it that way, and Shade didn't see the need to tell him. She had come to the place where she honestly believed her best chance of survival was with these two men. In her experience, if she could keep the two men guessing, she'd get more out of both. And, as the bruising faded from her face, it was easier to play up that tension with both men. Part of it may have been the physical bruising being gone, but, also, she felt more herself without the black, blue, and yellow anymore. She knew where she stood with Specter – at least for now. If their circumstances changed, she might try to cross that bridge, knowing it would be burning behind her.

But with Randal it was different. It wasn't a power thing either – although she had expected it to be. Strangely, both men seemed powerful to her: Specter in his physical prowess and surety, Randal in his own strength and survival instincts. Where Specter had brute muscle and force, Randal had a wiry tenacity. While Specter could plan an operation and execute it, Randal could fix things, repurpose and create new, practical solutions. Mentally, both men seemed on par with each other, just specialized in different areas. So she played off of both – not pitting one against the other and never overtly. She allowed both of them to drink her in with their eyes but limited their time at that well. She allowed both some physical contact but never sensuously and distributed evenly. And she let herself believe that she had such control because she knew that to think about it meant she'd have to acknowledge she was very close to two very masculine and virile men. That control, illusion though it may be, allowed her to focus on her training.

Randal saw Shade's focus on her workouts as an inspiration. If she was going to work hard, so was he. He guessed that's what Specter had in mind when he required the workouts. Specter also had him in the range every day, too, but that was pure fun for Randal. Specter's thinking was that, immediately post-workout, while tired, he'd train himself to "put lead on target," he'd said.

Randal took the opportunity. He had lived so long by his wits and knowledge; he took full advantage of such an opportunity. He'd been running long enough to know he might have to up and run quickly, but he didn't think these two would turn on him. But he was very aware of how quickly a gunfight could radically change a situation. That is, in a fight, he could find Specter and Shade dead at any time.

That's why he needed good gun control – 'putting lead on target' – as Specter had said. So Randal threw himself fully into the simulation.

So fully immersed was Randal in the simulation, that Specter, sometimes, for his own protection, had to quickly disarm him and hit him – however quickly and lightly – to get him out of fight mode. Often Randal would fight back. Specter let him, to a point, knowing it might benefit him one day.

It was after these evening workouts that Specter and Shade would start dinner. Letting Randal train on the range allowed them to shower and clean up before dinner was served, but Randal never had time to clean up before they ate. Randal was sure it was Specter's attempt for him to appear less appealing to Shade.

Chapter 24

And so it went. For at least a week, maybe two, the routine actually became that: each working on what he or she needed to in order to ensure the survival of all. As Shade's shoulder healed and she learned new techniques, as Randal worked on the webarmor goop and his marksmanship, as Specter maintained his strength and learned the tomahawks, they grew individually and as a team.

Their routine changed one morning when Randal announced he would be cooking that night. Specter and Shade agreed to let him have his moment, and Specter added, "I take it you have something for us?"

Randal replied, "Indeed. And you'll see soon enough."

And they did. Randal had made a fine meal of rice, black beans, canned vegetables and canned chicken. Simple ingredients made spectacular by his judicious use of herbs and spices. Shade was impressed. "You should have been cooking the whole time, Randal!" she said as she took another bite. Even Specter seemed impressed – or at least pleased he didn't have to cook. "We'll have to change the rotation," he said.

After they were through, Randal stood up and said, "Follow me." He strode right out of the kitchen, turned, and walked his familiar walk down to the practice range. Once there, instead of going straight ahead into the electronic practice range, he turned right. Shade was surprised to see an actual target range there. It wasn't large, but it did allow for live firing of weapons.

Randal had set up the room with two stuffed contractor's uniforms hung on wooden frames. There were two contractors' rifles on the right side of the room, Shade's tomahawks, and Specter's knife. Randal was smiling, obviously pleased with himself. He motioned Specter and Shade to their positions and began.

"We've been working hard, and it's finally time to show you what I've been able to do." Randal motioned to the rifles. "If you would be so kind as to pick up a rifle and shoot your respective dummy contractor – center mass, please. Only twice, though, please. Just two shots."

Specter and Shade jumped at the chance to fire some live rounds and both aimed for and hit their respective targets just to the right of the second button. Specter looked at Shade, and she looked back at him. Nothing happened. As Shade raised her weapon to fire again, Randal jumped forward with his arms up. "Hold on! Hold on!" he said. "The first two bullets were just normal ones." Randal saw their look of 'I thought so – where's the good stuff?' "I just need to make sure there's no difference in either loading or recoil or anything. You can fire two more rounds."

They did, and the reaction was immediate. The dummies' stomachs opened up where the bullets struck them – clearly going through the webarmor in the front and back. Randal had stuffed the dummies with multicolored towels, and both dummies shed towel remnants like the spurt of blood spray.

Specter and Shade were both impressed. Shade hadn't seen anything like it and, while Specter had seen it back at the road, he hadn't felt it. To Randal, it seemed like he had just given a new toy to kids who didn't expect it. Randal wanted to keep the feeling going. "Okay," he said, "put your rifles down and pick up your tomahawks and knife and check out how they work." The words were barely out of his mouth before they were attacking the dummies with the enhanced blades.

Shade was the first to strike the webarmored dummy, and it was amazing to see the flashing whirl of her tomahawks in action. It was dazzling but incredibly brief. Shade leaned in with her right and hit low to the dummy's left leg (gone), then up with her left tomahawk to the crotch (up to the gunshot entry). Then she spun around, her left tomahawk catching the dummy's left arm (off) while her right tomahawk cut through where the dummy's head would have been, slashing from the dummy's right side of his collar all the way through and out of the armpit. Only the dummy's right leg was left intact.

Specter's dummy fared much better. Once Specter had his knife, he stopped about twelve feet from the dummy, took the blade in his fingertips, and threw the knife. It did penetrate the webarmor and sink in but, although Specter was impressed, he knew it wouldn't be a death blow. As if he'd really actually throw his knife away. Specter retrieved his knife by the hilt and stabbed the same way, turning his wrist on the way back out and cutting an impressive hole. He reversed the blade and cut a diagonal swath on the dummy, the webarmor splitting at the blade like regular cotton cloth. Specter turned back to Randal and gave him that same look he did when he'd shown off his crossbow the first time. He was pleased.

That triggered Randal's memory. "I've gotten the arrow tips, your crossbow bolts, and your handgun ammo coated, too. I need to find some lead, though, in order to re-do your shotgun shells."

"You can do that?" asked Specter excitedly.

"Yeah, I found the reloading bench in the repair room and read an electronic book on it. The lead shot will probably hold the coating better than the rifle bullets do." Randal looked at the dummies. "But those seem to hold the coating pretty well."

"We'll get you what you need as long as you can get my shotgun working," Specter replied, clearly excited about putting it to good use.

"When do I get my new outfit, Randal?" Shade asked. She was excited, too, but very much looking forward to getting out and finding some more useful clothes of any material, let alone from webarmor. Despite that, Specter and Randal did not seem to be in that much of a hurry.

"We'll have to get more uniforms first. These two," Randal motioned towards the now destroyed dummies, "are the last we have. I'll have to get a large, flat tub or reservoir or something in order to make the cloth."

Shade thought better of playing the sultry, pouty babe and begging 'pleazy weazy.' She instead said, "I've got to get some clothes when we go out, and with these," she hefted her tomahawks, "I'm ready to go now!"

Specter looked at Randal. Randal just raised his eyebrows. Specter said, "Okay, it's settled. We go out just after breakfast – we'll need the light – and go on a trip."

"Where?" echoed Shade and Randal.

"Come on," Specter said.

Chapter 25

Specter led them upstairs. In the main room he fidgeted behind a sculptured vase, and a map materialized before them in mid-air. A little dot blipped on and off showing where they were.

"Nice technology," Shade said. "Is it manipulable?"

"Yes," answered Specter. "We probably need to add some things to it already, don't we?"

"Yes," answered Shade with a smile.

Specter walked up to the map and raised his hand. The map flickered, a white circle appeared then filled in, and then a little hand appeared. Once the map was able to be manipulated, Specter rotated his hand, and the map rotated, too. He said loudly, "Place marker." A red dot appeared and Specter moved his hand (and the little white hand) towards it, closed his hand (picked it up), then moved it where he wanted and opened his hand (placed the marker).

"That's about where we found you, Shade." Using the same process, he placed more markers and then said loudly, "Connect pathway." He looked back at them and then back to the map.

"We'll start here," Specter pointed. "This is where the scientist here," he jerked a thumb towards Randal, "set up his last stand." He traced the path as he spoke. "This is where we stopped to get supplies and horses. And, last, from where we found you, Shade, to here – although we took the lose-whoever's-following path to get here." He stepped back and motioned for Shade to step forward.

Shade moved to the map and manipulated it like a skilled artisan. Once she had placed her markers, she related her story along each point. She went further, too, showing patrol patterns as she had found them. Once finished, she stepped back and everyone regarded the map.

After a while of being left alone with their thoughts, Randal finally broke the silence. "What do you think?"

No one spoke. "Well, what do we need?" Randal asked.

"Clothes," said Shade.

"Clothes," echoed Randal. "Okay. Clothes could be found in towns, so which towns are closest?"

Specter moved to the map and pointed to the nearest ones.

"Kind of equidistant from each, aren't they?" commented Randal. "These were to be the sultan's fiefdom?"

"Maybe," answered Specter, "but we need to make sure our attacks are asymmetric so they can't trace us back to here."

"Okay," said Randal, "that means on the attack we either take the long way home or stay out for multiple attacks." He looked at Shade and winked. "But it shouldn't prevent us from getting clothes first."

"Agreed," said Specter.

"Great. Then which town would be the best to find clothes?" Randal asked.

"No," Specter interrupted.

"What?!" Randal was quickly on the defensive. "You just said that…"

"Wait," Specter interrupted him.

Randal caught himself and waited.

"What I mean," Specter said, "is that that's not the question to ask. Clothes can be had anywhere. The question to ask is, 'which town would best let us see what the pri-cons are doing?'"

"Oh," said Randal dejectedly.

Shade stepped towards the map. She was intently studying it and – just when Specter and Randal were each going to say something – her hands moved in a flurry and she spoke as quickly. "If the platforms were attacked here, the reinforcements would probably have come from here," and she pointed at the map. "Since this is the furthest town from there, that's most likely to have a unit with a former local in it. We want one closer than the farthest but further than halfway. Here," she pointed at the map.

As she turned, Shade looked directly into the eyes of Specter first, then Randal, and then she transformed herself. That was the only word Randal could think of. Shade seemed to flip a switch and turn on a super-sensuality. For Randal, it was a new palpable presence that could not be ignored. He was reminded of Specter's transformation at the store in Renna's Stream.

Shade waited until she had seen both men react – Specter less obviously than Randal, but still reactive. Once she knew that, she turned it off and said, "New men in a new place will be willing to give new people information."

Randal breathed a heavy sigh. How she could just turn that on and off like that was amazing! Then he thought, the only reason she can get to you is because you let her. He told himself to be careful.

Specter was impressed as well. He'd heard of women Hunters being trained like that – able to use sensuality and desire to their advantage. He wished he had a weapon like that. Still….

"It's settled then," Specter said. "We leave for Byland's Rest just after breakfast. Let's travel light but loaded. Cover story?"

"Two brothers and a sister?" Randal offered.

"How about two cousins and a wife?" Shade suggested. "I'll be Randal's wife and," pointing to Specter, "you be the second cousin."

Specter picked it up, "My father and Randal's grandmother were brother and sister. I was visiting. Now we're on our way back to…"

"Southwest…certain place?" Shade asked.

"Keep it open – but nowhere near here – way south, southwest," Specter replied.

"Just like that and I'm married?" Randal joked.

Specter was chuckling, too, "Don't worry, brother. I think you're about to be cuckolded tomorrow."

Shade just turned and headed for bed. "I'm only looking for information and a nice outfit," she said. When she got to the doorway, she turned her sensuality on again and, looking over her shoulder said, "I don't care who gives it to me." With a little dip curtsy and a shake she was gone.

Chapter 26

The well was a lot more dank than Randal remembered. He was coming up last and felt he had to hurry. The smell helped spur him on. Shade helped him up to the top. Once up and inside the cabin, he found Specter sitting outside on the porch. He had sat on the step and motioned with his hand to the two chairs. "Have a seat," he said.

They did. Randal looked at Shade, and she seemed to think this waiting was just exactly the right thing to do. He didn't. "I expected we'd..."

Randal was 'shushed' by both of them with vehemence and alacrity.

He kept his mouth shut.

As they sat there, still, Randal remembered waiting with Specter before crossing that clearing – the first time they saw Shade – how that Specter had sensed rather than seen Shade. Maybe that's what this was – some kind of calibration step to set the senses to 'outside.' He'd never done anything like it but apparently, looking at Specter and Shade, it was chapter two of the Hunter's Handbook.

Specter hadn't told Randal what clothes to wear, but they looked like they coordinated outfits. Randal had put on some of his older traveling clothes: some work pants with a lot of pockets, a plain grey t-shirt, and a long sleeved button-down faded blue shirt. You never knew when long sleeves would come in handy in the woods. Specter was dressed similarly, but his t-shirt was blue, and his sleeves were rolled up to his elbows. Both men wore their outer shirts untucked and unbuttoned.

Shade, on the other hand, looked a lot more like a refugee. She had found some skin hugging tights that she had on underneath the pants she was wearing when they met. She had cut the legs off to make a short pair of shorts, and she had cut the tights in places so they looked worn. Up top she looked more normal, a deep red shirt peeking out from a halfway buttoned up outer shirt, also with the sleeves rolled up to her elbows. All were dressed to look like weary travelers would look.

Randal forced himself to be active rather than just sit. He looked all around, keeping an eye out for anything out of the ordinary. He listened to the sounds around him. He felt the breeze and how if felt against his face and arms. He kept a 'watchful' attitude, trying to let everything sink in. After about fifteen to twenty minutes, Specter stood up, shouldered his pack, picked up his gun, and started walking. Shade and Randal followed suit.

After the wait in silence, no one felt the need to interrupt the natural sounds around them. They had already decided to stay clear of the previous platform battle site. Everyone agreed that there was nothing to gain by going back. They were headed directly east toward the town of Byland's Rest. Randal thought about how things had changed. Towns used to be hubs where people in surrounding areas could come and buy groceries, goods, eat at a restaurant, stroll the downtown shops.

Now a 'town' was more like a feudal fort. Those who had banded together to form the town lived nearby the old city hall, police station, hospital – wherever they had decided to meet. They would meet at least once a week, all together, and around here that meant Sunday. They pooled their resources and had some for trade, but mainly just what everyone needed. They all were the collective police and fire departments, and usually they would switch off teaching children. A lot of that instruction was hands-on practical stuff: how to sew, how to cook, how to skin an animal, how to cut wood. One of Randal's bigger fears was that if the Enclaves and Outerlands ever came together and tried to live together, the Enclavers would think the Outerlanders backward and uneducated. Conversely, the Outerlanders would think the Enclavers 'soft' and not able to find quick, practical solutions. Those misconceptions would lead to problems for years afterwards. Randal chuckled to himself without humor. If they ever decided to live together; fat chance, Randal thought. Just a few generations and then there would be no chance of a peaceful reintroduction.

Shade, following Randal, caught his snort. "Something funny, Randal?" she asked.

"Just the opposite, actually," Randal said. "Only the illusion of a pure democratic utopia."

Shade 'harrumphed' in agreement.

Specter led them along the ridgeline of the hills. They weren't necessarily in mountains, but they were definitely not on a plain. It being early spring, the woods were not yet impassable with new undergrowth, and the path Specter was making seemed to be staying in the deep woods anyway. Specter seemed sure of his way, and Randal suspected he had traveled to each of the surrounding towns enough to know the way to each one.

Not too long after midday, Specter stopped near the top of a steep hill. They each found a seat and Specter broke out the food. Specter watched as Randal bowed his head for about fifteen seconds before eating. As they ate, Specter asked, "How are you holding up?" His eyes directed the question to both of them.

Shade answered first. "I'm doing okay. It is good to get outside – actually move around outside. My shoulder feels good, too. Might be sore tomorrow, but it's okay now."

"I'm doing fine," said Randal.

"Good," Specter said. "We've got a lot more walking to go – especially if we're going to keep the illusion of heading southwest from Byland's Rest. We'll have to get out of town that way and then circle back around. Since we're new, we'll probably be questioned and definitely scrutinized."

"Will they know you, Specter?" asked Randal.

Specter laughed. "No, they won't. The only town I've frequented was the one you and I went to for supplies. I have traveled to all of the surrounding towns, but only to the outskirts, never inside the towns."

"Why?" Randal asked.

Shade jumped in, "He couldn't risk someone from one town running into someone from the next town and saying, 'Hey, I trade with this one guy from out of town' and the other guy saying, 'Really? I do, too,' and so on around all the surrounding towns because then there's the worry of a witch hunt or a 'fact finding mission'."

"Which wouldn't be a bad thing in itself," Specter said. "But I was waiting until retirement. It wouldn't be right for someone to visit me at the cabin and me not have any plants growing – not even herbs."

It made sense to Randal. Another thought came to him. "Why aren't we going to stay the night in Byland's Rest?"

"Because we can make some great time on the road before dark. That's why we'll get there in between lunch and dinner. It'll still be too early to expect a traveler to stop."

"With the troopers stationed in the towns around the platform battle site, we'll have to go directly to them," Shade said. "I can handle that part. We'll need to get our supplies and be on our way. We're loaded about as light as we can to not be too suspicious, but the quicker we're out of that town, the less likely we'll be remembered."

"Well, normally…" said Specter.

Shade looked at him and a flash of recognition swept over her face. "Oh. Right," she said.

Randal couldn't get 'what' out of his mouth before Specter said, "She's going to get some clothes and information, and she's going to look mighty fine doing it."

Randal understood then. Shade would be using her feminine wiles to get the needed information.

"She's probably going to get at least one teenage boy to go south looking for her," Specter continued.

"I see," said Randal.

Specter started packing up and said, "We'd better get on. We're just about an hour away."

They walked the next hour quickly, Randal getting more anxious with every step. He started getting nauseous as they got closer, especially when they started using the main road into town, now with him in the rear. When they caught sight of the downtown, Randal had a stern conversation with himself. He had been the one on the run all this time – he who knew how to get what he needed and what he wanted. Forget the fact that with these two there was just inherently more danger, despite their obvious ability to handle such danger. *Sell it and believe it*, he told himself.

Aloud, Randal said, "Hold up. I'll lead this show." And he strode past Shade and past Specter to the front and, to his surprise, Specter seemed content to bring up the rear. Randal motioned for Shade to come up beside him, and she did. She held up her tomahawks to Randal, and he took them. "In your pack," she said, and he put them there. And that's how they entered the town.

Chapter 27

As the three entered Byland's Rest, they were a sight. Everyone turned to look at them, and Randal was sure to give everyone a big "Hello!" His smile was natural and infectious and stood in stark contrast with Specter who, even though smiling, appeared distant and cold. Shade, though, was a different story. Somewhere on the way in she had turned on her sensuality switch, and every eye glanced over Specter and Randal to land on her.

This time, expecting it, Randal was able to detach himself (somewhat) from the effects and focus on Shade as she worked. It seemed as if she thrived and blossomed with the attention. Whether natural or trained, she certainly knew how to use it.

They passed a young man just old enough to be on the other side of puberty, and Shade stopped him by placing a hand on his arm.

"Excuse me, sir," she said, "but can you tell me where I can get out of these clothes?" She ran her hand down between her breasts and twirled just a bit as her hand reached her hips.

The poor boy was ambushed by her onslaught. He turned beet red and said, "Wha.." about five times before Shade spoke again.

"Oh, my! I'm so silly!" she pulled his arm closer towards her and touched his shoulder with her free hand. "That sounded so awful! Can you imagine me naked in the street? What I meant was 'where can I buy some clothes'" she laughed again.

The boy, to his credit, recovered surprisingly well. "You need to go to Aunt Lindsey's. She's got a lot of clothes."

"And where is that?" Shade said as she batted her eyelashes.

"Oh – right here," the boy said and pointed to the store just four doors down from where they were.

Shade kept it on. Maybe she hadn't worked out with that weapon in a while and needed the flexion, but all Randal could think was 'poor boy.' She pulled herself closer to the young man so that her breast was touching his arm and pointed to the store. "Right there," she asked, "right where I'm pointing?"

"Ye-yes," said the boy, "right underneath the sign that says 'store'."

"Oh, thank you so much!" she said and let the boy go. She made it a point to grab Randal's arm with her left hand, she on his right, and say loudly, "Let's go right now, pleeease?"

Randal was about to say 'okay' when Shade squeezed his arm and tapped with her index finger. As clearly as if she'd said it, he knew she had said 'turn right.' As he looked that way, he knew why.

There, about one hundred feet away, was a platform crew.

The plan had been to get her close to the pri-cons, so he turned that way and said, "In a minute." She gave him one quick squeeze that said 'good.'

Randal looked around but Specter was nowhere to be seen. As they approached the pri-con crew, Shade made a specific point to look to the left and point things out on the left. Once they got about twenty feet away, she looked to the right – and to the platform crew – for the first time.

That was when she squealed.

Randal wasn't sure what to make of it at first, and he found out it didn't matter. It was all her show. There were four pri-cons with the platform, but with her antics, the others came outside, from a barbershop it turned out. They had their helmets off, and Randal hoped Specter was ready for some more headshots.

Shade knew they had been looking at her since she stopped the boy. When she squealed, she had their direct, focused attention, and she made sure to play it up big and dumb and sexually charged, as charged as lightning. She needed to play this right, and she delved right in.

Randal saw Shade with that detached view, and he was thankful he didn't feel the full brunt of it. She was playing the excited schoolgirl for a guy in uniform. After the squeal, she ran up to them and said, "I've never seen a real platform before!" She turned back to Randal and half bent down with her hands on her knees and said, "You saw this all along, didn't you?" She then ran back to Randal and kissed him on the cheek. He was pretty sure she bent her left leg at the knee while she did so. Randal watched her bounce on back to the platform – clearly aware he'd never seen her run like that – and watched the pri-cons' reactions.

She asked, "Can I touch it?" And when the pilot said okay, she leaned against it and did bend her left leg at the knee. Then it was all kinds of questions – questions about the platform, about their uniforms, about their helmets, and about their guns. Randal was surprised how much information she was getting from them and how well she had mesmerized them.

She did finally turn back to Randal and said, "Oh, honey, I wish we could stay and talk with these fine men, but I really do need new clothes," and then she pouted like a two year old would.

Randal couldn't think too quickly, but if she was acting like she was two years old, he managed, "Maybe they'll be here after you get done shopping."

She turned, still pouting, towards the crew. "Okay, guys, sorry...." And before they could say anything and because Randal had enough distance, they didn't say anything to her as she ran back to Randal.

She grabbed Randal's arm and leaned her head close as they walked. She talked quickly so that Randal wouldn't be distracted by her closeness. She didn't need collateral damage. "I've almost got them, but I need you to give me more time. I'm going to rely on you to shop for me – get nothing frilly. Just get what you'd get but get it in my size." They were just shy of the middle of the street. "Say okay," she whispered, and then she pushed Randal away at arm's length and said, "Really!" loud enough to hurt his ears while bouncing on her toes and putting herself in between him and the pri-cons.

"Okay," Randal said, surprised.

"Oh, great!" she said as she dropped her pack and started undoing her pants. She bent over and slid down her shorts over her skin-tight tights. When she bent, he got a view of the platform crew and realized what she was up to. This had been planned before they left the cabin.

The torn tights focused the pri-cons' attention on her legs and butt, and that made the whole crew stop to look. She made a point of shaking and moving, getting the pants around her boots. She stood back up, handed him the pants, lifted both of her arms, and shook her butt in a little celebration dance.

"Oh," she said softly and started undoing the buttons on her shirt, speaking quickly. "The signal will be me jumping off the platform. Get all the clothes you can and stay inside until you see me jump off the platform. Then come out and say 'My God, woman!'" She looked him in the eye. "Okay?"

"Sure," he said.

With the buttons undone on her shirt, Randal could tell that what he had thought was a t-shirt was actually some form fitting undergarment, or it was three sizes too small. She started turning around and managed to take off her over shirt while turning. She put the shirt in his hands, and before he could drink her in, she said, "Don't lose it."

He looked her in the eye – knowing she didn't mean the shirt – and she winked at him. Then she said, "You're the best!" way too loud and she took his face in her hands and just as she was about to kiss him, her face went flat and hard and she commanded him, "Squeeze my ass, then turn." She said it in such a way that the sensuality was gone, and he was afraid of what she'd do if he didn't. She kissed him, and he did as he was told. He turned and forced himself to walk towards the store. He heard Shade say, "Hooray! I get to be with you guys!" Her use of double entendre was remarkable.

Randal looked back up the street, but there was still no sign of Specter. He reached the store and went inside. There was a nice woman at the counter, but it looked like she had just gotten there. Randal guessed she was looking out the window up until he turned the door handle.

"I'm Aunt Lindsey and welcome to my store. May I help you?" she asked. There was only one other person in the store, a young man with a full beard. He had the lady's eyes, though, and Randal knew it must be her son when she muttered something to him and he started stocking shelves.

"I need to get some clothes for my wife, Aunt Lindsey," he managed to say.

"I see," she said. "Any certain type of clothes?"

"Nothing frilly," he said.

She smiled a bit and walked up to him. She took Shade's clothes out of his hand and said, "These her size?"

"Yes," he said. He decided the less he said the better off he'd be. He would let the shopkeeper think he was being taken advantage of, that he had married badly, whatever she decided.

She walked towards the back left of the store, and Randal followed her. "Nothing frilly, huh?" she asked again. "These are to be work clothes, then?"

He thought back to what Shade had said about buying what he would. He liked work clothes. "Yes," he said.

She looked down her nose at him and asked, "Do you expect to make her get out and work?" She was pointing out the window at Shade.

This was a turning point. He could sense it. She wanted to like him, but she didn't know enough about him yet. He started playing his cards. "Miss, I sure don't mean to force a woman into doing anything." No response. "But when she and I got married, she made me feel like the only man alive." Still nothing. "But we've been traveling a lot going back to my home place…" A little softening of the eyes there. "And, well, she loves seeing new things and meeting new people. And I need to get her something presentable for traveling…" A bit of tension release in the forehead. "That'll last until we can get back home to my mom and sisters.." A bit more softening there – must have sisters. "And then – well my family works, miss." There it was; she was hooked. Time to seal it. "And some honest work, miss, I'm sure will work that traveling energy right out of her, and then it'll be back to her and me so's we can think of maybe having a family." He turned a wistful face from the woman to look outside at his wayward wife. There Shade was, in the center of all seven of the pri-cons, wearing the pilot's helmet and turning around, giving all of them various looks at her body.

The woman's voice had softened, "There's a lot that good hard work will do, boy, but there's a lot it won't, too." He wasn't sure he'd played his cards right. Her face looked hard still, but maybe it was more like a grandmother. "You two don't go making babies until you know she's going to stay there and care for them."

Chapter 28

He smiled. "Yes, ma'am." He paused and, looking out the window, he thought he might as well try to get some information. "Do you know why they're here? Do they stay here?" he asked.

She seemed curious herself. "There was some trouble up the way. They lost a platform crew or something. Bad, whatever it was. They think there's a band of murderers running around. They said there was some trouble up north along the road, and the people they think caused it might be headed this way," she said.

"Really," he said. "What do you think?" he asked pointedly.

She looked at him very closely, coming to some decision in her mind. Once she had, she said, "I think it's more like some people upset at the new pleasure dome that they're building up near Archer's Lake. Lotsa folks got run off their land by that one, and we're the closest town north of it. Lotsa folks pass through here tired of the Corps."

"But not enough to take on a platform crew. You'd have to be crazy, or have a boatload of people," said Randal.

She paused to think. "Well, there is that," she said.

She carried some clothes back to the counter and set them down. "These are all the right size. You pick out what's best."

It seemed like a challenge for him to pick out the right things, but Randal followed Shade's advice and picked out what he would get himself. He ended up with four pairs of pants, three t-shirts, and three over shirts. Then he got a belt and decided on another two shirts.

Lindsey, the shopkeeper, seemed endeared to him – or pitying him. She said, "You sure? Will she want to wear clothes like this and look like you?"

Randal just said, "She's got enough frilly things."

The woman wrapped up the clothes in Shade's shirt and tied the bundle with twine. "Now, what will you trade for them?"

Now Randal dropped all pretense. Now was the time to bargain, and he was in the hole. These were some pretty rugged, stout clothes. "What are you looking for? What do you need?"

She seemed to resize him. "Nothing you'd be likely to have," she said. She hurried on though. "The main things I need are a diesel engine, biodiesel fuel, good fabric, and white sugar. Got any of that?"

"Do you have beet sugar?" Randal asked.

"That's what we've been using. Have you ever had a cake made with beet sugar?"

Randal caught himself nodding and stopped. He was nodding yes – not because of the cake taste – but because this was his best set up and it was working.

"I know, I know. You just need to add a bit more vanilla, though, and it's passable."

"Hah!" she halfway laughed and harrumphed. "Vanilla! Ha! I'd let you have all of that for a bottle of vanilla!"

"What else would you throw in?"

Now she did laugh, heartily and at length. "Oh, thank you," she finally said. "I haven't laughed like that in a while." She grew more serious. "You ain't got no vanilla. Those plants only grow like in Africa or Mexico, and there ain't no more in stores. The only one who has any is too far away and charges too much for it."

Randal held her gaze. "So it'd be worth a lot to you."

"You ain't got no vanilla," she said again.

Randal could tell she was allowing herself to hope. He decided to go ahead and play his next card. "Well, do you have any vodka?"

It was like he asked her if she liked drowning puppies. It was the response he wanted.

"I most certainly do NOT! You make take your business elsewhere, young man. Good day!"

He had had this happen before, and he went with his standard response. With his head bowed he said, "I'm so sorry. I did not mean to imply you would keep vodka in your house – much less that you would drink it. I'm so sorry." He raised his head and met her icy glare. "All I meant was that you might have some in town for antiseptic reasons, like instead of rubbing alcohol. I'm sorry."

She seemed to pacify with his words. His apologies mollified her enough so that she focused on his face without seeing his hands. He had played this game before against many worthy opponents, and he was great at it.

She said, "It's okay. I just...Just don't worry about it."

"I only mentioned it because you would need some for this," and he held up about one inch of a vanilla bean pod.

She looked at it and, after her shock of thinking Randal was accusing her of being an alcoholic, here, in front of her eyes, was a money-maker.

Randal took her hand, placed the husk in her hand, and she immediately smelled it to verify it. "You need to put it in vodka for at least three months before using it. The vanilla bean and pod will flavor the vodka into a passable vanilla extract. You should be able to keep pouring off most of the liquid, as long as you keep a little left in the bottle, and then adding more for a long time," Randal said.

She looked at Randal, and he knew he had to move fast or she would bail – it was too good to be true.

"Worth at least some arrows, or gunpowder?" he asked.

She turned and went to the back. He looked behind the counter and saw a picture of a girl maybe twelve to thirteen years old. It was a picture taken a while back, maybe before the Breaking. He took a moment to focus on what was actually in the counter. There were some knives and some old guns. Nothing he could use but still a good selection. Maybe those people moving north needed provisions. He looked around. The woman's son was still captivated by Shade outside.

Oh, snap! He needed to hurry. Shade was still on the ground and not on the platform. So he had time.

Just then the shopkeeper came out of the back. She set three canisters on the counter. "No arrows, and I only have three," she said. "What else?"

Gunpowder. He could use it, but then he thought of Specter's shotgun shells. "Do you have any old wheel weights?" he asked.

"You a reloader?" she asked. Randal nodded. "I do have some – most of it spoken for – local needs. You understand." He nodded again.

"Any chance you've got a sieve and a cast iron ladle?" Randal asked.

She looked surprised, then walked to the back wall and came back with a section of screening with quarter inch holes in it. "Will this work?" she asked.

"Yes," Randal said, "And the wheel weights?"

Aunt Lindsey left and returned with a cloth bag of weights. She placed all on the counter.

"Do you have any sewing machine needles?" Randal asked.

"Don't tell me you've got power, too!?" she joked.

"No," he lied, "just need the needles."

She laid those on the counter as well. "Will that make it a deal?"

Randal felt good about this. He had gotten what he wanted and, finishing up, he was still giving her more than he was taking. She'd be more apt to trade with him in the future, too. "One more thing," he said. "Who is that in the picture?" he asked.

He immediately regretted the question. The pain on Aunt Lindsey's face was as visible as if he'd drawn blood.

She did answer, though. "She's my niece," she started. "She would be eighteen now."

"I'm sorry," Randal said.

"No – she's not dead. At least we hope not. She ran away when she was almost sixteen." She looked Randal in the eye. "If you see her, tell her she can come back, will you?"

"Sure," he said. And he would.

"You may want to make sure your wife gets to wear those clothes. Looks like she's getting away from you," Aunt Lindsey said as she pointed out the window.

There was Shade up on the platform with the pri-con crew looking up at her. Randal gathered up his stuff, secured it, and went to stand by the door. "Thank you," he said.

"You're welcome," Aunt Lindsey replied.

He turned and that was when Shade didn't jump off the platform – but back flipped off of it. His cue.

Randal was out the door and hollered, "My God, woman!" He was moving quickly and had almost crossed the street halfway when Shade turned to him.

"Oh, I'm so sorry, honey," she said with her fingertips over her mouth. She had squatted a bit for the pri-cons' benefit. Then she turned it all off and said loudly, "Our baby is going to be fine. It's just a little ball right now!"

Randal followed her lead. "That's my baby, too, you know. You've got to be careful. I've got your clothes, and it's late. Let's get going."

Shade came up to him and didn't even look at the pri-con crew. She took his arm and started going over his purchases. She said, low, "We've got to move straight out. Specter will catch up." So they made their way directly but not overtly quickly to the outside of town. Once there, they took an obvious turn to make sure they were seen heading south.

After they got a ways out of town, Shade stopped. "I need my clothes back," she said, "just the ones from today, not the new ones."

Randal handed her her shorts and started undoing the bundle of new clothes to get her shirt. He gave her tomahawks to her next, knowing she'd want them. Once done, he redistributed the stuff from the store into his and Shade's packs. He was just finishing when he saw Shade ready her tomahawks and stiffen. Randal didn't have time to react before Specter joined them. Shade and Specter kneeled down beside Randal.

Specter said quickly, "Ready to move?"

They both nodded.

Specter asked Shade directly, "Did you set up a meeting place?"

"Only generally. I said we'd probably only go ten more miles before stopping for the night."

"Too soon to turn back?" Specter asked.

"No," Shade said. "They're dedicated but no hard training in tracking. They'll stick to the road and not veer off unless they see something."

Specter addressed them both, "Any good information?"

"Yes," said Shade.

"I think so," said Randal.

"Good," said Specter, "Can we run? I'd like to have a wide circle before they get the balls to move out."

Randal and Shade nodded again and secured their packs.

Specter looked at Randal. "Count to three and then follow." He then looked at Shade. "Bring up the rear and let us know about any trouble. We're way too suspect if anything happens to that platform crew today." Specter then stood, nodded, and was off.

Randal and Shade stood, and when he counted to three in his mind, Shade patted his shoulder and he was off after Specter. It wasn't too overgrown, and it was easy to keep track of Specter.

Shade counted to three herself and then set out after Randal. It was easy to follow him, and Specter was heading at a good pace. At this rate, she thought they might make it back before nightfall. She wanted to share information and see what the others found because she was ready to fight back. She was ready to face her terminators, get them off her back, and, with Specter and Randal, maybe she would get her chance.

They were making good time, and she would periodically check behind, making sure they weren't followed. Out here, though, in the midst of all this wilderness, in between towns, it was hard to think there was a chance of that happening. From what she had learned, all the emphasis was on catching the perpetrators – maintaining a presence for the locals was just pretense. But there would be more to share later.

They paused only once on their way back just to make sure everyone was okay and prepared to continue on. They all took some water from the stream by which they'd stopped, and the cool running water made Shade think about her home. The smell of the damp earth and the babbling of the spring tugged at her memory. She felt homesick for the first time since becoming a Hunter. *Well*, she told herself, *soon enough*. They all stood and moved out again, making the last leg of the journey.

As long as we can lose them here, they thought, and kept pushing.

Chapter 29

Once back, they each cleaned up and rejoined in the kitchen. Specter had gotten some fresh rabbit, potatoes, onions, and carrots. Rabbit stew was the obvious choice, but Specter had devised another option. He had cooked the rabbit meat with sautéed onion, quartered and roasted the potatoes, and simply sliced the carrots. A simple enough meal, savory and tasty. Randal made mention of that fact and Shade echoed the sentiment. *But after only a light lunch, any big late dinner would taste good*, thought Specter while he said, "Thank you. My pleasure."

As the meal wound down, the sounds of eating were slowly replaced by conversation. It turned out that Randal was the hungriest, or at least the fastest eater. Since he'd finished first, he delved into what he had learned.

"The woman at the store had only heard of 'trouble' and knew it was something bad, like losing a platform crew, but she wasn't sure. She said the pri-cons think it's a roving band of murderers moving north to south because of some trouble up there." Specter and Shade shared a look, and he caught it. "What?" he asked, looking at each in turn. "They're not just there to protect the townspeople like she thinks?"

"Finish up," Specter prompted.

"Well, I still…Anyway, she's done a lot of trading lately with people forced to relocate from the Corp's annexation of land for a new pleasure dome to the south." Randal said.

Specter and Shade shared another look.

"Okay, what is it?" Randal demanded.

"You may be right about this thing to the south – but not about the roving band of murderers." Specter said and looked at Shade.

"The standard response," Shade explained, "is the opposite. If you're looking for a small group, you say you're looking for a large group. That empowers the small group to be more bold and less careful. They think they can run around and do whatever and, if caught, can always say 'it wasn't us – we're not a big group.' Plus, it may make them think they're not alone, like they've got comrades in arms," she said.

"Again making them think they can be more bold," said Randal.

"Right." Shade went on, "If you're looking for a large group you say 'small' and that way they get mad because they're doing a lot and don't want it to be seen as ineffective. Also, though, you've got the other side thinking they can overwhelm you because you're looking for a small group – when all the while, you're ready for them."

She paused as if remembering something, then she said, "So we know they're looking for a small group."

"Three," Specter interjected. When he knew he had their attention he went on. "I thought it might be better to pull away from you two just in case, and it turns out I was right. Apparently there was a local out hunting when he saw us leaving the road after we'd left the platforms burning. I found a guy who knew the guy. The local didn't have much of a description and thought we had taken one of the pricons because we tied him to the saddle."

"I'll take it that was me?" Shade asked.

"Yes," said Specter.

Shade went on, "Well, I got the fact they were working with a local, but not the story he gave them." She paused, and Randal could tell she was already trying to piece everything together. "That lady is right about the south. It's going to be a huge complex and will have everything you could want – if you want that kind of stuff. Operational, still a way from full completion, but they said some of their suppliers are nearby."

"Suppliers of what?" Randal asked.

"They didn't say. About us, I think we're in deep," Shade said. "They know what damage was done; they know we didn't keep a hostage. It must be two guys and a girl."

Randal tried to piece it all together, too. He asked, "So there isn't a band of murderers roaming north to south?"

Specter and Shade looked at each other and then Shade said simply, "No." They sat in silence, each trying to think a way out.

"Why not?" asked Randal suddenly. When he saw their blank stares he went on. "Why are there not roving bands of murderers?"

After blank looks again, Randal was determined. "Follow me on this, okay? You're looking for three people who took out four platform crews. That sounds like a very specialized set of people who could do that. Perhaps, though, with a lot more attacks it would be harder to believe the idea of it being only three people. That would make it easier to discount the witness as not having seen all the people who were there and make them think it really is a large group of people."

"We still run the risk of being seen again," said Specter.

"I can help with that," said Randal.

"How?" shot back Specter.

"Misdirection," Randal said. "Gaze re-focusing. It's actually easier than you think. If we attacked some more pri-cons and wrote some graffiti like 'give us back our land' or 'pleasure dome – not over my home,' they might think it is a band of disgruntled refugees." He went further, "And why can't we start some rumors of our own saying we heard it was seven, or seventeen, or thirty-four people?"

"The larger group would be easier to make people believe," Shade said. "Heck, it'd be easier for the pri-cons to believe."

"Especially if you play up their strength," Specter added. "That alone might make them think differently. From their point of view it could be that a Hunter did that, or two Hunters."

"Really?" said Randal, feigning hurt.

"Okay, two Hunters and the greatest Runner so far," said Specter. "But one thing I can see is this: we did that to get away, and now we're gone. Other than that, what motive do we have? Revenge? See – that's what I mean, it's still flimsy. Shade and I could disappear, and Randal has had years to get back at the Corps. Why just now?"

Randal drove his point forward. "That's just why I think it'll work. Once we're gone, or rather, since we're already gone, there's no reason to think it could be us. Now, they have a report that could match us, and revenge might be flimsy, but it is workable. If they have evidence of more attacks and notes showing up directing them to someone else, then they might give up the idea that it's us simply because three people couldn't do all that damage. You're forgetting that we don't have armor-piercing bullets, as far as they know. They won't believe that three people could do all that."

Shade picked it up, "And by giving them some other rumors, we'd be giving them a reason to believe what they'd want to believe:

that no three people, whoever they are, could take out platform crews." She nodded to herself. "We couldn't do many, though. We don't want the whole pri-con army to come here. Maybe four or five more attacks would be enough to throw suspicion, don't you think?"

"We couldn't do them all at once. Or we shouldn't," Randal said, remembering Specter's earlier admonition. "We could strike once and get back. But to make it look like a group wouldn't we have to cover more ground than we could on foot?" He looked deep in thought. "Could we take a platform?" he asked.

Specter took a moment to make sure Randal was serious.

Shade did not wait. "No," she said succinctly. Anticipating his question, she went on, "The platforms are activated through the voice of the pilot and a special code he enters as he gets on. It's changed each time for each platform. Even if you had a control panel, the code changes every trip. On top of that, the platform would only be effective on the road – not off-road. We'd have to be so high it would leave us open to counter attack. Too open."

"Do we need horses, then?" Randal asked.

"That or a few dirt bikes," Specter said flatly. In response to Randal's expectant face, he went on quickly. "No, I don't have any in the garage. And that would definitely stand out to any witnesses."

"Where can we get mounts, then?" asked Shade.

"I know," said Specter. "We'll go back to Renna's Stream. He nodded to Randal. "It's a hike on foot, but if we head straight east, we could make it in one full day. If we go to the north, take some more time, we could make a hit on the way there, get horses, and make another hit on the way back."

Shade seemed to agree. "Hitting two that close together, that fast, should lead them in a different direction."

"So how do we 'hit' them?" asked Randal.

"I'm open," replied Specter. "I was thinking we'd send one of us out, flag them down, and then mow them down, preferably before they can call for help."

"Just that simple?" Randal asked.

"Yup," Specter said.

"Too much and you overthink things," added Shade.

"Can we plan on an early morning, then?" Specter asked.

"I'll make some things tonight and be ready. Those shotgun shells will have to wait, though," said Randal.

Specter nodded.

"I'll cook breakfast, then," said Shade.

Chapter 30

They set a brisk pace from the beginning. They had packed for a few days, but they were moving like they'd get there and back before nightfall. Randal was having a hard time. Maybe it was the extra pack he had made for each of them. Randal had fashioned probably the worst looking things to represent people, but knew they'd work. Not up close, of course, and better on horseback – but better than nothing.

He had Shade wearing a harness like she was carrying a baby strapped to her chest. Specter was wearing a jig Randal had rigged to an old backpack frame. Specter had it lying around, and Randal had adjusted it so Specter could run while wearing it. It was meant to look like a person behind the wearer, but right now, it was packed with provisions. Randal's own pack resembled Shade's more than Specter's and was meant to look like he was carrying someone on his back. Randal was carrying other ones as well, to be used later.

Randal knew from experience that the disguises would work from a distance, but they would not hold up to close attention. What Randal knew would hold up was their resolve. He had invested too much time planning his own escape to have it not believed, and this would help. Both Specter and Shade seemed as dedicated to this course as he was. He knew they would have no trouble killing and, while he didn't look forward to it, he knew he was capable.

Uneventfully, they reached the highway sometime in the mid-afternoon of the second day. They had pushed hard to get here but saw only woods, heard only normal sounds from the woods, and smelled no fires. The travel was long, and they didn't stop for much or for long when they did. Sleep came easily after traveling, and they split the watch. The only prevailing thought was the fact that they were going forth specifically to shed blood.

They were some miles north from where they took out the other platform crews. According to Shade, the patrols would probably be going in twos, but regular traffic would still be singular. Those would be the ones to hit to get information if any information was to be had.

Shade had told them about her time on a platform crew, and it was very enlightening and informative. She mentioned stuff like where they would put officials and how they'd conceal them, for example. That'd be the mother lode – hitting a carrier transport – but it only happened rarely.

Specter and Shade picked the spot where they'd attack, and Randal set about putting his dummies up. "Anything that may help," he said, and Specter and Shade were fine to allow him. Randal set up some of the dummies where Shade's first and second shooting positions would be, then some around where they wanted him.

The way they had planned it, Specter would get them to stop in the right place, and Shade would take out those on her side of the road, using one of the pri-con rifles they'd gotten before, loaded with Randal's special bullets. Specter would take out the team leader and those on the far side of the platform. That left Randal responsible for the pilot. They had chosen a spot in the road cut through a mountain. That let Shade be up top for spotting as well as shooting and Randal at the base of the mountain, on Shade's side, where he could peek up and get a good sight line. Specter had the hard task of getting the platform to stop where the other two had a clear shot. The bank did provide Specter a little nook to wait in, though. Simple enough if everything worked. Then they'd collect everything, destroy the platform, mark the site, and be gone. Simple enough.

They waited until almost dusk for the right one. That is, many two ship patrols had passed but only two single transports. The first possible transport was going the other way, though. The next single transport looked to be the one, and Shade signaled Specter. Specter got out into the road with his hands out but his duster on. He started waving down the transport and, to Randal's surprise, it stopped.

The rest was over in a flash.

Eight flashes, actually.

Randal wondered if this was how bank robbers felt: easy to do the job – hard to live with it.

Once the platform stopped, Randal had the pilot in his sights. Not knowing that anyone had discussed a 'go' signal or anything, Randal acted. *I've got him now; I'd better go ahead*, thought Randal, and fired.

The pilot dropped, surprised, clutching at his chest as the left side of the transport was decimated. Randal thought he was the first to fire, and, though it was close, Shade had actually fired first. She had started at the back, though, so when Randal saw the man closest to the pilot fall, there were no more behind him.

Specter was as effective, drawing and firing as soon as he saw Shade's first kill. He stepped to the side as he dropped the team leader, so he could better wipe out the right side of the platform. The smoke from Randal's shot hadn't cleared before the platform crew were all dead.

They moved quickly then to get all the uniforms and rifles. Specter was up on the platform first, and he started with the team leader. Randal got up and started on the pilot. Shade kept her spot to act as a lookout. Specter and Randal worked quickly, piling helmets and boots in the middle of the platform, guns on the back, and uniforms over the side to the front of the platform. Soon enough it was done.

Randal went up to get his disguises and Shade came down. She helped Specter secure the weapons in a uniform. Once done, they packed the uniforms into Shade's fake baby pack, and she strapped it on. Specter shouldered his pack as Randal made it back down.

Shade took the sidearms from the pilot and team leader and walked toward the back of the platform. "Randal," she called, "get me two helmets and two boots, okay?"

So Randal did as she requested.

"Stay up there," she said as he was ready to come down. Shade tossed one helmet to Specter and said, "Write, or scratch, our demands on that." Specter brought out his knife and began. Shade aimed one of the sidearms and fired once into the platform and something started spewing out – fuel. She caught some in a boot, filled it, and then handed it to Randal with the words, "Cover them with it."

Randal did that with all four boots and the helmet. Once done, he was afraid he might light up. Shade hopped up on the platform and told him to back away. With Randal gone, she checked the magazines in the pistols and started shooting all the dead pri-cons.

Randal thought it a horrible display.

Shade stepped to the back of the platform, fired one shot near the guidance lever, and jumped off as sparks started flying. Specter set down the helmet he'd etched and started moving. Randal followed Specter as they made for the far side of the road. After a sprint for the wood line, they all crouched and looked back. The platform was burning, as was everything on it.

Specter spoke first, "I would've forgotten to shoot them; good thinking, Shade."

Randal, astonished, said, "What?!"

"Shooting them makes it harder to determine how they died. The burning helps, but with the multiple wounds it will take longer for them to know who they're looking for." Specter answered. "You did pick up your casings, right?" he asked Shade.

She patted her pocket, "Right here." She looked at them, "You get yours?"

Specter answered, "Randal's got a percussion revolver – no casing at all. I've got single action revolvers – my brass is still in the gun." He looked around at how high the smoke was getting. He rose with, "Let's get out of here," and was moving. Randal and Shade followed, each thankful, this time, for the quick pace Specter set.

Chapter 31

Specter kept moving at a good clip for the better part of an hour. He slowed to a walk and let Randal and Shade catch up. While walking, he reloaded his sidearms, keeping the casings in his interior duster pocket. He was reloaded when Shade got there. As they walked, he asked about eating. Shade and Randal both agreed to keep pushing until dark.

So they did.

Specter slowed the pace a little but not much. They ran on until just after dusk – until the risk of injury outweighed the need to cover ground. They were moving more easterly now and, with luck, would reach Renna's Stream by morning the day after tomorrow. It required them to push, but they'd be able to relax a bit more on horseback.

Specter picked out a campsite after about thirty more minutes of walking. After such a full day of travel, they all elected to go without a fire that night. Randal suspected it might be more to avoid any electronic thermal imaging sensors. Specter broke out some food and they ate. Bedding down, Shade took her pack and put it under her head. Randal stretched out and got as comfortable as he could. Specter took the first watch. Shade had elected to take the middle watch, saying she wouldn't have any trouble going back to sleep. She got no argument from Specter or Randal.

Shade nudged Randal awake, and he stood up quickly, letting her get back to sleep. He stood still for a few minutes letting his eyes adjust to the night. He stepped around his companions and found a spot not far away. He crouched against a tree and let the sounds of the woods wash over him. He thought of those times when Specter would wait and just listen. He didn't know if Specter evaluated himself during such times, but he used the time that way. Just as he listened to the natural sounds in order to hear when some foreign sound came up, he used the time to see what was off in his life.

Committed as he was to this path, Randal had some trouble accepting his role in it and justifying his actions. He had determined that there probably was no justification, but perhaps there was forgiveness. He found it amazing how, in his mind, he could compartmentalize his actions. He guessed that was everyone's spiritual dilemma. So he spent that time alone with his God, the woods an unwelcome intruder.

As the dawn rose up through the trees, Randal awakened Specter and Shade. They didn't waste much time getting ready and even less on breakfast. They started moving before it was fully light. Walking to mitigate the risk of injury, Specter led them out into the day.

When it got light enough, they picked up the pace and started making some good time. They ate their lunch while walking and refilled their water at the next stream. They kept pushing forward and saw no sign of any pursuit or any patrols. The second day of the trip back to Renna's Stream was looking to be blissfully uneventful.

And it stayed that way. Through the midafternoon on into the evening, the only things they ran into were small game and birds. Despite being uneventful, it was exciting. The path Specter took was far from anything developed, and the natural beauty of the woods kept each traveler's attention. They kept very little conversation going, due in part to the pace but more so to the majesty of the outdoors. It just demanded each keep his or her own council and each one left the other two to their own thoughts.

As darkness fell and their place slowed, Specter said, "We're about two hours away from Renna's Stream. We've had a good day and could probably try a campfire if you want" Shade agreed and Randal didn't argue. They took some precautions for the fire so it wouldn't be seen and lit it with Randal's fire piston.

Shade asked about the piston, and Randal gave her the story of compression and lighting an ember. He was demonstrating it again for her when Specter jumped in, "Let me guess, it's one of the things you got before you started running."

It kind of took Randal aback, being referenced to as Prey again, but he saw no malice in Specter's face. He answered good naturedly. "Yeah, it was. Didn't you get some things when you knew you were going to run?"

Shade seemed to pick up on it and joined in, "I sure did. I loaded up on guns." With their surprised faces, she went on, "Just because I got caught with only my tomahawks doesn't mean I don't like guns!" she said, laughing.

It struck Randal there in the dim light of dusk how really beautiful Shade was when she was enjoying herself. Her laughter smoothed her face, and the firelight painted highlights on her face like a natural makeup. He watched her as she turned toward Specter. "What did you grab up, Specter?" she asked.

Specter sat back down with some biscuits to warm in the fire. "Bullets," he finally said. "When I knew it was coming, I got bullets. And primers."

Randal couldn't resist. "Little primers like books to teach you how to read?" Randal said it with a smile, but there was a tense half second before Specter chuckled.

"Not to read, Randal, to reload," he said.

Shade slipped in seamlessly, "I noticed you had quite the set up there in the bunker. All that for reloading?" she asked.

"I just decided it'd be smart to use what the guy had there," Specter said. "After all, they're not making bullets anymore." Randal couldn't believe it but it looked like Specter was opening up. "I went around everywhere looking for bullets and primers," Specter continued, "and I stockpiled a lot."

"Did that take a lot of money?" Randal asked.

Specter looked at Shade before he answered. Randal followed his gaze and Shade looked down and to the right. *Remembering something?* Randal thought. Specter answered, "It might not be commonly known about Hunters, but we get what our Prey had." Specter let that hang in the air for a bit before continuing. "What a Hunter does with that, after recompense is paid, if any, is up to the Hunter."

Randal could tell this was upsetting to Shade but he didn't know how to segue into something else. Thankfully, Specter did. He said, "I wish I'd bought up more canned food." Then he took a bit of biscuit and – did he pout?

It was so out of place, both Shade and Randal started laughing. Specter never seemed to complain, and what he wanted he just seemed to take. That big bite of biscuit and his expression just got Shade and Randal going.

Specter joined in a bit later. Maybe it was the pressure of being hunted that Specter and Shade were just feeling, maybe it was being able to actually fight back, and maybe it was just a full day of traveling. But it felt good to laugh. It felt really good.

The rest of the evening went as well. As Randal lay down, he thought they had bonded – each of them a little closer. And he thought Specter understood a lot more about leading a group than he let on.

Chapter 32

The morning held the promise of mounts, and what a difference they would make. For now, they decided to use the disguises, but they would leave them prior to going into the town proper.

Arriving at the far edge of the town, on the ranch side, Specter stopped and crouched down. Letting Shade catch up, Specter waited. "Okay. I'm going in. Just me." He looked at both of them to make sure that was clear. Shade seemed to have some reservations. Specter explained, "They know me as one person. Maybe sometimes with one other person. Further, they trust me. I'll be back with mounts, and we might be able to strike again before heading back to the bunker."

"Be quick," Shade said simply.

Specter pulled a bundle from his pack and started off for the farmhouse. Randal lost sight of him as he went along the tree-lined lane to the barn. Shade seemed to trace him a bit longer. Randal sat with his back to a tree and, after a bit, Shade came and sat down beside him.

"Do you think he's turning us in?" Shade asked right out of the blue.

"I hadn't thought about it, really," Randal said. Then he did think about it. "No, I don't think he is."

"What made you trust him?" Shade asked.

Randal realized that Shade didn't know how he and Specter had met – not the full story anyway. He tested the waters. "You do know he and I met as Hunter and Prey, right?"

Shade put her hands down on the ground and pivoted away from the tree. "Really? I remember Specter saying something like that, but nothing more," she said. She seemed genuinely enthralled. *Probably more about how Specter let me live*, he thought.

But he went ahead anyway. "I had set a trap so I could stop running, and he fell into it."

"Really?" she asked, getting – excited? – again.

Randal went on, "Well, it wasn't just for him. It was for anyone who would've found me." Shade smiled. "It was in the morning, and I had him in my bow sights when I asked him if we could have breakfast before he killed me."

"No way!" Shade exclaimed, laughing. And Randal realized he was recounting that first day like Specter was an old friend.

"Anyway, I made my move – rigged the floor and was about gone when the house erupted. The pri-cons just started firing at everything."

"Oooh," Shade mouthed with concern showing on her face.

"So I opened the trap door for him and made him a deal, so I had to trust him. I thought he would honor the deal anyway. He called me on it later, and then I had to make a choice. So I guess I had to trust him," Randal said, remembering.

"But you decided to, right?" Shade prompted.

"Yeah, I guess you're right," Randal said. "I think what drove me there was the fact that he could have killed me anytime he wanted to – but didn't."

"Yeah," Shade said, slapping at his leg, "that not being dead makes you really want to trust that someone who didn't kill you." She was enjoying this.

"Okay, okay," he said. "In that moment he called me out, I felt our survival was intertwined. So, not trusting him was more like – not trusting myself."

Shade chewed on that for a while, digested it. "I've never looked at it that way, Randal," she said. Then she smiled and winked at him, "Kind of like you're married to him, right?" She kicked at his feet with hers.

He did have to chuckle; a trust described like that did seem intertwined. "Well, what about you?" Randal asked. "What made you trust him?"

She got a coy, surprised look on her face. "What makes you think I trust him at all?"

This surprised Randal. All he could get out was, "Well, you're still with us."

She looked him right in the eye and said, "I owe you two a blood-oath. You saved my life." Then she looked at Randal as if really seeing him this time. Then, she kind of half-squinted her eyes and asked, "Who's to say that it's not <u>you</u> that I trust?"

Randal brushed it off. "Yeah, right," he said.

He watched as she shrugged her shoulders as if to say, 'Okay, if you don't believe me.'

Randal hurried on, "I am pretty trustworthy, though." He looked at Shade and wasn't sure of her expression. He looked into her eyes and said, "Either way, we're all together, we will get through this, and we won't have to run anymore." He put his hands on the ground and started getting up. He looked at her again and said, "We will be okay."

Surprised, Shade felt a little ember catch light in her for Randal. His sweetness oozed out and seemed genuine. But, here, for – not so recently – Prey to try and comfort a Hunter – that had to be a first. She made a mental note of it. It was rare that someone expressed care for her. Rare and welcome.

Randal was headed back towards the tree line when Shade caught sight of Specter. He was on his way back with what looked like four horses. She came up behind Randal and pointed over his shoulder toward where Specter was. Then she patted him on the back and just said, "Thanks." She turned and walked back toward the clearing where they had set their stuff down. Randal joined her as Specter reined in. Randal was pleased to see the same two mounts he and Specter had before.

Specter dismounted quickly and seemed in a hurry. The horses were each laden with a bag of feed, and one was carrying five bags. *This must've cost a fortune*, thought Shade. Specter was getting something out from his pack. She went to help him.

Specter pulled out a pie tin and acted like it was heavy. He pulled off the cover, a cloth, and then she could tell it was hot, not heavy. The smell hit her then – fresh biscuits!

"Easy, easy," Specter said, "it's not just biscuits." Then, as Shade picked up a biscuit, she could see the stew underneath. She took a bite of the biscuit and could taste the stew. It was rabbit stew, with some carrots, potatoes, and hints of fennel and basil. After two days of bland travel fare, it was delicious. No one spoke as all three of them dipped their biscuits in the stew and ate.

Once done, Specter said, "They wouldn't let me leave without it. And they gave me something else." He looked at their expectant faces and said, "Information."

Randal was quicker than Shade as both said, "What?" at almost the same time.

Specter began, "It's not looking too good for these local folks. Losing four platform crews in a day is pretty serious for the pri-cons, and they're out for blood. Apparently our activity the day before yesterday is adding to that anger."

"Are they taking it out on the locals in any way?" asked Randal.

Specter looked him in the eye, and his face belied the dilemma. Specter explained, "It's complicated. The pri-cons are upset – we expected that. They've increased patrols – we expected that. But they've gone to selective interrogations."

"That's not normal, not this fast. What does it involve?" asked Randal.

"It's actually more of a selective intimidation. They'll pull people at random, they say, and ask them questions in a closed room. That's probably what the pri-con crew was doing in Byland's Rest. But what they do is really just try to scare the hell out of whoever they talk to. Now, we did expect it, just not this soon."

Randal thought about it. "But what can they do? They can't bring charges. They can't haul anyone off to jail. They'd have to...."

Specter waited for the realization to set in. When it did, he said, "Right. And that's what they're threatening to do. They've even threatened to wipe out entire towns."

"Then how can they expect cooperation by making threats like that?" asked Randal.

Shade chimed in, "It's a double-edged sword. No law out here means you can't enforce things too easily. On the other hand, though, there's no accountability. The pri-cons could wipe out a town, and no one could do anything about it." She paused and then went on, "That's where the collective peer pressure builds in, and it's what they rely on. So you're not just hurting yourself – you're hurting the whole town."

Specter drove the point home, "They don't expect cooperation; they demand it."

"So, if we keep going, they'll destroy a town?" Randal demanded.

"That's the dicey part for them," said Specter. "If they don't know who's doing it, they can't very well single out a town and destroy it. Because people will know. The actual witnesses, if there are any, will know, and that'll lead to hatred towards the pri-cons instead of just tolerance for them. So they have to tread lightly until they have hard proof."

"What do we have to do then?" Randal asked.

"We have to avoid towns and we have to strike a lot more," Specter said.

Shade, nodding approval, said, "The more we spread it around the less likely they'll focus on one town."

"And the less likely to think that it's us," Specter added. Then he went further, "We need to wear those disguises."

"Is there more or are we headed out?" Randal asked, his anger motivating his need to be up and in motion.

"That's all from me," Specter said.

"Thanks for the biscuits," Shade said as she strapped on her fake baby. She took the reins that Specter gave her and started getting to know her mount.

Randal helped Specter get on his disguise and then put his back on. He also took his reins from Specter, and his horse seemed to remember him. Specter kept the pack horse, and Shade helped secure the rifles and uniforms on it. So equipped, they rode following Specter's lead, guns loaded, anger hot. Resolved.

Chapter 33

Seen from a distance, Specter, Randal, and Shade looked like a group of six. They had set a quick pace from Renna's Stream but wanted to really make some long miles, so they ate their lunch dismounted and walking.

To take advantage of the daylight, they decided to push the horses. They were making for the highway south of where they had first met Shade, but that would be hard today. Sometime mid-afternoon in a clearing, Shade spurred her horse to ride alongside Specter. They talked for a few minutes, and they all slowed to a walk. Then Shade dropped back and rode beside Randal.

"We're going to get close to the road by this evening and just observe. We'll plan on hitting a transport in the early morning maybe," she said.

"Why not push on right now, hit one, and then make for the bunker?" Randal asked.

"If we push now, we won't be able to push the horses later, and, if something happens, we may need to. It's safer," she answered.

Randal just nodded. It was already decided.

Specter pulled up finally in a small horseshoe-shaped clearing ringed by scrub pines on one side and dense rose bushes on the other. A relatively secluded spot. He dismounted and the others followed. They secured their horses so that they could graze yet not get away. Dropping their gear, Specter led them back out of the clearing and towards the road.

They still had good light, and they crept up to the edge of the woods and looked out at the highway. This section of road looked much like the others; nothing remarkable differentiated it. Each of them spread out from where they were and settled in.

Specter found a tree, sat down, and leaned against it. It was back far enough from the tree line to keep him hidden but still afforded a good view of the highway. Randal found another tree about twenty yards to his left. Shade was propped up against a rock probably forty yards to Randal's left. It was still a couple of hours until sunset and, hopefully, they would get some information from the movements of the pri-cons.

They didn't have to wait long. The first platform to pass them came only about fifteen minutes from when they had settled in. Nothing stood out about it to Specter, just another platform crewed by eight. What Specter found interesting was that about ten minutes after that one, another platform went by, and, another ten minutes after that, another went by. There was a break then and three more went by, ten minutes separating each. So they were traveling in threes.

Specter wanted to do a little experiment but didn't want to take the risk. Perhaps he could ask Shade later on. He was almost certain that the three platforms were linked, so that if one was hit, the other two would respond. That would eliminate all plans of taking the last platform out. It would force them to figure out how to attack three platforms at the same time.

Watching the sun creep closer to the horizon made Specter think more about what they were getting into. Here he was, one of the Corp's best, a Hunter, cast aside like trash. Worse, he was more like a pet that bit someone – something you can't just let go, but you have to destroy. Randal may have gotten used to being a Runner, but Specter hadn't had much time to process everything. Or he hadn't taken the time.

He allowed himself to do so now. The betrayal…the distrust. But distrust enough to turn to hatred? He knew killing, that's for sure, but what were they doing here? Continuing on this path would eventually lead to retaliation. How much was he willing to pay for the chance of living the rest of his life free? Randal had tired of being hunted – how much more so would he? But was it worth living with the blood of a whole town on your hands? He thought for a long while.

I'll see your moral dilemma and raise you survival, he thought; *expediency and survival always trump morals.*

The hard part was accepting that his life really did come down to a business decision.

Someone decided. Some board may have voted on it, but some one person made the decision to eliminate the Hunters knowing full well that everyone in that division would not get a pink slip but a toe tag.

That made him angry. But, as he examined himself, he realized he wasn't angry enough to risk a town. He had enough blood on his hands already. No. Just a few more hits, divert the attention, and vanish.

Specter was almost thinking about what he'd do once he'd vanished when it rolled into view. There below him was the first truck he'd seen on the road in over a decade. He knew trucks traveled this road, but he hadn't seen any in such a long time. It was just a utilitarian transport truck – and empty at that.

It was led by a platform and followed by another – still traveling in threes – and the truck had a driver and a passenger. His mind started running the numbers – doing the probability calculations. Specter sat back and let his mind work. It was no formal theorem and no specific set of equations. It was the mathematics of death, and he'd been using the same calculations for years. His mind simply figured out if it could be done and sent the answer to his gut. His gut decided whether to do it or not.

Now his gut, finished with its deliberations, had a strong answer for him.

Patiently, they each waited until dusk and only got up when Specter did. They saw no more traffic. As they got back to the horses, Specter handed Randal a bag and had him start on dinner. Specter drafted Shade into helping with the horses. Randal finished just before Specter and Shade. They joined Randal and got ready to eat the biscuits, carrots, cucumbers, and pickled squash from Renna's Stream.

Specter waited while Randal bowed his head and prayed over his food. Once done, Specter began before anyone could take a bite. "The truck today got me thinking. We need to hit a truck." Specter then started eating like that was all he had to say.

Shade picked it up, "We would all like to hit a truck, but you do realize they're traveling in threes now," it came off more a statement than question. "So how do you propose we do that?" Shade phrased the question not as someone who thought it couldn't be done, but as a call for ingenuity in figuring out the best way. She really did seem intrigued by the question.

Specter turned it over in his mind again. How would you do that? He'd been thinking most of the afternoon about it.

Shade prompted him, "I know you've got something. Go ahead. It'll at least give us something to work from."

He did. "First, we get you, Shade, on a high point, sniping. Second, we have you, Randal, on the opposite side with a path you can run along. I, then, will work my way through the crews, mopping up what's not already taken care of. The key is to let Shade start the show and then have the crews focus on Randal as he runs along, shooting all the while, until Shade gets those she can and I root out the rest."

Shade said, "I can see it."

Randal had his doubts. "So I'm supposed to be the bait?"

Specter shook his head, "Well, not really. With an ambush they'd be trained for, there's usually just a line of attackers shooting at them. Knowing that, if we have you run back and forth shooting, they'll think you are that line of attackers. That'll make them leary at first, but after a few rounds, depending on their training, they'll begin to wonder how many are out there. Once they know it's only you, they'll be a lot more willing to keep their heads up, giving Shade a good shot. Those who are well trained or smart enough to know something else is going on will be my responsibility."

Shade seemed pleased. "I think it'll work. We'll have to find the right spot, though. Plus, how long do you think we'll have? I didn't see anything too close together."

"We'll probably have plenty of time – at least as much as last time," Spector answered. "We'll have to be fast anyway because the more time Randal's out there, the more likely it is the pri-cons will figure out what's going on."

"You're right – they have gone to having three travel together but they haven't made them start running in convoys yet," Shade said.

"So that's it?" Randal asked. "Just like that? That's the plan?" He was upset, but not sure about what.

Specter answered, "It seems like a good plan to us," he held out his hands, "but if you've got a better idea, we are both willing to listen and implement as best we can." He looked at Randal with sincerity. "I would remind you that the only reason we are able to attempt such an action is your special coated bullets and that this is a shot at a life without running."

Randal was mollified. He didn't have a better idea; he just needed to be sure he understood – and could do – what they needed him to. They spent the rest of the waning evening light going over everything. All slept that night, but each one went over the plan in his or her mind's eye while manning the watch.

Chapter 34

Morning found the trio fed and mounted. Specter had awakened early, and discussed the plan with Randal – on watch – and decided to wake Shade a little early, too. They ate biscuits and some jerky, washed it down with water, and were ready to move as the first fingers of dawn tickled the earth awake.

They walked their horses south along the road looking for their best spot. After finding a couple of passable spots, they found what they wanted. Here, the road appeared to be cut through a mountain. Despite that, it afforded a good view of the road in either direction. The sides were closer and high, and the southernmost slope on the left side was smooth and gentle. They took the horses on Shade's side and tethered them about thirty yards on the far side of the road.

They walked up to where she'd be positioned. "Do you have enough ammunition?" Randal asked. She did a quick check and said, "I think so. I won't be laying down a lot of effective cover fire, though. I'll just be taking one out at a time. I'll get some other non-coated magazines, though, just in case."

Specter and Randal verified they were loaded as well. This would definitely be the last attack before resupplying. Everyone was getting low. They had enough for today, they all hoped, as long as everything went according to plan.

Specter led Randal to the opposite side of the road and inspected the slope more closely. It wasn't too steep, but there was a lot of vegetation in the way. Specter led the way, using his knife like a machete, cutting a path for Randal. Once near the top, he told Randal, "Wait here for me to get down." Randal waited as Specter made it back down. When he got down, the first platform traffic of the day hovered past. They each waited in place for all three to go by.

Specter stepped out into the road once all was clear and yelled, "Run down – but stop when I say and mark the path." Randal did. He would stop when he heard 'stop' and mark the path with two crossed sticks. Once down, Specter trotted over to him, just inside the tree line. He was carrying the disguises. "This should help a little," he said. "Maybe at least draw some of their fire. I'll help you set them up." Since there were only three main ones, it didn't take long. They walked back down and, at the bottom, Specter turned to look at Randal. His face was all seriousness.

"The success of this depends on you. By that, I mean, our lives here today depend on you. When Shade takes out the driver of the truck, you are to start shooting. Your life depends on you running to those spots I told you and firing. If you stay in one spot for two shots you'll be dead. Run, shoot once – don't waste too much time on aiming – don't blind fire either – then run again. Go up and back, though, not all in one direction or you'll be dead." Specter looked at him. "Got it?"

Randal looked overwhelmed. "No pressure," he said.

Specter put his hand on Randal's shoulder and looked him in the eye. "You'll do fine," he said, more of a command than as reassurance. "You've got three replacement cylinders?" Randal nodded yes. "Then use two going up, and I'll attack as you reload." He looked at Randal again. "You'll do fine," he repeated. Specter looked up at Shade and gave a thumb's up – she returned the gesture. Specter turned from Randal to find his own ambush spot and yelled, "Think alive!" so both of them could hear.

The waiting followed.

There were spurts of activity but all in threes and no trucks. The first few were the worst for anticipation. Randal was on edge for a good two hours there – ready, waiting, thinking each time he'd hear that sound, that it would be time. Then the sounds started sounding different to him – but still the same platforms. After such a long time, Randal was worried that he'd still be on top of his game.

Specter had disguised himself much like Shade had that first day. He was lying down, covered with dead leaves and branches, ready to spring into action. Shade was on the far hill, Randal couldn't make out where, but he knew she'd have three or four positions to shoot from.

Shade, being the one who was going to start this show, waited patiently for her chance. She knew Specter would be used to waiting and felt confident with him on the ground. Randal, though, she was concerned about. If all went according to plan, Randal would cause just enough confusion to allow her and Specter to do their work.

She was about to wonder whether they'd have any luck before lunch when, just as they'd hoped, a truck appeared on the highway. The lead platform looked like every other one. The truck looked similar to the one they saw yesterday, but the canvas cover was up on the back of this one. She waited as the vehicles approached, watching for the far platform. It came around – like the others.

Well, here it was.

She'd have to plan it as best she could so the truck would stop at least near Specter's position. She sighted in on the driver, wishing she had a scope. When the lead platform was just about alongside Specter, Shade sighted in on the driver of the truck. She had a clean shot. Shade squeezed her trigger and saw the bullet hole in the windshield of the truck – along with the blood spray. She shifted to the following platform and tracked the pilot. The platform followed the truck as it veered off the road, and she heard Randal's revolver go off. The pilot's head tracked the smoke from Randal's gun. Before the pilot could react, though, she put a bullet through his heart. She watched briefly as the platform lurched and started going down. She switched her gaze to the lead platform to get its pilot, but she saw it already down near where Randal started his run. She decided to focus on the far platform, leaving the rest for Specter – at least for now. As she looked back to finish the trailing platform, she caught sight of something coming down the highway.

Another platform!

Her heart would sink if she let it, so she focused directly on the trailing platform. *This is going to get messy*, she thought as she dropped the trailing platform's team leader.

Randal had a clear view of the truck, despite the closeness of the lead platform. When he saw the truck cut to his left, away from the median, he felt sure it was on. The platform was close, and he was worried it might be too close, but he still aimed at the pilot and pulled his trigger. He ran without looking to see if he'd hit. He stopped at his first spot, looked out, and saw the truck but no one in it. Then he looked right, sighted, and shot at the lead platform. He ran. Two – he had to keep track of that! His next stop allowed him a view of the trailing platform. He sighted and fired. This time he ran back towards the lead platform. Specter had said to keep changing direction. He poked out, sighted on the first pri-con he saw and fired. He ran – *that's four bullets – two more*. He ran past his furthest point so far, sighted on the trailing platform, and fired. He ran on, stopped at his next spot, sighted on the trailing platform again and fired, but his target – the last visible on the platform – dropped as he fired. Shade's, he guessed. He started reloading and, by chance, looked up the road and saw the unexpected platform. Processing it quickly, he started back down the hill thinking, *we'd better be done with this when they get here.*

Specter was amazed at Shade's timing; she was almost perfect. The truck stopped just short of running into the ditch, the result of some quick thinking and reacting by the guy riding shotgun. That guy managed to get the truck stopped with the passenger door right where Specter was. Specter was on his feet and up at the truck in time to hear the pri-con breathe a sigh of relief. Specter rewarded the rider's quick thinking with a quick shot to the temple.

Specter was about to jump down when he looked to his right and saw the lead platform down only about forty feet in front of him. *Randal got the pilot!* Specter thought. Specter used the cover of the truck and shot the team leader, who had turned around, square in the chest, blowing him back and off the platform. The effect was immediate; Specter watched as those remaining pri-cons froze in fear at the loss of their leader. *Things are going my way!* he thought. A pri-con dropped as he watched, the close report telling him it was Randal's work.

Specter sighted on one, gone. Another, gone. Specter loved the feeling of the kick in his hand, the smell of gunpowder, and the adrenaline rush of combat. Years before, he had been afraid of how much he liked that rush, but he had learned to allow himself to drink it in without choking on it.

He did that now, swinging up onto the hood of the truck, pulling his left revolver and, using both – Pop! Pop! Pop! Pop! – ending those left on the lead platform.

Instinctively, he dived off the hood and rolled under the truck. He shoved two shells into his left hand gun and fully reloaded his right – listening. That was the sound of automatic gunfire. *Not instinctively, then*, he thought, *that's what I heard*. That wasn't coming from Randal or Shade.

There must be another platform out there!

He rolled out from under the truck and got in its cab. Mr. Quick Thinker was equipped with a rifle, and Specter took it and a couple of magazines. He took the butt of the rifle and smashed the passenger side mirror at the top. As quick as he was in, Specter was out and back underneath the truck. He picked up a shard of the mirror and crawled to the back of the truck.

Specter could see the trailing platform behind the truck. He listened more carefully to the gunfire. He reached out with the mirror and looked up through it. Stationed right above the truck – and him – was the other platform. Apparently, the platform hadn't seen him or was concentrating on Randal and Shade. He didn't have much time. He crawled about halfway out from underneath the truck and rolled onto his back.

When Specter rolled over, he got his shock of the day. There was a young woman looking out of the back of the truck! Her eyes got very wide, and Specter knew her gaze had gone right for the rifle barrel. It probably looked big enough for her to fall into. He yelled, "Get back to the front of the truck!"

Her shock was going to be too much. Before he could do anything, though, a bullet ricocheted off the truck's tailgate. *Shade's still good with timing*, Specter thought. That shot got the girl back into the truck quickly. Specter rolled all the way from under the truck and aimed at the platform in the same place Shade had shot, the fuel tank. He emptied the whole clip into it, even after it started smoking. The steady gunfire cut off. Specter got to his feet and changed the clip as he followed to where the platform was going down.

Shade knew she was pushing it, but she had to clear that platform! After the pilot and team leader were gone, only three didn't hit the deck, and somehow they managed to delay hitting the ground. Randal dropped one, and then she got the last one standing. The others were down. She picked up her rifle and scooted down the hill, checking her magazine on the way. *Damn*, she thought, *only six more bullets*!

Shade hit her second spot prone and ready to fire. As luck would have it, the platform went down with its top facing her. The four pri-cons left on the platform thought the action was up where the truck was, so they were content to sit still. Randal must've winged two of them; she could see them tending their wounds. She focused on the one peeking his head around the front of the platform. She took him high in the chest, she aimed toward the right, fired again, and spun him around. A lucky shot, but it had the desired effect of freezing the remaining three. She took the far, right pri-con with another shot to the chest. The two wounded pri-cons realized where she was now, so she took the nearest and then the remaining one while they dropped their bandages and went for their guns.

Shade was up and running downhill as the last one fell. She'd be no use up there without coated bullets. She had made it almost all the way down the hill when gunfire exploded around her. The tree she was behind at the time saved her life. She hit the ground hard but alive. She crept forward to where she could see something, maybe get her last shot off, but instead she got the second shock of her day. There were people in the truck!

The ground in front of her erupted in gunfire. They hadn't really stopped; they just caught sight of her again. She hoped Randal was keeping his head down. She rolled, crawled, and scooted until she found a good spot and peeked out again. This time she was watching the truck. She saw a girl lean out the back about the time she noticed Specter beneath her with his gun up. She readied her rifle and decided the tailgate was the best option; after all, she couldn't shoot Specter, but maybe she could save the girl. She fired.

Randal shot one on the lead platform – at least he thought so – and then ran down the hill for his next shot. He hit his spot, looked and sighted, but didn't fire. He caught sight of Specter and hesitated just a second. The sight was horrific, and Randal couldn't even see his full face. Randal shook his head and ran up the hill to meet the last platform.

He reached the top of the hill as the platform was coming in. Something didn't look right about it. They hadn't seen him because they weren't shooting, so he aimed for the pilot, tracked him, and fired. As he pulled the trigger something strange happened. The woods around him started humming to life, and Randal thought that he had stepped on a hornet's nest. He moved and knew that wasn't right. Luckily for him, he tripped and flailed out and down. That saved his life. His mind started going fuzzy, and he was afraid he was going into shock.

He lay there and forced himself to recall what just happened. When he fired, one of the pri-cons actually dove in front of the pilot and taken the bullet, but also…

The gunfire around him didn't let up and, although it was throwing dirt and rock into his face, it wasn't hitting him yet. He forced his memory open. The pri-con he shot had yelled and – that was weird to begin with – there were nine people on that platform. Those in the back of the platform had pulled that ninth guy down and covered him. He was an official! Then the humming and whining had started. He felt dumb – that was them shooting at him!

They were still firing, a steady drumming. He'd better move soon or they would connect with him. He listened for a change or a slowing. Then he did hear something different. Right after that, the shooting did slow and then stopped. He rose up and looked out.

Randal saw the platform going down, smoking, and from where he was, he had a straight-on view of Specter striding forward.

Murder was on his face.

The way the platform was going down, though, exposed the crew to Randal but not Specter. Randal saw three of the pri-cons, including the team leader and pilot, taking the official back towards the woods on the opposite side of the hill from where he came up. One of the pri-cons was down, the one who jumped in front of his bullet. *Strange he did that*, Randal thought, *they were both wearing webarmor*. The other four pri-cons had divided up into two teams of two on either end of the downed platform. He looked back at the official getting away.

Randal had a quick decision to make: either stay with the dignitary or stay and help Specter. He cursed himself – him help Specter? He started down the hill to try and cut off the retreating pri-cons.

Shade started down the hill as soon as she heard Specter start firing. She broke onto the roadway, tomahawks in hand, in time to see Specter reload. A flash caught her eye – the girl in the truck. She ran to the truck.

The girl was trying to get out when Shade arrived. Shade put the flat of the tomahawk blade on the girl's arm and said, "Stay in the truck."

The girl caught her eye and froze Shade in her tracks. The girl grabbed Shade's tomahawk and said pointedly, "They'll kill us all." It was the same desperation, the same resignation that Shade had seen in her Prey lately. There had been no more selfish, egotistical, evil people trying to negotiate, bribe or beg for their lives. Just more people like this girl, damned either way and desperate that the people they care about are okay, negligent of their own fate.

"Not today," Shade said. She looked the girl back in the eye and willed her back in. "Get in and stay down." The girl knew not to trust her, despite Shade's motives, so Shade decided to use it. "Or I'll kill you myself," Shade said and nudged the girl with her tomahawk. The girl complied.

Shade turned around just in time to duck. The pri-cons had cleared the downed platform and were firing at her. She rolled away and started to circle when she realized the girl was right. The pri-cons weren't firing at her. They were after the girl in the truck! That realization made her next move a lot simpler.

The pri-cons were almost past her and were paying no attention to her. She turned and, as Specter opened up with the rifle, the pri-cons turned towards him, away from her, but did not stop advancing toward the truck. Shade threw her tomahawks in quick succession. The first took the closest one square in the back. The second hit the other pri-con in the upper right shoulder. Shade was moving almost before the tomahawks hit, pleased the pri-cons were arrogant enough to disregard her as a threat. She grabbed the first tomahawk out of the pri-con's back and drove it into the neck of the other pri-con, beheading him. Shade then took both tomahawks and finished up the other pri-con. She looked up in time to see Specter kill two pri-cons.

Specter had reloaded the rifle and braced himself for a full team frontal attack. He hoped Shade would come up soon and help out. At least he had his duster on; he knew full well they were one bullet away from disaster. He crouched, rifle at the ready. Two pri-cons cleared the left side of the platform, so he focused on those two. He fired and shook the first one back, but the second did the same to him. Knocked down, Specter expected them to come by and finish him off but, instead, they had one direction and were of singular purpose. They didn't even bother to make sure he was dead.

That pissed him off.

Specter rolled up onto his feet with his guns drawn. He saw Shade dealing with two other pri-cons out in his periphery. He took aim and fired. Pop! Pop! And those two were dead. He wheeled back around for the counter attack he expected, but there was none. He looked back to Shade, and she was looking at him. He motioned around the platform. She nodded back.

Specter went left and Shade went right. They sprung around the platform, ready to deal death – and found nothing. Shade pointed back up the road. Specter followed her gaze and had just the slightest glimpse of a person moving into the woods. They were trying to run!

Specter knew they were in trouble. They couldn't have much time before another three platforms came through. Those last pri-cons were dead set on killing the girl in the truck, so unless they had acted fast enough, the pri-cons had probably already called for reinforcements. He made a snap decision. He looked at Shade and told her, "You get that girl to the horses. I'll get these guys and meet you there." Instead of instant obedience, Shade asked, "What about Randal?"

Specter had forgotten about Randal. He hadn't heard his revolver since the last platform opened up. "I'll get him and meet you. Move." Shade moved then.

Specter was off after the running pri-cons. He made quick time and, for whatever reason, they were not. He found where they had entered the woods and bounded after them. He knew he had to make time, so he pushed the needle into the red, trusting his training and instincts. He counted four pri-cons and noted when the last two peeled off. *You won't shoot me that easily*, thought Specter. He didn't slow but dived into the spot where he saw them split off and rolled to the right giving the pilot, it turned out, both barrels. Specter spun on his back to shoot the other and watched the pri-con's helmet shatter while his own bullet exploded the pri-con's chest. Specter spun – Randal!

Randal was quick and to the point, surprisingly confident and commandeering. "Team leader ahead with an official. We need him alive. Count to thirty in your head. If you don't have him by then, kill him. If you haven't by the count of sixty, let him go. I'll be back at the truck." Randal, clearly done talking, knelt and starting getting the pri-con's uniform. Specter only had time to think, *Trust the Runner this time*, before he was up and moving again.

Specter did as Randal said and started a clock in his head. He ran full tilt toward the two in front of him. He made good time on them. Despite being panicked, the official was not used to activity, and the team leader stayed with him. Specter counted to seventeen before he knelt and shot both men in the leg – one with his right revolver, one with his left.

Specter was on them before they could bring their sidearms up. Kicking them away, Specter ripped off both of their helmets. The only way to be sure they hadn't just switched helmets was to look them in the eye. Men of arms, fighters, Specter had learned, always had a look of losing a hand of poker after going all in, whereas those in power, officials, always had that look of fear. Kneeling down between them with one of his revolvers above the face of each, Specter looked left and saw the man looking back at him. He looked right and saw the man looking cross-eyed at the barrel in his face, whiter than a bleached sock. Specter pulled his left trigger without looking away from the official.

The shot shook the official in a kind of all-over body shake. The man focused on Specter as Specter started getting the team leader's uniform. Amazing how much faster it was when you could cut it off. Specter thanked Randal's coated blade.

The shock was wearing off the official enough for him to want to talk. Specter turned his full attention to him. Looking him straight in the eye, he was very direct. "I'm sorry you had to see that, sir. Are you hurt anywhere else but the leg?" Specter used the team leader's undershirt as a bandage, tying it just above the gunshot wound. He'd hit the man's calf. Specter went on quickly. "We had been aware of his activity, but we had to wait until he moved before we could act." Specter dug into his pocket for the same type of needle he'd given to Shade to knock her out. *Time to test this official*, thought Specter. "I'm sorry we had to keep our presence secret, putting you at risk like this, but the conspiracy reaches the highest places. I need to inject you with this, sir, before we can brief you on all we know – once we're safe, of course. Will you, sir?"

The official took the needle as Specter said, "Leg, sir." The official then plunged the needle in and depressed the plunger. "Thank you, sir," Specter said smiling. He took the syringe, capped it, and put it back in its place. In his experience, only pompous, self-absorbed, egotistical, selfish people injected themselves. In such a stressful situation, only those type people imagine themselves part of such a grand scheme that they would inject themselves with something they don't know given them by someone who's just killed all those assigned to protect them. Specter picked the official up over his shoulder and started back out of the woods. He rejoined his count – fifty-one? *Things were going well this morning.*

As Shade turned from Specter, she worried she was going to be hard pressed to get even a few uniforms – they had to move! Shade reached the truck and lowered the tail gate. Looking in, she had the third shock of the morning. *Strike three*, she thought. There were five people in the truck bed! The girl she'd met, two other girls about the same age, and two younger boys – only slightly younger, she amended. Fear and desperation looked back at her from their faces, but their eyes shone with a hope and a firm distrust of that hope.

Shade remembered her training when dealing with children, but it mostly applied to younger children. She decided these were close enough to adult to handle the truth. Shade directed her words to the girl from before, but she let her voice carry and her eyes wander so they all knew they were part of the decision.

"We've killed all the pri-cons," Shade began. That got their attention. "We didn't plan on anyone not a pri-con being here. You're free to go." *More fear*, Shade thought; *they want protection.* "We can't have you giving us away either." *Confusion.* "If we let you run, you'll get caught, and give us away." *Clarity, then fear.* "If you want to stay here, you can; there'll be another three platforms coming in," she thought quickly. Maybe they had fifteen minutes. "Seven minutes and I'm sure they'll take you on to where you were going." *Horror.* "You can all move with us and we'll make sure you get to where you <u>want</u> to go. But you have to help us get the uniforms and the guns." The decision was evident in their faces.

The first girl rose and asked, "We get their uniforms off them and you'll get us out of here?" Shade thought the girl would pee herself with joy.

"No," Shade said. "We need their guns, too." She turned and walked towards the closest pri-con. "Your call," she said over her shoulder. *That will let them think they've got a choice*, she thought. Sure enough, by the time she had her second uniform, most of them had their first.

They had all of the pri-con uniforms from the four they'd just killed, the lead platform, and truck, along with the weapons – the boys got those – and were hurrying back to the original trailing platform when Shade caught sight of Randal walking towards them carrying uniforms. They all converged on the original trailing platform and started getting the uniforms.

Randal seemed too nonchalant for her liking.

"Are you okay?" Shade asked.

"Sure," he answered. "You hire some new hands while we were out?"

"They were in the truck," Shade said.

Randal kept working but he was…off.

As Shade was about to ask him another question, she felt a hand on her arm. "He's adjusting," the girl said.

Randal looked up at the sound of her voice, dropped everything, and stood up, looking at the girl.

Shade stepped in front of the girl, thinking, *Oh, shit, he's lost it.*

But Randal seemed to…coalesce.

He addressed the girl, "You're Aunt Lindsey's niece."

The girl elbowed Shade out of the way, "I'm Jess. You know Aunt Lindsey?"

Randal had regained himself. "No," he said. "We just met. You can come home any time. She told me to tell you."

The girl started crying the long tears that no longer shake the body but come unbidden and simply roll over the eyelids. The tears that come when something you've long ago given up hoping for is promised again. "Please take me back," she stammered.

She had just finished talking when Specter startled all of them, "I told you to get to the horses. We have to MOVE!"

The girl wiped her eyes. One of the boys announced that all the uniforms were collected. Shade cursed under her breath for not having everybody at the horses.

Specter looked around and called the boys over. "Give me the guns," he ordered, motioning to Shade and the girl to get going. To the boys he said, "Now, take him." And Specter laid the official down. The boys both recoiled and Specter knew the official had hurt them. Specter bent down and clapped his hands hard above the official's face, in the boys' faces. "See?! He's out. Once we get out of here you can help me cut him up, but now we've got to MOVE!" The boys picked him up at the shoulders and ankles and followed Shade as she started moving for the horses. Specter grabbed

Randal's arm and said, "We're on your show now, Randal. Get us free of this or we are totally screwed, okay?"

Randal announced, "We're going to Byland's Rest as fast as we can – your call on the route." He turned, picked up the guns, and followed the others.

Specter started reloading his guns and thought how well the day had gone. All around a pretty good job for three people. He let out a yell, "Whoo, yeah! Let's GO!" He rushed to the front trying to encourage – and rush – the rest, knowing that if they could make it through the next seventy-two hours, they might have a shot.

Chapter 35

Back at the horses, Specter was faced with a dilemma: four horses and nine people. He had the boys throw the official over the pack horse and tied him on. Shade, helping him, asked, "How long will he be out?"

"At least until morning," answered Specter. "Do you have any doses?"

"I've got two," she answered.

"And I've got one more," Specter said. "So maybe three days? At the outside?"

Shade smirked, "Two, unless you want his brain to turn to mush."

"We shouldn't need it," Specter said. "We'll be in Byland's Rest tonight, if we push it."

Shade crossed her fingers in front of her face so Specter could see. Specter smiled; neither of them knew if these kids could travel.

Specter then secured the arms and the uniforms to the same pack horse. One down, three to go. He had an idea. He grabbed Randal and Shade and took them to the side. "The pri-cons are going to be mad now," Specter started, "but they're going to start by going as far out as they think we've gone, searching, and then coming back here and searching out, right?" Shade nodded the affirmative. "So," Specter continued, "let's take it easy now and then start bolting, okay?" Specter noticed Randal's blank stare. "We go slowly from here while they try to work backwards, then we speed up when they try to look from the beginning to where we are."

"Oh, okay," Randal said, "as long as we can use their standard protocol against them."

They returned to the group.

"Which one of you can run the longest?" Specter asked them. One of the boys, the younger one, raised his hand. "You ride. Who's second?" One of the girls raised her hand. "Really? You just want to ride?" Specter asked. The girl showed her steel. She said, "We ran for four days before they caught us, and Jake and I could've run three more if we'd found something to eat."

Specter softened. Randal was reminded of Specter's change back at the store in Renna's Stream. It was hard to believe that this man who was just recently reveling in killing could change like that. Specter stopped, looked at her, and said, "I hope so. In order for us to get away we're going to have to run, too. So you and Jake?" the girl nodded. "Jake, take the time and rest on the horse first, because when we need to go, we'll have to move, okay?" Jake and the girl both nodded.

Specter looked around and found the girl he'd seen from under the truck. "Brave girl," he said, "you ride, too."

"Jess," she said simply.

Specter only nodded.

Specter looked around making sure everyone was loaded and ready. He said, "We're walking right now and we're going to eat. We're also going to push once we get out a way. You all do as I say, and we'll all get out and away." He looked at the boys. "Then is when payback comes – not before. Listen, we can't survive another fight like that. I will – but not all of you will. If you can't do something, you tell me quick. Like ride. You can all ride?" They all nodded; it was rare to find an Outlander who didn't know something about horses. Specter resumed, "No questions," he looked around, "that's it. Think alive."

With that he started walking.

Chapter 36

They hadn't walked too far when Specter broke open his pack and got out their biscuits. He told Jake to keep moving and handed him a biscuit. Specter worked his way back, giving each of them at least something to eat.

They ate as they moved, and it was a tense time. They walked with anticipation of when they'd have to move and how far they'd have to go. Randal decided to let Shade and Specter decide when they had to move. He understood it was like trying to walk a path through a series of pendulums; you had to time it just right.

As he ate his biscuit, Randal tried to get his mind around some things. First, he didn't know whether to trust these kids. Why were they with the pri-cons? Why did they run from them? When he talked with Jess, it seemed the one thing she wanted to do was to go home, so why hadn't she? Had the pri-cons held her against her will? He'd never heard of that, but why would they ever do that? And the others? Were they all in the same situation?

Randal hadn't seen it, but Shade had told him when they were getting uniforms that the pri-cons didn't care about anything but killing the kids. The way she'd explained it, they had split into two teams – both with the singular purpose of killing the kids. What made them so important that they had to be killed? And what about the official? What caused him to be traveling down this way? And, even more importantly, why did the pri-con jump in the way of his bullet when both of them were wearing webarmor? Could they have known about the webarmor-tearing bullets? They'd been so careful, though. Could they have done an autopsy yet? Maybe on that first team leader. Even if they did the autopsy and knew about the bullets, did they know it was <u>him</u>? Would an autopsy on a burned body even have any webarmor fibers left – any that would indicate they'd been torn by a bullet?

The revolving litany of questions was exhausting him.

It was a welcome relief when Specter stopped everyone, switched the runners and the walkers, and they took off. Specter led the way, the girl and Jake behind him. Jess rode on Specter's horse and held the reins of the pack horse. The other girls doubled on Randal's mount, and the other boy rode on Shade's mount. Randal and Shade brought up the rear. Specter set a good pace and didn't start out faster than the girl or Jake could handle. Randal knew he would pick it up, though, so he let the steady drum of horsehooves in front of him drive his questions out, letting the steady pounding of his stride be his only focus.

After a long while, Randal came to himself and realized the sun was down. They hadn't stopped, rested or switched – as far as he knew. *I'd remember that*, he thought. Once he came back to himself, the questions came back, and Randal realized he may have zoned out but his mind had kept working.

Randal's focus was honed now, though. He knew what information he needed. First he needed Jess and her friends to tell their story. Second, he needed – wanted anyway – the official's story. Those two sources would probably be able to answer most all of his other questions. Maybe they could get started tonight.

Specter was pushing hard. They probably should be stopping soon, but Specter showed no signs of slowing. Randal noticed that Specter led them more from clearing to clearing, taking all advantage he could from the failing light. Soon enough, though, his concern for the horses made him call a halt. He walked back and got Randal and Shade.

"Randal, I want you to keep walking with everyone. Shade and I will look for a spot to camp where we can build a fire," Specter said.

Jess had turned her mount around and was listening. "Aren't we about two miles from Byland's Rest?"

Specter, interrupted, answered curtly, "Yes." He turned back to continue.

Jess, boldly, interrupted again, "Why don't we use my aunt's barn?"

Specter harrumphed and was going to let loose when Jess, sensing it, ventured more. "It's isolated, there's always someone on guard, there're plenty of provisions, and there're some secret smuggling places."

Specter started to argue more but Jess again showed her mettle. "In fact, that sounds real good. You are certainly welcome to join us, of course. It's on the outskirts of town, right behind her store." And she turned her mount and started off. Her friends, who had been listening in, followed in behind her when she called over her shoulder, "You can get your horses back once we're there."

"Wait," Specter said. "The pri-cons might know about your family and try to recapture you."

Jess looked back at Specter with a look like she was eighty years old and bone weary. She said, "They didn't even ask my name." And she continued riding.

Chapter 37

Shade spoke first. "I thought she had a lot of spunk, but she's lost everything, and she's not going to lose this chance. I'm going with them." This didn't totally surprise Randal. "It's hard to put all that effort in," Shade said, "then just let them go. I feel like I need to protect them." *We all feel that way*, thought Randal. "At least until we know they're safe. See you there!" And she was off.

Specter quickly said, "You're with me." Apparently Randal didn't have a choice. Specter set off at a trot. Randal kept up, trying to stay light on his feet.

In just a short while, they were at Byland's Rest. Specter told Randal, "Go to the store, tell the aunt everything, and wait for me." And then Specter was off. Randal entered the town alone. It wasn't too long after sundown, but the town seemed asleep already. Randal strode resolutely to Aunt Lindsey's store. The door was locked, but he saw a light on in the back. He knocked at the door.

Aunt Lindsey came out of the back with her lantern. She held it up as she got to the door to see who it was. Recognition lit her eyes as she saw his face. "We're closed, sweetie," she said.

Randal didn't expect that. He just said, "Please."

Whether it was his face or the way he said it, she unlocked the door. "Quick mind you," she said, and opened the door. He walked in as she asked, "Where is your lady friend – I mean, wife?"

He turned and said, "Funny you should ask that." He stood still, crossed his arms, and made sure she could see his face. Then he said, "She's actually watching out for Jess."

Aunt Lindsey, nonchalant, said, "Oh, really? And who is this Jess person?"

Randal continued to hold her gaze. She seemed upset that he just stood there, so she just waited for a response. Randal didn't speak until he saw her eyes flicker towards her picture of Jess. At that moment, he said, "We found her."

Aunt Lindsey's hope would not allow her to trust. She transformed much like she had when he had asked her about the vodka – but a lot worse. She drew up to her full height and filled her lungs with air so she could cuss him up one side and down the other. That's the moment Specter picked to come inside.

That distracted Aunt Lindsey, and Specter said to Randal, "You can see the resemblance, can't you?" Aunt Lindsey seemed to hold that breath she'd taken and her eyes widened even further – easier to see as she held up the lantern to see Specter's face. Specter pointed toward Aunt Lindsey and said, "I bet you she and her sister get confused with each other all the time." This sent Aunt Lindsey into apoplexy – Was it true? Did he know? Was she back?

What happened next was totally unexpected for Randal. He had seen Specter earlier today with death written on his face. He had seen Specter, also earlier today, transform into a kind and caring man. He had not seen Specter transform into the demon he now saw.

Specter had gone directly from sort of joking around into an evil being. Seeming interested in helping Aunt Lindsey find her niece, he had been moving closer to her and now, with his left hand, he grabbed her hand holding the lantern. With his right, he held Aunt Lindsey's throat.

Randal was shocked. He moved forward to stop Specter and said, "Hey, wait," before Specter's voice stopped him in his tracks. Like a voice from the grave, Specter's words echoed around the shop, "Get back or I'll kill her now." Those words held more gravity because Randal was certain that Specter would do exactly what he said. Randal stayed where he was. Randal could see the evil face Specter was displaying, but thought it uncharacteristic from what he knew about the man.

Aunt Lindsey didn't know about Specter, though.

Specter's face in the lantern light radiated the evil of certainty. He would do what he said.

He spoke slowly and articulated each of his words as if they were a precious commodity, weighed and used specifically and appropriately. "Yes, we have your niece. I and my men have ridden hard, though, and we're hungry. You've got twenty minutes to get enough food for ten men to your barn, and then we'll talk about you getting your niece back – or which piece of your niece you'll get back first."

Aunt Lindsey looked pale gray and Specter relaxed his grip, but tightened it back, and shoved her down. "I've spilled blood to get that girl, shopkeeper. If I see any sign of a pri-con or someone who looks like a pri-con, I'll burn your niece alive while I burn your barn."

Specter let her go this time for good. She grasped at her neck. Specter set the lantern down, picked her up by her shoulders, and slapped her lightly on her cheeks. "We'll see you in twenty minutes, okay?"

Specter turned and walked out, calling for Randal to join him as he left. Randal, with a quick look at Aunt Lindsey, followed Specter out. Joining him in the street, Randal barely heard Specter's whisper, "Not now." They turned in behind the store and started making for the barn.

When they arrived at the barn they found everyone inside, including the guard they always had on duty. Shade had him tied up and gagged in a corner. Surprisingly, Jess and her friends were sitting quietly in the center of the barn. They were using boxes as seats.

In fact, the barn was actually more warehouse than barn. There were a lot of dry goods and other goods stored here – even hay and feed.

Shade came up quickly as they entered. "How'd you play it?" Shade asked Specter. "Did you go for display of strength?" Shade even looked excited.

"Yes," Specter said, "I said enough food for ten men in twenty minutes."

"Keeping me on my toes!" Shade exclaimed, then looked abashed. "They are mine, right?" she asked.

Specter nodded.

Randal had had enough. "I will not stand by and let you kill these people."

"Shh!" both Specter and Shade voiced in unison.

Specter looked at Shade and jerked his thumb at Randal. Shade stopped Specter and said, "It's real bad," indicating Jess and her friends. Specter nodded and walked over to Jess and her friends.

Shade took Randal by the shoulder and invaded his personal space. To an observer, they would look affectionate, but she was all business and spoke quietly and directly. "We can't afford to battle the pri-cons again. This way we can see how many people will fight, maybe not against pri-cons, but for their own. If Specter scared Aunt Lindsey enough, we might get half the town to show up. But we also need to know if there's someone who would tell the pri-cons about us. The ones who show up here will probably know who that is." She looked down and then continued. "Look, this is not foolproof, but it works ninety-five to ninety-seven percent of the time."

Randal nodded toward Jess and her friends. "That's how you got them to sit there like they're prisoners?"

Shade looked straight up and then into his eyes. He could feel her empathy. "All I did was mention the pri-cons and they got very obedient," Shade said. "I think they'd fly if you told them you would keep them away from the pri-cons. Something real bad happened to them. They told me a little, but not all."

Randal breathed a sigh of relief. "I'm glad you're not planning on killing anyone." Another question occurred to him, "What about the official?"

Shade said dismissively, "Oh, I gave him another shot."

"I would like to talk to both of them," Randal asserted.

"We'll see," said Shade. "I've got to run."

"What? Where are you going?" he asked.

"I'm going to make sure we're not ambushed," Shade replied.

"Really?!" Randal said, surprised.

"It's amazing," she said, "almost no one backs up their backups." And she was gone, her tomahawks leaving their afterimage on Randal's eyes.

Chapter 38

Randal walked up to where Specter was talking with Jess and her friends. He caught Specter saying, "…almost there – just keep calm and look scared. We may have to fight, and if we do, I'll tell you. We're almost there."

"Close now, huh?" Randal asked.

Specter clapped him on the shoulder. "Close," he said. Specter started walking Randal toward the main entrance. "Unload your revolver and don't do anything. Don't fight back or give them a reason to hurt you." Specter looked him in the eye. "Just a bit longer and the ruse will be over. Then we'll get some answers, okay?"

"Sure," Randal said. Specter walked back nearer to Jess, and Randal decided he was just bait for one of Aunt Lindsey's backups. Still, he removed the primers from his revolver so it wouldn't fire – easier than unloading a packed and waxed cylinder. He got ready for a long wait.

Thankfully, Aunt Lindsey wasn't too long in delaying. Randal figured Specter asked for food because he could estimate how many people were contacted before the food showed up. The people could always blame the food for taking longer to prepare and cook – rather than telling the truth – that they'd run down the center of the street crying out for help.

In any case, Aunt Lindsey walked up to the barn, carrying a tray loaded – presumably – with food. As she neared Randal, he knew it was food. It was past dinner time, and the savory smells wafting up from her tray hit him harder than he would've thought. When she passed him, though, she spit right at his feet – slapping him emotionally.

Randal followed her to where she stopped close to Jess's group. The resemblance was unmistakable, and each welled up with tears.

As Jess got up to run to her aunt, Specter ruined the reunion moment by grabbing her arm and stopping her.

Aunt Lindsey's knees got weak, but Jake's friend – the other boy – jumped up quickly and steadied the tray as Jake himself helped to steady Aunt Lindsey.

"What have you done to her, you bastard!?" Aunt Lindsey screamed and cried.

Specter had gone cold again. "There, there, little Auntie. She's right here, but I've got to get paid." He emphasized the last word by pulling Jess to her knees. "Now, what can we trade?"

Despite her emotion, Aunt Lindsey composed herself and held up a key ring. "This, the store," said Aunt Lindsey, "all of it – just let me have my niece!"

"Sure, sure. And as soon as you're gone, your people come in and cut us open? No way," Specter said.

It was then that Randal felt hot breath in his ear and a cold blade on his throat.

"Where are they?" Specter demanded. "Bring 'em out!" he yelled as he pulled one of his revolvers and placed the barrel to Jess's temple.

He didn't have to repeat himself. Aunt Lindsey was close enough to see that Specter meant what he said.

"Come out! Please, God, come out! My niece!" pleaded Aunt Lindsey.

She was near hysterics and the man holding Randal grabbed his arm, put it behind him, and started walking, never letting the knife slip from his throat.

"I'm here," said the voice – too loud – beside Randal's ear. "Now put the gun down unless you want to lose your boy."

Randal never wanted to hear that again.

Quicker than anyone could think, Specter, appearing weary and irritated, cocked the gun at Jess's head and said, "I said everybody."

Nothing happened, and Specter's words hung in the air.

"Okay, then," Specter said. "If that's the way you want to play it." And he dug his fingers in Jess's hair, stood her up, put his gun to the back of her head and said, "Bring out everyone or this is as close as you'll get to her alive, but you'll taste her brains in death."

Aunt Lindsey hit her knees begging and pleading for the life of her niece. She wailed and begged everyone to come out. She started calling people by name, and more and more people appeared from various hiding places. There were about ten men, and they formed a ring around the group.

Randal's holder had the knife so tight that Randal was afraid to swallow. The man addressed Specter, "Don't be dumb, man. Let her go and you can leave here alive."

Specter looked around Jess's head at the man and said, "You think it's just us two?" Randal felt the man stiffen just as Specter spoke again. "How many you got?" Specter yelled out.

"They had two snipers up here," Shade called back. Randal's holder laughed with his breath. If he didn't have his mouth right by his ear Randal would've missed it.

"Come back down," Specter yelled to Shade.

Just then, Shade must've entered, because Randal heard gasps and muttered curses.

"Bring them here for Knife-man to see," Specter ordered.

She walked by them leading <u>four</u> men bound and gagged.

Knife-man cursed under his breath, right into Randal's ear. Aunt Lindsey just broke down crying.

Specter didn't let the situation get away from him. "Which one of you is loyal to the pri-cons?"

That question took them unaware, and no one said anything.

Specter let his voice echo, "I ask a question, you give an answer."

Knife-man spoke at Randal's ear. "No one here has any contact with them. We leave them alone, and they leave us alone."

"Then who ran and told them about some platform going down and people getting away – riding off into the woods?" Specter asked.

One of the men on Specter's left said, "That was Paul Robertson. He was saying that." Then, from behind him, "Soap-making Paul or trader Paul?" The same man on Specter's left answered him, "Trader Paul."

Knife-man cursed and then raised his voice, "You are the three that took out the platforms, aren't you?" He didn't wait for an answer. "We all applaud you for that, and no one will mention it to another. So moved?" Every one of Aunt Lindsey's men said, "So moved."

Knife-man continued, "All we want is the girl. We can pay. No one has to get hurt."

Specter broke in, "All we want is her story, something to eat, and we're gone." He looked around, that had caught them off guard. Specter added, "So moved?"

At the nod from Knife-man, every one answered, "So moved."

Specter looked at Randal – or Knife-man. He said, "Let my man go as a sign of good faith?" Only then did the man release the tension on the knife. He then shoved Randal away from him – not hard, but clearly separating himself from Randal.

Specter then said loudly enough for all to hear, "Sorry we had to do it this way, but you need to know who's going to fight and who you can rely on. You've got to keep these kids protected and safe now." Then he released Jess while he holstered his revolver.

Jess, free of the ruse, ran over to her Aunt Lindsey and hugged her as they cried. Shade started untying the snipers she'd captured. Randal rubbed at his neck and only got a little blood.

Jess's friends went for the food and Randal, seeing it, remembered he was hungry, too. Shade found her way to the food as well. Specter, on the other hand, had gone to speak with Knife-man. After some brief words with him, Specter rejoined Shade and Randal.

Aunt Lindsey must've had help to get all the food together that fast. There was some ham, scrambled eggs, green beans, some stew and dinner rolls. They must've cobbled together some people's supper to make all this. Randal didn't mind, though; he ate up.

Specter told them that Aunt Lindsey's son had gone to fetch Jess's parents and that Knife-man's son had gone with him. Her parents had moved away after they couldn't find her; too much pain, apparently. They'd be here in two days if everything went well. Knife-man, Jeff was his name, said they'd be paying trader Paul a visit in the morning.

After they had all eaten, there was a lull in activity and conversation. It was getting late, and Specter got up and went over to Jess and Aunt Lindsey. He knelt down before Aunt Lindsey and said, "I'm sorry for having to behave like I did."

Aunt Lindsey didn't see it that way and didn't understand it, but she was more happy to have her niece back than she was angry.

Specter asked Jess if they could talk about why they were with the pri-cons. He included everybody in the question. All of Jess's companions looked toward her and, above the objections of her aunt about it being too late and her being too tired, Jess agreed. Everyone at the barn gathered around Jess and her companions.

"Before I start, though, I'd like some whiskey, please," Jess asked.

Aunt Lindsey seemed dismissive as Shade got up and left the group. Aunt Lindsey said, "Oh, sweetie, it is wonderful to have you back and it's certainly cause for celebration, but that's not a reason to start drinking. We can celebrate without alcohol."

Jess got her hackles up and was about to argue when, apparently, she thought better of it. She repositioned everyone so that her friends were all around her. They formed a kind of semi-circle with Jess in the middle, the two girls next, and the two boys on the ends. They seemed to have certain positions within the ring – like they had done this before.

Everything got quiet and Jess said, "This will be hard to hear. It'll be harder for me – us – to tell. Bear with us." Then Jess and her friends joined hands. In unison, they said, "We are not victims. We are survivors. We have life, and, as long as we are alive, we can fight. They can break our bodies, but they cannot touch our souls."

They must've been saying that for a long time. It seemed to strengthen them and bond them together. It also seemed to demand someone share something. Jess began.

"I was walking alone two years ago when I was sixteen," Jess started. "A group of men came upon me and took me." There were gasps from the audience. "They put me on a platform, bound and gagged me, and didn't say anything to me." She looked directly at Specter and said, "They didn't even bother to ask my name. They took me to a house that had huge gates, and they told me there that they were taking me – and others like me – to a pleasure dome, where the richest of the rich would go to indulge their fantasies. It wasn't until I got there that I realized I was there for other people's fantasy. Mine – ours – was the rape fantasy."

Jess faltered. Shade was back and passing her a bottle of whiskey. Jess said a little "Thank you," and Aunt Lindsey said nothing. Shaking as she poured a little into a cup, she took a sip, held her head up, and continued.

"I was 'processed' first, where they made me presentable. Then," she hesitated. "Then they put me in a suite of rooms with a man who…"

"It's okay, Jess," said Aunt Lindsey.

Jess continued, "He raped me and took my virginity. I found out later that they pay extra for virgins."

Aunt Lindsey, ash white, asked, "All this time, child?"

"Yes," Jess confirmed. "They would house us together so we could commiserate, plan, and scheme. Apparently that kept us more adept at getting away from the rapist. They had actually been doing it long enough to know that. And, yes, there were some times when we would get away. There were even some who would pay extra for that."

"Unfortunately for us, the people we were going to..." Jess faltered again in the telling. "They wanted to see – they got off on – the pain, the tears, the screams."

There was a still silence.

Someone from the back finally broke that silence, stunning realization clear in his voice, "I thought the people there were volunteers, that it was their job."

"Most of them are," said the other girl, "but the people we saw would pay extra for the real thing – not for someone playing the rape victim – but being the rape victim."

Specter asked a question knowingly and somehow, almost clinically, separating the emotion and the empathy and the anger. "So you would have repeated ... encounters ...with the same rapists – for the continued horror and pain. And turnover is high – for the same reason."

"Yes," Jess answered.

"So you managed your escape but were recaptured, and they were taking you back to the pleasure dome," Specter ventured.

"No," Jess said, "they were taking us to a new pleasure dome for more of the same. Too easy to break out of the same place twice."

There was not a person within earshot who was unaffected. There were clearly a lot of upset people. This information flew all over them. They would act. Randal recognized it right as Specter acted on it.

"This first place," Specter began, "how far away from here is it? Where were you walking, and how long were you on the platform?"

Jess thought for a minute. "I was on the old Patterson farm – in that field that borders the river." She thought. "I was out there half of that day and half the night maybe."

"Do you remember where the sun was?" Specter asked.

Everyone could tell she was focusing totally on that day. Finally she said, "I remember the sun being on my face but not directly. I remember being on my stomach, facing right, and," she turned, "the sun was," she indicated, "here." Southwest.

Specter asked Shade, "How far can a platform go in a day?"

"Two hundred miles, non-stop, pushing it," Shade replied.

Specter stood up and looked directly at Jess. "Thank you. I'm sorry for your ordeal." Then he looked around the room at everyone there and said, "I'm going on a hunting trip. I'm leaving in a week, and it's going to take about twice that long. Whoever wants to join me is welcome – just bring your own food."

Although his announcement was met with many nods of assent, there was also dissent.

One voiced his concern, "I don't have any love for the pri-cons, but if this is going on, we need to tell them so they can fix it."

"Friend," Specter said, "it is the pri-cons who are doing this."

"No," the man said, "she said a group of men took her – not pri-cons."

"Right," said Specter, "and they put her on a platform." He let that sink in. Then he drove it home. "Do you go to town on your platform? You got a platform I can borrow to carry my hay?"

Before the man could respond, the girl who ran spoke up, again showing her steel. "The pri-cons themselves were the worst. A lot of pri-con crews see gang rape as a team building exercise." She almost spit the words. "I'll be going hunting in a week. Then I can go home." She then stood up and walked out. The boy who ran with her, Jake, went after her.

"You see?" demanded Specter. "The pri-cons are doing this, or are at least complicit in it." He moved around so he could look at each person directly, his voice rising. "You can't demand someone to stop something they're doing unless you can make them stop. Especially when it's something illegal." He grew even more emphatic. "Illegal, hah. That whole concept kind of died with the Breaking, didn't it? Well, I'm going up there because what they're doing is wrong whether or not it's illegal." He stopped walking around. "I'm going whether any of you want to or not. All I'm saying is that whoever wants to is welcome to come with me."

There would be no more discussion. Specter said, "Go home. Kiss you wife. Hug your kids. Think about it. I leave in a week." He sat down to signify that the time for talk was over.

The men all sort of milled around before heading home. They left alone or in small groups of two or three. They did have a lot to think about – a lot to absorb. Most of the men wanted some time alone to think. The others needed it.

Chapter 39

As soon as the men started leaving, Jake and the girl came back and joined the others. Specter asked the two boys and Jess to follow him. As Specter passed by Randal, he asked him to join them. They didn't go far, but they did get away from the group.

Specter began. "I had expected as much when we found you in the truck. Pleasure domes offer all sorts of entertainment, including the adult kind. And I've had some dealing with the type of men who use the back rooms and order off the menu in pleasure domes." He was all business to the point of being cool, just shy of cold. "My dealings were strictly in an official capacity, but now that's changed."

Randal saw the looks the kids had. "He used to get paid to kill people," he said by way of explanation. "The kind of people who would do such things." The kids seemed to expect as much.

"Anyway," Specter continued, "What do you know about the official?"

No one spoke up, and Specter seemed to expect that.

He continued, "The reason I'm asking is that we've got to interrogate him soon, and I don't know if there's something specific we need to get from him." Specter paused, thinking. "Look, I can get everything he knows, but it'd be better if I knew what I was looking to confirm."

Specter turned to Randal. "When we were tracking them down you told me he was an official and we needed him. Why?"

It was Randal's turn to think. "What made me think that was that the pri-cons on the platform used their bodies to protect him and the pilot – even though every one of them had webarmor. My first thought was that they couldn't know we had the...," he looked around, "the special bullets." He looked down. "That and he must be high up to have that level of protection."

Specter answered that one. "Not really too high up. He has to be there in order to have pri-con protection but only one team means he's on the lower level of those having that protection. In fact, the really high ups have their own specialized protection. Interesting about the bullets, though."

Specter turned back to the boys. "What do you guys want to tell me?"

They didn't say anything.

Specter turned to Jess, "Tell them they can, okay?"

"You can, you know," Jess said. "They won't let you get hurt."

Specter added, "You don't get to go in there with me without talking."

At this there was some interest.

"Really, we get to be there?" Jake asked.

"If Jess grants you permission to be," Specter answered.

"Will it help them?" she asked.

"I think so, but I'm not a doctor," Specter replied.

"Okay, then," she said.

The younger boy started first. "We were his slaves. Anything he wanted done, we did."

"Or?" Specter prompted.

Jake dove in as if Specter hadn't spoken. "We didn't just fix him dinner or carry his things. We had to do everything including wiping his ass."

"He never touched either of us," the younger boy said. "I guess we weren't his type."

Jake added, "He'd use us for demonstration when he wanted to show his friends how to beat a disobeying servant. He never did that to those he raped."

"We knew he'd kill us if we disobeyed," the younger boy added.

"How?" Specter asked.

"He always has ten of us. Once, very early on, one guy just refused to do anything. Chairman Jones, that's his name, took him, brought us all together, along with his pri-cons, and took a bat to him, and then a knife." He swallowed hard, as if it had just happened.

"He threw the pieces at us," Jake said.

"He didn't smile or yell or anything the whole time. Expressionless – like it was a waste of his time," said the younger boy.

"Anyone else?" asked Specter.

"There was another – the last guy," said Jake.

"Did he kill him the same way?" Specter probed.

"Yes," said Jake, "only he used a sledgehammer and a hatchet."

"What did he do, boys, as his job?" Randal asked.

"I'm not sure exactly. We were only on his house staff, never on his traveling staff," answered the younger boy.

"Why wasn't there any staff with him when we found him?" Specter asked.

"I think it was because it wasn't a planned trip. When they caught us he said he was mad that the pri-cons wouldn't let him take his staff, but it was only supposed to be an hour long trip. He told us he had to leave them behind – no space – but that he was taking us back to kill us," Jake said.

"Sure he was," said Specter. "You disobeyed him by running away." He turned thoughtful. "I'm going to talk with Aunt Lindsey. You both get some sleep tonight, if you can. Try at least. I'll wake you up early, before his sleepy juice wears off."

The boys left to set about finding a place to sleep. Jess turned around with another question for Specter, "Are you sure they will be okay with this?"

Specter looked right at her and put his left hand on her shoulder. "After what they just said, I know they will absolutely be okay. I only wish we had the other eight slaves here."

Jess smiled at him and then walked away.

Specter turned to Randal. "You need to get some sleep, too. We'll have to have a bit of drama, but I think we can work it. After we get done, though, we'll need to ride back to the cabin. We need more bullets, and I'd like my shotgun back if you can work it."

"Okay," said Randal, and Specter turned away from him in search of Aunt Lindsey. Randal needed to get his bedroll, so he looked around for Shade. Seeing her, he walked over to her and asked her where the horses were.

Shade said, "You tired, too?" When Randal nodded, she added, "Come on, I'll show you where we stowed our gear." She led them around a few stacks of goods to their packs. Once she had grabbed hers and handed Randal his, she took his hand and said, "Come on, I'll show you where we're sleeping." As if the sounds of the words alerted her to their meaning, she squeezed his hand and then just let go. Shade led him towards the rear left corner of the barn and entered what looked like a small feeding stall.

As Randal watched, Shade opened the false floor of the stall and started down. Just underneath the ground level was another level – the one Jess had spoken of earlier. They had cleared some of it, and Randal could see some cots set up. The only light came from two bulbs – each connected to its own car battery.

"The kids will sleep in here," Shade said, leading him back further. They went through a very dark and narrow hallway to a larger room. "And here is where we sleep," she said spreading out her arms. There was only one car battery light in here.

Randal looked at Shade and asked, "Are we doing the right thing? I mean, abandoning our attacks on the platforms to go and do this?"

Shade answered, "It might not be the best thing for us to do – for ourselves. But I'm convinced it's the right thing to do." Shade looked him in the eye. "You know that, too, don't you?"

"Yeah," Randal said looking down. "I'm sure." He added, "It's just rare that I have a chance to do anything but keep running."

Randal's eye went for the official, Chairman Jones, and he asked Shade, already knowing the answer, "We make sure he doesn't get out?"

Shade looked at him, "Yes," she said, "but we also don't let them come and get him." And she started unrolling her bedroll. "I'll be here," she said, "but I've got the first watch tonight. We watch in that room with the kids and sleep in this room, okay? Specter will have the middle watch and you the third, but I think you'll be doing your thing pretty early. I'm going to pull a third watch anyway. Just in case. You grab some sleep – we're going to have a busy week," Shade said and was gone. Randal laid out his bed roll, looking at Chairman Jones, wondering what other evils this man had committed. He lay down and, as he lay there, he said a silent prayer for the man. He prayed also for those who would bring justice to him.

Chapter 40

Randal woke with Specter's hand on his shoulder. "It's time," he said.

Randal got up and looked around. There were two lights in here now, and they were in the room with two pri-cons!

Randal jumped back and looked again. It was the two boys in pri-con uniforms. They each held an axe handle without the axe head. Specter held out a tiny box to him. Randal shook his head and finally shook the sleep away. It was a hand-held video recorder! Randal hadn't seen one in – well, it had to be over a decade! "How did you...?" Randal got out.

"Aunt Lindsey is very resourceful," Specter informed him. "Apparently somebody rigged up a bicycle to generate current, and she charges batteries that way. She says there's about a minute of recording here but we only need about thirty seconds."

"What's the plan, then?" Randal asked.

Specter smiled. "I'm going to let the boys give Chairman Jones some of his own medicine. I need you to film it. Then we'll switch out and Jake there will get down beside him and you get behind Robbie (*so that was his name*, Randal thought) so all you see is his back and then pan down to Jake's face. What Chairman Jones sees looks like Jake being beaten, then we give the Chairman the 'go' juice and he feels his legs and starts telling us what we want to know."

They all got into place and Specter dropped his hand. Jake and Robbie started wailing on his legs. Like men building a railroad, they swung in tandem, one striking while the other hoisted the handle over his head. Over and over it went. There was no audio on the camera; but they still worked in silence. Then after an indeterminate time, Specter guided Randal by putting his hands on his shoulders to Robbie's back and Jake moved. He was up – halfway out of the uniform – and down when Robbie got out of the way and you could see Jake's face. Then Specter tapped Randal hard on the shoulder, and Randal cut the recording. Thirty-five seconds.

Playing it back, it looked good. *Well*, thought Randal, *that's what Specter wanted*. They got set for phase two. Robbie left and then reappeared with a wheelchair. They put Chairman Jones in it and left the room.

Specter said, "You go out with them and then come back once I turn my back to you, okay?"

"Right," Randal said.

Specter gave him a syringe. "You present this to me and say, 'Sir, there are men approaching,' okay?"

"Okay," said Randal.

Randal got to his spot and was relieved to see Jake and Robbie. They got their places set while Specter got Chairman Jones awake.

Once Specter had his attention, he said, "Sir, I apologize for the inconvenience. We are getting ready to travel further, but I thought you would want to see this." And Specter showed him all the footage they had just filmed and Jake, Robbie, and Randal could all see that Chairman Jones liked it. Seeing the beating aroused him.

Specter then stepped in front of the wheelchair and showed his back. Jake elbowed Randal in the back even as Randal started walking. He delivered the syringe and the message. Specter looked shocked but he wasn't breaking character. He immediately jabbed the syringe into Chairman Jones's thigh – apologizing while he did so.

Chairman Jones, groggy from the medicine of the past day, seemed to become more aware. Jake and Robbie left their hiding spot when Specter gave the injection and arrived at Chairman Jones's wheelchair just as he was getting fully awake, axe handles behind their backs.

With no regard for another, Chairman Jones began giving orders. He told Jake and Robbie that this was unacceptable. He needed his two domestic slaves right then. He wanted Jake and Robbie brought to him at once so he could see if any bones were broken and see what did need breaking, and what he could do to make that happen.

Specter jumped in with, "I'm sorry, sir, but that is not possible."

Chairman Jones was livid. "That is not acceptable you incompetent piece of <u>trash</u>! If you can't do your job then get me your supervisor and..."

Specter interrupted, "I <u>am</u> the superior here – your superior."

Chairman Jones wasn't believing any of it, "You think that... well, I will; you can't..." Then he focused on the two pri-cons, "You two – arrest this man! You will be commended by me personally to Commandant Halsey and..." Specter interrupted him again, "Go ahead, boys." And Jake and Robbie raised their heads so that he could see their faces.

Chairman Jones sputtered and opened and closed his mouth like a fish out of water.

"I do believe we've given the chairman here an acute case of apoplexy," Specter said as he walked around behind the chairman. Specter bent down to his ear and said, "That man in the video was you. You've got about two minutes before you start to feel that pain."

"I don't believe this nonsense!" Chairman Jones said, the blood visibly draining from his face.

Specter asked him, "Then why don't you stand up and walk out?"

Randal could clearly see Chairman Jones think it over. And then, as Specter suggested, he tried to stand. Propping himself on the arms of the wheelchair, Chairman Jones almost made it to a standing position, but when he tried to put weight on his legs, they gave way. Almost involuntarily, Chairman Jones put one leg out to catch himself but he went on down with a hair-raising "AAaarh!" as something audibly snapped.

Specter was quick, "Pick him up, boys." They did so, and Specter motioned for them to sit back down as he walked in front of the wheelchair. "Now," he said to Chairman Jones, "Let's you and me talk."

"We have nothing to say," said Chairman Jones curtly.

Specter took out his knife and showed it to Chairman Jones. "This is what's going to happen. You're going to tell me what I want to know. That's the given. And," Specter nodded to Jake and Robbie, "we're going to beat you and cut you up. Now, what I injected you with will counteract the sedatives you've been getting and it's also a stimulant, so you'll be awake and able to feel everything. Plus, I have some hypercoaggulant powder so you don't bleed out too quickly."

Specter squatted in front of Chairman Jones, looked him in the eye, and said, "We will kill you today. How fast we do that is up to you."

Chairman Jones spit right into Specter's face.

"Thus it begins," Specter said almost to himself.

After wiping his face, Specter then calmly removed Chairman Jones's right shoe and, with Robbie and Jake holding Chairman Jones down, Specter sliced down in between Chairman Jones's pinky toe and the next one until he got about to the ball of his foot, and then neatly cut off Chairman Jones's pinky toe. The screaming went on for a while.

Once the screaming had subsided, Specter held up the toe to Chairman Jones, who was now sweating profusely, handed it to him, and asked, "Are you going to spit on me again?"

Chairman Jones's eyes belied his grimace. He must be feeling the full effects of his pain now.

"No," Chairman Jones managed.

"Good," Specter smiled. "Now, what do you do, Chairman Jones?"

"I provide very exclusive products for very expensive tastes," the chairman answered.

"Specifically, Chairman Jones," Specter said evenly.

"I provide experiences that my clientele pay dearly for, experiences they cannot otherwise have," Chairman Jones said.

Specter said, "I said 'specifically,' Chairman Jones." He looked to Jake and Robbie. "Left arm, boys. Mind you don't hit his head."

Jake and Robbie brandished the axe handles and lit into Chairman Jones's left arm in the same way they'd dealt with his legs. Finally, Chairman Jones was able to withdraw his arm to his body. Specter stood and took Robbie's axe handle and showed them how to pry the axe handle between Chairman Jones's body and use it as a lever to lift the arm away from the body.

Specter handed the axe handle back to Robbie and let the boys continue. Randal was amazed at what they could do – how they could focus – with Chairman Jones screaming so loudly. After Robbie had pried Chairman Jones's arm away for the umpteenth time, Jake took a well-placed swing and was rewarded with a teeth-clinching crack.

Chairman Jones's arm dangled there on the outside of the wheelchair; he was unable to move it.

Specter stepped in then and the boys stepped back. As they turned, Specter searched their faces and saw that they had not yet released their pain. This was not enjoyable to them as much as a necessary fulfillment of justice. Specter would need more time to make it repugnant to them.

Specter gave Chairman Jones a drink of something – made him swallow it actually. When Chairman Jones had choked it down and was just breathing heavily, Specter said in the same even tone, "What do you do, specifically, Chairman Jones?"

This time, Chairman Jones had diarrhea of the mouth. "I put up fighters in the ring – gladiator style – death matches. I also run the murder fantasy." Chairman Jones stopped to spit on the ground, while Randal told him, "Explain."

Chairman Jones continued, "People pay me so they can kill someone. We set up whatever scenario and let the patron kill – with proper protection for the patron, of course."

Specter looked at him with disgust and said, "And people know you do this?"

Chairman Jones became defiant. "Everything we do is sanctioned by the Corps. We only use prisoners. We offer a solution. The fights are one thing. Everybody wants to be one of the new gladiators, and everybody wants to sponsor them. It's too easy to make money there. Small time money, though. The murder fantasy is the upper echelon exclusive; the big money is there. But we offer the fair chance to the prisoner, they get out, they go free."

"Free?" Specter interjected.

"Yes," Chairman Jones said, totally believing, "free to live in the Outerlands, like you people."

"But you also protect the patron. How?" Specter asked.

"We send a pri-con team with them. If the prisoner wins, we can protect the patron until the threat from the prisoner can be neutralized."

Specter looked at Randal and winked. Randal understood. The pri-cons with Chairman Jones on the road were that type of team, that's why they dove in gunfire – to protect the patron.

"How often does the prisoner win?" Specter prompted.

"Often enough," said Chairman Jones.

Specter grabbed Jake's axe handle from him – he was closer – and swung at Chairman Jones's broken arm as it laid outside the wheelchair. He connected square in the back of the wrist, and it made a sound that Randal could only associate with opening an old pop-top soda can.

Chairman Jones's scream hit Randal palpably in the gut.

"Specificity, please, Chairman Jones," Specter said evenly.

It was Specter's nonchalant calmness that was beginning to unnerve Randal.

"On to other matters, Chairman Jones. What else do you do?" asked Specter.

Chairman Jones either hesitated or was dying.

Specter did not wait for him to respond, but instead walked over to Randal, taking him aside with his arm around to the entrance of the room. Once there, Specter whispered, "It's going to start to get nasty in here. You're looking a bit pale and nauseous. Maybe you should wait outside."

Randal didn't hear anything after the fourth word. '*It's going to start to get nasty?*' he thought. "Yeah, I need to get out." Randal looked at the boys. "Let me take them, too," he asked.

Specter looked...divided. "No," he said. "They have some other things to learn here."

Randal couldn't get enough saliva in his mouth to ask his next question. His voice came out as a rasp. "What could they possibly learn here that won't scar them for life?"

Specter looked at Randal and decided something. "Go get some water, boys," Specter ordered Jake and Robbie. They complied.

Once they had left, Specter asked Randal, "Did your parents ever catch you drinking?"

Randal was taken aback and didn't understand why Specter would ask that question – especially now.

Specter continued. "I'm not being flippant; this is relevant. My father did. I came home from practice after sneaking a few beers and he acted like that was the best thing, his son, a man. So he and I drank together that night. He and I drank a lot of whatever. Then, the next morning, he got me up early and we started again. By lunchtime, I hurt all over and was retching every five minutes. Now, my father didn't win any parent of the year award that day, but he showed me there's a lot more to being a man than drinking a lot of alcohol." Specter paused and Randal could see the dilemma within him. "One thing you seem to be forgetting is that these boys are already scarred for life. This piece of..."

Specter was pointing to Chairman Jones, and Randal could see that Specter was almost in tears. Randal got very scared.

Specter continued, "He took every kind of chance at a normal life the boys had and cut it. What we're doing is looking at the scar on these boys. It's always going to be there, but we can go in now and break up that scar tissue around the cut. Breaking up that scar tissue hurts, but it's necessary to healing. I know this is hard but it's supposed to be. These boys don't have people who will make sure they get life-long counseling. No one gets that here in the Outerlands. Maybe after today these boys will know what justice means and how hard that is to mete out. Maybe they'll get some closure over that part of their lives. Maybe through this we can work on their scar so it won't define them for the rest of their lives."

"Or maybe you're just teaching them how to torture," Randal said.

Specter got in Randal's personal space and said, "I didn't say you had to like it."

Randal could feel the heat of Specter's glare. This was going to happen whether he got in the way or not. Despite his qualms, Randal had to believe that Specter thought this was beneficial to the boys. Specter stepped back, motioned towards the exit, and gave Randal a pat on the back. "We won't be too much longer."

Reluctantly, Randal left them and went back through the first room, out of the barn itself and into the morning air. He drank it in. He let the smell of dew, the woods, and the barn wash over him, hoping it would cleanse away the dank smell of sweat, the sickly-sweet smell of blood, the distinct smell of hopelessness.

Shade came up to him and offered him a cup of coffee. Randal took the cup and drank from it, letting the heat of it shock him back to this world of life rather than the dark dungeon of death.

Shade looked him over, and, thankfully, gave him some quietness to let him find himself again. After some minutes of just sharing coffee, Randal looked over at Shade. She took it as an opportunity to talk. "Not what I expected our first cup of coffee alone to be like."

Randal was surprised. He smiled.

"First time you've sat in on one of those?" asked Shade.

"Yeah," Randal answered, at a loss to say more.

"Remember why," Shade said. "That helps sometimes."

"Thank you," said Randal. They sat on in silence, Randal thankful that Shade was giving him space.

"We're not in danger here, are we?" Randal asked when his mind turned to it.

Shade said, "No, they've got sentries posted that will tell us if they see any pri-cons."

They continued to wait in silence. Randal could not imagine what might be happening in there. Nor did he want to. The waiting, though, seemed interminable.

At last, Jake and Robbie came outside much like Randal imagined he did, drinking in the morning sun. Only they were rubbing at their eyes, too. Robbie didn't stop when Jake did. He kept walking until he got a little way past them and then he dropped to his knees and vomited. Shade patted Randal on the knee and then went to Robbie.

Specter came outside, took in the situation, and went to Jake. "You okay?" he asked. Jake nodded. Specter clapped him on the back, "You get some lunch, okay? Robbie's going to need some, too. You have to get your strength back. Make sure you don't eat anything you like; you won't be able to eat it again for a while." He raised his voice so Robbie could hear, too. "He's never going to hurt anyone else again; that's over." Specter then motioned for Randal to come over.

When Randal got close, he thought that Specter had been crying, too. *What happened in there*? "You okay?" he asked, the way one asks when he already knows the answer is 'no.'

Specter looked down and spoke softly, "I can still tell myself that I'm slaying demons. That keeps me moving." Randal waited for more and thought Specter was done talking when he added, "Your God may tell me differently one day, though."

"You need to make sure of what He's going to say to you," Randal said.

Specter dismissed it with a wave and said, "Go get something for us to eat. We're going back to the cabin." Randal complied.

By the time he got back, Specter had the horses ready. Specter was even taking the packhorse. Randal didn't understand why until he saw the horse laden with uniforms, feed for the horses, and some other bags. The horses they would ride would only be carrying them. That meant a fast trip.

Saying some quick goodbyes, they left about midmorning. Randal was thankful for the distraction. Justified though it may have been, Randal still had trouble stomaching the death of Chairman Jones. The ride, though, at the pace Specter was setting, demanded Randal's full attention, and he was relieved to give it.

After about an hour, Specter slowed and brought his horse to a canter. Randal followed suit and stayed behind Specter. Rather than dropping back to talk with Randal, Specter kept his pace. *Apparently he needs his time, too,* thought Randal. With just enough time to let the horses rest, Specter looked back at Randal and gave his hand signal, 'move out.' They pushed the horses hard, only slowing to wait to cross the road. Eventually they came to a clearing where Specter dismounted. Randal also dismounted. They led their horses up to a ridge where they could look down on their cabin hiding the bunker.

Everything looked intact at the cabin. There didn't appear to be anything out of place. Specter waited and watched much like he did at the road. After seeing no sign, they led their animals to the cabin. They arrived with no incident. They tied their horses to the rail on the front porch, and Specter broke open a bag of horse feed on the porch for them. They both started unloading the packhorse.

Once inside with all the gear stowed, Specter made a quick dinner. Early as it was, both wanted to eat something and then begin their work. As they finished eating, Specter said, "Remember that you can have a snack later if you want one."

"Right," said Randal. "I'm off."

"Hold on," Specter said.

Randal waited while Specter went to fetch something.

Specter returned with some of the bags from Byland's Rest and some other things in a box. He said, "Follow me." Specter led him to where he had set up his bathtub and everything to break down the webarmor. Specter set the box down. He said, "Here's some dye for the webarmor. I want blue. Shade wants red. You can be either, but we also got green. Aunt Lindsey said you might need this." He held up a half gallon bottle of bleach.

Randal couldn't believe it. "I thought bleach was all but gone," he said.

"Aunt Lindsey had some in her special stash. Having her niece back put her in an especially giving mood."

Randal saw a problem. "Specter, I've got to have another bathtub, though."

Specter said, "I know, but – follow me." He led Randal just in the next room over, and there, in the floor was an old garden tub, circular, with an almost five feet diameter.

"Is it fiberglass?" Randal asked.

"Yes," Specter replied, "I had to look all over for it. Can you use it?"

"I think so," said Randal. "Where did you find it? And when did you get it?"

"When you were working the first time, making the coating, I got out to some old houses. This was in an old mobile home and just so happened to be the easiest to get out. It took a couple of days, but I got it." answered Specter.

"Awesome. I do need something else, though," Randal said. "I need a small wooden frame made that will just fit in here. Wide as we can make it, but it needs to fit flat on the bottom. And it needs to be covered in a metal screen."

"Like a screen door screen?" Specter asked.

"Well," Randal thought, "like a two-ply of that."

"I can get that. I'll just get a lot of screening and help you make what you need." said Specter.

"Deal," said Randal. "I'm guessing you want this all done in about three days?"

Specter smiled, "If you can, yes. But you can have four days if you have to."

"I thought as much," said Randal. "I'd like to have a full week, but we'll do what we can."

"Good," said Specter. "I'll go and get that screen. Oh – almost forgot." He walked through another door into a room Randal hadn't noticed before. "Here's all the other stuff you may need."

Randal looked in and saw shelves full of all kinds of chemicals, cleaners, solvents, everything.

"Car batteries are in the back. Use as many as you need," Specter said.

"Awesome," Randal said. "I can probably find what I need in here." He looked down and saw a whole shelf of bleach in gallon containers. "Did you know you had all this bleach?" Randal asked, concerned.

"I knew we had some, not how much." Specter looked Randal in the eye. "Sometimes it's better to let someone give you something she thinks is precious – and not let on that it's not precious to you. Sometimes it's just better." He started out of the room. "Go ahead and get started, Randal. We can always fill up Aunt Lindsey's bottle and tell her we didn't have to use it anyway."

Randal accepted that and then went back to the first room and retrieved his notebook. He made sure he'd have enough chemicals to start and estimated how much he'd need. He then carried the uniforms into the room and counted them out, making sure he'd have enough chemicals. Randal then went through each uniform – all thirty-two of them. With just 6 uniforms left over – there was a lot of trial and error – that made thirty-eight total, so that would be...He did the math in his head. He could probably do eight runs. He'd have to see where they were after six runs, but he could plan on at least seven. So, with clothes for Shade, himself and Specter that should leave a good batch for coating bullets, and some left over if something happened.

Specter came back in with two rolls of screen.

"I thought you were going out somewhere to find that," Randal said.

"I was," said Specter, "but as I looked back at the cabin, I noticed the windows. They're specially sized and the screens are, too. Plus, they're metal."

"I'll start measuring," said Randal.

Specter gave him a tape measure and started laying out the screens. Randal came back and marked everything on the screen on the floor. Then he did the same thing on another screen. Randal positioned the other screen perpendicular to the first and said, "I need these screens set like this, stretched taut and secured – only make sure the wood doesn't get wider than this," and he showed Specter.

Specter only said, "All right," took the screens, and left.

Randal started in on the uniforms, removing buttons, zippers, and anything in the pockets. That usually was not very much. Shade had said that before the pri-cons went on patrol they would empty their pockets so that, theoretically, they could carry more ammunition. These uniforms were no exception. Randal found nothing of note in any of the pockets.

He did find one anomaly, though, in the eighth uniform he looked at. As he was cutting out the zipper, he noticed something red on the waistband. Looking closer, he could see that someone had sewed the numbers seven, three, two and one, two, zero in the inside waistband of the pants. The numbers were separated by a gap so they looked like:

7 3 2   1 2 0

The thread looked normal, and the sewing was definitely homemade. Looking closer, the thread only showed on the inside; there was nothing visible from the outside. It was red thread, so maybe it was a pilot's uniform. *He must have run through a lot of needles*, thought Randal.

Randal like to play with numbers, though, so he started to play with those numbers – just to pass the time. $7 + 3 + 2 = 12 + 0$. Or, $7 + 3 + 2 = 12.0$. Or, $7 + 3 = 10$ times $2 = 20$ so that's 1, 20 or one, single 20. He imagined the pilot flying his platform calling his homebase: 732, 732, this is unit 120. We see a red fox. Please advise. Kill or let live. Unit 120, this is 7-3-2 homebase 7-3-2. Advise to kill with prejudice. Enclave Chairman reports fox is wearing his wife's new stole, so no body shots unit 120, copy? 732 homebase, unit 1-2-0 copy, no body shots.

Randal kept playing around in his mind like that until all the uniforms were ready. He then turned his attention to the garden tub vat. He would have to align the webarmor fibers in there, so he went and got some wire and an old light switch from the shop area. Randal made some rigging, went back to the shop, and got a light bulb and some more wire. After what seemed just a short time later, Specter brought in the screen and told him it was pretty late. Randal felt they needed to test the tub, and Specter acquiesced. They put some water in the garden tub, put in the screen, connected the wires, and then, making sure they were both clear, Randal flipped the switch. The light came on, and Randal knew the circuit was running correctly and would align the fibers in the right way.

They took a break to sleep and, after a quick breakfast, started planning the work day. Once planned and fed, they began.

Randal started by showing Specter how to make the shot for his shotgun shells. They got a sheet and spread it out on the ground in the back of the cabin, supporting it so it was taut but did not touch the ground. Randal, estimating the drop from the top of the cabin down to there was about forty feet, climbed up to the top of the cabin with Specter's ladder. He took the wheel weights, the metal ladle, and the metal sieve from Aunt Lindsey's. Once on the roof, Specter handed him a deep cast iron pot with charcoal briquettes in it. When Specter had told him they had those in the bunker, he was amazed. So many things this 'sultan' had planned and prepared for – it was amazing.

Specter followed Randal up with the rest of the wheel weights and said, "I figured it would save time." He then lit the briquettes, and Randal went back down into the cabin. The kitchen table in there was light, really not much more than an old card table, so he took it and three sheets back outside. He spread the sheets out and then set the table on top of them, all in the backyard. He folded down one side of the table's legs and set it down on that angle. Randal went back into the cabin to retrieve two bed slats, about the length of the table, and then tacked them on the long sides of the angled table. By then, Specter called down and said the fire was ready.

Randal climbed up on the roof again and walked over to the chimney where Specter was. Specter had set the cast iron pot on top of the slab covering the chimney's flue outlet. Specter already had the ladle in the coals. Randal grabbed gloves, put the two hot mitts on his hands, and dropped two lead wheel weights into the ladle. The weights liquefied almost immediately. Randal picked up the sieve with a long pair of channel locks, picked up the ladle, stepped to the edge of the roof, and then poured the molten lead over the sieve. The droplets of molten lead fell down and landed on the sheet below. Replacing the ladle in the cast iron pot, he told Specter to follow him, and got down from the roof.

Once down they went to the sheet. Randal picked up a lot of little lead pellets. "Higher up would be better, but this will work." He explained to Specter, "Pouring the lead over the sieve gives uniform droplets that will form into a ball by gravity as they fall. They also cool as they fall."

Randal then took some lead pellets from the sheet, placed them on the high end of the table, and let them roll down. "Round pellets," Randal said, "the ones we want, will roll straight down. Odd ones, oval ones, bad ones will roll to the side." He picked up one lead ball about one quarter of an inch in diameter from the bottom of the table. "Will that work?" Randal asked.

Specter said, "It's a good size."

Randal took another lead ball from the side of the table along the slat, a nicely shaped oval. "This goes back to be melted and dropped again. We could use it if we have to, but it'll fly truer if it's a sphere." Specter nodded knowingly and Randal immediately regretted giving a Hunter a lesson in ballistics.

Randal ended with a quick, "I'm going downstairs." As he left he couldn't shake the feeling of Specter staying outside and doing manly work while he went inside and did womanly work. He was comforted by telling himself this was not simply sewing but material making and tailoring. He shook it all off. *Either way*, he thought, *it has to get done.*

While he started the dissolution bath, he put the first uniforms in to soak and went upstairs. He went into Shade's quarters, the harem room, and started going through the underclothes and nightgowns. He found what he needed and turned to go back downstairs.

Specter was there in the hall when he came out. "Do you work better wearing women's underthings?" he asked, laughing.

"No – it's for the filter," Randal tried, but Specter was laughing too hard.

"Next time I have to go to the bathroom I'll make sure you know so I won't catch you doing your own thing," Specter said, laughing all the while.

Randal allowed himself to laugh as he walked back down to his vat and stirred.

Chapter 41

Specter brought him dinner about seven o'clock that evening. He watched as Randal took some liquid from the large bathtub, poured it into a large conic colander, like those used to make jams, while the liquid was caught in a five gallon bucket. What Randal needed was caught on the once white satin nightie he got from upstairs.

Specter was proud of the fact that he got the bathtub boiling. The fountain pump from the water sculpture worked perfectly to circulate the water from a stock pot on a hot plate to the tub and back. Randal said it was the other two hot plates under the tub and the fact that the mixture had a lower boiling point than water – but whatever – it worked.

Randal had requested finger foods, so he'd brought him some frozen chicken nuggets, two boiled eggs, and sliced cucumbers. Randal would take a bite, do something (stir, drain, transfer), then repeat. Specter had decided to eat down there with Randal and see what he could pick up. He made sure to always be eating when Randal turned around, though, specifically so he wouldn't be asked to literally pick something up.

Randal would take the nightie and the colander over to another five gallon bucket and pour the bleach over it, then transfer to yet another bucket and rinse again in the same bleach. In fact, he did that repeatedly. Finally, Randal took the nightie, stretched it out and took the goop – the 'filtrate' Randal called it – and scraped it off the nightie and put it into the garden tub. Aunt Lindsey was responsible for the pump in there, an outside fountain pump from one of the swankier houses in Byland's Rest. She said they'd gone to the Enclave and wouldn't miss it.

Randal had a lot of goop in there, Specter thought, but he kept adding more and stirring it in with his cut off wooden broom handle. The garden tub was blue now, thanks to the dye. Randal had adapted the screen with another piece of wood on each corner. He'd attached it perpendicularly to the screen frame so he could lift it out of the tub. *And not get electrocuted*, thought Specter.

Presently, Randal flipped the switch. He said, "It's going to be about twenty minutes and then I'll turn it, and twenty minutes later turn it back, and so on and so forth for at least three hours, maybe four." He motioned towards the pile of uniforms. "What do you think about that thickness?" he asked.

Specter felt specifically for the thickness. It was a bit thicker than denim jeans but still a rugged, hefty feel. "I like these. I know Shade will; she's used to them," he said.

"Great," said Randal. "That's what I'll shoot for then."

Specter could tell he wasn't happy. "That would be the best," Specter said. Still no response. "Is there anything I can do to help?" It was an honest offer.

Randal thought. "No, not really. It's just the every twenty minute thing. I can sleep in between, wake up, switch it, sleep, repeat. If you get up early, though, I could use some coffee. This'll all run through faster if I keep it going." He looked at Specter, "I might sleep a whole day after that, though," he said with a short laugh.

Specter saw that the laughter did not touch his eyes. He smiled back but wondered if there was something he could do to make the work easier. He was at a loss. He stood up to leave – and it came to him! "Look, I'm going up to bed. I'll get up early and bring you some coffee." He looked at Randal but Randal was still looking down. "And thank you for this. You let me know if you need something, okay?"

"Sure," Randal said.

It was time to use it. "Hey, for what it's worth, I'll put in a good word for you with Shade." That did pique his interest.

"Thought you and her…" Randal started.

"Nah," Specter let that hang in the air as he turned and walked out. "Night, man," he said.

"Night," Randal replied.

That should keep him up for a little while anyway. *I'll still get him some coffee early, though*, thought Specter.

Chapter 42

Morning found Specter up early making coffee and breakfast. Remembering about bite-sized food, Specter fried up some country ham and scrambled eggs, flat though, and then portioned it out for biscuits. Once the biscuits were ready, he put it all together and then quartered the biscuits. He figured that would be bite sized enough.

Taking everything down to where Randal was working took only a few minutes. Randal, though, looked like he'd only slept a few minutes. He was in good spirits, though, and thankful for the food. Specter offered to help him again, but Randal reassured Specter that he'd be okay; he just needed food and drink.

Throughout the day Specter provided that for Randal. In between Randal's set times to stir, or wash, or turn, Randal was still working. Specter saw that Randal was working on patterns for the clothes and, it seemed, Randal was making some adjustments to the regular fatigue pants and shirts.

Randal did have Specter bring him some specific measurements, which he wrote down, and he also asked if there were things Specter wanted in his clothes – like an extra pocket or if he'd rather not have a pocket somewhere. Specter told him what he could, he had always made clothes work, never had a say in how they were made. Randal asked for Shade's clothes, too, her old ones – those she was wearing when they saw her for the first time. Specter found them and brought them down, including the new shorts she cut out of her old pants and the almost discarded pant legs. On a later snack trip, Randal asked Specter for some of the clothes they'd bought that first trip out. Because they weren't planning on running into Jess and her friends, Shade had left some clothes there.

Specter did not spend his day idly. He took advantage of his time and hit the gym and the bag. He worked hard at that, focused on eradicating any second thoughts about Chairman Jones.

Specter also spent some needed time with his map. It was a bit outdated, but it was extensive, and he could adjust things he knew had changed. As he worked the map, he tried to find the most probable locations for this 'processing' house Jess had spoken of. He put in markers, plotted travel times, and plotted travel distances based on what Jess had said. Specter then overlaid what Chairman Jones had said – or rather rasped – because Jake's axe handle had broken off so many of his teeth.

The map Specter came up with seemed pretty accurate. Now came the insurance part, the part that he had to do but might not ever need. Looking at all of the other possible places, going back over terrain, settlements, population, water, and so on ad infinitum. That stuff that he might never need but that his life would depend on if he did need it. That took time, but it was good – he was Hunting again.

Around dinner, Randal had an interesting request: "When you and Shade would work out, Specter, did she wear one thing more than another?"

Specter just raised his eyebrows. Randal clarified, "I'd like to pattern a shirt like it if it's possible."

Specter shook his head with exaggeration to egg him on, "Yes, yes, a gift for the sweetheart."

Randal, unfortunately, was too weary to play that game. "I'm a grown man, not an eighth grader. And, yes, I would like to look good in Shade's eyes."

"Sorry, man," Specter said. "I'll bring it down if I can find it."

"Thanks," Randal said and went back to working.

Dinner for both was not memorable. Specter fixed something that was simple and fast. In order to focus on his planning, Specter opted for calorie density rather than nutrient density. Specter was taking the food down to Randal when he stopped. He put the tray down at the top of the stairs and checked his memory.

Shade had complained about clothes, but she had found some she liked – or at least kept wearing. He remembered one top that she wore that was like a combination camisole and jog bra. He went to the closet in her quarters and, sure enough, there were three different ones there: same style, same color, three different ones. He stuck one in his back pocket.

He delivered the meal, and Randal was very appreciative. As he turned to head back upstairs he remembered the top in his pocket. He turned around and saw that Randal had turned around, too, back to his work. Specter said, "Hey." and as Randal turned around he tossed the top to him. "I remember her wearing this a lot," Specter said. "There are two others up there, and she probably has some more with her. Check it against the one she was wearing first. I don't know if she likes it or whether it's the only thing in the drawer she could tolerate."

Randal just waved thanks and as Specter was going up said, "Hey, hold on a minute," and Specter turned. Randal asked, "Where am I going to be able to sew these?"

Specter felt bad. He was so worked up in planning, he hadn't shown Randal where the sewing room was. "Got a minute?" he asked. It turned out he did. Randal followed Specter back upstairs, then back down again where Randal's room was, and then Specter took a different turn and there was another door – a new door that Randal hadn't noticed before.

Specter opened the door, and Randal was awestruck. Randal had had experience running a sewing machine and knew a lot. That Specter would keep quiet about this and not tell anyone bordered on betrayal in Randal's eyes. "Why didn't you tell me about this?" Randal asked.

"You weren't making clothes. Now you are," Specter replied simply.

The room was a large twenty by twenty room with machines lining one wall and, Randal counted, five rows of all kinds of different cloth. Specter interrupted Randal's looking around, "The guy who had this thought that, like in ancient times, clothes would be a sign of wealth, so he had a big supply to that end."

Specter watched as Randal went from the fabric to the machines, then to the work/cutting table. Randal's timer started beeping – his time was up. "You've got free reign, Randal," Specter said. "Will you be able to find your way back?"

"Sure will," said Randal. He looked thoughtful and then asked, "How many of these bunkers do you have, Specter?"

Specter just smiled.

"Really," Randal pushed.

"Enough," Specter conceded.

Randal was off to his fabric. Specter returned to his maps. They spent all evening at their respective tasks and, after Specter brought by some late snacks, they both worked well into the night.

The next morning Specter brought down breakfast, and Randal was still at it. He set down the ham biscuits and coffee and said, "I thought you would be sewing by now."

Randal looked up at him, haggard and tired, but excited and not exhausted. "I'm trying something new!" Without waiting, he burst forth, "I can't ever remember if we – or anyone really – had ever tried to anneal the fibers onto another type of fabric. It just happened. I was thinking we could try this and that it could make so many more options available. Plus, it would lead to a lot more tailored clothes. And so I'm trying it, and I've got the other material swaths done and they're drying, but it might put me a little behind schedule."

Specter let that all wash over him. "You need me maybe to coat the bullets or something?"

You would've had the same reaction if you'd have kicked him in the gut. Randal looked shaken. Then he started cursing. Specter wondered idly, is it really cursing if you just say the same single word over and over? Specter felt he needed to jump in, "It's okay – calm down – you're hitting a manic phase. You still have plenty of uniforms left, right?"

"Yes," Randal said. "But I won't have time to sew <u>and</u> coat the bullets unless we take some extra time."

"Okay," Specter said. "Get your material done. I'll get the bullets streamlined. Will you just dip them there in the garden tub?"

"No," Randal said. "In the bath tub – that first tub. And all we have to do is get the bullets the right temperature. Oh, snap!" Randal again had that look on his face. "Did you melt down those wheel weights?"

Specter said, "Yes, the first full day we were here. And I know how to reload them, so I just need them coated, and I can do the rest."

"Okay," Randal said, and Specter could tell he was desperately trying to tie up ends that shouldn't be problematic.

"Hey, just keep working on the material, and we'll see where we are, okay?" said Specter.

Specter got out of there. Randal's mania was getting to him. He walked to the guns, took one of the rifles, and carried it down to the workshop. He removed the magazine from the gun and took out a bullet. Specter then tried to size up the casing and the outer rim of the cartridge. He then took a small piece of wood and drilled a hole in it. The bullet fit through and the outer rim of the casing caught short, too big to go through. Specter took another, longer piece of wood and started drilling more holes the same size. This way, he could dip a lot of bullets at the same time. Judging by the amount of bullets they had, it would still take a while.

Specter kept busy until close to lunch time. He had a bunch of slats together for the bullets, and he took one down to Randal. Randal, he found, was wearing down. His excitement and fervor were still there, but they were muted by his weariness.

"You okay?" Specter asked, trepidatious of the answer.

"Yeah," Randal said. "I'm better anyway." He looked up at Specter. "Listen, I've got to get some uninterrupted sleep or I'll mess something up." He paused. "I don't know if that puts us too late," he said with resignation, as if he <u>did</u> know. He looked up at Specter for his determination.

"I thought we'd be leaving today," said Specter, deflated. "Well, I need to get back, debrief Jess, see if I can make it mesh with my map – specifically about that compound and house – then come up with a plan to free anyone who might be in there. Also, I need time to go over what we learned from Chairman Jones with Shade, and you, too, if you're up for it."

"I'm sorry, Specter, but there's just no way I can make that. Not unless you've got some extra 'go' juice." Randal looked up at Specter.

Specter sighed. "How much time do you need?"

Randal answered right off. "I've got the goop ready for the bullets, I've coated the scissors and the needles so I'll probably get all three uniforms done in say, four and half hours? I think sooner but, if something happens…." Randal trailed off.

"How do I coat the shot? I've still got to load the shotgun shells."

Randal thought for just a minute. "Do it like mine. Actually, do some for me, too. I've got some in the left top drawer of the dresser in my room. Heat the shot in a cast iron pan in the oven at one hundred degrees for about ten minutes. It doesn't have to be too hot because you don't want to melt or deform them. Then take them down here, put the pan in the bath – that first tub – and just get some liquid in there, then swirl it around. Next, set it down, let it come to room temperature, then drain the liquid back into the bath, and remove the shot by dumping it on a towel or something. Once dry, you can use it." Randal stopped. "Too much? Too fast?"

"No," Specter said. "So, you're telling me you could get done and we leave before it gets too dark and be there tonight?"

"Sure, if I don't fall asleep on my feet and if, importantly, I'm not so tired that I make mistakes."

"Okay," Specter turned to go. As he walked away, he said, "Get your stuff, and I'll meet you in the sewing room."

Randal did.

When Specter got in, Randal had spread out some material and was starting to transfer patterns to it. He looked up as Specter walked in, but his gaze focused on Specter's hand. Specter held up the syringe for Randal to see. As Specter got close to Randal, he recoiled. "Geez, Randal, have you not taken a bath since we've been here?"

Randal said only, "I'll do that once I'm done. What's that?"

"It's 'go' juice," Specter said, "as you so aptly put it."

"Shoulder or leg?" Randal asked.

"Since you'll be using your hands, we'll say leg," Specter said. "Don't go through your pants – but don't drop 'em until I'm gone. Just pop it in the side of your thigh, push it all in, and then work fast." He looked him in the eye. "This is a one time thing and probably a misuse to begin with, but no more unless you're dying. Last thing, when that wears off you've got about five minutes from when you first feel woozy until you hit the floor, so find a spot and lay down quick."

Randal said, "Thanks."

"Do I have to heat the rifle bullets, too?" asked Specter.

Randal nodded and said, "Same way."

"What about your arrow heads?"

Another thing Randal had forgotten about.

"No, well, it won't hurt," Randal said.

"So do them last and see how time is?" asked Specter.

"Sure," said Randal.

Specter saw that Randal was about asleep, right there, having a conversation with him.

"OKAY!" Specter yelled and Randal jumped about a foot in the air. Specter continued with, "Get that in you first thing, okay?"

Randal nodded and Specter left.

Specter focused on getting the bullets ready. This was the one task they had to get accomplished or the hunting trip would probably end in disaster. So he focused on getting the rifle bullets done first.

In between rounds, he got the shot and Randal's pistol shot coated. Then, on a whim, he coated his handgun bullets in the same way. He had plenty of reserves, but he would need to spend a week or so reloading and restocking. But that would be later. Specter finished with all the bullets and then coated every crossbow bolt he had. Having some time, he got all of Randal's arrows and coated those. Only then did he ready his reloader.

Wondering whether he should or not, Specter finally decided to check on Randal. He creeped up to the door and only peered in. He could see Randal at work on a sewing machine. Specter looked just long enough to make sure Randal was doing okay and then, satisfied, Specter returned.

He didn't think it took him long to get done, but he was surprised when Randal came, hair still wet from his shower. "You already done?" Specter asked.

"My sewing skills are pretty rusty, but I did better than I thought. You?" said Randal.

"Yeah. I've got these few more – maybe another twenty minutes," Specter answered.

"Okay," said Randal. "I'll pack us a supper and get everything loaded up?"

"Sure," Specter said. "Just make it something we can eat on horseback."

Randal waved his hand as he walked away to say 'okay.'

Specter finished up as Randal finished with the food. Simple warmed chicken patties were the fare tonight – filling, not messy, easy. Specter wondered if anyone would get power again to run a freezer. *Shoot, power to run anything*, he thought. It was amazing how you could take this stuff for granted. Specter was thankful he had planned ahead. Way ahead.

In any event, Specter was eager to Hunt again, but they had to get back to Byland's Rest before he could. That meant they needed to saddle up.

Specter and Randal worked together to get their gear up, the horses loaded, and everything ready to ride. It was late and both of them knew it, but Randal only handed Specter his dinner and motioned for him to move out.

They did.

They made the time they could in the failing daylight. Specter wanted to be across the road before it got too dark and, pushing, they made it. Specter wasn't as careful as he normally was, but he judged that speed outweighed spending the night outside.

As the night settled in, both dismounted and walked their mounts and the packhorse. They were blessed with a full moon, though. Specter took advantage of it as he could, staying in the open areas. Even up and walking, it wasn't long before Randal said, "I feel a bit woozy."

Specter got him up on his horse and then tied him to the horse much like he had with Shade. It was a good thing, too; Randal was out before Specter had finished tying his knots.

Specter tied the horses together and then continued on. It took a lot longer than a daylight ride would have, but at least they'd be there, rested, in the morning. Specter felt secure in approaching Byland's Rest even so soon after the attacks and events with Chairman Jones. Jones himself was probably not high enough to pose a problem, and the replacement procedures were most likely in their favor. That is, Chairman Jones's replacement was probably already trained and ready to take over his duties and then make sure any questions about Chairman Jones's whereabouts or condition were met with continuity measures and production numbers to further make his memory fade into the background.

As it was, Specter strode almost up to the barn door before being challenged. He knew he was being tracked – by Shade – but he didn't let on. As he had suspected, she had Jess and her friends on their own watches.

Robbie was the one who finally stopped him, rather blatantly, by stepping from behind the barn and charging a pump shotgun. Specter thrilled to that sound and wondered how long Aunt Lindsey had had that stowed away. "Stop," Robbie said simply and had the barrel up towards the left side of Specter's torso. While Robbie wasn't loud enough to wake the town, maybe because of pri-con presence, he was clear and direct in the silence. And within arm's reach. Specter, wearing his duster, took advantage of the teachable moment.

Specter reigned in his horse, but his left hand shot out and grabbed the barrel of the shotgun as he spurred his horse – dragging Robbie to the ground. Specter had the gun and was dismounted with the barrel at Robbie's face in an instant.

"Two things," Specter started, "Number 1: never get too close. With a shotgun, you don't have to be close enough to cut them in half in order to kill. And Number 2: never give up your weapon or allow it to be taken."

Specter replaced the barrel of the shotgun in Robbie's face with his hand. "Okay?" he asked.

"Yes," Robbie said as he took Specter's hand. Specter helped him regain his composure before moving on into the barn.

Shade appeared, a look of obvious concern on her face.

"Relax," Specter said. "He's just sleeping. I gave him a stim shot earlier so we could get everything done." Shade raised an eyebrow. "He agreed; I told him about it." He winked at her. "He was making something for you."

Only because he was looking for it did he see her quick response. *So that could get to her*, he thought. Gone as quickly as it was there, she said, "I was worried he might not be able to make any more bullets."

"Let's get inside so we can talk," Specter suggested. Shade motioned 'okay' with her hand. Specter untied Randal and carried him inside as Shade and Robbie unpacked and unburdened the animals. They set everything down in the far chamber, the one that Chairman Jones died in. Specter noticed the new sand covering up the larger bloodstains. Someone had lit a fragrance candle – some kind of vanilla derivative – that did a great job of redirecting the nose from sweat and blood.

They laid a little pallet out for Randal and set down all the ammunition from the packhorse. Shade commented on Randal's bow and Specter's shotgun. "We're loaded for bear," was all Specter said.

Chapter 43

Once they had unloaded everything, Robbie took care of the horses while Specter, Shade, and the others sat in the outer, first room and talked.

Shade was very direct as she told Specter about the last four days. Not much had happened in the way of pri-con intervention. Only one platform had been through town, and the locals, after hearing the young women's stories, were a lot less hospitable. The pri-cons had caused no trouble, and the town had let them leave unmolested. *That change in behavior might be a red flag in itself*, thought Specter.

Shade went on, discussing her work with Jess and her friends. "We've been going over each one's memory of the Creep and..."

"What's the Creep?" Specter interrupted.

Shade explained, "We couldn't decide whether it was a walled off house, a castle or what – so 'castle' and 'keep' together with what went on there – we've taken to calling it the 'Creep.'"

Specter nodded and Shade continued. "Jess and Natalie are..."

"Natalie?" Specter asked.

"The feisty one," Shade said, "the runner."

Specter nodded.

"McKensie is the other girl, the quiet one. You know Jake and Robbie," Shade added.

Specter nodded again.

"Well, Jess, Natalie, Jake, and Robbie are training with the rifle. They can already break it down and clean it. We've been doing drills. Aunt Lindsey did have some bullets, but not enough to amount to much. They know what a recoil feels like, but that's about it. We have been dry firing, but that's just not the same."

"McKensie?" Specter asked.

"McKensie has shown a predilection for and a fascination with knives. She's a much quieter person than the others but, interestingly, she's a knife-in-your-ribs kind of girl. I've been training her most intensely on hand-to-hand techniques, but also on blades. She actually whittled us out some knives and we've been practicing with those."

"Well, now. What do you know of this 'Creep'?" Specter asked.

Shade was more hesitant than usual, but it wasn't in her nature to hold back. "Jess is the most knowledgeable about it. Her parents got here yesterday. Let's sleep on it tonight, and we can go over everything – with her there – in the morning."

Specter could sense she was doing this for a reason. He would go along. "Okay," he said. "But we start early."

Chapter 44

They did indeed start early. Specter was used to getting up early, but Shade woke him earlier than he had thought. They were up for their morning run, and Shade thought it only fair to ask if Specter wanted to join them.

He did.

He soon found out, though, that this was no early morning stroll. Shade had actually built a makeshift obstacle course around the barn area. Most of it was running, but it was interspersed with great training ideas designed to make it more fun in a try-hard-and-puke sort of way. They ran between two buildings where they had braced two by six boards between the buildings and then secured old ladders on top of them – a kind of poor man's monkey bars. They ran from there on to another barn where they had run some solid iron bars in three horse stalls. The first three did pull-ups while the other three did push-ups, and then they switched. Right after, they had set up some solid wooden crates. The object there was to jump from one to another, always higher, to a balance beam on the top of the barn, then a rope climb back down to the ground. Running back to the first barn, there was a big surprise for Specter. On the outside of the barn, they had set up a rock climbing wall. They said they got the pieces from a now defunct gym and had repurposed them into a way to the top of the barn. Once up there, they hopped down on other crates to ground level. The circuit was reversed by a rope climb back up to the top of the barn, down the rock wall, and everything in reverse.

Specter was pleased the kids had such release. He was happy to see Jess join them after their first circuit and even more impressed to see Randal join them for their third and last one. He was not surprised to see Shade take an extra round to go through alone with Randal, though.

Specter had tried to make sure they could work and, more importantly, fight together. In such situations, however, it was not uncommon for a heated romance to develop – heated, because it usually ran hot and burned out quickly. After that, though, fighting together suffered. Knowing this, Specter had made a note to broach the subject with Shade.

For now, though, he followed Jake and Robbie to wash up and get ready for the day. He didn't interact much with the two; they would do better without a friend like him. Randal came in not too much later to the makeshift men's locker room – a room in the barn with two pitchers of water. "You feeling okay?" Specter asked him.

"Feeling good," Randal said. "Glad to be outside and active."

"Will you be up for some planning discussions today?" asked Specter.

"Yeah, sure – is that what we're doing?" Randal asked.

"Unless you've got other plans?" Specter asked.

"No, no," said Randal, abashed. "No, I just need some time on a range if we can work it."

"We'll see," said Specter. "I don't think it will be a problem." He thought a moment. "May I ask why?"

"That new idea I had, remember?" Randal replied. "I haven't had a chance to test it yet."

"And just what would that mean?" Specter began. "I know you're excited about it, but why?"

Randal looked really surprised. Then, he started to say something and then stopped. Twice. Then he asked, "What would you do if you knew you could wear what looked like regular clothes but were really webarmor – really bulletproof?"

Specter hadn't really thought about that before – not realistically anyway. Every kid has dreams about being a bulletproof superhero. Every soldier prays to be bulletproof. Every Hunter works very hard to be where the bullets are not.

It's different when you are not obviously armored up. Pri-cons are easily identifiable in their webarmor. He himself had seen the difference in those who recognized his duster as webarmor and those who didn't.

Randal broke into his thoughts, "You hadn't really thought about it, had you?" Randal was getting excited again. "Can you imagine what that would mean?"

Specter interrupted him, "No matter where you could go and how far you could get, you could still be dropped by a headshot."

Randal started to say something else, but Specter said again, "Headshot."

Randal just nodded and walked away.

After breakfast, Shade, Specter, Randal, and Jess and her friends all sat down in the barn. Shade stepped up and spoke first. "We're here today to go over everything we know about the Creep. I'm going to let Specter start us off and tell us what he needs."

Specter stood and unrolled a paper he was carrying. The map back at the bunker not only showed in three dimensions but would also project a two dimensional map onto a wall. One could then trace any map onto a role of paper with time and a pencil. Specter had already set up some boxes to hold it up and tacked it in place. It was an overview map of the area.

He began, "We are going to find this 'Creep' as you call it. Judging by Jess's recollection, it was a day trip from the Patterson farm. That's here," he pointed on the map. "With the range of a platform, that's roughly this area." Specter traced a circle around that field. "So, somewhere in here should be the 'Creep.' Using what Jess remembers of the sun on that day, we're thinking it's in this direction," again indicating it on the map.

"We also have information from the late Chairman Jones. The nature of his information was more directed at the pleasure dome itself, but, inadvertently, he did provide us with something useful. He said the few times he'd been there took a full day and a half of travel by platform. That puts us from here to somewhere in here." He drew another arc that intersected the circle of Jess's description.

"Looking at the intersection of these two, I have been able to narrow it down to four different possible locations. The maps I was using don't take into account new construction, so I was hoping to get a better idea of which place it might be."

Shade stood up and motioned at Jake and Robbie. They stood up and moved quickly around behind Specter into the boxes of Aunt Lindsey's inventory. Shade explained as they went, "We have something that's going to help you with that. It turns out that these kids are pretty adept with their hands." She looked pleased, like a commander pleased with her troopers' performance and allowed to show them off at review. Which probably was close to the truth. She looked at Specter, "You have maps of all the potential places?" she asked. She asked more for permission to look at them; she already knew he had them.

"Sure," he said, giving her what roll was left in his hand.

Shade called McKensie to help her hold out the different maps. The one she wanted turned out to be on top. "Your first choice?" she asked.

"It was the place I would've chosen, and it matches the distances," Specter answered.

All talk stopped, though, when Jake and Robbie came back. They were carrying a four by eight sheet of plywood with a mound of something on top of it. As they got closer, Specter and Randal could see that it was a model. Specter's eyes went wide and he turned, smiling, towards Shade. Randal caught on a bit later.

Jess and her friends had made a model of the Creep that Jess had described. Shade was proud of their handiwork. "It is to scale," she said. "1:18 ratio. That scale seemed to work better than anything bigger and seeing things helped bring back memories and other recollections. Working together, they all fed off each other." Shade was positively beaming.

"Just saved me a day of work," Specter said, smiling.

Jake and Robbie set the plywood sheet on some boxes Natalie and McKensie had set up. Everyone gathered around the model. No one spoke for a while as they all took it in, Specter and Randal seeing it all for the first time, everyone else watching their responses.

Specter kept looking at the model and then at the overview map. He would step around the model, ask a question or two, refer back to the map, and so on and so on.

Two things that struck Randal were the detail and the accuracy. Looking at the map, made from an aerial photograph, it looked for the most part like what you'd see if you climbed up on the rafters and looked down on the model.

The words came out of Specter's mouth without him being aware. "This didn't come from one person."

Shade picked up on it. "Once Jess had broken the ice, McKensie and Natalie opened up, too. It turns out that they would set up pick-ups mainly monthly, but we're still we're working that out. Jess just happened to be there only a couple of days before that scheduled pick-up. McKensie got there just a few days after the last pick-up. Natalie had about two weeks there."

"All at the same place?" Specter asked.

Shade took on a different tone – more of a military commander. "It appears that all around this area, these crews are going around and kidnapping girls and boys. There is also a second unit that goes farther out and does the same thing. There is some speculation about other areas like this one, but no credible evidence as yet."

Specter stopped walking around the model, took a few boxes, and made a high seat for himself. Climbing up, he said, "Why don't you tell me more about your model." It wasn't a question, and, seated, he was giving his full attention.

Shade had expected this and pulled out an extendable metal wand. Randal wasn't sure if it was part of an old metal grabber or an old car antenna. Shade, using the wand to point with, started at the road. "We may need to do some adjusting of the elevations here if you've got a contour map." Specter nodded, he did. "Great. First, for an overview, it looks like this place was built specifically for trading in human flesh and has been operational for some time. In other words, this place was built for defense, and it looks like no expense was spared. As you come up the road you notice a lot of switchbacks. This acts to slow vehicles, but it also provides multiple spots for sniper fire."

Shade motioned to McKensie before going on, "Looking at the angles and back planning, we think the most likely spots would be here, here, and here. McKensie put long, straight pointers on the road corners that pointed back to three spots. Randal saw that the pointers were just straws inserted together on ends – but reasonably straight.

Shade continued, "We may have to fine tune those locations if we have to adjust for elevations in your maps, Specter. But as you can see, it looks most likely that the best vantage spots are on the roof. The others are possibles, though."

"Next is the gate – or portcullis might be more accurate. From the road, this is the only entrance, and the only way to get a vehicle into the compound." Shade pointed to a second gate like the first. "There is a second gate that is never opened when the first one is. If that is just protocol or if the doors are designed that way, we don't know."

"Anything trapped between the gates is assuredly dead. It appears mostly as a searching place, but it's manned and guarded, and that makes it a killing field."

"As we get inside, though, it's a bit more open." With that, Shade lifted the top of the model – the roof – off.

"I am truly impressed," said Specter.

Inside the main building, all under one roof, was a 'U' shaped building that curved around a central open area. "You can see that there are three stories above ground. We're not sure how many are below. But you'll all notice there are no windows on the first floor, just on the upper two levels."

"McKensie overheard that was where customers would wait. The kidnapped were paraded on the grounds, and they chose which ones they wanted. Notice also on the front of the building the lack of windows until the second floor. So, no easy access from the front or from the inside courtyard. There are three doors opening to the inside, one on each side of the 'U': the bottom one set towards the middle, the two others set near the ends.

Shade opened the tiny door on the right of the 'U.' "We know from Robbie's trips there that there is a hallway directly across from the door and two stairwells going up, one left and one right. We assume it's the same on the left, but we're not sure."

"While we don't know much about the first floor," Shade said as she removed the third floor, "we do know some about the second floor." With the third floor removed, all could see lots of rooms, and it seemed like these would be the holding quarters. Shade confirmed it, "you'll notice all these rooms; these were – are – being used to house the kidnapped girls and boys. We know from McKensie that the doors latch locked when closed, and, while one person opened the door whenever it was opened – meals, bathroom – we can't say if that is the only key."

"On the opposite side of the rooms are more specialty rooms. Bathrooms at the two corners, here and here," Shade pointed them out. "They have showers, commodes, only three sinks. Then there is a salon on this side and an infirmary on the other. Those are exaggerations, of course. The salon is a chair where they cut your hair the way they want it, another at which they paint your face the way they want you, and a spray booth at which they paint your body up the same way. The infirmary has a couple of beds, some gauze, some tape, and not much else."

"There are stairs at the ends of the 'U' and another room at the base, but we don't know much about that room." Shade replaced the third floor and roof.

"Any information about the third floor?" Specter asked.

"No," Shade said. It was clear she wanted more information to give but couldn't produce it. "We know that people live there, so there's that. The workers and guards have to live there, so their quarters have to be somewhere, but up or down we don't know."

Specter got up from his makeshift chair and started down. Everyone waited for him to get down, waited for his insights and observations. Once down, he said, "I am thoroughly impressed." He paused for effect. "I think you have all done a marvelous job on this model and with the intelligence." He paused again, and most were waiting for the other shoe to drop. "Why don't we get some lunch and then come back after that?" Specter proposed.

"You don't like it," Shade said, naming the devil.

"It's not a question of like or dislike. It's a question of completeness," Specter responded.

"What do you…" Shade started but stopped when Specter held up his hand.

"I have no doubt that you have done a remarkable job. I've just said as much. But I'm also sure that there's more to fill in here, and the more we can fill in might mean the difference between living and dying," Specter said. To punctuate it, he added, "That doesn't just go for us. That goes for everybody inside there, too."

Everyone piled their own feelings into the resultant silence, filling it with whatever demons each sought to purge from this earth – all with the subconscious hope that they might be able to banish some of their own demons in the process. Each wondered what failure to do that would mean – what life their possible failure would give back to the demons. Randal waded first into that murkiness. "Let's just break, get some food, and then come back and see if we can push that much more."

They all broke up and went to find something to eat, except for Specter and Shade. Specter made it a point to seek her out, and they were talking animatedly as Randal looked back. Aunt Lindsey had been very generous, and they hadn't wanted for food. Jess's parents had brought out some sandwiches from the town proper, and Randal snatched up a couple. He found a little seat off to the side and listened as Jess and her friends talked.

The girls seemed visibly upset and the boys less so. By the boy's tone, though, they were upset as well, just more adept – or practiced – at hiding it. Most of the talk centered around what wasn't good enough for Specter, how they'd gone over everything so many times already, what Specter thought – did he think they were holding something back? When the conversation turned that way, Randal felt obligated to chime in.

"Specter does think you're holding something back," Randal said as he stood and walked closer. "But not the way you think. He thinks if he can hear you describe your experiences, he may be able to get more information from you."

They all started to object, but he held up his hand and they waited.

"Specter has been trained to pick up things other people overlook. He's one of the best out there. Now, look, he's not saying Shade didn't do the same thing and that this may be a waste of time. He's saying why not try just one more time?" Randal pressed his advantage, trying to use their focus on the negative and redirect it.

"Try to see his side of it, too. We don't know how many people are in there. We don't know how many are being held hostage. At the end of that day we attack, we will wipe out that house, that's a given. But can we do that and still save those being held inside?" Randal could see them thinking.

"Would you like to be locked in your room, hear gunfire and screams, and then your door opens and someone is shooting at you? Or open your door and someone says, 'Come on, we're going to take you home'?" He paused, giving them time. "What Specter's doing is trying the hardest he can to make sure we can save as many innocent people as we can while killing as many guilty people as we can. If a little more questioning and thought are required for that, then what are you really upset about?" Randal turned around without waiting for an answer.

Chapter 45

To his surprise, Specter and Shade were watching him. They were close enough to be in earshot, but their presence hadn't been enough for him to lose his hold on the kids. They had had their attention on him. Randal walked over to where they were standing.

"Good words," said Specter.

"You really had their attention," Shade said.

"I just see the importance – and was trying to get them to see," Randal replied. "You guys get everything worked out?"

Specter and Shade looked at each other. Shade said, after a pause, "Yes. Yes, I think we have come to an understanding." She reached for a sandwich and started eating. "The important thing is that we have as much information as we can – no matter who gets it."

Specter reached for a sandwich, too. After taking a bite he asked, "Do you know how many of them want to come along?"

Shade answered, "I think it's unanimous for them," she paused and looked at both of them. "They all want to stay here." Shade was pleased with Specter's and Randal's reaction.

"Really?" Randal asked as more of a statement.

"They all want to learn to shoot and want access to weapons, but they want some time away from action. Even Natalie, who seemed so ready that first night, changed her mind. Jake may have convinced her otherwise. Yeah, even Jake and Robbie, who talked very rough and ready, seemed to deflate after talking with Chairman Jones." Shade stole a quick look at Specter with her eyebrow raised in a question. "You know anything about that, Specter?"

Specter was looking down, and he didn't respond right away. It was almost as if he didn't hear the question. Shade looked at Randal, and when Randal opened his mouth to speak, Specter finally said, "Good." He didn't look up; he then repeated, "Good." Specter repositioned himself and said, "They know what it means to mete out justice, and how it changes you to carry out a death sentence. They won't rush to spill blood without a clear conscience. That's one hell of a lesson to learn that early, but it will stick with both of them, and they'll be better men for it. They won't forget that."

No one wanted to break the silence that followed.

Specter finally did. "Speaking of lessons to learn, Shade, do you think you could teach Randal here the finer points of a pri-con rifle?"

The question took her aback, but she responded quickly nonetheless, "If I had enough time, I could."

"Well, you've got the afternoon, then," Specter announced.

"What?" Randal and Shade asked together.

"Look, I think I'll do better with...," Specter pointed to Jess and her friends, "if I'm alone. And Randal, while effective so far in our engagements, is not assault trained. I think he'd be more effective at a distance and not up close." He looked at Randal. "No offense meant, but I need to make sure that only bad guys get shot. That's hard to tell in the half second after you open a door, but that's what we need." He paused to take another bite of sandwich. Mouth half full, he added, "Plus, I thought you needed to test something on the range. And, didn't you have something to give Shade?"

Randal's embarrassment was overtaken by his thirst for knowledge. He had forgotten about testing the new webarmor fabric. "I've got something for you, too, Specter," he said.

"I left some regular bullets in a pack," Specter said. "We don't have an unlimited supply of bullets, but if no one's going with us, I'd just as soon we use as many as we need to make sure Randal can hit what he's aiming at."

"And you want us to go now?" Shade asked.

Specter didn't miss a beat, "Well, right after you eat, yeah."

"And out until?" she asked.

"You can bring us dinner; we might be done by then. If not, well, we'll see," said Specter.

Shade picked up another sandwich and said, "We sure will!" She started out of the barn and Randal, not wanting to be left, hurried to catch up.

Shade turned around abruptly and almost ran into Randal. He put his hands up to catch her to avoid a collision, but she stopped short. Randal was left standing there with his hands up.

Shade looked at his hands – up as they were – about the height of her breasts. She looked at him and asked, "You were going to run into me, and that's how you were going to stop us from running into each other? By my breasts?" She delighted in the different shades of red Randal turned. After he spluttered and spurted a bit, she laid her hand on his shoulder. "I was joking," she said. "We need to get the rifle and ammo before we leave."

"Right," Randal managed.

She withdrew her hand and then stepped past him on her way to the cache. The exchange made Randal think about her outfit. He went to his things and packed her red outfit, her special shirt, and her special shirt fabric remnant to test. He went back up and saw Shade talking to Jess's parents. He walked up and, just before he got there, Jess's parents walked away, back towards town.

Shade turned as he approached. "Sorry I broke up your conversation," Randal said.

"I was just asking them if any pri-cons were in town. She said 'no,' but it might be worth a check," Shade answered.

"Can we not trust her?" Randal asked.

"I'm sure we can," answered Shade.

"Then let's trust her," said Randal.

"You want to get shooting, don't you?" she asked.

"I do have something specific to test," he said.

"Well," Shade thought about it and came to a decision. "Okay. Let's take the horses, though."

"Great," he said.

And so they were off. Apparently Shade had had time to explore the surrounding area. She led them both out of town, heading more easterly, all the while setting a good, quick pace. It seemed she needed to ride something out, so Randal did what he could to stay close and quiet.

After about three or four miles, she slowed and he pulled alongside. They rode in silence for a little while, until Randal felt he had to say something. "Do you have a certain spot picked out?" he asked.

"In a sense," she answered. "It's away from town and in a valley. It will also allow for hiding if we have to run."

They rode on, and Randal thought about a saying he'd heard long ago: "Don't start nothin', won't be nothin'." It was said in the context of a fight and may actually have been the words setting off the brawl. But Randal had used it for motivation ever since. If he didn't take advantage of this time to try and get to know Shade, he might not get another chance.

So, reciting the motto to himself, he asked, "So, Shade, are you alright with what happened back there?"

"I'd rather not talk about it," she said flatly.

Randal doubled down. "Don't you think you should, though?"

Shade looked at Randal, judged his motives, and sighed audibly. "We spent a lot of time on that. The kids did anyway. I grilled them over and over on what they remember and what they remember other people saying. And then, Specter comes in all, 'I can get more out of them' like I hadn't tried that already, and then the kids think they're not good enough and…"

"Or that he thinks they're holding something back…" added Randal.

"Yeah," Shade looked over at him surprised. "Yeah, they think – hey!"

Her accusatory tone caught him by surprise. "What?" Randal asked.

"What're you trying to do? Why do you want to know?" she asked accusingly.

Randal was surprised and taken aback. But more so, it made him mad. He spurred his horse forward and cut her off. "Where do you get off? I want to know because we're friends – or at least getting to be friends, I thought – and we've fought together and are getting ready to fight again. And I'd just like to make sure you're okay."

Shade didn't back off and said heatedly, "Yeah – or what?"

That caught Randal by surprise but in the opposite manner. He actually laughed. He said with a smile, "Or I'd try to help you be okay would be what." He chuckled again while watching Shade.

He could almost read her thoughts through her expressions. First, there was embarrassment for what she'd said. The smile that started in her eyes showed she knew it sounded funny. And then there was – a warmth. A warmth that rose from knowing that she had a friend who cared for her.

"I'm sorry for being smart. I just…" she trailed off searching for the right words. "I hate feeling inept," she finally mustered.

Randal looked at her with as much compassion he could put in a smile and said, "Welcome to the human race."

Shade smiled. She smiled warmly at him. *Well*, he thought, *don't start nothin' won't be nothin'*.

Randal found he was not prepared for the afternoon, though. Once they reached the little valley, he was in for some intense training. The pri-cons – the only real military of the day – had specific step-by-step instructions for firing a weapon. Shade, having been through that, put Randal through that. It was no afternoon picnic.

Whatever Shade was going through or feeling was easily pushed aside. She did not lose sight of the fact that she had to teach him how to shoot, and she focused and led the training based on that.

Randal was an avid hunter, though, if avid means if you don't kill something, you don't eat. Hunger tends to make avid hunters. Through his hunting, Randal had learned to keep still, focus his breathing, and keep his hands steady. All that helped him in learning the finer points of the rifle.

And Shade made him shoot and shoot. Always a controlled shot, never a rushed shot. Shade told him, "In a gunfight – as you know – you are amped and jacked and you will be faster, but you've got to learn the basics slowly so you won't be inaccurate when the pressure is on." And then she put more pressure on.

The afternoon wore on, and they were about out of bullets. They had shot mostly at trees and, as they were winding down, Randal stopped for a minute.

"I need to try something," he said and brought out a blood red piece of cloth.

"What is that?" Shade asked.

"You'll see," he said. Randal then went and, unrolling the cloth, saw how long it was and found a tree of just the right width. In the valley area, the side of the bank they were shooting towards was very steep, and the ground formed the perfect backdrop for the bullets. The tree Randal had found quickly found itself tied in Randal's dark red cloth.

Randal ran back the fifty yards and, sure enough, on that tree you could see the two to three inch strip of red cloth tied to it. Taking the rifle from Shade, Randal got prone, sighted at the cloth, and fired.

"You missed it," Shade said.

Randal shot again.

"Unh-uh," Shade said.

Randal used that as he stood up. "'Unh-uh' sounds a lot like 'uh-huh' which neither sounds like 'yes' or 'no.' I didn't see anything so I think you said 'no'. Either way," he held out the rifle, "will you please put a bullet through it?"

Shade smiled and took the rifle. Standing, she sighted in, waited, then squeezed the trigger. "That's odd," she said, and she was already sighting again. This time she fired two shots, one right after the other. "That did it," she said.

Randal said, "Let's go see." He walked by his horse and picked out her shirt. He was going to give it to her anyway – the bulletproofing would be the extra. He folded it up and carried it behind his back as he followed Shade up to the tied tree.

Once there, he was greeted with what he did not want to see. The cloth had been shot and was not intact – not fully intact anyway. It was obvious where the bullets had hit, and while not every bullet got all the way through, most of them did. The double tap Shade had shot last did stick into the tree. The first bullet made a hole in the tree (deformed the cloth to the bullet hole in the tree), but the second bullet got hung in the same hole. The cloth held it there, but it was torn through.

Shade, surveying the damage, spoke first, "Well, it's better than nothing, I guess. Is this your next step up from coating bullets?"

"It was supposed to be," Randal said, upset that it was back to the drawing board. He turned to walk back when he realized the shirt was in his hand. He turned, "Oh, well, you can have this," he handed it to Shade. "I thought you might like having another one of those. I was hoping it would be bulletproof, but..."

Shade took it and was genuinely thankful. New clothes were always a commodity but, well, she hadn't had a gift from someone who genuinely liked her and cared about her for a long while.

At least she's making me think she likes it, Randal thought

They got everything together and started back towards town. Shade started out the ride with, "How did you choose a color that looks like dried blood?"

That started a long explanation of the acidity of the bath, what makes the fibers of webarmor accept colorant, the dye that Specter supplied him with... Randal realized too late that he had talked too much about himself. When that hit home, he wrapped it up with, "Well, really I like dark red and wanted to see you in it."

His abrupt ending made her smile. "Fair enough," she said. They rode in silence until she said, "I do thank you for it." And she looked at him and smiled. It must've been what he wanted, because he positively beamed.

They rode the rest of the way in silence. It would be tomorrow that they were scheduled to ride out. There were a lot of questions surrounding that trip. Did Specter get more information from Jess and her friends? How many people would show up to go with them? What were they going to do with the people they saved? Many more such questions clamored for attention in their minds. They each hoped those questions would be answered, and they rode back with that hope.

Chapter 46

Arriving at the barn, Shade and Randal tended to the horses and then went to find Specter and the others. What they found really surprised them. Opening the doors to the barn, they saw probably thirty people. They looked like regular people, but they were armed. They were pretty well distributed, maybe fifteen to twenty men and ten to fifteen women. Most were middle aged, although some were older. Few were as young as Jess and her friends.

Specter found them and came up. "I've been looking for you two."

"Need somebody to cook supper?" Shade asked. She could see that the jab hurt him. No one else could probably see that, but she did.

"No," Specter said simply.

"You're waiting on us to go over the plan?" Randal asked.

Specter's look of surprise seemed out of place to Randal, and, when he looked at Shade, he could tell she thought something was out of place as well. Specter directed them back outside and away from the door. Randal had never seen him like this, had never thought to see him like this. He seemed...out of his element.

"Waiting on you for the plan?" Specter started. "What about having a plan? You think of that?" His tone spoke of anger but his face told a story of desperation.

Randal wanted to jump in before Specter got too wound up. Shade, seeing him about to speak, laid her hand on his arm, clearly telling him to be quiet. He patted her hand as he ignored her. "What exactly is upsetting you so badly?" Randal asked.

Specter whirled on Randal, and it drove Randal's mind back to the road and the death machine that Specter had become that day. Now all of that was focused on him. But part of Randal's make up included an overdeveloped sense of justice. And Randal felt that the anger directed against him was not justified.

Randal, against even his own instincts of self-preservation, matched Specter's venom and vituperation, and he stepped into Specter's personal space, poking his finger into Specter's chest as he said, accentuating each word, "You back off."

Specter seemed shocked and further angered, and he drew back his hand, but then he opened his fist and looked down. He took a deep breath and spoke to the ground. "These people are all looking for me to have a plan, some kind of idea of what to do." He looked up at them. "I don't have that. I know what I would do, but I have no idea about how to use thirty people. That's what I was waiting on you for – so we could get a plan together. These people won't follow unless it looks like we know what we're doing. More importantly, I don't want to put them into harm's way unless I know we've got a good plan."

"Really?!" exclaimed Randal, incredulous. "That's what you're so upset about?"

"I know individual tactics, not small unit tactics..." Specter began.

Randal interrupted him, "You need to relax, Specter. Just let everybody give their ideas and shoot down what's wrong with each idea. When someone finally says, 'What's your idea, then?,' you just combine the best parts of each."

Shade stepped in, literally, and used her command voice, a tone that brooked no dissent, "Dismiss them for a meal. We'll eat by the model and discuss the plan. Let me give the overview and, as each brings forth a plan or suggestion, take note, and incorporate the best you hear." She put her hand on his shoulder, "These people want something you cannot give them. Deep down they know that. All they need is an outlet for their pain and frustration, a means for them to do something, a means to act when they haven't yet had the opportunity."

Randal caught on to what Shade was doing and saw that it was working on Specter. "Most of these people probably have had kids in Jess's situation – missing – and they think they'll be sitting there in a room when we attack. The reality is that most are probably already dead. You can't give them what you don't have." He paused. "Shade's right. You give them a chance to do anything other than search, and they will follow you – good plan or bad."

Specter took another large breath in. "I'll go tell them to take an hour and eat. That'll give us time to get a rough plan together. We'll expand that as we need to."

Randal stopped him. "They've already got something to believe in. They just need the excuse to act."

Specter nodded and went back in the barn to make the announcement. Randal started to follow him but was stopped by Shade's hand on his arm.

"You had better watch yourself," she said as he turned around.

Randal tried to laugh it off, but she took his shirt in her fists and pushed him, then pulled him – shaking him up more than just physically. "You have no idea how close you just were. You could have been dead."

"So you're showing me just how close I was?" Randal asked.

Shade was close enough to Randal that he saw her pupils dilate at the same time he saw her right hand rise. The fire then bloomed in his left cheek as that hand connected with his face. Her eyes never released his, and her words echoed in his ears, "There are times to keep quiet or you get killed. One more like that and you are dead." Her intensity radiated over him and seared her words into his memory.

Shade let go of his shirt, patting his chest there with her hands and smoothing his shirt. "You've been told. Next time you're on your own." She wiped at his face and hair. "You need to apologize for that to Specter."

"That is going too far," Randal said. "I appreciate your concern, but he's got to learn to control his anger."

The shock on her face shocked him in return. "Our responses keep us alive, and it's not easy to check reflexes." She patted his chest and then patted his cheek. Something strange started happening to Randal. Shade's demeanor and actions made him distinctly feel like he was a corpse and she the undertaker prepping him for viewing – making sure he looked as good as he could in death.

"I've told you," she said and brusquely turned away.

Randal's feeling of being already dead was intensified with those words. He thought that this must be what Jesus felt when Pilate washed his hands: discarded, done away with, abandoned. *Fair enough*, he thought; he resolved to speak with Specter.

Randal followed Shade into the barn and just avoided the efflux of people coming out. He had stepped just inside the door and was blocked by people filing out. He looked at each one as they filed past.

Randal was struck by the wide range of ages represented, the parity of just about as many women as men, and the wide range of weapons. But, more importantly, he was struck by the group emotionally.

Naturally some were angrier and some were happier or, at least not as angry. But underneath all of the surface looks burned an intense need for action. These folks wanted to do something and, more, they looked like they had wanted to do something for a long time. They would tolerate some delay, but not much. This was going to be a fast dinner.

Once all had exited, Randal wasted no time and went straight up to Specter. Looking him right in the eye, Randal said, "I apologize for my outburst earlier. I..."

Specter interrupted. "Stop. I appreciate the sentiment; enough said." He looked back at Randal and asked, "Did she tell you to apologize?"

Randal swallowed and said, "She may have mentioned that it was in my best interest to do it, yes."

Specter regarded Randal. "You are the third person who has ever done that to me, though," Specter confided.

Randal couldn't believe that. "Even growing up – and in your line of work?" Randal asked.

"Well," Specter smiled, "three that I've left alive after doing it."

Randal swallowed hard and said, "I will try to remember..."

Specter interrupted again, "Your place? Now all that you're trying to do is keep me from killing you."

Randal could feel his face getting hot, his neck getting red, his sense of justice being trampled on. Instead of calming it, he used it.

Distinctly and with visible effort, Randal kept his voice even. "I will try to remember that you result to violence more quickly than most in the future." He continued with difficulty, getting angrier with each word. "Regardless of what she said, I see the utility of working together, and I freely acknowledge that I haven't done that in a while, and it may come off as abrasive. But understand this," he held up his finger, that same poking finger, "I mete my words carefully to pay the thoughts that I give voice. I invest each with value..."

Specter interrupted him again. "You mean what you say and you won't apologize for it, right?"

"I shouldn't feel like I have to apologize for it," Randal responded.

Specter looked at Randal and did so in a long, considering way. He folded his arms and finally spoke. "You should feel free to speak your mind. It's hard for me to work with people after working alone for so long. I'll try to hold back my temper and give you the freedom to speak your mind."

"I'll do better, too," said Randal.

Shade came up, "We okay here?"

Randal looked at Specter as Randal said, "We're wasting time. Just as Specter said earlier, we've got a plan to make because these folks want to know something."

"Very well, then," said Shade, "let's get started. I've already asked McKensie to bring us something to eat."

And so the planning started.

Chapter 47

They first went to the model. Jess and her friends were working on it. *Probably adding what Specter found out*, Shade thought. There they were, indeed adding things. After working with the kids for as long as she had, the changes stood out clearly to her. For starters, there was an exercise room, a fountain in the courtyard, some small rooms on the third floor, and a large open room, also on the third floor, replete with a bar.

There were other additions as well, but those were the main ones. Natalie noticed her looking at the model and told her that Specter just kind of asked some weird questions and such. Shade told her she was glad he asked those questions. Unified front and all that. The bottom line was like Randal had said, though. Anything they knew would help. They would be fine; it would be the people captive inside that would be in trouble.

Looking at the model, Shade acknowledged that this would be difficult. Again she blocked out the thought of how easy it would be to just go in and fight through. At least the pri-cons they killed wouldn't do it again. Seeing the faces in the barn tonight, though, she knew that wouldn't be an option. Hell, with even the best plan there was a good chance everything would start going to hell, and they'd shoot their captives anyway.

As McKensie gave out the food, Shade took hers and listened as Randal and Specter went over the assault. She had to admit that Randal was a pretty smart guy. He had some good ideas, some insights, but some of the things he asked about were totally way off base. Mostly, if a question seemed out of place, Randal would justify it or at least explain his rationale for asking it. To his credit, he seemed to pick up on things quickly and learn as he went along. *Probably what made him such a good Runner*, she thought.

Specter for his part seemed to be taking it as more of an educational exercise, giving – it seemed – two reasons why every idea wouldn't work. That included his ideas. Maybe that was how he planned, but it seemed to her that mostly he kept going back to how many Creepers – those inside the Creep – he could take out before they killed the captives. Specter would focus on individual tactics and neglect the advantage that squad tactics would provide.

Shade put her own ideas forth, too, and each seemed tactically sound until Specter started picking it apart. It didn't take long to realize that the plan would have to center around having someone inside. Whether already there or in there pretty fast, they had to get someone inside.

Randal put forth the best worst idea – that of simply running ladders up to the second floor windows. Specter was quick to point out that ladders are heavy and make those carrying them slower and easier to shoot, how they slow people when climbing them, along with the burden of carrying a large ladder on a long journey.

Because no one could think of a better way before people started ambling back inside the barn, they decided to go with it and hope they heard a better idea during the meeting. Shade felt sure they would think of something better, but she set about helping McKensie make a few ladders out of sticks and string. It was actually more of a selfish thing; she did her best thinking while her hands were occupied. Specter also told her that he'd take the meeting anyway; she wouldn't have to. That meant she could sit towards the back and hear the talk that wouldn't reach the front, all the while just acting like an unobtrusive, simple helper.

As Specter called everyone's attention, Shade moved towards that back left of the group, more to where the vocal holdouts had positioned themselves. She had been trained as a Hunter, but one of her natural strengths was picking out the dissenters in a group.

Something rang in her ears when she walked in a crowd. Somehow she was specifically attuned to those who didn't agree with the rest of the bunch. She insinuated herself not in the group, but just beside it, and close to the few she'd have to impress so she could win them over later, all the while just tying string and stick together.

Specter gave a brief introduction to everyone – interestingly (and thankfully) not mentioning his or her past. He took some time showing the overview map and discussing the best routes up to the Creep, as it would be referred to for at least this operation.

They decided on the location where they would rendezvous because a group this large would make it too difficult to travel all together. Once that had been taken care of, Specter brought out the model and then started going over all the aspects of it. He stayed away from tactics and just explained all they knew about the Creep. As Specter finished explaining, he moved to the side and asked, "Now, how do we get the kids that are there now out alive?"

He was met with stone cold silence.

Randal jumped in quickly and said "We've got an idea but want to hear your insights."

"What's your plan?" Shade asked loud enough for those around her to hear, but for Randal only to barely pick up. Loudly she said, "You first." Shade got some approving nods from her neighbors.

Shade gauged the feel of the crowd and found one overwhelming motivation. Just as she had intuited earlier, these people wanted to act more than anything. Most, in fact, were strong proponents of tactics that would shed a lot of needless blood if they felt the alternative was no action at all. That sentiment seemed to slow progress a lot. Perhaps some here had been counseled into not acting before.

At one particularly tense time, Randal showed some good diplomatic skills by getting louder than either arguing side and saying, "My goodness, folks! We are not arguing about if we're going to go or not. We are going. We're discussing," he stressed the word, "which way we can do that without losing half the people here."

Doing that seemed to rejuvenate and refocus everyone on who the enemy was and the purpose of the meeting. Everyone – after that – worked better together and directed their energy to finding solutions and not faults. Specter would point out problems with ideas while Randal acted as a good diplomat, mainly helping people let go of bad ideas.

Shade took it all in, adding her two cents, snickering or balking when needed. She had worked her way into the dissention ranks and gently helped them to go where she wanted them to. She knew the bigger payoff would come in the fight, though. She knew these people would have to trust her in order to put themselves in danger during a fight. She would trade on her place now to get them to do what needed to be done in the fight, and she knew they would. It was a lesson she had learned early on. In blood.

After about two hours, it seemed like all had been decided. Their original plan had been modified; there were some competent people in the barn that night. And that thought set Shade's mind in motion. As soon as she thought of it, there was almost not time to react. She ran up to McKensie and Natalie, telling them, and then Jake and Robbie. As she turned, she was face to face with Randal.

"What's up?" he asked.

"I need a code," his face went blank as she spoke. "Something that these folks can remember and that we can use to know each other."

Randal asked, "And tell those 'not us' people apart?"

"Yeah – and quick!" She looked as Jake and Robbie appeared armed at the barn door and McKensie and Natalie, also armed, got on the second floor where they had good shots.

"Hey, how about..." Randal started.

Shade interrupted him. "Great, I like it. Tell everybody when I give you the chance." *This should be the perfect exclusionary tactic*, she thought. She jumped up on some boxes and addressed the crowd. "Before we break up and head up to the Creep, I think we all need to second guess ourselves." She delighted at the quizzical looks. She caught sight of Specter, and he tapped his fingertip on his nose and pointed to her, signaling that she was doing the right thing.

She went on. "We've been talking about some pretty seditious stuff – things that the Enclaves don't want us talking about – things that pri-cons question people about." That riveted their attention to her. "Do you know everyone here?" She let the question penetrate like she had just doused them with gasoline.

Then she gave them the lit match. "Is that person next to you a pri-con?" Murmurings rose up, and, instead of letting it conflagrate, Shade threw dirt on it. "Calm down. Calm down. What I'm saying is that we want to save these kids at the Creep and get kids like Jess back to their parents, right?"

Shade knew she had them as they all said, "Right!" She kept the pressure on. "We want to make sure they don't do that stuff ever again, right?"

"Right!" the group echoed as one.

"We want some clue about those we've lost, right?"

There was a muted response on that one. It sounded like some had just made a groan while others had started to say 'right' and stopped halfway through – conscious of their loss. It was exactly what Shade wanted to hear.

"That's right!" she continued. "That's right because it hurts, right?" She poured it on, "Well, we can damn sure make sure that no one else has to feel that pain, right?!"

"Right!" echoed the group.

"Now. Let's make sure we don't get sabotaged right from the start. Look around you and each of you get five people that you know," she held up her hand, fingers out. "Get to know them if you don't, but everybody gets five. Go!"

Everyone there started getting to know each other. It went way beyond five, but a lot of the people had come with someone they knew. It wasn't a crowd of five hundred people, so it was easy for most to meet everyone. Even the very reclusive, introverted people felt the obligation to get five people.

Shade got back down; she knew some would want her to be one of their five. She also wanted to implant the faces in her memory. After a sufficient time, she stood back up on her boxes and addressed them again.

"Okay, okay, everybody. Everybody got your five?"

"Yeah!" everyone said together.

"What about you?" she singled out a guy halfway back.

"Yeah!" he yelled.

"Well, who are your five?" Shade asked pointedly.

"Well, right here we are!"

Shade picked out the woman beside him, "You're one of his five?"

"Yeah," she answered. Then the woman went on with names and pointed out each one, names of their collective kids, and some quirky fact about each of the five.

"Okay," Shade said approvingly. "That's what I want. That's what I want so when we meet at the rendezvous we will know everyone there. So we will know who <u>doesn't</u> belong there." She let the implications of that sink in. "Now," Shade continued, "does anybody need some more time?"

There was not a cheer so much as a collective groan of approval. Everyone then turned and talked with their neighbors a lot more intently – like their lives depended on it, which they probably did. In the interim, Shade found Randal and dragged him up to the boxes with her. "Don't let me down," she said to him. "Everyone listen up!" she said. "Randal here has a password for us all to use." Then she motioned for him to go ahead.

"It's kind of weird," he started, "but it should be memorable. Most all of us remember making words on a calculator. Well, what we're going to spell stands for 'obliterate Enclave establishments'. It's three, three, zero. That can be: 3.30 or 33.0 or 330. When we rendezvous and you don't recognize someone, you can say 'it took me 3.30 days to get here.' Or 'I came 330 miles to be here.' Or 'it cost me 33.0 bottles of whiskey.' The person you're talking to will then answer back with something similar that has 3-3-0 in it." Randal finished, hoping that was clear to everyone.

Specter drove that point home from the back. "If you give that password or challenge to someone at the rendezvous point, and that person does not answer in kind," he paused making sure he had their attention, "you can assume that person is a spy from an Enclave or a pri-con." Pausing again for full effect, he continued, "That means you should shoot that imposter as soon as you can." Specter looked around at the group. "See the importance of the challenge?"

There were murmurs of assent.

"What is the number?" Specter asked.

"330," was the clearest number Specter heard. He looked up at Randal and loudly said, "Hey, you, up front! I just ate 330 raisins."

Randal looked a bit surprised but then said, "I was born 330 miles from here."

Specter looked back at the crowd. "See how that works? Before we get everybody there and no one recognizes you as one of their five yet, start by using 3-3-0. If you get no response, consider the other person hostile and kill that imposter as quickly as you can."

The seriousness had returned.

Shade spoke up, "I know we don't expect it, but it could happen, so if the pri-cons pick you up, say nothing. If they torture you, hold out. When you can't hold out, give them the number: 1-3-3-0. When they ask you why, it's for 'Obliterate every Enclave insider'. Backwards that's 1-3-3-0.

The friendlier mood had shifted back a bit to a halting trust seasoned with trepidation. Everyone seemed glad to have a group of them together, but there was no more denying their real purpose.

They were going out to kill. And that was serious business – that had ramifications.

Specter stepped forward in the silence. He knew the thoughts of those present. He realized this might be the first time some would face conflict – let alone a life or death action. He tried to keep it simple. "We've all had a lot to think about here. Shade, Randal, and I are leaving tomorrow. The way I figure it, it'll take about six days to get to the rendezvous – five days if you push it. We're going to attack the eighth day, so be ready and rested."

He could see the fear in some faces, the eagerness in others. In all the faces, he could see the purpose they had – the drive. "Make no mistake, there's going to be killing on that eighth day. If you're not ready for that or think twice about that, that's fine. Nobody here will fault any who don't show at the rendezvous – or if they show up late." He knew he had just given some of them the out they needed.

"But remember this. We're going up there because they are kidnapping children and handing them over for all sorts of hideous and heinous things. And these self-serving sons-of-bitches don't give a goddam. So we're going up there to make sure they don't hurt anyone else – ever. So sleep on it. Think about it. If you're still clear, join us eight days from now to set things right."

Chapter 48

The meeting broke up quickly. The group had a lot to think about and they had a lot of traveling to do. There would be time for reflection tonight in the quietness between wakefulness and sleep. For some, that was when their demons held their sway. For others, it was only a delay, necessary as sleep. The thing that kept Randal, Specter, and Shade from sleep was packing. Randal helped Specter load the guns and ammunition for the pack horse while Shade tended the other horses. They would head out early, and they all wanted everything ready.

Once finished, Randal called them over to his pack. He could have made a big deal of the presentation but, in the interest of sleep, did not. He simply handed Specter a dark blue bundle of clothes and Shade a blood red bundle of clothes. These were their new webarmor clothes, and Specter and Shade were very pleased with them. Randal assured them they were bulletproof – tried and tested. Specter and Shade, trying them on right then, were impressed with the custom fit. Shade showed her appreciation with a big hug and a kiss on the cheek for Randal. It was the wink she gave him after the kiss that stuck in his mind, though.

After they had packed everything, they let Jake and Natalie stand watch for them so each could have some uninterrupted sleep. They took advantage of that time, knowing that there would be time for introspection on the long days of travel. They would have the time to explore their motivations. Some would need no further such exploration. Randal found himself in the latter category.

Randal didn't expect to find his thoughts leading him to the same conclusion. He had felt generally conflicted for most of the time he'd been with Specter and then with Shade, but not now. After Jess's story, he was certain this was the right course.

When morning came, they ate breakfast, and set out directly after preparing the horses. Some rain started early, but stayed light. Randal followed Specter, and Specter set a good steady pace starting off. Shade brought up the rear and made sure they were not followed. One concern she had was that some of the children of the town would try to trail them. She was thankful for the rain which acted as a natural deterrent to freeloaders. Shade was more thankful for the sun when it decided to come out before midmorning. She felt it bode well for the journey.

What Randal didn't expect, though, after the sunshine, was the weather over the next few days. It turned out that they had been traveling for four days and had seen two and a half days of rain. Rain on the trail was something he was prepared for, but the sheer volume of this rain was something he hadn't seen in a few years. And so it was that after a day and a half of good weather, they saw two and a half full days of rain. That was when Specter started adjusting their route.

Early on, Specter had led them in the woods as much as possible to lessen the rain's impact. After they were thoroughly soaked, however, the lines were straighter and corners and bends started straightening up, too.

That little change, the decision to straighten up a little, turned out to be the butterfly's wing flap that caused a typhoon on the other side of the planet. That series of random decisions turned out to be a primary bifurcation point for Randal, Specter, and Shade. That little change put them on a collision course with a farmhouse in the woods.

Chapter 49

It was late afternoon, but the rain had blotted out the sun, and they knew they'd have to make camp soon. There was some debate later about who saw the farmhouse first because, almost on top of each other, Shade said, "I smell smoke" while Randal said, "I see lights." Following both, Specter led them toward the light and the smell of smoke, into the front yard of the farmhouse. Shade said, "I'll check the door." She dismounted and went to the door to knock. She rapped loudly at the door.

Specter kept his horse and scanned the house. The lighting looked electric because there was no flicker of light, just a steady glow. That made it easier to pick up movement. He picked up movement in four different windows and knew there had to be at least the same number of people inside. From the yard alone, he knew that; you couldn't keep a yard looking that well-manicured and tended without help and time. He couldn't see behind the house, but Specter noticed some corn already starting to sprout and figured they had a pretty big garden.

Shade, as well as Specter, heard the front door latch disengage, and Shade stepped back as the door cracked open.

A woman's voice came from the crack, "Who is it?"

Shade answered, "I'm Shelly. I'm here with two men, Reevis and Spencer." Shade gave fake names by habit.

"What do you want?" the voice asked.

"Shelter. A dry spot where we can rest and get dry, maybe have something to eat," Shade replied.

Randal barely caught a glimpse of the woman inside as she peered around the door. She looked to be about sixty years old. Shade stepped in between them, and Randal lost his view. He heard Shade say, "Please, we're soaked and we can pay, do chores, help, whatever."

Then, unexpectedly, the door flung wide open and a child, maybe three years old, ran onto the porch and hugged Shade's leg. As surprised as she was, Shade hugged the girl back with her left hand as she gently turned to the right so she could replace her tomahawk without being obvious. Shade said, "You scared me, little girl! How are you? I'm wet, I know!"

Shade picked the girl up and held her.

The woman did not shut the door back. She looked out at Specter and Randal and waved them in. "You can put your horses under the lean-to and, well, you may as well come in."

They did so.

Randal and Specter decided to leave most of their gear with the horses and, although Specter unbuckled and left his gun belt in his pack, Randal kept his on. As they came back up on the porch, they saw that Shade and the lady of the house were standing just inside the door. Randal was shocked to see the woman he thought was sixty years old. She couldn't have been older than thirty, but she was obviously frail and sick. Randal figured either cancer or anorexia. Randal introduced himself, she gave her name as 'Ginger,' and he was afraid he was going to break her hand as he shook it.

She shuttled Randal and Specter into a front room and told them they could change into dry clothes and then took Shade on down the hall to another room. Something had set Randal on edge, and he didn't feel he could relax. There were too many discrepancies – too many things that didn't match. He mentioned it to Specter as they got into dry clothes. Specter asked, "What things?"

Randal said, "Well, having a young lady who looks like she's way older?"

"Disease," Specter answered simply.

"A hitching post way up here with no horses?"

"Neighbors have horses," Specter said.

"Lights – electric lights?"

"Generator. Solar. Whatever. Pre-planning, like the bunker," Specter replied.

"A girl too scared to talk – yet runs out to Shade and won't let her go?"

"Kids," Specter snorted.

Randal gave up – for now.

Changed, they went back to the living room. Shade was already there, and she was surrounded by children. *Maybe that's why she's so aged and frail*, Randal thought. There had to be – Randal counted – ten children around Shade, and not one could've been older than twelve years old.

Specter went right into the room and started playing with the kids. Rather, he tried to, but each child drew away from him. The woman, Ginger, said, "It's just because you're new. We don't get many visitors. Gordon should be back home soon, and," she looked right at Shade, "he's going to be happy to meet you all."

Randal stayed on the edge of the room, afraid of going all the way in. Something in his gut told him something was horribly wrong here. There was a smell you couldn't smell, a scent you couldn't detect but knew was there. An odor detected by the mind and not the nose. And both Shade and Specter seemed oblivious.

Ginger made no further moves at hospitality, and Shade seemed pre-occupied with the children so everyone just watched them play. Randal's admiration for Shade grew as he watched her with the children. She was a natural with making them laugh, hugging and playing with them, and talking with them. And even as he watched how good Shade was with the kids, he watched her – closely. He saw it briefly. Maybe she did sense it. The children were hug happy and – finally – he caught Shade's eye as she was being hugged yet again.

Randal's eyes held Shade's eyes and he made a face, expressing as best he could that something was off. All he could think of was to act like he smelled flatulence. As he did, Shade winked at him, but there was no humor in her face. She <u>did</u> sense it. Something here was, well, wrong.

That was when the front door opened and a man walked in. Gordon, Randal thought. The way Gordon came in, he could only see Randal and Specter. And Gordon came in with his rifle in hand. Randal was not trained in weapons like Specter or Shade – like Hunters – but he, being Prey for so long, had seen many hunting rifles. He'd seen many rifles that put food on the table, and Gordon's rifle was <u>not</u> a hunting rifle. It looked like one, probably was the right caliber, but his mind followed his gut, and he could not bring himself to call it a hunting rifle.

Ginger was on her feet immediately and going over to hug Gordon. Gordon let her hug him, but his eyes never left Specter.

Specter, apparently oblivious to the clues setting Randal off, stood up almost as quickly and went over to shake Gordon's hand. He said, "Thank you for your hospitality. Your wife was kind enough to let us in to change, but I apologize if we're overstepping our bounds."

"Just you and him?" Gordon asked as he pointed to Randal.

Specter said, "Well, us, and Shelly. Shelly, this is Gordon; Gordon, Shelly."

Gordon stepped up into the room to see Shade and, as he entered the room, there was an obvious shift in the children. A shift toward silence and in movement towards Shade.

Shade stood up politely to shake his hand, but Gordon took her hand by the fingertips and bent to kiss it. Shade looked at Randal and made the I-smell-feces face he had to her earlier, but she let Gordon kiss her hand.

Gordon held out his rifle, keeping his eyes on Shade, and Ginger went right to it, took it from him, and then exited the room with it. She must have put it away, because she was back quickly.

Gordon, with not even a look at anyone else but Shade, said, "Ginger, you got supper ready, right?"

"Yes, sir," she said – as Randal shared a look with Shade. "I've got some good rabbit stew ready. It's been on all day."

"Let's get it on the table for our guests, then," Gordon said, more like an order.

That last sentence made everything click for Randal.

It had happened a couple of years into his Running. Randal had been trading with a local merchant, but one day as he was getting the supplies he needed, he got taken. It wasn't forcible, but if Randal hadn't gone with them it would've been. They took him to the leader of the town – a self-important potentate who was trying to establish a kingship. The guy wanted Randal to do some things for him, things the trader knew only Randal could do. As Randal was trying to decide what to do, the potentate said, "You got that drink ready, right?" A woman had brought him a drink which he didn't want and didn't drink. The man said, "She can't even serve a drink without messing it up, can she?" The potentate then got up and summarily beat the woman right in front of Randal. Whether to show his own power or to scare him, Randal didn't know. Randal, making the excuse that he had to wash her blood off, made his escape on the way to the bathroom.

It all fit into place now. Gordon was abusing this household. Everyone in it. Even the children.

Randal saw his way out – just like the last time. He stepped forward and said, "Excuse me, Mr. Gordon, sir. May I please wash up before eating, sir?" Randal ignored Shade's look of puzzlement.

Not surprisingly, Gordon said, "Down the hall on the left." As Randal took his first step, Gordon said, "The left mind you – don't go to the right." As an afterthought he added, "It leads to the basement, and we ain't got no lights down there."

Randal looked Specter in the eye and jerked his thumb.

Specter, obviously not sure why, got up and said, "Me, too," and had filed in behind Randal even as Gordon waved his hand in dismissal, returning his attention to Shade.

As Randal led Specter down the hall, he waited for the door on the right and, when he got to it, reached for the handle.

Specter put his right hand on Randal's right shoulder. Randal turned and looked at Specter. "Do you not see it?" Randal whispered.

Specter just stood there, looking like he was not sure what he had missed.

Randal turned the door handle and opened the door. There before them was a small hall with two doors on each side. Randal went for the first door on his right and opened it up. There was a small room there no bigger than three feet by three feet, but tall. It would've looked like just a closet except for the shackles chained to the wall. The size was unmistakable. Such shackles could only hold children.

Randal looked inside and then at Specter. Randal caught Specter at just the right time. The tumblers in Specter's head finally turned, aligned, and he knew. Randal could see it in Specter's face even as it blossomed and was replaced almost immediately with stone.

Randal opened the door on the left, still on the right side, and there was a closet full of tools and accoutrements for torture. Specter had switched to the left side and opened both doors. The one on the left had shackles in it like the one on the right, its opposite. The one on the right, though, was empty.

The room was indeed empty, but Specter sensed something. His mind now aware of the situation, he put his hands in all the corners. He felt air in the back right corner. Pushing and feeling around, he was rewarded with a click, and the back of the little closet opened, revealing a circular staircase going down. Specter said, "You go watch the door." His tone brooked no dissent.

Specter was gone a long time. Randal could hear the wind moan and whine through the old farmhouse. There were going to be problems if Specter didn't get back soon, and Randal's fears were realized when he heard Gordon from the kitchen, "You about ready to eat, boys?"

Randal opened his mouth to answer as Specter came back up out of the closet. Randal's breath caught in his throat. Specter came out beet red and obviously, absolutely teeming with anger. Whatever he saw in there was bad. "Yes, sir," Specter said. "Be right there." Specter's tone and his countenance didn't match up. That mismatching added to Randal's sense of wrongness. "We're in the kitchen," Gordon called.

Specter only laid his index finger over his lips and shook his head 'no' at Randal. Randal got it and didn't say a word. He followed Specter back towards the kitchen not knowing what to expect. When just about to the corner, Specter turned and put his hand on Randal's, which, by habit, he had put on his revolver. Specter shook his head 'no' and in that barely audible whisper of his said, "Kids." Then Specter removed his hand.

When they turned the hall corner, there sat Gordon at the head of the table on the far side of the room. The table was about six feet long by four feet wide. Shade was seated at the foot of the table with her back to them. Ginger sat beside her on the right.

Specter went up to Shade, putting his left hand on her left shoulder, and leaning his head down to hers. He whispered, "I need this," as he ran his right hand down her waist to where she kept her tomahawk.

"You looking for her shingle makers?" Gordon asked.

Specter looked him in the eye as Gordon, with his left hand on the table, lifted one of Shade's tomahawks with his right.

Gordon began, "I decided that…"

That was all he got out, and those were the last words Randal ever heard Gordon speak.

Randal watched as Specter used Randal's own trick from that first day at the cabin. Already low, Specter had put his right hand on the table edge when he found no tomahawk on Shade, then he had moved his left hand to the table when Gordon opened his mouth. For Specter, seeing both of Gordon's hands was his 'go' signal.

Specter put his whole weight behind the table and drove it straight into Gordon's gut. Ginger flew out to the right, and Specter drove until Gordon hit the wall. Specter immediately raised the table using Gordon's lap as a pivot point. Once up, Specter slammed it hard to the wall, trying to sandwich Gordon's head between the wall and the table. Then, almost in one fluid motion, Specter shoved the table toward his right and off Gordon's lap. The motion shifted Specter to the left, so that Gordon was on his right and, as Gordon just sat there, dazed, hands in his lap, Specter put the top of his foot on Gordon's forehead. Specter's kick sent Gordon's head into the wall, crushing the sheetrock in a rough circle. Gordon rebounded from the wall, and Randal caught sight of Gordon's eyes rolling back in his head. Gordon was out cold.

Specter, however, was not sated. He whirled around to his left and came at Ginger with murder in his eyes. Ginger had stood up from where she'd been knocked back and had reflexively grabbed a fork. She was gripping it tightly with both hands, with the tines held at gut level. She was going to defend herself, and that fork was as good as welded to her hands.

Specter started yelling at her, and she looked down, clutching her fork, taking the verbal onslaught. Randal knew it immediately. Ginger was used to this. She had taken such cussings before, and the only thing different was the person giving it.

Randal, even right there in the same room, couldn't make out everything that Specter was yelling. Randal did catch him ask, "How long have you known?" and "When did you stop listening?"

Specter kept on for a good while, but at last he ran down. When he did, he worked visibly to compose himself, and asked, "Where are the children?"

Ginger gently pointed her finger and said nothing.

Specter told Shade, "Bring them here."

Shade left, and soon the hall became full as overflow from the kitchen spilled out into the hallway. When Shade came back, there were all ten children together.

Specter picked Gordon up, and some of the children gasped. All of them got out of the way. Specter led them all down that small staircase in the back of the closet and into the large room it opened up into. Specter dropped Gordon down by a wall that had some more chain shackles on it and let him lie there. Gordon was still unconscious. Specter motioned to Randal and for Shade to get Ginger and, leaving the kids in the main room, they all walked to a little room off the main one – the only other room down here.

Specter opened the door. There was a little twin bed in the room, but the walls of that room were covered in pictures of child rape – with Gordon as the rapist. No one went in, but Specter grabbed Ginger by the arm and pushed her inside with, "You wait here." Specter closed the door quickly and said to Randal and Shade, "The more you can think about something else, the quicker this memory will fade."

Shade raised her hand a bit – about chin level – and asked, "Did I see a gun in there?"

Specter was quick with his response, "I don't think so. I'm sure it would only have one bullet in it, if there was one in there." His expression never changed.

The kids' expressions were fixed as well – in terror. They did not want to be here. *Naturally, they don't*, thought Randal, *they were tortured down here.*

Specter grabbed a sledgehammer from along the wall and went over to Gordon. Specter turned him on his side and spread his legs some. He turned and looked at the kids. "Hey, everyone! I know this is a bad place, isn't it?" Specter had turned on all the charm he could muster. It seemed to be enough. "This man, Gordon – is that what you guys call him?" Some nods.

"Mr. Gordon," one said.

"Okay, Mr. Gordon. Well, kids, Mr. Gordon is a very bad man. Did you know that?"

Some nods on that, too.

"Yeah. He was – is – a very bad man. But I can't put him in jail."

"Why not?" one asked.

Specter was quick. "I don't have a jail," he intoned with distress. "Do you have a jail?" he asked.

"No," that one said.

"Well, we have to punish him, don't we? So he knows never to hurt anybody ever again. Right?"

There were some nods, no words.

"Did Mr. Gordon ever hurt any of you?" Specter asked.

Most all of them nodded. Shade turned away with her hand over her mouth. Specter swallowed hard, and his face turned stony. Randal imagined Specter taking that lump in his throat, reshaping it into anger and energy and swallowing that. Randal imagined that because that's what he was trying to do.

"Did any of you try to run away from Mr. Gordon?"

Some nods again. A little girl of about five held up her hand and said, "My sister tried but she didn't make it. Mr. Gordon said he'd catch anyone who ran. He let me have her feet. I didn't get to say good-bye, but we buried her feet in the yard, and that's kinda like saying good-bye. She's with Jesus now."

Specter stood there immovable, like he was cold cast in bronze.

One of the smaller girls, maybe two years old, went and hugged the girl who had spoken.

The only thing that moved on Specter was the tear that overran his non-moving eyelid and fell to the ground. Almost simultaneously when the tear hit the ground, Specter whirled and was over by Gordon, his back to the children. Specter retrieved one of those Hunter syringes and laid it on the ground beside Gordon.

Specter addressed the kids over his shoulder, "I'm..." he choked out but could not go on. Specter's head titled up and he spoke to the ceiling, "I'm going to make it so Mr. Gordon can't catch anyone else, okay?"

"Okay," most said.

Specter shook his head violently once to clear it. Then, with skilled aim and practiced swing, he let the sledgehammer fall full force on Gordon's left ankle. Before that awful bone-crushing sound had even faded, Specter did the same to Gordon's right ankle. Then, Specter picked up the syringe and injected all of it into Gordon's left thigh.

The response was rapid, and Randal was sure it was exactly what Specter wanted. Gordon woke up and tried to take in the situation. As he did so, he got in an almost push up position and pulled up his left leg and tried to stand up but fell screaming back to the ground when he tried to put weight on his ankle.

Some of the kids were distraught at Gordon's being awake, regardless of if he was in pain or not. Specter jumped in quickly, "All eyes on me, okay? I have some more questions I need to ask you. But first, my friends are going to wait outside and make sure we're not interrupted." With a nod, Shade and Randal were dismissed. It was an order – and not one to be disobeyed.

Just as they reached the staircase, they turned at the sound of a gunshot. They looked at Specter, and he waved them on with the back of his hand, saying, "It's right on time. There's only so much you can refuse to see and only so much you can see once you have to see."

Once at the top of the stairs, Shade looked in the adjacent room at the small shackles. She looked at Randal, and he could tell she was about to lose it. Randal held out his arms and she rushed into them, burying her head in his shoulder. He felt her shudder a couple of times, going through a silent sob. His eyes went wet as well. And then, just like that, she took a deep breath and backed away.

Chapter 50

Shade seemed embarrassed for crying and, although she didn't say it, Randal felt she was ashamed or sorry for crying. He tried to comfort her by saying, "We're all human." She took the comment with the sentiment attached, but she said, "Not all of us. Not all the time." Shade wiped her eyes, and all trace of the sadness was gone.

"Not while I'm Hunting," Shade looked at Randal. "So let's Hunt."

Randal was all too happy to do something else. They first reclaimed Shade's tomahawks. "Why did you let him take them from you?" Randal asked.

"Ginger had the rifle on me and, since you guys were here, I just decided to play the docile, subservient woman. I knew something was wrong – was off – but it seemed better to see what was going on before taking action. Come on."

They started searching the level they were on. Gordon and Ginger had their room on this level. Shade and Randal turned it upside down. They found a handgun, but nothing they could use. They did find a well-stocked pantry and, adding to the wrongness of the whole house, there were new things in there. New things like salt, sugar, flour, and crackers and cookies. Randal showed Shade, who had found Gordon's rifle.

"Strange," was all Shade said.

They moved to the upstairs and went room by room. The kids' rooms were upstairs. Nothing was out of the ordinary in the rooms, unless you'd count the lack of toys. That made Randal think about the basement, those kids. Shade's voice startled him. "Randal, I've got something."

He found her in the attic. "What's up there?" he asked.

"You'd better come up," she said.

He followed her up and was indeed surprised. It wasn't a large space, but there were three crates there all labeled the same way, and Shade had the lid off the top one. The contents were pri-con rifles. These rifles Randal recognized as those based on the Belgian FAL type rifle, not the Kalashnikov frame.

"Yeah," Shade said. "And these aren't the general issue ones. These are special, the ones used primarily in personnel protection."

Randal thought. "But we didn't see any of these with Chairman Jones," he said.

"Yeah, not these kind." She thought for a bit. "These would be much higher profile protection…"

"Or?" Randal prompted.

"Or prisoner transfer," she said, looking into Randal's face.

Randal felt like he'd been punched in the stomach. "Oh, no," he breathed more than said.

Shade reached out to steady him because the color had bleached out of his skin.

Randal reached out for her hand, which seemed to secure him and restore his blood flow. It anchored him. Randal stammered, "This place is like the Creep? But for children? Why aren't there more guards? Wait, are there more guards?"

"Calm down," Shade said. "Let's see." She continued her inspection and found nine full ammunition boxes. Then a whispered, "Jackpot!" escaped her lips. She had found a case of medical supplies, chiefly the syringes she and Specter carried – the 'go' juice – and the powder to stop bleeding.

As Shade was looking, Randal looked more at the room itself. It was well lit even though he could see no bulbs lit. It was all indirect lighting. He noticed four windows. *Each aligned on the compass directions, probably*, he thought. On a whim, he went to one and looked out. He couldn't see much in the darkness outside other than the raindrops on the window. But, looking out at the right time, Randal was treated to a view of the grounds by a serendipitous flash of lightning. There was another building behind the lean-to where they'd put those horses.

Randal's attention was so riveted on the outside building that when the lightning stopped, there was Shade's face in the window!

Shade patted him on the shoulder. "Just a reflection," she said.

It did serve to get his blood pumping and made him eager to explore that building. Shade seemed just as eager.

It was still raining, so they did the best they could to stay under cover. There didn't appear to be any way to get access to the building Randal had seen by going through the lean-to. Randal remembered how Specter had found the hidden downstairs door, took a step back, and looked again. There! He went to a spot and tried pushing/pulling/kicking – no luck.

Shade and Randal decided to get wet and walked around the lean-to. There was no obvious door to the barn. Randal then tried the same tactic with the same results. He stepped back and looked again. Randal felt he saw it, and moved up to the door. This time, he did find it.

Shade helped him get the doors open. They were large bay doors, not a regular domestic door. Once open, there was a large open space in the middle with smaller stalls and alcoves around the sides. It was Shade who found the power box and threw the lever.

There was only one light hung from the top of the ceiling which gave plenty of light to see everything but probably not enough light to work by. They went through everything there and only found horse feed that they could use. Shade appeared ready to go and she was moving towards the door when Randal stopped her.

"Something's wrong here, isn't there?" Randal asked.

"Yes," she said. "There's all kinds of stuff here we can't use," and she started for the door.

"Wait," Randal said. "Really." He was not really paying attention to her, but searching for what was off. He talked, more to himself than to Shade. "Why such a large barn and no horses? Lot to do for neighbors." He would walk around and get different views, looking for what was off. Walking more, he started kicking at the floor. He stopped and grabbed a shovel and started sweeping the ground with the flat part of the shovel.

"Really?" Shade asked disdainfully.

"Have you ever been in a barn with a floor?"

Shade came over to look and, sure enough, Randal had uncovered a board about three inches below a layer of dirt. That made her take a second look. *If this were like the barn in Byland's Rest, the entrance would be...*, she thought. As she walked over that way, she kicked at the floor there and found wood, too.

"You find some, too?" Randal asked. And, being only about fifteen feet apart, came over to look. "Yours is different from mine," he said, looking at the wood.

"You think?!" Shade said, joking and playfully shoving his shoulder.

Randal got the double entendre but said, "The wood over there is tongue and groove. This isn't." He looked at her and tick-tocked his finger, "Don't go there," he said. He looked closer. "There's a lot of straw here. A door?" He began clearing the straw, and Shade helped. Indeed, it was a door set into the floor.

Raising his eyebrows, then winking at Shade, Randal grabbed the recessed ring handle and pulled on the door. It came open easily, as if well-used, revealing a set of steps going down. They went inside.

There was a fifteen foot by fifteen foot room at the bottom of those stairs with an eight foot ceiling lit by two single bulbs. At first glance, it seemed like a root cellar, complete with jars of canned foods along the wall. But to Randal and Shade, self-trained to escape and trained to locate, respectively, it looked like subterfuge.

Without saying a word, they each took an opposite wall and started looking for a hidden door. Randal didn't have far to go. Looking down, he could see tracks leading into the wall. *It's the little things*, Randal thought.

"I found it," he said. "I don't have the switch yet, though." Shade came over to help look. She found the switch on the closest shelving unit and pressed it. The door swung away from Randal, the motors audible while the door moved.

The door opened onto a dark, narrow hallway. Randal looked at Shade. "Shall we?" he asked. Shade mimicked a curtsy. Randal took the first step inside, and a light overhead bloomed to life. "Motion activated," Shade said, "nice touch."

Randal made his way forward, and somehow his revolver found its way into his hand. "Are we outside of the barn now?" Randal asked as they walked.

"Probably," Shade answered.

"But we're going away from the house, right?" asked Randal.

"I think so," Shade said.

After a good one hundred feet, they came to another door. This one opened inward to the hallway as the last door did; they could tell by the marks on the floor. Here, though, was a light switch with two switches. Looking at Shade, Randal hit the top switch.

The door opened and lights went on in a circle going counter-clockwise from the door and circling back. Randal was following the lights when he was bumped from behind. He looked at Shade pass

by him and then to where she was going. There was a platform.
There, in the middle of the room, a platform!

Randal started going around, looking at the edges of the room,
worried they may have surprised a pri-con crew. Shade let him,
telling him after he'd made it around that they were clear. Shade
took everything in and looked in each area.

"I guess this explains the food in the pantry," Shade said.

"How do you mean?" asked Randal. "So Gordon put together a
platform and hid it down here. How does that explain the food?"

Shade was surprised. "You don't see it?" she asked. Randal
shrugged. "We're in a platform hangar," she said stressing the word.
She jumped up onto the platform and started pointing out things.
"This is set up exactly like all platform hangars. Maintenance keep
their tools over there, cleaning has their area over here, staging area
for troops right there, and fuel – fuel should be right there." She
jumped down, and Randal met her over where she had pointed. Sure
enough, underneath a tarp sat the gas tanks, and they were huge.
With that much gas, you could run the place on generators.

"But how do you get it out of here?" Randal asked.

Shade realized he hadn't looked up. She looked him in the eye
and simply pointed upward.

Looking up, Randal could see a line in the ceiling right above the
platform and, tracing back, he saw some huge brackets – or at least
pivot points. It looked like the ceiling would open up like a
drawbridge. Randal wondered if they could…"Can you fly it?" he
asked.

She jumped back up and looked around. "No," she said simply. "I
could if we could find the control panel. We could search the house
again?"

"Sure," Randal said, "let's go."

Chapter 51

They hurried back, ready to tear the house apart to find that control panel. They snapped back to reality as soon as they entered the house.

There in the living room were the ten children, obviously shocked, obviously distressed. Specter came in from the kitchen as he heard the door. His face was stone, and Randal wasn't sure if it was because he was angry at Gordon and what he'd done or if he was willing himself not to let his guard down and break down. Either way, the effect was the same.

"There you are!" said Specter, relieved. "Did you forget about supper?"

Randal certainly had. "I'll help," he said, walking to the kitchen.

The kids, most anyway, had swarmed back around Shade. "I'll stay here," she said, and she didn't have to say more. The mood of the children had already improved with her back.

Thankfully, Ginger had made plenty of rabbit stew. There was enough for everyone. Specter had not done much to clean up, just set the table back up. Specter had set out bowls, though, so Randal set about filling them with stew from the stockpot on the stove.

Specter was occupied with getting drinks set out. There was some kind of colored drink in the refrigerator, and Specter portioned it out.

Randal remembered seeing some crackers in the pantry and retrieved those. He also grabbed some cookies he saw there. Specter raised his eyebrows at the cookies. Randal saw it and said, "We have…"

Specter interrupted him with, "We have time after dinner to talk, okay?"

"Sure," Randal said, a little abashed. "Fine."

Specter found a tray and started making trips out to the living room. Randal filled a cake pan with drinks then started making his rounds.

They all ate in the living room, and there was little talk. Shade managed to get a spurt of conversation going among the little ones about games they liked, but it was short lived.

As Randal started getting all their stew bowls up he listened as Specter talked in a soothing, deep soft voice to the children. He was laying down some ground rules and the kids, of course, were going along with them. But Randal was pleased to hear Specter involving the children in the decisions. He wondered if Specter had had children; he certainly seemed to have a way with them.

Randal dumped the cookies into three bowls and then poked his head around the corner. Specter nodded to him and said to the kids, "You do know what happens when everybody obeys, right? We get cookies!"

Randal came around right on cue, but it was clear that the young ones didn't even know what cookies were and that the older ones knew they weren't allowed to have them. Randal felt horrible. As he stood there, one boy said, "Those are Mr. Gordon's and we can't have any or we'll get in trouble."

Randal reacted without thought, "Oh, no, they're not. These are my cookies, and I get to say who can share them and who cannot." He pulled himself up high and stuck out his chest. He handed a bowl to Specter and Shade. Then he pointed to that boy who had spoken and asked, "Have you been a good boy today?"

"Y – yes," the boy stammered.

"Well, then, I allow you to share a cookie with me." And Randal proffered the cookie to him.

The boy took it but did not eat it.

"We will take the first bite together," and Randal made sure the boy mirrored him and took a bite. It was obvious the boy liked the cookie. Randal couldn't think of any ten year old who hadn't had a cookie – even after the Breaking.

"Now," Randal continued, "Who else has been good today?" More hands up. "Everybody? Does everybody have a hand up?" He spun around, and then everyone did have a hand up. "Then we will have cookies all around! Everyone grab your cookie!" He, Specter, and Shade, passed cookies around. "All together now, share!" and everybody took a bite.

That set everything off. The kids seemed to loosen a bit and forget – at least for a bit – that their whole world had changed. He got a special wink from Shade. She even came over to get one of his cookies and share her kind, and she said quietly to him, "Very impressive out there. You're good with kids." And then she was gone before he could reply.

Specter let them eat cookies and play for a good while. When there were a couple of meltdowns with the youngest kids, he got up and announced bedtime. They didn't argue and went up to their rooms. Specter and Randal started cleaning up while Shade went to help the children get in bed and tuck them in. When she returned, they all sat down to talk.

Specter started off. "What did you find?"

Shade gave the breakdown. The rifles, ammunition, and medical supplies in the attic. The barn, the hidden hallway, all building to the discovery of the platform. She finished with, "If we can find the control panel, I could fly it."

"Why," Specter asked. "What do we need with a platform?"

Shade's mouth dropped, but Randal flew into the gap. "Are you serious? That's our ticket into the Creep! We swoop down in that and we've got people on the second floor in an instant. That single fact will save lives!"

Specter put his hand on his chin as if he was thinking. "Hmmm…," he said. "We'll probably need this," and he reached behind his chair and pulled out what looked like an old electronic tablet.

Shade's eyes got large quickly. She knew exactly what it was – the platform control panel! "Where'd you get that?" she asked.

Specter related his experience. "We were showing Mr. Gordon what being mean is when he blurted out that he had a platform. I was concerned. I felt we didn't have much time after my kick," he looked at Shade. "I was worried about coup/countrecoup brain injury, and I thought maybe it was affecting him a lot sooner than it should have."

"But it wasn't," Shade prompted.

"No," Specter continued. "He went on about it. The more his situation became real to him, the more desperately he talked about it. Well, I figured I'd humor him and asked him to prove it. He kept it in his little room. I told him that changed things, and then it all came out."

"He started by talking like he could take me wherever, then he could get me whatever. I asked him where the kids came from, he made me promise again to keep him alive, then said the kids come from the girls at the Creep. He called it the Castle, but whatever. If a girl up there gets pregnant, they keep her up there and wean the baby, and then they either sell the baby for adoption or, if they can't do that, bring the baby here. The kids get taken to the pleasure dome for more of the same."

"The end?" Shade prompted.

"Well, I pressed him on the Creep. There are two lower levels. The lowest level is where the mothers and wet nurses are kept. The level above is the guard quarters. The rest is pretty much what we know. The end? He said I promised, and I asked the kids if he had ever broken a promise to them." He left it there. His narration ended.

Randal needed to know. Shade looked like she already did. Randal could guess but... "Well?" he found himself asking.

Specter looked at him as if it were self-evident. "He had," he said simply.

"So you killed him right there." Randal said.

"Well, later. Yeah." Specter said.

Randal thought and finally said, "I just don't know, but that seems harsh to kill him in front of them."

Specter looked at him, and in that look Specter managed to convey the weariness of one who had spent a long time cleaning up after evil people and trying to set things right – and the weariness of being second guessed by those people who were ignorant of that process. He spit.

Randal knew he was in the wrong before the spittle hit the ground.

"He's making it right again...," Shade said in the voice of one who is beyond arguing – not because of the futility of convincing another, but because they are so secure in their position that they don't have to convince others.

"Let me tell you a story, Maker." Specter's use of his Prey name caught Randal's attention, the derision in the appellation not lost on him. "There was a man, Chesterton was his name. He was writing for a newspaper and came across this woman who didn't want anyone to tell fairy tales to children. The lady didn't believe in them and didn't want to scare the kids." Specter paused as if making sure he was relaying everything properly.

Specter continued, "Well, Chesterton wouldn't have it. He called hooey on it."

Randal interrupted him, "'Hooey'?" he asked.

Specter spat again. "Chesterton was a religious man. He called bullshit on the lady, but he was religious, so he probably just called hooey on it. Okay?"

Randal just said, "Sure. Go ahead. 'Hooey'."

"So Chesterton," Specter continued, "says these kids already know monsters, know evil. No made up story of the boogie man can compete with the shadow monsters they make up in their minds. The kids know those monsters are out there ready to gobble them up."

"But Chesterton tells this lady the fairy tale tells the kids that monsters can be killed. That there's a force out there – he called it a 'knight of God' maybe – that slays the dragon. So the fairy tale isn't about the monster so much as your reaction to it. It shows you that you can fight back when you're scared."

That's what these kids need, thought Randal.

"And that's what these kids need," continued Specter. "They need to know there's no monster out there that they can't fight," he paused again. "They need to believe in fairy tales again. They need to know good can win."

"Where'd you hear about all that?" Randal asked before he could stop the words.

Specter's exasperated sigh spoke volumes. "One of my first Prey was a guy like Gordon here, a child abuser – no, child rapist. Before he died he started spouting all kinds of bullshit, and the guy called me the 'knight of God' and himself the dragon. So I looked it up; he was right, that Chesterton said it."

"And you killed him," Randal said, knowing he had.

"I killed him in front of the boys he'd been abusing." Specter saw the appropriate amount of shock in Randal's eyes. "You take away the fairy tale; you leave them to fight alone." Specter looked into Randal's eyes, but he spoke the words into his core. "They're already stranded in the blackness of midnight, far from home, far from help. You take their justice from them, and you make them fight alone to get back home. You let them see justice, though, and you give them back the fairy tale. You give them justice and you give them an ally stronger than any evil person, any dragon, or shapeless, black, fang-mawed demon of death – you give them hope.

And hope is what helps them fight on until they find their own happily ever after."

The silence that followed demanded the time, demanded the reverence for those so affected. Specter, and Specter alone, could break that silence, and he gave it its due.

"I'm not a psychologist," Specter began, "I'm no choir boy, and I'm damn sure no knight of God. It just seems right to me to give some poor bastard a shot at something better than they've gotten so far."

Randal looked at Specter and waited until Specter met his gaze. "You can tell yourself that you're no choir boy, but that's you talking. That's not God talking." Randal got up, patted Specter's shoulder, and walked back to the living room, leaving Specter and Shade alone with their thoughts.

Chapter 52

Shade woke Randal for the last watch. She told him that Specter had found a lookout point from the attic, and Randal found it easily enough. He settled in and waited for day to break. Randal was getting more accustomed to just sitting and listening in the woods. He chuckled a bit to himself, thinking that listening was only done in the woods. He figured you could listen anywhere for the sounds that made that place, that place. Then you would know what was out of place.

As he established his baseline, he thought back to the evening. After he had gone to bed, he heard Shade and Specter talking. He couldn't follow their conversation, though. He was either too sleepy or too exhausted to listen in or to make sense of the snippets he'd heard. Now, though, in the early morning stillness of the night, he did wish he could remember more.

Randal let it go; they could hash that out later in the morning. *Right now, though...,* he thought, and just let himself feel the morning. He had a good vantage point up here. Randal thought about the Creep, thought about the vantage point they would have from up there. It put him in the mindset of what a guard at the Creep may think of a platform coming up. Did they see a lot of platforms? Would they recognize this one?

Then he had an idea. Why not use that? If you can't surprise others, you need to focus their attention on something else. His mind started spinning fast. They were already carrying ladders. They wouldn't expect the platform, so they would be suspicious about it. Maybe if they disguised the platform, especially if they recognized it, maybe they could make the guards think that Gordon had been attacked and was forced to lead his attackers to the Creep.

Why? His mind fought. Why?

Because they were angry parents or neighbors, and they didn't like it. *Kind of like – exactly like – we're doing*? he thought. But yes. His mind fought on again. What would make me leave this crow's nest? Why would I get down from here to fight some farmers? Fire. Fire would require everybody to help put it out. Fire was also a double-edged sword and could work against you. But what if they could make it work? And maybe have the platform wheel away as people ran from it. They would have to send out people then, if only to get the platform back. Wouldn't they? His mind fought its internal battle until the sun forced a truce.

When he went back down to wake Specter and Shade, he found out he didn't have to. Randal found them already awake and in the kitchen making breakfast. With all the kids. Specter looked at him and said, "Kids don't sleep in, and these got up early." It turned out the kids ran their regular routes – pretty involved chores for kids. Then Randal realized the penalties for not doing everything right, and he shuddered. Regardless, the kids had gotten in the eggs and milked the cows.

Shade came by and elbowed him in the ribs. She said, loudly, "You didn't raise an alarm when you heard the kids getting eggs and milking."

Before Randal could say anything, one of the girls said, "Oh, no, he did not hear us! We didn't make a sound!"

Specter chimed in, "We've been hearing so much about how quiet these kids were, we wondered if they were lying."

"We are not lying!" said one girl almost in tears as she stomped her foot.

Uncharacteristically, Specter crouched down and said, "I think you are telling the very most absolute truth, little lady."

The little girl shook her head up and down once, and then shook her finger while she said, "Don't you forget it!"

It was certainly cute, the origins behind where she got it were sad, but it was, overall, hopeful.

Specter had fried some country ham, scrambled the eggs, and everybody ate well. Randal was slowly coming to terms with the fact that they had ten kids to take care of now. Little kids on top of that. They could do some things, but they would have to have someone look after them. Apparently, Specter and Shade had already addressed the issue.

"Randal," Specter said, "You and I have babysitting duty today."

"I'm sorry, Specter, but you were talking and all these kids were so loud I couldn't hear you when you said 'just kidding'," Randal joked.

Shade smiled and said, "You guys are going to help me get that platform out and then watch the kids."

"And you're just going to fly off into the sunset?" Randal asked.

"No, I'm going to get my wings back, fly over to the rendezvous area, and pick up some baby sitters," Shade replied.

"Can you actually do that? Fly over woods like that?" Randal asked. "Is it safe?"

Shade smiled again and said, "It's expedient." She winked at Specter.

Specter sighed and gave his reasoning. "We – Shade and I – need to be on this assault. The people who will help, will help. They are Outlanders so they hunt. They'll be helpful. Shade and I <u>Hunt</u>. We're necessary."

Specter let that sink in. "Now, in order to plan the best way to get the platform to that second floor is for Shade to do some scouting, which I need to do, too, and that means we can't be here, and that means we need baby sitters."

"We don't have to get the platform to the second floor, really," said Randal. He continued despite Specter's look of incredulity. "Those platforms are loud and you'd have to be high, but…" He felt pressure. "They might recognize that it was Gordon's platform. If we have smoke, then a fire pulls all the…" He stopped, realizing that he was rambling. "Do you have a minute?" he asked.

Specter laughed and clapped him on the back. "Yeah," he said. "Yeah, I've got all day. Let's get Shade going first, though, okay?"

Randal agreed and, leaving the older kids in charge of the little ones, everybody walked to the barn, into the hallway, and into the hangar. With everyone standing well back, Shade took the control panel, inserted it into the platform, coupled them, and then hit the ignition.

The sound was more than Randal had expected. He looked back, and all the children had their hands over their ears. As Shade had expected with the layout, the hangar release was integrated into the control panel and only became available once the engines were running.

The hangar opened more like a draw bridge than anything else Randal could think of. He was surprised at how much thickness the hangar doors had. They were solid but also carried about two feet of soil on top. There were trees spaced around the jagged edges of the hangar doors. It was clear that this hangar was meant to be hidden from the air and the outline very camouflaged. But the weight of the doors was huge.

The power drain just to operate the doors had to be substantial. Specter came up beside him and put his head close to Randal's ear, and yelled, "Clandestine military." Randal gave a quick thumbs up, showing he understood. The whole area seemed to take on a different aura when observed through that filter.

Here was a remote outpost that had easy access to major highways. Things start going south – or to hell – and then this place is kind of on its own. The soldiers here get entrepreneurial and start trading. No. Probably those stationed here wanted some action and started grabbing girls for their own fun – then started trading the Creep their old women. And thus a mutually beneficial relationship was born – with no regard for how morally repugnant their actions were.

Shade edged the platform up higher as the doors opened and, when she could, shot free of the hangar. They all watched as she rose higher and then, as planned, she activated the doors to close.

"Fill in your own story, right?" Specter asked more like he was making a statement.

Randal shook his head, "What?"

"How a military operation can go from sworn to protect straight to human trafficking. There's a myriad of ways that could happen. You can fill in the one you want to believe," Specter said.

"Hmmn, I guess so," said Randal. "At least we get to write the ending, though, right?"

"Right on that one," said Specter. "But what about your story? Fill me in on how a handful of adventurers attack a fortified castle, kill the evil minions, and still rescue the damsels in distress. No dragons, mind you," Specter said, shaking his finger.

So, as they rounded up the children and started walking back to the house, Randal began to tell Specter his plan.

Chapter 53

"First of all," Randal began, "there is a chance that the people at the Creep will recognize the platform as being Gordon's. Second, I think they probably have some other form of communication so they know when he's coming and vice versa. So they'll be suspicious of the platform already. Let's use that." Randal looked for any kind of sign in Specter's face, but caught nothing.

"Anyway," Randal continued, "we try and focus their attention on the platform. We have Shade fly it but put Gordon up there beside her like he's flying it and..."

Specter interrupted, "A dead man? Three to four days old? Stinky."

Randal responded, "Okay, how about we get..." and then an idea hit him so hard he wondered if Specter heard the 'pop.' "We get his head and body – cold, embalmed, whatever – so it won't stink – and go towards the gate with some folks. We yell out that we're going to kill them for what they're doing, and then cut off Gordon's head and throw it at them. Their attention is focused on the thrown head and seeing whose head it is."

"We then start a little fire on the platform like we've blown an engine or something, and we'll get more attention. Shade will then fly up and over the building to make sure everybody looks out to the right side, presumably to see the platform crash. But we switch and re-do it, flying back over back to the front, or left, side. That way, doing it faster, they won't be able to get back to the front, and that's the side we crash into. Shade will hit the wall right at the second story windows, and you go in on the second floor, protecting the women."

"Shade will then drop to ground level like the platform is damaged, and the others with the platform do two things. First, we get Gordon's body – stuffed with explosives – up by the wall and burning, so that maybe he'll blow a hole in the wall – maybe. But second, those on the platform get down and run off. That should drive some guards out to hunt them down."

"Then to finish it out, Shade flies around to a set location and sets down the platform so it looks like she crashed it. That, at least, should pull some guards out. We have folks lying in wait to see how many are coming and from where."

"If we set it up right, I think Shade could set the platform down and then take it out. What I mean is, from the Creep they see the crash signs, send men out to retrieve it, and we have an ambush for those people. But Shade only acted like she crashed the platform, while the whole time, she's ferrying people back to the Creep from the woods."

"Then we just keep at it until we have everyone dead or in chains," Randal finished and kept looking for some kind of look, some clue of how it was received.

"We can't have the people get off and run. Too likely they'll get shot – but more importantly, they won't chase after them," Specter said. He looked at Randal. "I've spent a lot of time re-assessing my opinion of you, Randal." Specter thought. "That plan might actually work."

Randal was glad his idea wasn't shot down immediately. "One thing, too, is that since we've got the ladders coming already, we could position a group on the far side of the building using them to get to that second floor. Maybe sneak underneath their radar."

"Dangerous," Specter said, but he was thinking. "So dangerous that it might be enough to either get them in or get the guards separated enough so each group could deal with them. How many people you thinking?"

Randal was caught off guard. "I wasn't, really." He did think now, though. "Not more than ten I'd think." Then he thought better, "Heck, I don't know. I really have no idea. I was thinking six, three carrying ladders, three covering them. Three teams of two, one carry, one cover."

Specter gave Randal a kind of grimace nod. "That's kind of what I was thinking, but I'd put two more good shots out in the woods to serve as cover for them."

"Good idea," said Randal, "I wouldn't have thought of that."

"I'm glad you like it. I thought you might be one of those providing cover," Specter said.

Randal was taken aback. "I, well, uh, thanks for the thought, but I'm not sure I'm that good of a shot. I'd hate to put people in danger because I'm not the best."

Specter held up his hand. "Everyone going up there is volunteering. You didn't hear anyone asking for others to qualify on the rifle range, right?" He made sure Randal was hearing him. "You'll do your best just like everybody else. And you're all right in a fight. You keep your head and get your job done. That goes a long way." He looked at Randal. "Okay?"

"Yeah," Randal said.

"You've got good instincts, and I think you'd be better up close to the house. Plus, Mr. Gordon left something special for you," Specter said.

Perplexed, Randal asked, "What?"

"It's a customized rifle like Shade helped you out on, so you know the basics. We'll let you get some practice around lunchtime if you want." Specter told him.

"Great," Randal said.

"Now," said Specter, "let's refine the finer points of this frontal assault diversionary attack."

Chapter 54

It turned out that Specter and Randal spent most of the day planning the attack and not much time watching the kids. When Shade got back that afternoon, she learned that they had kept the kids fed and alive and not much else. The kids were going through a transition time to be sure, so a few hours – a day even – of not much attention should be okay for them. At least there was no negative attention. Shade pried Specter and Randal away from their planning and introduced them to Don and Ruby. Don and Ruby were among the older people who'd shown up at the meeting. They were Shade's top choice of those at the rendezvous site. Don had taught elementary school before the Breaking and Ruby had worked in a daycare. Shade hadn't known that when she had asked for volunteers; she had known the two as tavern/inn keepers, and quite the liquor makers.

Shade knew the two would be good with the children. She just hoped the kids would be okay adapting to their new situation. As she looked at the kids playing, she knew the scars they bore were internal. Evil had touched them. Now it still sat there in the dark places of their minds, somewhat forgotten but spreading its taint over every interaction, every gesture, every basic trust they would ever have.

Shade went round to each child, giving a hug and telling each about the meeting. Next, she stood in the middle of the living room and said loudly, "I announce the meeting! Come one, come all, get in here out of the hall!" When she had all the children sitting down in front of her, she said, "I know you all have had a pretty eventful last two days. And now, I'm going to introduce another person to you, two people actually."

"Kids," Shade said, motioning for Don and Ruby, "this is Don and this is Ruby."

Don and Ruby looked at all the kids. One of the older girls stood up and said, "Hello, Mr. Don and Miss Ruby," in a perfunctory, wary voice.

Don knelt down and said, "Hello, there. But I'm not Mr. Don. I'm just 'Don.' Mr. Don was my dad, okay?"

The little girl just nodded.

Ruby said, like an aside to the girl and the others, "You can call him Don or Donnie, just don't call him Ding-Don!" and she laughed in just the right way so that the other kids would join in.

"Now," Don said, "Who is going to show me through the house? I don't even know where I can poop!"

The kids were all smiling, if not all laughing.

Ruby said, "Well, I know you can't poop in your pants!"

That got all the kids going.

Don and Ruby let the kids lead them out of the living room, giving Shade a chance to get caught up with Specter and Randal. "So what's had you two so wrapped up you couldn't play with the kids?" she asked.

Randal, rather than looking abashed, said, "Just planning on saving lives, Shade." He winked at her. "Wrapped up in saving lives."

She raised her eyebrow at him.

"Don't look at me in that tone of voice!" Randal said in mock exasperation.

Shade had to laugh.

"Really," she finally said, "what do you have?"

Specter started out by asking her, "How did the platform handle?"

"Well," she replied.

"Are your reflexes still good? Can you still maneuver a platform?" Specter asked.

"I'm sorry, Specter, but can you still shoot?" Shade answered, a bit shocked. "Yeah, I can still fly and make that platform perform."

"Good," Specter said, "I had no doubt, but I needed to ask – to make sure you were at the same place. What we have depends on some exact flying. And people." He stopped and looked up. "How many were up there at the rendezvous?"

"There were nine. I took two, so seven up there now," Shade said.

"Have they been watching the Creep?" asked Specter.

"No," said Shade, "but they are now. So far there's no indication that the Creep knows we're there. The people there had set a watch, but I told them to go in twos and observe the Creep with eyes on it all the time – without being detected."

"How long does it take to get there?" Randal asked.

"We probably need right at three hours. Next time I can fly us straight to the rendezvous site," Shade replied.

"How much fuel to get there?" Randal asked.

"Not much, but it can add up if there's a lot of flying around once we're up there. I don't like to rely on finding fuel there in order to get back." Shade pulled up. "Wait. We are coming back here, aren't we?"

Randal looked surprised. "I had just assumed we would. I hadn't thought about it."

"Did you even feed the horses today?" Shade asked.

Specter dismissed that. "Some of the older kids did that just after you left." He thought. "It's probably better for us if we keep moving." He looked at their questioning faces. "These people had supplies, and even assholes have friends. If we stick around, we're more likely to meet them. And to be friends with an asshole usually means you're one, too, so meeting their friends might not be too good."

"It'd probably be better if we move everybody up there to the Creep once we take it, if it's salvageable," Specter finished.

"Really?" asked Randal. "Won't it be better for the kids to stay here until we can move them somewhere more permanent? It'll be awful bloody up there."

Before Specter could respond, Shade said, "I think we should bring all the people here after. We just stumbled on this place. People know where the Creep is. Plus, this place is surrounded by woods, but the Creep is open around it for what, one hundred and fifty yards?"

Specter nodded like he knew what that meant, Randal didn't. "How does being wooded make a difference?"

Specter said, "You ever try to shoot a deer through the trees?" Randal nodded his head 'No.' "Exactly. If either place got attacked and overrun, people would stand a better chance of running for their lives from here, in that classic run-for-your-life scenario."

"Oh," Randal said.

Into the silence, Shade said, "So let me have it from the beginning until we get back here."

"We're going to have to make a lot of trips tomorrow – getting our supplies up there and bringing – did you already bring Don and Ruby's horses?" Specter asked.

"They didn't have horses; they pushed hard," Shade said and, as she put her hands on her hips she showed more of her Hunter side and spoke clearly and succinctly. "Tell me the plan for the Creep." Her tone intimated that there would be consequences for disobedience.

Chapter 55

Randal and Specter started together and both stopped. Randal said first, "Let's go to the kitchen and the map."

Once there, Randal let Specter do the honors.

"First I'll give the overview, and then we'll get into details. Due to the familiar noise of platforms and communication between here and the Creep, the platform will be a focus of suspicion, and we'll capitalize on it. We need to put Gordon down there on ice or something so you will fly maybe six people and Gordon's body up towards the main gate. I'll be...," he faltered, "somewhere, maybe under a tarp with the body – or bodies if we take Ginger." He forced himself to stop rambling.

"Overview," Shade said commandingly.

Specter nodded once. "Right. We fly up to the gate and raise a ruckus and say we know what you're doing – evil pigs – all that. We throw Gordon's head and act like the platform is damaged, smoke and everything, and you'll fly us up and over to the far side of the Creep. Hopefully, that will pull guards over to that side. Then – bam! – you fly us back up and over and, here's where your skills come in, you smash the second story windows like you're crashing, and I'm off the platform and inside as the others have pushed Gordon's corpse onto the ground at that spot. We'll rig the corpse to catch fire or explode or both. Either way, you'll fly like you're damaged down the hill to a spot we'll pick out and act like you've crashed. That's where our ambush is. When they go out for the platform, we get them. Chosen aptly, though, you'll be able to set the platform down and get people and then ferry them around – without being seen – back up to the Creep."

"Leaving you alone to be inside until I can get a group up there?" Shade asked, obviously displeased at that prospect.

"No," Specter quickly replied. "From the first time we fly up, Randal will take seven people or so in four teams of two from the opposite side of the Creep. Three of those teams will be ladder bearer/cover, with Randal and another providing cover fire for the teams who will try to sneak up to the second floor as we discussed back at Byland's Rest.

"Won't the guards hear Randal's team's fire?" asked Shade.

"They'll shoot only when they have to," Specter answered.

Shade looked right at Randal and then at Specter and asked Specter point blank, "Do you think he's a good enough shot to give cover fire?"

Rather than be upset, Randal considered it an honor that Shade was committed to the mission's success and was secure enough in their friendship to honor her legitimate concern. He was more surprised with Specter's response.

"I think it's important enough to have him there. He's reliable in a fire fight. We've seen that. I think we need him out there; he's the only one, besides you, who I trust, and it's the only part of the attack that you or I are not involved in. I don't know that we could trust this to someone we don't know. Plus, Gordon left a sweet customized AK-47 with a good scope. We'll get him some practice on it," Specter said.

"Fair enough," Shade said matter-of-factly. She did flash Randal a quick wink, though, as he watched her.

"So that's the overview. Any questions right off?" asked Specter.

"Well, first off, what are the windows made of? It might be better to hit either just above or just below, and take out part of the wall to be sure. Second, why would we hold so many in reserve for the ambush? Well placed, we could switch the numbers and get more in faster. Third, what's the plan for holding the hostages? I don't want to rescue someone only to watch her get shot while trying to get to safety. Fourth, what are our plans for those inside who surrender? Fifth, about the fire/explosives in/on the corpse, how do we make sure that nothing goes off prior…"

Thus a long night of planning began.

Chapter 56

After that first night, Specter, Shade, and Randal pretty much agreed that what they were going to do was not really present the plan to those at the rendezvous so much as announce it as *fait accompli*. The intervening two days were hectic for all of those involved.

For Specter, he spent the sixth day and night up at the rendezvous so he could get the feel of the camp and the lay of the land surrounding the Creep. Coming back on the seventh day, he took some time to rest his body and prepare his mind. He checked all of his weapons and grilled Shade and Randal about the finer points of the plan.

Shade had lots of time to think on her multiple flights back and forth from Gordon's house to the rendezvous area. She carried food, weapons, and fuel. She practiced her flying techniques and looked into how she could reinforce the front corners of the platform. She also had volunteered to be the group's inner voice. She and Specter would confer about who was where, and she would talk to each one specifically. She encouraged those afraid, mediated among those with conflicts, and doused those whose bloodlust boiled too freely. Because of her efforts they were all about evenly tempered the night before the attack.

Randal found himself swept along with the current. Everything seemed to move inexorably toward the killing and death via a strong current, a current he did not want to fight. He practiced with Gordon's rifle until he felt secure, if not comfortable, with it. He practiced alongside the woman who would also be providing cover fire until he felt proficient. He put eyes on the side of the Creep his group would be attacking, looking for the best cover and the most likely positions for the Creep guards to take or fight for.

When the night before the attack came, though, it seemed all was ready. The webarmor-piercing bullets had been distributed, as well as rifles. In the very early morning hours all twenty-eight attackers gathered at the rendezvous. Twenty-five people had made it out of the thirty present back at the barn eight days go. Shade would be taking seven with her, including Specter. Randal would take eleven with him – his cover fire partner and five teams of two to make their assault. That left eight to ambush any Creep guards, Creepers, once sent out after the 'crashed' platform. As they readied for the now inevitable battle, Specter stepped forward.

"It's almost time," Specter began. "We are ready. We are prepared. Whatever reason compelled you to come to this place, on this day, use that and solidify your resolve. We will spill blood this morning. May none of it be ours. May your hands be steady, your aim hold true. May your bullets be deadly; let's do what we're here to do. Think alive."

And with that, everyone stood and got with their respective groups. Then, with nothing left to wait for, each group moved out.

Chapter 57

Randal's group had the furthest to go, and they all wanted to be there early. Each followed Randal's lead, though, and he had to make sure to walk quietly enough not to alert the Creep. Everyone had walked the route at least once, and all were confident of the route. Those carrying ladders had dampened the moving parts to cut down on the squeaks that might give away their position. Those providing coverage had done the same with their weapons. No clicks, no metal-on-metal clangs. All was relatively quiet. Finally arriving at their spot opposite the far wall, they took their positions, ready for the distraction.

Shade made sure the ambush crew was off and moving. She relied on their preparation to be on time and in position. She watched over the loading of the platform, the careful loading of Gordon's and Ginger's corpses. In order to keep them, they made use of their own freezer, eating the food that was in there. The heads had been thawing for a day. They were in a bag, ready to throw. They had crudely opened up their bodies, removed the internal organs, and packed them back with gunpowder, plastic containers filled with gas, and some various caliber cartridges. Rather macabre, but hopefully effective. They'd decided to set the bodies down on the far side of the Creep due to the potential stray bullet. When loaded, Shade took her spot at the helm of the fully-fueled platform.

Specter calmed his breathing and made sure the bodies were carefully loaded and secured aboard the platform. The drop was supposed to break open the gas containers, not the ride itself. He went ahead and lit his slow fuse. He would be the one lighting the kerosene they had found at Gordon's house. It would mimic fire aboard a platform more closely than anything else they had at hand.

They had mixed it with some old motor oil so it would be thicker and not slosh around as badly. As it was, they had fashioned a crock of sorts that would allow enough air in to burn and produce enough smoke. It was a balance and, like this operation, a lot depended on everything being in balance. As the platform lifted, he refocused on finding his inner balance.

As the sun rose and warmed the world out of its nightly rest, Randal tried to quiet his heart and relax. He thought of Shade's words previously about slow, accurate shots. He looked at those around him. Poised. Ready. Above that, eager to have the opportunity to act. He watched with the others for the platform.

As Shade guided the platform up the driveway, she was ready to break free and fly straight at the gate. But she kept steady, as if the platform wasn't responding or the pilot was a novice. As they came up on the penultimate turn in the drive, a voice boomed out from the Creep. "Stop your vehicle." It said. Shade did not, and the voice boomed again with the same message. Shade only slowed as they approached the gates and, acting on a nudge from Specter, one of the men stood up and yelled, "We found out what you're doing here, and we're going to stop it!" He pulled a head out of the bag, Ginger's, and his friend pulled Gordon's head out of the bag. "Give up or we'll kill every one of you – you heartless cowards! Just like we did them!" yelled the other guy, as both men tossed their head at the two Creepers who had come outside.

Specter lit the fuse in his pocket from the slow fuse and dropped it in the crock as the heads were in the air. The Creepers fired once they saw what had been tossed. Specter fired back once they opened up. Specter took one Creeper guard out in the first burst of activity, but Shade spun up and away too quickly for him to get another shot off. There was a good amount of smoke, and, as Shade took them up over the far side of the Creep, Specter lit the two fuses on the corpses. Shade banked just right so that they dropped the dead right beside the building. Shade then banked back and up towards the other side of the Creep, but Specter did get to see the flame burst from the bodies as they hit the ground, the gas liberated and lit by the fuse.

Randal waited for the first view of the platform and waved everyone forward as soon as he saw it. Then, behind his tree, he looked through his scope at the spots Specter had pointed out. He heard the first bursts of gunfire while he scanned. He spotted one Creeper on a walking patrol – as they had seen before – and Randal watched the guard's chest disappear as he heard his partner's rifle report.

Randal kept scanning, trying to give the teams a chance to get close. He heard 'Right roof' and immediately had his scope there and saw the Creeper reach for his right shoulder. Randal squeezed his trigger, the Creeper's chest blew outward, and the Creeper fell, knees first, then down, still with his left hand reaching to his right shoulder. Then...he was calling on a radio, like police used to do! Ahhh! Randal cursed himself. Of course they still make batteries in the Enclaves, so these Creepers would still be able to talk to each other. They had to react fast. "Think alive," he said as he saw the platform careen back into view.

Shade could feel the heat they were under. Apparently most of the Creepers were out to get the platform. *Good*, she thought, as she banked again. Shade was focused hard on exposing as little of her underbelly as she had to. But she was still giving good looks for her crew to shoot back, she thought, but she didn't hear much firing from her crew. Specter's clear, "Get on your triggers! Think alive!" told her why.

Shade rose up and banked hard to get back to the front side of the Creep, showing her belly to everyone. If she could just – *ha*! *Made it*! Shade picked out her spot, banked to the opposite side, and said "Hold!" just prior to slamming into the wall right at the top of the second-floor windows. She felt a wrenching twist and shifted away. Shade heard the welcome sound of shattering glass. With welcome relief, she turned and watched over her right shoulder as she ran the back right side of the platform along the windows, smashing all she could. She paused for an instant and yelled, "Now!" and held steady as Specter, already primed, was off the platform and inside almost as the word left her mouth. She pivoted back toward the left and started down the hill, trying to appear wounded.

Specter hit the ground and rolled, coming up with his revolvers in hand like he had practiced so many times. He was in the infirmary and, thankfully, it was deserted. He went down the infirmary towards the front of the Creep to the door closest to the stairwell.

Specter popped his head out and back quick as a flash twice – looking right, then looking left. All clear. He stepped out. He needed to make sure these doors stayed closed because the girls would be safer in there than out. He looked at the door to the stairs – a lever door opening to the stairs. Specter ducked back into the infirmary, grabbed an I.V. stand and, kicking off the base, jammed it through the lever and bent it to the outside of the door frame. Secured. At least the Creepers would make noise getting through.

Specter ran down the hall, stopped, popped out looking right, and saw no one. He ran on down that hall, saw nothing, and again popped out, looking right. A Creeper was at the door going to the exercise room, going inside toward a window where the corpses were on fire outside. Rather than risk a bullet, Specter holstered his right gun and drew his knife while he quickly and stealthily made his way after the Creeper.

Specter got in the room, and the Creeper was looking out the window and talking to himself. He listened as he got low and close. "There's something burning down there, yeah." Without waiting for more, Specter was up and had slit the man's throat just as his finger let off the 'talk' button. Specter took the radio off the Creeper and turned back toward the hallway. The Creeper's blood covered the window overlooking the burning corpses and framed Specter in a familiar portrait of death: a bloody demon with a distinctly frightening smile. He was Hunting!

Randal heard the crash of glass from where he was and was thankful for the sound. The teams were almost there when he spotted a Creeper coming from around the front of the building. He was shooting and not radioing, so Randal wasted no time in dropping him.

At the wall the teams were setting up the ladders. Those covering the ladder carriers were the first ones up, smashing the glass windows with their gun butts. It was taking too much time, though. The teams saw it, too, and doubled up. The glass finally came away, and the first one was in.

Randal felt they could go. "Move up," he said. They did, one down and covering the building while the other ran forward. Randal reached the building first, resting his back on the stable, rock-solid feel of the brick building. He was on the corner of the building. He was watching his counterpart run forward when she dropped and started shooting. Randal looked around the edge of the building to his left and saw about five men converging on his partner. She was holding them back, but Randal worked quickly.

Starting with the furthest one away – knowing she'd get those closest – he picked them off from her, dropping them one right after the other. She realized they were gone, and she started to get up, but was back down in an instant. Randal peeked out and saw five four wheelers! It shocked him – to have the fuel for that! But these guys were riding two to a vehicle and shooting at his pinned-down companion. So he sighted on a driver and started dropping them. Randal's back-up stood out as she sighted on the passengers just after Randal ended the driver. The Creepers tried running them down, but Randal shot true three times, and the other four wheelers turned away down the hill.

Shade weaved and wobbled as she went down the hill, not enough to slosh the kerosene mix out of the crock, but enough to seem damaged. When she set down behind the little knoll they had designated, one of the ambush crew lit another pan of heavy kerosene, kerosene mixed with oil, and it generated a lot more smoke, just as if Shade had gone down.

Rather than take off right away and risk being seen, she decided to deviate a bit from the plan and wait. She didn't wait long, though. Once word got passed down that four wheelers were on the way, she took off and around, trying to stay low and out of sight. She would drop these guys where she dropped Specter, go back for the ambushers, and maybe they'd be done in time for a late lunch.

She stopped herself. Things were going too well; something unforeseen was going to happen and change everything. She needed to stay focused.

Specter heard the crashing in the back of the Creep that told him Randal's crew was getting inside. He started for the stairs beside the exercise room when he heard some banging on the doors where the victims were kept. He knew they were safe inside, so he moved on towards the stairs. That was when he heard a muffled yell from a room that sounded like 'gas,' and just then his stolen radio spoke, "Gas deployed in commodities quarters. Use PPE." Specter cursed and kicked down the door he was in front of. He was not prepared for what happened, but he reacted fast.

Specter should have given some warning, because when he kicked the door, the girl behind it took the full force of the door with her face. Staggering backward, she looked and just started screaming when she saw Specter. Specter saw the faint haze in the room and wondered what gas it was. He ran back across the hall and got the rifle of the Creeper he'd just killed. Coming out of the exercise room he saw Randal's crew coming toward the screaming. Specter yelled, "They're gassing them. Get the girls out and to the infirmary!"

Thankfully, they understood and started acting. He ran back in and told the girl, "Get to the infirmary." Shocked she wasn't dead already, she took her chance to run. Specter checked his magazine and used the rifle butt to shatter the window. He fired three quick, well-aimed shots at the window directly across the courtyard from him. He saw the bullet holes, but the glass didn't shatter.

With no time and the wrong angle, he turned and ran down the hall, running past the ladder crews and grabbing the last crew member he saw, a woman. He burst through the door to the room overlooking the courtyard directly across from the entrance, the holding quarters on their left and right. Specter pointed and said, "Shatter the windows, not the people." The woman from the ladder crew wasted no time, and shattered the window in front of them. Standing side by side, Specter on the right, they started shooting out the windows of the holding rooms starting with those farthest away, those near the stairs. At this angle, the bullets shattered more glass, thus allowing the gas an exit, giving the girls more time.

Catching a glimmer of light from above, Specter tackled his partner, and they watched the floor get shot to pieces where they just were. Close as they were, Specter yelled in her ear, "Get the girls to the infirmary and let the platform get them out."

The woman nodded, and they crawled and scraped to get to the door. Once there Specter broke for the stairs. Nobody was going to stop him from Hunting today!

Randal barely caught sight of some other four wheelers going down the hill. He picked up the smoke from Shade's location and said a quick prayer for her safety. He chastised himself – she was a Hunter and knew combat intimately, like a lover. Randal shook his head to clear it and asked God for everybody's protection.

His shooting partner came up beside him, and they gave each other a fist bump. They were up to the Creep and the plan was for them to go on in, but something felt distinctly wrong about that to Randal. And he had survived by following his gut. He said, "Come on," and ran around the back side of the Creep. He peeked around the right edge of the wall and saw two, maybe three, Creepers putting out the corpses' fire – probably not knowing they had gas inside them. Anyway, Randal looked at his partner and said, "There's three out there, you take the one on the right, okay?" She nodded, and he scurried out three or four steps, knelt down, sighted on the one furthest left, and fired. Both got their targets, and the third Creeper caught one bullet from each of them in the chest.

Randal ran back to their first spot, and he caught sight of Shade coming up alongside the Creep to deposit her crew. But he saw something was wrong; she was just sitting there. He looked out and then back up, then stepped out and, looking up, got shocked. They were loading girls up on the platform. His mind raced ahead. He told his partner, "To the wood line – you're covering the platform and getting those girls covered and safe. Move!" She did so with only a nod.

Just then, Randal picked up movement above the platform and had his rifle up when he saw the Creeper's rifle flame to life.

Shade knew something was wrong as she pulled alongside the hole in the second floor windows. There were way too many people, and not one of them was Specter. Wrongly, a lot of them were girls.

Unexpected, but something you deal with, she thought. Quickly she yelled, "All but three out the back!" to her crew before she fully stopped. "Five girls!" Shade yelled to the closest of the ladder crew, and he passed it on even as the girls started getting on.

Shade felt too open, too exposed. *This was taking too…*then she felt a white, hot, searing pain in her shoulder and arm as she was driven to her knees. She ended up looking down on the ground and saw Randal with his rifle raised and her first thought was, *he shot me*! Followed immediately by, *no, he wouldn't do that*, followed immediately by a hard 'chunk' on the deck of her platform. Turning to look, she saw a dead Creeper had fallen on her platform. *That's who shot me and who Randal shot*, she thought in an instant.

Shade stood and used her arm and shoulder to test them – hurt bad but not broken. "Hold on!" she yelled and banked away from the wall. Shade flew straight to where she had seen Randal, banking to protect her passengers, but also so she could see. Once she caught sight of Randal, he waved her on toward the tree line. She got it and trusted he had somebody there. When she got there, Shade saw her waving and sat down the platform. "Get off and stay down. You three help her form a perimeter. This'll be over soon," she yelled.

As they exited, she took a syringe and gave herself some 'go' juice as Randal called it. Randal saved her life today. But she had runs to make. Once the girls were clear she lifted up and banked hard right and then immediately left and watched with satisfaction as the Creeper corpse was jostled off the platform.

Shade circled wide to the right to swing in line with the second floor windows and sat in quickly in the same spot. The girls didn't waste time getting on. She shouted to the closet ladder crew person, "Ten girls! Wait, one of you guys, too!" He stopped a girl and pulled another crew member onto the platform.

Shade jerked as the ricochets sounded above her. She had been a lot faster but Randal was ready, too. But gunfire made clear it was time to move. Shade swooped down, away, and towards her new rally point.

Specter ran down the hall and grabbed two ladder crewmen, a man and a woman, and simply said, "You're with me." They followed in behind him. He checked the stairs down and up and saw nothing. He went up, preferring a top-down approach. Two snipers on the roof wouldn't hurt either.

They took the stairs until they couldn't and broke out onto the roof. Turning around quickly, Specter stuffed the Creeper's rifle in the door to block it open. Turning again with revolvers drawn, he scanned for people. He went to the far edge, looked down, and saw Gordon and Ginger slowly cremating, with three Creeper bodies nearby. But no one up here. There was a low wall, and he crouched down and ran along it, motioning for his helpers to follow. They were back to just above where the ladder crews had come up and still no one. Turning and running back down the other wing, back to the front of the Creep, Specter did see someone. Specter shot him in the torso just as a shot came up and made a mess of the Creeper's head. Specter ducked, not wanting to be mistaken. He got to where the Creeper had been and raised his hand guns over the wall. Then he peeped over the wall. Randal! Specter stood back up and gave a thumb's up, but something caught his eye. It was the ambush crew. He looked back at Randal, pointed to his eyes, and then pointed to the crew running up the hill. Randal looked, then gave back the thumb's up.

Specter was about to go down, but he had forgotten about the courtyard. Edging up, he looked over the wall. Down there, ready to move out, was what had to be Big Man's car. Whoever ran this place was going to try and get free in some large vehicle that didn't look like anything Specter had seen before. It was some kind of jeep/truck combination.

Just then across the courtyard, movement caught his eye. One of the ladder crewmen on the second floor was looking out to the courtyard, too. Specter stood up quickly waving his arms. Specter caught his attention! Specter mimicked like he was bench pressing, then throwing a football and pointed down to the vehicle and mimicked driving. The man held out open palms, probably saying 'what?' Specter pointed back hoping the man would go into the exercise room and see the weights.

Specter couldn't wait, though. He told the two with him, "Don't let anyone in that car. Spread out, circle, and don't pop up in the same place twice. Shoot anything getting in that."

They nodded and Specter started running back to the other side of the Creep. There was no roof access from this side. As he went around, he was pleased to hear a crash and, looking, he saw a dumbbell on the hood in its own dent. Specter hoped they could get the windshield.

Randall looked toward where Specter had pointed and, sure enough, here came the ambush crew. Randal whistled for help, and a woman saw him, signaled the others, and they all ran up and took cover with Randal.

"How'd it go?" Randal asked.

"Got 'em all!" the woman replied. "You?"

"We're in, but something's wrong because they're getting the girls out," Randal replied as he pointed to Shade on the platform.

Without thought of aught else, the woman asked, "Where do you need us?"

Surprised but clear, Randal responded, "Send two of your best shots over to where they're holding the girls," he pointed, "and let's get the rest of you inside by the ladders."

With a nod from her, they were gone.

Shade dropped off her load and saw people running towards her, and she didn't like that. Then she recognized them as from the ambush crew. Two broke off and continued to the girls, and the rest went for the ladders.

Shade got going and started her last run. There were only five girls left, and once they were out, Shade would be free to move as she wished.

Back in the stairwell Specter faced a dilemma: clear the third floor or go for the lowest floor. Knowing that they already gassed the holding cells, the decision was clear. He went down to the second floor. He went past the dumbbell thrower, telling him to get the windshield. Specter was going around to the infirmary when he saw the ambush crew coming up the ladders. He told a ladder crew member to get a team and clear the third floor.

Once the ambush crew was all up, he said, "You're with me." They went down the stairs to the lowest floor, the floor below ground level. Rather than divide them, Specter kept them together – himself and six from the ambush crew. They broke out and down the stairwell to the lowest level. Checking the door, they found it clear. Specter's radio hadn't gone off again, so he was hoping there was no gas down here. *So far so good*, he thought. The crew bracketed the first door they came to. One of them kicked the door open, and then Specter burst in and looked over the first room. He had spoken too soon. He shut the door back quickly. The rooms did not cover both sides of the hallway down here, just the inner side. Specter had everyone stand back from the doors from then on. He checked the second room; only he looked in. No one should have to see this. A woman with a baby, whether it was hers or she was just nursing it, both shot in the head. He closed the door and heard a muffled shot from the end of hallway.

Specter took off like a rocket down the hall, desperate to be there before the next gunshot. He whirled around the corner as the murdering Creeper was opening another door. Specter's first shot was meant only to get the Creeper's attention, but it hit the man in his left side, a lucky shot for a man on the run. Not trusting his aim, Specter ran full speed and slammed the door shut with his shoulder. Skidding to a stop and turning, Specter saw the Creeper raise his gun at him, even as the first ladder crewman running behind Specter fired a burst directly down into the man. Specter turned again and looked down the hall to his left, all clear.

Going back, the ambush crew cleared all the remaining rooms and found that, of the remaining eleven rooms, only five were occupied – five wet nurses and five babies. Going back over the eight rooms he had run past to begin with, Specter saw they were all occupied. All inside – without exception – shot once in the head. No child older than two. Specter was ready to meet the owner of this Creep; and that meant now.

He directed four of the ambush crew to escort the women and babies out of the Creep and told them to rendezvous with those already rescued. Specter and the remaining two made their way up to the next level, the guard quarters, and then swept through that floor with no resistance. Apparently everyone had been called up and into service. They did count the occupied rooms, though, and it looked like thirty Creepers were here. The bonus was the extra webarmor uniforms they had; it looked like each man had five extra uniforms. *Randal's going to love this*, Specter thought. Well, Specter's gamble hadn't paid off – but it had to be either first or third.

They went back up the same stairs to the third floor, looked left, and this time Specter barely got his head back before the wall erupted in gunfire. So, this was going to be the stand-off. Specter readied his gun and, as he raised it, looked out. This second look was more informational. There were two Creepers right there and Specter took the one on the right with a head shot.

Ducking back, he held up a finger to his companions. "You want to give up?" he yelled to the Creeper.

The response he received was gunfire, just as he wanted. Once the gunfire stopped, Specter popped out, revolver raised, and shot the Creeper between the eyes as he looked up from reloading. Specter and his team checked the first room on the left and found nothing. The room on the right looked to be something like the guard's workout room. It was deserted as well. Specter said, "What do you bet this guy is in the back?"

They heard gunfire on the far side of the Creep but no way to tell where. They kept on checking rooms, kept on seeing empty ones. But each one was ornate and richly furnished. "That's why we didn't have much intelligence about this level – it's the Big Man's," Specter said.

Before breaching the left hall, Specter peeked around.

He thought about it, something in his gut telling him there were people there. He finally said loudly, "I've fired three hundred and thirty bullets today."

An answer came from around the far side of the hall, "Seems like we've been at this for three hundred and thirty minutes."

They both looked out. It was the ladder crew sent to clear the third floor. Apparently, these two rooms were the last to be searched. Specter motioned, and they hit the room on his left – the other team's right, the room facing the courtyard. It looked like a bar area, but it was certainly deserted. Specter gathered the crews together and whispered to everybody, "We're sure this is the last room?" There were nods of assent. "Let's get in there then, because we may have missed a secret passage or something. Think alive."

They set up on the two doors and, just to try, Specter knocked on the door and said, "You can give up, you know. That is an option you have."

An answer came back, "Please come in, then."

Specter threw open the door and saw a man seated behind a large desk (Big Man, Specter knew), and he was flanked by two men who were most likely his body guards (Big Boys, Specter named them). There were six other Creepers in the room, three on each door.

Specter had been to this dance before. He knew the steps, and he knew the finale. But having danced the dance with Randal, Specter knew to keep his eyes open.

He said to Big Man, "The six guards, arms up. Out the door."

The Big Man dismissed them and they went. Specter told those guarding them, loud enough for all to hear, "Take them to Shade. If they don't do exactly as you say the first time, shoot them."

Specter then walked in and made sure the men stayed outside. No sense in losing more than one to stupidity, he thought. But he said, "You do know to kill everyone if something happens, right?" He got a nod of assent, and then he addressed the seated man.

"Thank you for giving up so easily," Specter began. "It will save so much time later on."

"Sir, I think you are mistaken. This is a negotiation, not a surrender," the man said, dripping with condescension.

"Well, sir," Specter replied, playing the game. "What do you have to negotiate with that I haven't already taken?"

"Ah, you may have certain things here, but there are far more things elsewhere that I have to offer."

Specter was having a hard time maintaining his temper. This man actually thought he was going to get away. Caught up in the adrenaline of clearing a building and the ghastly sight of what happened downstairs, Specter had to focus hard on maintaining his composure.

"Elsewhere doesn't affect me that much," Specter said. To Specter's credit, his voice sounded rock solid.

"Well, sir, there is so much more beyond this place, beyond these wooded Outerlands," he said. The man really thought he was offering Specter the world.

"No, I know," Specter began, intently watching Big Man's face. "I gave up an outside view high rise apartment in an Enclave to come and live out here." And there it was, the condescension. This man would not believe that a reasonable person would choose to live in the Outerlands. The man's ability to compartmentalize his feelings and emotions must be extraordinary.

"Well, sir, I'm sure that…"

Specter shot the Big Boy on the man's left right between the eyes. Specter could see the man was used to violence. Interesting, he thought. "So nothing to offer here?" Specter asked. The man's face showed a mix of incredulity and exasperation. It looked like he really couldn't understand that this was happening.

"Hey, I thought of something – hope. Can you give my friend some hope?" Specter began.

"Well, I feel certain that I can…"

"She came here," Specter interrupted, "and seems like she lost her hope here. Have you seen it? Can you give that back to her?"

"Well, sir, I'm sure that…"

Specter shot the other Big Boy in the gut as he was talking, and then got what he wanted – a real emotion, not a controlled response.

The Big Man rose up and put his hands on the desk in front of him and sneered, "Hope is the most insolent of emotions. It's the last to be eradicated and easiest to spring back up. Hope is useless. It's like a wish, faint and insubstantial – so useless." The Big Man almost spit the last as he spoke.

Specter didn't like that. "I take issue with that," he said, drawing his knife. "Hope is not like a wish." Specter walked up and grabbed the man's left hand, pulling him halfway onto the desk. He took the man's left index finger in his left fist. Specter looked into Big Man's eyes and saw only contempt there. "You can hope I don't cut your finger off. Feel that? That's you hoping I don't cut your finger off." Then, quick as a flash, Specter slammed his hand on the desk and cut the finger off. After the man's scream, he said, "Now you can only wish you had your finger back. See the difference?" Then Specter released his grip.

The man's unbelief still refused to let him accept the situation. The man instead started raining down curses on Specter, his spittle and blood spraying the room. The man came around the desk, used to violence, used to command, used to <u>his</u> rules.

Specter stopped him by putting his revolver on the man's forehead. Specter watched his eyes. "So much hate," he said. "Do you realize you're going to die here?" Specter, through experience, could see in the man's eyes that he did not.

As the man breathed in, Specter squeezed his trigger. Whether he was going to curse more, dare him, whatever, Specter knew he'd never have to hear it.

Specter holstered his gun and told those there, "I'm sorry it was over that quickly. He was…non-remediable." Specter paused a moment. "We need to run another full sweep from top to bottom. No one goes in the basement. At least not yet."

Shade dropped the last of the girls off at the rally point along with five other members of the ladder crew. After she made sure they were secure, she took the platform back to the Creep. The crew had said everything was wrapped up but she hadn't seen Specter yet. She was waiting on him to call everything over.

She set the platform down by the ladders, and was about to climb up when she heard "Shade!" It was Randal. He came running over; he must have seen her coming back. When he got close, she expected him to stop, but she barely had time to get her hands up as he enveloped her in a hug. She heard an involuntary "Unnh" of pain escape her lips as he put pressure on her shoulder.

Randal released her quickly, saying, "Oh, my, I'm so sorry. Your shoulder. Are you okay?" He was talking too fast, probably still caught up in the fight. She was about to slap him, just to calm him down, when something dawned on her. "I thought you were okay because you kept flying. You just whizzed by. I got the second one, though, I had a good spot," Randal went on. *He hasn't mentioned anything but me*, she thought. All this planning, the ferocity of battle, the adrenaline, and his thoughts were only for her. It caught her off guard and she distrusted her own feelings for him. Almost as a reflex to that realization, she slapped him.

Randal visibly calmed. She felt good about that. *Put that in its place*, she thought. "I'm sorry," he said. But then Randal did the unexpected. He reached out and brushed the hair from her face and cupped her cheek in his hand. She heard him say, "I'm sorry, but I'm glad you're alive," as he bent and kissed her forehead. Shade was taken aback at how much she responded to his touch, to his feelings for her.

Randal, steadied by her slap, turned and started up the ladder. "Let's go find Specter," he said as he climbed. Shade followed, letting motion help her keep her emotions in check; this wasn't finished yet.

Specter knelt down beside gut shot Big Boy. Specter pulled the man's shirt out of the way, got some of the stop-bleeding powder, and applied it. He slapped at the man's face until he came around.

Big Boy was shocked to see Specter. He looked down at his gut, at Big Man dead on the floor, and then back to Specter.

"Anything you want to tell me?" Specter asked.

Big Boy studied Specter's face. "Yeah," he finally said. "Don't kill me. Let me go."

"It's good you haven't lost your sense of humor," Specter replied. "But you know how this goes. You've seen it; probably done it." Specter looked up and sighed. "Easy or hard, friend."

Big Boy didn't hesitate. He knew that Specter would get the information, one way or another. He turned out to know a lot: schedules, names, places. Specter dragged a chair over and used the corner of Big Man's desk to write down what he needed. It turned out that there were other locations like this one, other houses like Gordon's. None nearby, but a network that reached across what served as the country after the Breaking. Specter was looking at the underbelly of the pleasure domes, this Big Boy just one scale on that belly. Even Big Boy didn't know how many there actually were, certainly more than five. Specter had to focus on his penmanship to avoid ending Big Boy's narration himself. Specter would double-check what he could with whatever papers Big Man had laying around. When he finally ran down, Specter asked, "You or me?"

Big Boy said, "If you'll give me your blade?"

Specter handed it to him.

Big Boy took off his shirt, raised his arm, and then cut his left brachial artery directly below his armpit. "Sorry if you wanted to keep the carpet," he said as he gave Specter his knife back, handle first.

Specter took the blade, sheathed it, and turned to leave. "Thanks, man," he said as he walked out. Specter stopped as he passed by the guard outside – a ladder crew member. He pulled the guard close to him and whispered, "Give him ten to fifteen minutes, and then," Specter tapped the guard twice on the forehead, "double-tap him."

The guard nodded and Specter walked toward the stairs, eager for an exit.

Shade and Randal found that those left in the building had gathered at the ladders. They arrived just as the Creepers from Big Man's office were escorted onto the second floor. The crewman leading them walked right up to Shade.

"Specter said to take these Creepers to you," she said.

Shade took it all in, saying, "Did Specter have any special plans for them?"

The woman shook her head, "None that he mentioned, just to shoot them if they didn't do what we said."

Shade smiled a wan smile. She addressed the Creepers, "Do you know what that means, gentlemen?"

No one answered.

Shade put her hand on the woman's arm who brought them down. "I need a room where I can talk with these men," Shade said.

The woman turned and led Shade and Randal across the hall. "This is where Specter and I shot the windows out of the holding cells so they couldn't gas the girls," the woman said. "Will this do?"

"This will do nicely," Shade replied. "That's why we had to get the girls out?" she asked the woman.

"Yes, ma'am," the woman answered. "They were gassing the rooms."

Shade looked at Randal and asked, "Will you excuse us, please?"

Shade waited until he was gone and addressed the woman. "We don't need the Creepers. Specter said that so that I'd know we'd have to...deal with them."

"We need to kill them?" the woman asked.

"Well, in a word, yes," Shade answered. "We can try to get some information from them, but otherwise we are judge, jury, and executioner. As such, I need to know if you're okay with that."

The woman was quick with her response, "Yes, ma'am."

"Okay," Shade said. "Who else would be, too?"

The woman thought for a minute and said, "Bethany and Roddy, probably."

"Why?" Shade asked.

The woman answered, "Bethany saw her older sister get taken but no one believed her until you all came and Jess told her story. She's been waiting and preparing for payback since then. Roddy, well," she hesitated, "Roddy used to be a judge. He's fair, and I think he'd even be fair to them."

"Interesting choices," Shade said.

"Well, when you said 'judge,' I thought of Roddy. With 'executioner,' I thought of Bethany. That leaves us two to be the jury," the woman replied.

"Good enough," Shade said, and walked back into the hall. She addressed the crew escorting the Creepers first. "Please take these men in here," she said, gesturing to the room she had just left. Shade continued, "I need Bethany and Roddy."

A woman and a man stepped forward and Shade motioned for them to stand to the side. "Randal," Shade said, "I need you to take the rest of our people and take them to where the girls are being held. Once we're done here, we'll come out and then we'll all start the clean-up process. Let me make that clear: we'll come out to you, okay?"

Randal simply said, "Yes, ma'am." He then turned and started walking back to the ladders. "Come on, then," he said to the remaining crew members.

Shade steeled herself against the pang of just dismissing Randal, but she had to harden her heart for the work ahead.

Randal and the others made it back to the edge of the woods and joined with the rescued girls and their guardians. It was obvious that they were still on high alert and didn't know the battle was over except for the clean-up. He went straight to his partner and said, "It's over." Then, raising his voice, he addressed the whole group, "It's over. The rest are finishing up."

There was no cheer, no celebration. Just sighs as people sat down and relaxed. The girls huddled together, still crying. It wasn't clear if the tears they shed were tears of joy or commiseration. Freedom for them was too much to hope for and fantasy to them once realized.

Randal made his rounds among the fighters. Each group talked about what had happened to them, catching up on what events had transpired, each filling the other in while trying to piece everything together. Randal had a lot clearer picture of the day by the time he saw people walking towards them from the Creep.

He could make Shade out before he could see the others' faces clearly enough. He'd overstepped his bounds with her and had gotten slapped for it. He knew that now, but he was still happy to see her alive.

As they got closer, Randal recognized the woman who had brought up the Creepers, the two people Shade had called out, and a noticeable lack of any Creepers. Randal waited until they got close and was going to call out, but Shade pointed to him and motioned for him to join her, away from the group. He had the sinking feeling in his gut that he was going to the principal's office.

Shade led him a little way into the woods, out of sight and earshot of the group. He tried to speak first and deflect the brunt of her anger/admonition/rancor whatever. "Shade, listen, I'm sorry." Shade stopped walking when he spoke, but she did not turn around. Randal continued, "I overstepped my bounds and I shouldn't have and I apologize."

Without seeing her face, Randal couldn't judge her reaction. He could only see that her back was set. After a minute, she asked, "Are you apologizing for your feelings or for telling me about them?"

The question was not what Randal expected but he was secure in his answer. "Your slap was clear evidence that I should have kept my hands to myself. So I'm apologizing for my obviously unwanted advances."

"What if they weren't unwanted?" she asked.

Shade's question struck Randal as strange. "Then I'd ask you why you slapped me instead of tilting your head back and kissing me?"

At his response, Shade did turn. "Could you chalk it up to shock?" She took the few steps over to Randal and took his hands in hers. He let her. She got close to him, looked him in the eyes, and asked, "Can you forgive me for that?"

"Probably," he said.

"Can we try it again?" she asked, putting his hands around the small of her back.

"I'm glad you're alive," Randal said, and, pulling Shade close to him, kissed her.

They broke the kiss slowly, with a shared promise for more. "We'd better get back," Randal said.

"Yeah," Shade replied. She unfolded herself from him and they walked back to rejoin the others.

Chapter 58

Specter led the few remaining crew members out to where the group was waiting for them.

Randal was checking out Shade's shoulder as Specter walked up. "Everything's clear inside," he said. "You get shot?" he asked Shade.

"Yeah, I took two good shots. Randal took the guy down, though."

"Good," he said. "Randal, you okay?"

"Fine," Randal replied.

"Good again," said Specter. "Everything's clear inside, but we need to pack everything up and get gone before any old friends drop by."

They all nodded, but knew this would take time.

"How many girls were there?" Specter asked.

"Twenty-four," Shade said. "They may have been due for a pick-up soon. Any idea why there were no boys?"

"The boys were picked-up two weeks ago," Specter replied.

Randal noticed they were all looking at those rescued girls. "They're going back on foot, right?" he asked.

"Yeah, I'll take them, and we'll go by Gordon's farm, pick up the kids, see if we can reunite any, and then see if we can get some back home," Specter said.

Their conversation was interrupted by shouting and wailing. Turning to look, it appeared that one of the assault crew had found a loved one among the girls.

"Looks like one's going home," Randal said.

"Yeah," Specter echoed. "Shade, I hate to ask but…well, I've got a basement of dead women and children, and I'd like a hand with it – even if you're just there for moral support."

"I can help," Randal volunteered.

"No," Specter said. "Shade and I are used to seeing things no human was designed to see. Those images would stay with you to the grave." Specter paused. "Speaking of that, though, you could get a grave detail going or a funeral pyre, whichever they do here."

Chapter 59

They each threw themselves into the work. Getting all the bodies together was a chore. They decided on two funeral pyres: one for the Creepers, one for the others. Having the use of the four wheelers did make the job easier, but it still took time. Laying the bodies of the mothers and/or wet nurses out was tough. No one recognized them, though. Specter didn't know if that was better or worse. It was definitely better than when Specter and Shade carried out some small bundles wrapped in sheets.

Once the bodies were taken care of, though, something flipped in Specter. It was odd for him, and he wasn't used to it. Through the whole clean-up process, there was not the raucous celebration Specter was used to seeing after combat. There were few slapping of backs in celebration. More often there were simply hugs and pats on the back – pats that meant 'we made it,' 'we live another day.'

The people shared a camaraderie that came from want and misery – the same feeling of commiseration that you used to see in hospitals before the Breaking. You never knew if the person you passed in the hall was going to sit with a dying loved one, or get test results, or have a grandchild – and it didn't matter. You were both there and quietly wished the other good fortune and good wishes. It was the whole 'what I'm going through is bad, but I know you might be going through something worse' attitude.

It extended to the division of the spoils. Specter put the claim on all the webarmor uniforms, but weapons, food, fuel, and other clothes were up for grabs. There were those who clearly needed much more but were afraid to take what they thought might be too much. The whole mindset was foreign to Specter. Oddly to Specter, they ended up partitioning out the spoils based on how many kids each had. The highest prized spoil surprised and shocked Specter. White sugar. They divided it out like every granule was a gold coin.

These men and women had risked their lives for something they believed was right. The spoils were extra, and these people wanted to be sure each had enough. It was no wonder that the Enclaves had worked so hard to quash such sentiments. It was Specter's first time on the other side, and it really cut him to his core. His mind forced him back to Lloyd and how Lloyd had only wanted to ensure his people could make it, could have a fair shot at a life he remembered. Specter again saw Florentina trying to hold Lloyd's head together. As he remembered, Specter felt the same familiar regret: that of him not being able to take that shot back. He shook his head to clear it. *Too many like that to go down that road,* he thought.

Randal happened to join Specter when that feeling was hitting him especially hard. It was the second day after the attack. One group had already left on foot for Gordon's farm, and the other was loading up and heading out. Specter was going with the second group. Randal and Shade were taking the platform back. The plan was to rendezvous at Gordon's farm, divide the farm's spoils there, and then go their separate ways. Whoever was closest would assist each girl getting back to her home.

Randal could sense something was bothering Specter.

"You okay?" Randal asked.

"Yeah," Specter said. "I think I'm going to do more of this."

"Load supplies for people?" Randal joked.

"No," Specter said. "Seek out situations like this and set things right."

"Really?" Randal asked.

Shade walked up behind Randal. Specter, winking at Shade, said, "Yeah, and I'm going to ask Shade to come with me unless you ask her first."

"He already has," said Shade. "But what were you going to ask me, Specter?"

Randal broke in, "He's going to be a television show."

"What?" asked Shade and Specter together.

"You remember television shows before the Breaking. The lead character would find a problem in the first thirty minutes of the show and then solve it in the last thirty minutes. Specter wants the lead in a television show." Randal, though, even as he joked about it could see that Specter was dead set.

"You <u>are</u> serious, aren't you?" Randal asked.

Specter didn't move a muscle.

"You are – you're like mid-life crisis serious," said Randal. "You like it that much?"

"I get off on it," Specter said.

"Great way to get back on the Enclave radar and get a hit put out on yourself," Randal stated.

"Are we free from that? Do you think they're convinced we're dead?" Specter countered. "You two don't feel it? You don't feel the 'rightness' of what we did here?"

Randal took it up, "What, balance the scales or something? Really, three people against the Corps? What could we hope to accomplish – other than being laid to rest?"

"It could be done. Little by little. A piece here and a piece there," Specter said.

"We're not talking about eating an elephant, Specter," Randal added. "The logistics of keeping up a fight against the Enclaves is phenomenal."

"But you've thought about it, haven't you?" countered Specter.

"A person would have to go underground – spend time setting up a network of hide outs and safe havens," Shade said.

"What if that were already in place?" Specter asked.

"What if those safe havens already had contacts established – trusted, loyal contacts?" Shade asked.

"Look at what wc did here with just a week of recruiting," Specter added.

Randal broke in, "I see what you two are doing. You're trying to say that all this is set up, you two can merge your contact networks and safe houses, and we can spend our lives fighting against the injustice of the Corporations?"

Specter and Shade only looked at Randal.

"Can't we stay dead for at least a year?" joked Randal.

"So it's settled, then? I'll see you back at the bunker?" asked Specter.

"Yeah," Randal said.

Randal and Shade looked at each other and smiled.

Shade added, "But don't wait up for us."

Randal took Shade's hand as they walked back to the platform. He looked back over his shoulder at Specter leaving with the second group. Randal did mean what he said; he would meet Specter and continue the fight. This campaign was the first time Randal had fought back. That was only because he had Shade and Specter with him. Throughout his Running, Randal had always turned and run, leaving those he saw mistreated or abused to fend for themselves. It felt good to use his talents to right wrongs, to fight against those from whom he would normally run, to fight for those people who couldn't fight back.

But now Randal had a woman by his side, and she a Hunter at that. He felt he could stand. And with both Specter and Shade, he felt confident they could do some good in the world. *And*, thought Randal, *isn't that what we're supposed to do?*

THE END

Bibliography

Spider silk body armor
http://news.discovery.com/tech/body-armor-spider-silk-121015.html
http://en.wikipedia.org/wiki/BioSteel
http://www.postnatural.org/PNOM/BiosteelGoat.html

Fire piston
http://en.wikipedia.org/wiki/Firepiston
http://www.primitiveways.com/fire_piston.html

AK-47 Kalashnikov Rifle
http://en.wikipedia.org/wiki/AK-47
http://world.guns.ru/assault/rus/ak-akm-e.html

FN-FAL Belgian Rifle
http://en.wikipedia.org/wiki/FN_FAL_50.63#Variants
http://world.guns.ru/assault/be/fn-fal-e.html

Pitch and Tar
http://www.primitiveways.com/pine_pitch_stick.html

Platform
http://en.wikipedia.org/wiki/Avrocar_(aircraft)
http://greyfalcon.us/restored/Project%20Silver%20Bug.htm

Daedalus
http://www.pantheon.org/articles/d/daedalus.html
http://en.wikipedia.org/wiki/Daedalus

Pharaoh's Curse
http://en.wikipedia.org/wiki/Curse_of_the_pharaohs

Alexander the Great and the Phalanx
http://en.wikipedia.org/wiki/Army_of_Macedon
http://www.mlahanas.de/Greeks/LX/MacedonianPhalanx.html

Mongols and the Stirrup
http://history-world.org/mongol_empire.htm
http://www.globaled.org/nyworld/materials/mongol/Howdid2.html

G.K. Chesterton
Tremendous Trifles (1909), XVII: The Red Angel
http://www.gutenberg.org/ebooks/8092